Giguhl lea
banquet
his

"Ahem?"

"What?"

"You don't really expect me to hang out in this hairless carcass, do you?"

I removed a set of sweatpants from the bag and rose again with a sigh. "We'll be right back."

Carrying the cat under one arm, I made my way through the crowd toward the bathrooms. Ignoring the speculative glances from the females in line for the ladies' room, I went to the men's door. I pushed it open and tossed the cat and the pants inside. Leaning against the wall, I crossed my arms. "Giguhl change forms," I called out loud enough to be heard inside the john.

Two seconds later a pop sounded. Green smoke wafted under the door, bringing with it the scent of rotten eggs and urinal cakes.

"What the fuck!" a deep male voice shouted from inside. "Keep that thing away from me."

"Don't flatter yourself," Giguhl responded in a bored tone. "You couldn't handle The Pitchfork."

Praise for the Sabina Kane series

"A seriously wild ride!"

—*RT Book Reviews* (4.5 Stars)

BY JAYE WELLS

SILVER-TONGUED
DEVIL

JAYE WELLS

www.orbitbooks.net

Copyright © 2012 by Jaye Wells
Excerpt from *Blue-Blooded Vamp* copyright © 2012 by Jaye Wells
All rights reserved. Except as permitted under the U.S. Copyright Act of 1976, no part of this publication may be reproduced, distributed, or transmitted in any form or by any means, or stored in a database or retrieval system, without the prior written permission of the publisher.

Orbit
Hachette Book Group
237 Park Avenue
New York, NY 10017
www.orbitbooks.net

Orbit is an imprint of Hachette Book Group.
The Orbit name and logo are trademarks of Little, Brown Book Group Limited.

The publisher is not responsible for websites (or their content) that are not owned by the publisher.

Printed in the United States of America

First Edition: January 2012

10 9 8 7 6 5 4 3 2 1

ATTENTION CORPORATIONS AND ORGANIZATIONS:
Most HACHETTE BOOK GROUP books are available at quantity discounts with bulk purchase for educational, business, or sales promotional use. For information, please call or write:

Special Markets Department, Hachette Book Group
237 Park Avenue, New York, NY 10017
Telephone: 1-800-222-6747 Fax: 1-800-477-5925

*For Mom, who knew I should do this before
I realized it's what I wanted all along.*

SILVER-TONGUED
DEVIL

1

Blue lights flashed off the undersides of leaves. Off the tall brick buildings. Off the stoic faces of New York's finest. The cops formed a tight circle around a tarp-covered body next to a Dumpster. Its lid gaped open like the mouth of a shell-shocked witness.

After three months on a steady diet of bagged blood, the aroma of a fresh human kill hooked me by the nose and dragged me toward the crime scene. The humans around me could smell the stink of trash and acid rain and gritty city. But they couldn't detect the coppery scent that made my fangs throb against my tongue.

Delicious. Seductive. Forbidden.

Bright yellow police tape cordoned off the entrance to the park. Spectators gathered in a tight clutch on the sidewalk along Central Park West. Their morbid curiosity clung to their faces like Greek tragedy masks.

I shouldn't have paid any attention. I shouldn't have stopped. And I definitely shouldn't have pushed my way to the front of the crowd.

But the blood called to me.

A male in a black Windbreaker with the word CORONER on the back lifted the tarp. His expression didn't change as he surveyed the carnage. He looked up to address the detective and uniformed cops waiting to hear his verdict. "Anyone located the dick?"

A young patrolman lurched his head over the side of the steel box and vomited.

"Hey, rookie, you contaminate my crime scene and I'll give you something to puke about."

The white-faced recruit wiped his mouth with his arm. Raised a gloved hand. "Found it."

"What's that he's got there?" The question came from a blue-hair standing next to me.

All around people started voicing guesses.

"Maybe it's a finger."

"A toe?"

"That has to be an ear."

I bit my lip. Giguhl was going to be so mad he missed this. If he'd been there with me, the Mischief demon probably would have said something like, "Sabina, dicks in Dumpsters are no laughing matter." Then he'd move closer for a better look.

But Giguhl wasn't there. He was waiting for me to get home. I should go—

The coroner knelt next to the body and frowned. "That's odd."

I halted my exit, curious despite my best intentions.

"Dick-ectomies usually are," the detective replied.

The coroner ignored the joke and frowned. "Considering the extent of the wounds, there should be a lot more blood."

"You think he was killed somewhere else and dumped here?" the rookie asked.

"Negative." The detective shook his head. "There are signs of struggle over there." He pointed to the tree line, where stubs of broken branches littered the ground.

"There's blood spatter over there, too," the coroner said, rising. "Just not enough for an arterial wound like this." He sighed and put his hands on his hips. He scanned the area, as if searching for the answer—or the perp—among the crowd. When that gaze landed on me, I stifled the urge to shy away. To pull my collar higher and duck my head so he wouldn't see the guilt on my face. But then I remembered that, while I shouldn't be there, I wasn't responsible for the human's death.

Not this time.

But given everything I'd just heard, I knew who was. Or rather, *what* was responsible.

A vampire.

And a clumsy one at that. Slade was going to be pissed. Especially if the vamp was a new arrival who hadn't bothered to pay the blood tax. Either way, once Slade found out, there'd be a reckoning. I almost wished I could be there with a bowl of popcorn when he found the guilty party.

But he definitely wasn't going to hear about the botched kill from me. Vampire politics weren't my business.

Not anymore.

That reminder shook up a cocktail of emotions. Longing and jealousy mixed with something else. Something about being a spectator to someone else's kill. Something about secondhand adrenaline leaving me hollow. Something about . . . loneliness.

A siren demanded attention. The crowd split apart, their eager eyes tracking the arrival of the medical examiner's van. As I backed away, the phone in my pocket vibrated. Fishing it out, I glanced at the screen.

Shit.

"Hi, Adam."

"Where are you?" he asked.

Ogling a crime scene. "Across the street."

"You better hurry. Giguhl is already pacing."

"Tell him to chill. The concert doesn't start for an hour."

In the background, I heard Giguhl's deep voice asking if it was me on the phone. Adam affirmed the demon's suspicion. "Tell that misbegotten daughter of Lilith to get her scrawny ass home already. I don't want to miss Pussy Willow's opening number!"

Guilt made me cringe. I should already have been up in that apartment, preparing to head out to Vein. Instead, I was standing in a crowd of mortals eyeing a crime scene like a voyeur. "I'll be up in a sec."

"Okay," Adam said. "Love you."

My stomach jumped. Surprising how those three little words could still pack such a punch. "You too." I clicked the END button and shoved the phone back in my pocket.

The coroner watched his assistant load the body into a black bag. I couldn't get past the feeling that the bag looked a lot like one used to collect trash. For some reason the sight made me feel...heavy. Like someone had thrown away a perfectly good life.

I shook my head to clear away the maudlin thoughts. I had a date with a hot mage, a Mischief demon, and a drag queen fae to get to. With a sigh, I turned my back on the bagged body, the eager bystanders, and the scent of blood.

A block or so ahead and across the street, the spires and turrets of Prytania Place loomed. To some, the mage fortress with its gray stone and gargoyles might seem macabre, a Gothic anachronism crouching sullenly between ambitious skyscrapers. But the warm golden lights beaming from all those arched windows and the promise of friendly mage faces waiting inside called me home.

As I walked, bright night eyes peeked from between the leaves and branches of Central Park's tree line, beckoning me like crooked fingers toward memories of darker times. Back when using humans like fast food was standard operating procedure and my motto was "kill first, avoid questions later."

But that was then. Now, I shook off the cold fingers of those shadow memories. That old life was over. I was happy now. Settled. Safe. I'd left the cold, blood-soaked world behind in favor of one filled with warmth and magic.

I finally reached the gates set into the base of the building. Entered my code, scanned my hand, spoke into the intercom. The gate popped open and I slipped inside. But I couldn't resist turning for one last glimpse of the commotion.

A flash of red hair down the block caught my eye. I took a step forward for a better view. She turned her head, giving me a clear view of her face. I didn't recognize her, but she was definitely a vampire. If the hair hadn't been a dead giveaway, the smile on her face as she watched the scene told me everything I needed to know. Yes, she was definitely a vamp, but was she also the murderer?

I felt eyes on me, a palpable but unmistakable sensation. Figuring the chick had spotted me, I kept my eyes averted. Acknowledging her presence would be asking for trouble.

Instead, I focused my gaze across the street, where the coroner and his assistant hefted the body bag into their van. Somewhere in the city, a roommate or a partner or a mother expected that dead guy home at any minute. My stomach cramped at the thought of some gray-haired woman learning that her son had been slaughtered and left to rot like garbage. To her, only a monster could discard human life so carelessly. And she'd be right.

Funny. I never used to think of vampires as monsters. Back when I lived as one, human life was no more valuable than a Big Mac. I gripped the small cooler in my hand tighter. The bagged blood inside was more than just sustenance. It represented my new life among the mages, one where I'd learned to control my baser instincts.

So why did my fangs still throb?

The apartment Adam and I shared in Prytania Place sat on the third floor. I opted for the stairs for two reasons. One, the ancient elevator usually took twice as long as hoofing it up the steps. And two, after the crime scene, I needed to work off some excess energy.

Were I human, I might have found the staircase creepy with its dark wooden risers and shit-brown walls. I had no idea why the mages hadn't updated the decor since the Victorian era, especially since a remodel would require only a few spells.

I climbed the last few steps and pushed open the door to the hall. I'd made it just a few steps when the air shimmered outside my door. The rise of magic made the hairs on my arm prickle. I braced myself and crouched into a fighting stance. Since I was inside the mage stronghold, an attack was unlikely, but the violence I'd just witnessed left me edgy.

Two seconds later, my twin sister materialized. I let out the breath I'd been holding. Her back was to me, so she hadn't noticed me yet. I took a few cautious steps forward, not wanting to startle her. "Maisie?"

It happened fast. One second, I was reaching out to touch her shoulder. The next, she swung around with a snarl and a flash of fangs. I jumped back, more from surprise than fear. The cooler scuttled across the landing and hit the wall.

"Oh, no!" Maisie gasped, rushing forward to help. "Sabina, I'm so sorry."

The rage on her face when she'd turned had dissolved into red cheeks and a frown. I forced a smile and made a mental note to make more noise next time I approached her from behind. "Not your fault."

She bent to grab the cooler. Handing it over, she gave me a wobbly smile.

Please don't cry.

"Thanks, Maze."

She nodded and shuffled her feet. Her awkwardness wasn't a surprise. This was the longest conversation I'd had with my twin in weeks. The silence welled up around us like rising water.

After a few tense moments, we both spoke at once. Our words tangled in the air like alphabet confetti. Self-conscious laughter followed. "You first," I said.

"I was looking for you."

"Oh?" My eyebrows shot up. Maisie lived on the top floor, in a penthouse apartment complete with gargoyle guards on her rooftop terrace. Since we'd returned to New York, she'd made that place into a plush hermit's cave. "Did you need something?"

She shrugged. "Not really. It's just…been a while. Thought I'd see what you were up to."

As much as her seeking me out warmed me, my stomach tightened. "I was just going to drop this off." I raised the cooler. "Why don't you come in and say hi. I know

Adam and Giguhl will be excited to see you." Without giving her a chance to refuse, I opened the door and shooed her in.

The minute we crossed the threshold, the shit-talking began. "Thanks for joining us, magepire. What the hell took you so long?" This from the seven-foot-tall demon standing in the center of my living room. He tapped a hoof on the hardwoods and shot a glare that would make a lesser woman piss her pants. But when he spotted Maisie, his black lips morphed from a frown into a surprised smile. "Maisie!"

Adam ducked his head out of the kitchen. "Did I hear—" His warm gaze landed on me. Then he saw Maisie and stood straighter. "Wow! It's so good to see you, Maze." A chord of tension braided through his overly enthusiastic greeting. He approached her cautiously, like he was afraid she'd run. He reached for her, but she shied away.

She backed against the wall, crossed her arms, and curled into herself, as if buffering her body from the sudden attention. "Hi." The word was barely above a whisper.

Adam recovered quickly. He changed course and gave me a quick kiss on the lips. "Hey," he whispered. I looked into his eyes and offered a silent apology. His tight smile told me not to worry about it.

"How have you been?" he asked my twin.

She shrugged. "Fine, I guess."

I bit my lip to keep from challenging her claim. True, her frame had lost its heroin-chic thinness and her coloring was better than the ghostly pallor it had been when we'd returned from New Orleans. In fact, she looked better than she had even a week earlier. I took this as a sign that Rhea had convinced her to take her weekly infusion of bagged blood like a good little vampire. Still, her slumped shoulders gave her a brittle appearance and black memories lurked behind her blue eyes.

Back in October, our maternal grandmother, Lavinia Kane—who was also the Alpha of the vampire race—had kidnapped my sister as part of her campaign to start a war between all the dark races. When we'd finally found Maisie inside the crypt that was her prison, she was barely more than a skeleton and out of her mind with bloodlust. I stifled a shudder as memories of that night threatened to take over. I blinked and tried to focus on the here and now. Maisie might be fragile and haunted, but at least she was alive.

We all were, thank the gods. I glanced at Adam as if to reassure myself. Even though Lavinia was dead and the remaining members of the Caste of Nod had been hunted down and killed by the Hekate Council's Pythian Guards and Queen Maeve's faery knights, I sometimes caught myself bracing for attack and searching the shadows for threats. Old habits died hard, I guess.

Maisie looked around the room and said, "Where's Pussy Willow?"

"She's at Vein doing her sound check," Giguhl said. "Her first show is tonight."

"Oh." Maisie frowned. "I didn't know."

Adam and I shared a tense look. We hadn't specifically decided not to invite Maisie. It's just that, well, with her pulling the hermit act all the time we'd just assumed she wouldn't want to go out in public.

"Don't let me keep you then." She turned to scurry off.

"Maisie, wait," I said, jumping forward. "Do you—I mean, I don't suppose you'd want to go with us, would you?"

She paused with a foot at the threshold, tensed for flight. "I don't want to intrude on your date." Something about her tone made my conscience prickle.

Adam stepped up to her. "It's not a date. We're all going."
The hurt drained from her expression. "I don't know."

I gritted my teeth. Why was it still so hard to talk to her?

"You should totally come," Giguhl said. "It'll be the balls."

Maisie looked to me for confirmation. "He's right. Pussy Willow is an amazing performer." A memory of the first time I'd seen the faery perform at the drag club in New Orleans made me smile. "Her shows are not to be missed."

Adam shot my twin his trademark Lazarus smile, the one that usually charmed my pants off in five seconds flat. "Come with us, Maze. You'll love it."

And then a miracle happened: My sister smiled. Her hand flew up like that smile had escaped despite her best efforts to remain miserable. "It has been ages since I've been out."

I stifled my urge to laugh out of relief and continued as if what she'd just done was a normal thing. "So how about it?"

"I—" She hesitated. "Will there be lots of people?"

I reminded myself to be patient. "Yes, but it'll be safe. Promise."

"I'll be your personal bodyguard," Giguhl said.

"Sabina's allowing you to go out in your demon form?" She frowned at him. "Isn't that kind of risky?"

"No, she's not." The demon glared at me. "But don't worry. I'm a badass attack cat when I need to be."

I laughed. "Yeah, right. If anyone gives you trouble, he'll hump their leg like a berserker."

"Hey! I haven't humped anyone in months." The demon pursed his lips. "Anyway, we'd better head out soon." He shot me a pointed look. "Someone made us late."

"Sorry, guys," I said, holding up the cooler. "I ran into some hassle at the blood bank."

"What happened?" Adam asked.

I sighed. "Just a misunderstanding. They have a new girl on staff who wasn't aware of my 'arrangement.' But we got it worked out." My "arrangement" being that the bank supplied me with their diseased or almost-expired blood. Yeah, I know. Gross. But it beat the bullshit I used to deal with by feeding from live humans. "Anyway, after that, I got distracted by a crime scene across the street."

I'd considered not mentioning the murder at all, but (a) only a blind man would have missed the flashing blue lights coming through the wall of windows in the living room and (b) they'd see the scene on the street when we left anyway. Not mentioning it would have been even more cause for speculation.

Giguhl rushed to the window, smelling drama like a bloodhound on the trail of a prison escapee. "Ooh! What happened?"

Adam looked curious, but not overly concerned. This was New York, after all. Crime and the city weren't exactly strangers.

"They found the body in a Dumpster. Seemed pretty nasty, but I moved on before I could get the whole story." I forced a casual shrug to cover my evasion.

"Aw, man," Giguhl said, coming back from the window. "Looks like they're already wrapping things up. You know I hate missing drama."

I pushed down my conscience. Giguhl would have loved to hear the sordid details I was keeping to myself, but sharing them now would only open the door for questions I didn't want to answer.

"Anyway," I said, and cleared my throat. "I just need to grab a quick pint and we can be on our way." I opened the cooler and removed a bag of blood. "Maisie? Do you want some?"

Her eyes jumped to the bag of blood I held toward her. She recoiled like I'd offered her a cobra. Her face swung wildly side-to-side. "No!"

Before I'd offered excuses for my tardiness, she seemed fine. Now her complexion had gone ashen and a fine sheen of sweat coated her brow.

"Maze?" Adam said, moving toward her. "What's wrong?"

I pulled the bag away and hid it behind my back. With my free hand, I reached for her. "Shh. Maisie, it's okay."

Her eyes were wild. "I-I can't." Magic crawled up my spine. In the next instant, Maisie disappeared.

I watched the spot in shock, my stomach sinking. "Shit."

"Nice going, Red," Giguhl said.

"I didn't mean to—Oh, gods, I didn't mean to upset her." My chest clenched with guilt.

"It's not your fault," Adam said. But we both knew that was a lie. His stoic gaze met mine. "I thought she was getting better."

"Are you kidding? That *was* better," Giguhl said. "Remember how she was when we first got back from New Orleans?"

Of course we did. I'd been there when Adam pulled the lid off the tomb where our grandmother had confined her. Saw the feral beast lurking behind her gaze after a week of starvation and being fed upon by her own flesh and blood. And all that was before Lavinia unleashed my blood-crazed sister on Adam, a horror that almost resulted in his death. When Maisie finally killed our grandmother, I'd hoped the poetic justice would alleviate some of her guilt over nearly killing Adam, but, if anything, the violence had only intensified Maisie's issues.

The simple truth was Maisie still needed time. According to Adam's aunt Rhea, my sister's condition was what mortals called post-traumatic stress disorder. The physical wounds resulting from her captivity had healed quickly, but three months wasn't long enough to heal the emotional damage.

"Do you think it was the mention of the murder scene that set her off?" I asked.

Adam shrugged. "Who knows? It could just have easily been the blood."

Since trying to figure out the source of her distress was a futile endeavor at that point, I didn't respond. But I did briefly consider going to look for her. However, since I was the one who set her off, I probably wasn't the best candidate to comfort her.

"Adam, call Rhea and have her check on Maisie." He hesitated. Clearly he was thinking of going after her himself. But Maisie and Adam had their own issues, which made him almost as bad a choice as me. Finally, he nodded and went to grab the phone. Adam's aunt was the only mage who knew how to handle Maisie's...issues.

While Adam went to the kitchen to call his aunt, Giguhl murmured some vague excuse about getting something from his room. I shot him a grateful smile for allowing me a few minutes alone. The last thing I wanted right then was another postmortem about one of Maisie's episodes.

I grabbed my discarded bag of blood and took it with me to find some solace in the view. One of the things I loved about our apartment was the full wall of old sash windows overlooking Central Park. Usually, gazing out at the park's shadowed treetops with the sparkling city lights beyond calmed me. But that night, the blue lights demanded my attention. Tried to seduce me down dark serpentine paths.

But I'd seen enough darkness for one night. I turned my back and focused on ignoring the coagulant aftertaste of my meal. Thus far, my night was not amusing me. And frankly, despite my claims to Maisie that Pussy's show would be fun, I was so not looking forward to going. But I didn't have a choice. Pussy Willow was my friend and I wanted to support her. Besides, if I begged off, I knew I'd just sit around all night brooding about my twin.

"Rhea promised to check on her and give me an update," Adam said, returning from the kitchen. I nodded and speared another bag with my fangs. I used my full mouth as an excuse to avoid talking about what had just happened.

"Red?" Adam's tone was quiet, careful.

I swallowed the last few drops and lowered the empty bag. "Yeah?"

"You okay?"

My first instinct was to fire back with a caustic retort. But this was Adam. He'd see right through it. "I just never know what's going to set her off."

"She's going to be okay. Eventually."

I blew out a shaky breath. "Maybe I need to get Rhea to teach me a patience spell."

The mancy chuckled and wrapped his arms around me. "Red, there are some things even magic can't fix."

I thought about my sister, the once vital, earthy female who used to paint her dreams and loved to laugh. "Tell me about it."

Getting to Vein was something straight out of a spy movie. Adam flashed us to the alley behind a hole-in-the-wall Chinese joint in Hell's Kitchen. To the dark races, this area was known as the Black Light District, where vampires, mages, werewolves, and faeries came to indulge their favorite vices. Vein served as headquarters for the BLD, and its owner, Slade "The Shade" Corbin, ran prostitutes, drugs, and the dark-races underworld out of the club.

As usual, I was thankful for Adam's skills with interspatial travel that allowed me to avoid public transportation. I might not feed off humans anymore, but that didn't mean I wanted to press up against them in a tin can hurtling through a dark tunnel. I kept asking Rhea to teach me how to travel magically, too, but she held me off, saying I needed more experience in basic magic.

Once we arrived, I hefted my large tote bag up on my shoulder. The ugly canvas thing didn't go with my black ensemble at all, but it made lugging my hairless cat demon around town easier.

"We need to put you on a diet, Mr. Giggles," I complained.

A blue knit cap and two batlike ears appeared over the top of the bag. "Bite me, magepire."

I rolled my eyes. Giguhl was always so bitchy in his cat form. Probably because of the ridiculous sweaters and cat toboggans he was forced to wear to protect his hairless body from the frigid New York winter.

Adam crossed his arms. "Are you two done? We're running late."

I held a hand toward the entrance of Pu Pu Palace. "Lead the way."

Adam shook his head as he passed me to the entrance. The place held maybe six tables out front. When we entered, the few mortal customers kept their heads bent over bowls of steaming noodles and General Tso's chicken. Slade must have paid the owner of the restaurant well to not notice the parade of vampires, mages, and faeries who came through the restaurant on a nightly basis. Although, knowing Slade, he'd bought the original owner out and kept the restaurant running as a front for his more illicit businesses.

We went back through the swinging door to the kitchen. Peanut oil droplets and the scent of MSG and mystery meats hung heavy in the air. The cooks sweated over large woks and prattled in a steady stream of Cantonese.

I grabbed an egg roll off a plate and dropped it in the bag for Giguhl to make up for my comment about his weight. A muttered "thanks" reached my ears over the kitchen racket. Adam opened the door to the walk-in freezer and shooed me in. I closed it behind us and pulled the lever to open the hidden passage. Two minutes later, we'd made our way down the stairs and into the tunnel that led to the entrance of Vein.

The regular bouncer, a Mohawked vampire named Joe,

sat on the stool. Word of PW's show must have spread because the line to get in was ten beings deep. Since Adam and I were regulars, Joe waved us past the line. A few disgruntled mutters rose from those who had to wait. I ignored them and high-fived Joe as we passed.

Earl, Vein's fanged barkeep, was busy filling drink orders for the large crowd who'd turned out for Pussy Willow's New York debut. I waved to get his attention and held up three fingers. Earl wasn't exactly the chatty type, but he did deign to nod vaguely in my direction. The move was both a greeting and an acknowledgment that he'd send our drinks over to the table. After the night I'd had so far, I briefly considered changing my regular beer for a double Bloody Magdalene, but knew the move would only earn me The Look from Adam. On the bright side, the beer would go a long way to help scrub the chemical taste of coagulant from my tongue, courtesy of the pint of bagged blood I'd chugged earlier.

Adam beelined for our usual spot—a booth along the back wall that gave us a perfect view of the stage. I scooted in and opened the canvas bag. Giguhl leapt out and onto the vinyl banquette, the move knocking his blue cap askew.

"Ahem?"

"What?"

"You don't really expect me to hang out in this hairless carcass, do you?"

I removed a set of sweatpants from the bag and rose again with a sigh. "We'll be right back."

Carrying the cat under one arm, I made my way through the crowd toward the bathrooms. Ignoring the speculative glances from the females in line for the ladies' room, I went to the men's door. I pushed it open and tossed the cat and the pants inside. Leaning against the wall, I crossed my arms. "Giguhl change forms," I called out loud enough to be heard inside to the john.

Two seconds later a pop sounded. Green smoke wafted under the door, bringing with it the scent of rotten eggs and urinal cakes.

"What the fuck!" a deep male voice shouted from inside. "Keep that thing away from me."

"Don't flatter yourself," Giguhl responded in a bored tone. "You couldn't handle The Pitchfork."

The door burst open and a very large, very pissed-off werewolf exited. As the door swung closed, I was treated to an unsavory view of naked demon ass as Giguhl pulled on his sweatpants. And here I was thinking I was clever for making him change forms in the bathroom. If I didn't know better I'd think Giguhl enjoyed flashing me. Which was likely, considering he was a Mischief demon.

Two seconds later, the seven-foot-tall, green-scaled, black-horned demon emerged. He wore a pair of faded black sweatpants that ended a good six inches above his hooves. He looked ridiculous, but it was better than sitting next to a naked demon all night.

"Did you have to antagonize the werewolf?" I asked.

"That's a rhetorical question, right?"

I rolled my eyes and pushed his shoulder. "C'mon, the show's starting soon."

As we walked back to the booth, I bumped shoulders with a familiar mage. He stopped when he recognized me. "Oh, sorry, Sabina."

I waved away his apology. "Hey, Marty. No worries."

"What up, homeslice?" Giguhl raised a claw to high-five the mage, who we knew casually from around Prytania Place. He was some sort of low-level administrator for the Council, but a nice enough guy.

Marty smiled and slapped Giguhl's claw. "You up for another round of hoops, G? I want a chance to win back that twenty you took off me last time."

"You're welcome to try," Giguhl said, and laughed.

We said our good-byes to Marty and headed back to our seats. Cinnamon, one of Slade's nymph waitresses-slash-prostitutes, had delivered our drinks while we were gone. Giguhl dropped onto the bench and chugged down half his beer. When he paused for a breath, a loud belch escaped his black lips.

"Nice, G." Adam raised his own drink to cover his smile.

"I can't help it," the demon said. "I'm so nervous for Pussy Willow."

"Why?" I asked. "She performed all the time in New Orleans."

Giguhl shot me a bitch-please look. "Yeah, but that was lip-synching. She's been practicing her vocals but she's still really nervous."

"Wait," I said. "You mean she's actually going to sing?" I exchanged a worried look with Adam. He shook his head slightly. Apparently I wasn't the only one who thought there might be a very good reason PW used to lip-synch during her drag shows.

The demon nodded and took a nervous sip of his beer.

"So how's the Roller Derby stuff going, G?" Adam asked, deftly changing subjects before Giguhl could work himself up into a frenzy like an overprotective stage mother.

Giguhl sat forward, warming up to the new topic. "Pretty well. I've recruited six chicks so far."

Up until a few weeks earlier, Giguhl had been the reigning champ of Demon Fight Club. The setup had been simple: Two demons faced off in a fight pit located in Vein's basement. But an incident involving a Lust demon and a mage with attention deficit disorder brought that to a screaming halt. Luckily, I'd missed that ordeal, but according to Giguhl, the whole thing was quite upsetting. "Sabina, some things cannot be unseen," he'd said. Apparently, several of Vein's patrons agreed and Slade was forced to shut down DFC for good.

Never one to let a little difficulty prevent him from making a fast buck, The Shade, as Slade was known in the Black Light District, started looking for new ideas to entertain his customers. Giguhl suggested he bring Pussy Willow up from New Orleans to sing at the club one night a week. The suggestion hadn't been without ulterior motive. Ever since we'd returned to New York, Giguhl had been moping about missing the changeling.

When she arrived, Pussy Willow admitted she'd been looking for a chance to get out of the Big Easy. "Everyone there still thinks of me as Brooks," she'd said. "Even Zen had a hard time remembering I'm a full-time lady now."

Brooks was the changeling's given name. He used to live his life as a full-time male and part-time drag queen. But after an attack by a group of crazy cult members, Brooks had decided he felt safer behind a wig and stilettos. That's when he became Pussy Willow full-time. And, since everyone in New Orleans knew Brooks, the changeling believed coming to New York would give her a chance at a fresh start among people who didn't know her past.

"I feel just like Mary Tyler Moore," she'd exclaimed the night she arrived. "And Giguhl is my Rhoda."

Anyway, after the success in bringing Pussy Willow up, Giguhl went to Slade with the Roller Derby idea after watching some movie. And that's when the idea for Hell on Wheel's Roller Derby Night was born.

I leaned forward to look past Adam at my minion. "I didn't realize you were already recruiting for the team."

The demon nodded, his enthusiasm palpable. "I convinced Slade to host the first match here next week."

I blinked. "Wow. How many team members do you need total?" This wasn't an idle question. Ever since he'd first brought up the idea of putting a team together, I'd been waiting for my invitation.

"I'd like ten. That way we'll have plenty of subs. So far I have three mages, two of Slade's nymphs, and, of course, Pussy Willow."

"No vamps?" I asked. "Or weres?" I added at the last minute so it wouldn't look like I was digging.

Giguhl pulled the label off his beer bottle and started shredding it. "That's the problem. I don't know any vampires in the city. And all the weres I know are dudes."

I stilled. He didn't know any vampires? "Um, Giguhl? Not to point out the obvious or anything, but…I'm a vampire."

"You don't count." He waved a claw.

"What's that supposed to mean?"

He shrugged. "You're not going to be on the team." He said this like it was the most obvious statement in the world.

I set down my beer with deliberate slowness. "And why not?"

Adam tensed. He knew I'd been waiting for Giguhl to ask me to be on the team.

"Don't give me that look, trampire," Giguhl said. "It's nothing personal."

"You just told me you need warm bodies for the team. And in the next breath, you say you don't want me. How am I not supposed to take it personally?"

Giguhl finally noticed the sharp edge to my words. He

shot a look at Adam. "Um, I'm not asking friends to be on the team."

"But you just said PW is on it!"

Giguhl cradled the beer between his claws and sighed. "Look, Red, no offense, but you're not exactly a team player."

My mouth fell open. "How can you say that? What happened to us being Team Awesome?"

Two dubious male stares greeted that statement.

"What?" I demanded. "I know I had some problems remembering the team thing in New Orleans but I'm much better now. Right?"

Adam shifted uncomfortably. "I think what Giguhl means is that since he's your minion you won't take coaching from him seriously."

I grabbed my beer and sat back with a huff. "That's the most ridiculous thing I've ever heard."

"See?" Giguhl said, looking at Adam. "She's already undermining me."

The lights dimmed. Giguhl's eyes widened and he swiveled toward the stage. But if he thought this conversation was over, he was sorely mistaken. How dare he imply I couldn't be a team player?

"Here we go," Adam said under his breath. He tried to pull me closer but I remained stiffly distant. He sighed and leaned in. "Oh, come on. You didn't really want to play Roller Derby anyway."

He was right, of course. I thought the costumes and nicknames the teams used were silly. Still, Giguhl's rejection stung more than it should have. But none of that was Adam's fault, so I scooted closer.

Onstage, spotlights flashed and a machine belched smoke. PW's backup band appeared and took their positions, accompanied by lackluster applause from the crowd. A few moments later, they began to play a swingy baseline.

"Ladies and gentlemen." Pussy Willow's voice came from the speakers. She stood just offstage in the shadows with her mic. "Vein is proud to present the Black Light District's newest musical sensation—Pussy Willow and the Catnips!"

Giguhl looked over his shoulder. "The band name was my idea!" He looked so proud that I smothered my urge to roll my eyes. Instead, I shot him two thumbs-up. When the demon turned back around, Adam squeezed my thigh and smiled.

With the lights still down, the Catnips switched the melody into the opening notes of the first song. Instead of the upbeat dance songs PW performed at Lagniappe in New Orleans, this had a jazzy lounge sound. Sounded vaguely familiar, but I couldn't call the title to mind.

In the shadows, Pussy Willow's silhouette rushed across the stage to take her place. A few seconds later, a single spotlight illuminated the piano. The faery draped across the top like a mink stole. She wore a long, blue-sequined gown and Lana Turner waves spilled over her shoulder.

She lifted the microphone to her bright red lips like a phallus. The first words were something about making it through the wilderness but not knowing how lost she was. I frowned. Where had I heard this song before? The words were familiar but the bossa nova beat threw me off.

But then she got to the refrain. With her false-lashed eyes groping the audience, she sang, "Like a virgin, touched for the very first time."

A snort escaped my mouth. I couldn't help it. Adam bit his lip. Giguhl shot a glare over his shoulder.

It's not that Pussy's singing was funny. She actually was

doing a pretty good job. But her choice of song was hilarious. I had to give her some credit, though—she was a pretty sexy woman ... for someone with a penis.

I looked around to gauge the audience's reaction. The crowd at Vein was used to screaming for blood at Demon Fight Club. But I was pleasantly surprised to see most of the patrons enjoying the performance. Especially the nymphs, who gathered in a clutch near the back of the bar. The nymphs usually didn't take kindly to other hot chicks getting male attention on their turf. After all, they made their living seducing Slade's patrons. But that night a few of them even sang along with the changeling.

As I watched, Marty approached Tansy, one of Slade's most popular nymphs. She was known for providing services to more adventurous johns, like a certain Mischief demon who shall remain nameless. Marty spoke to her briefly and handed her something I couldn't see. She palmed what he offered and took his hand to lead him to the back rooms.

Dismissing the exchange, I started to look back at the stage, but a familiar auburn-haired male near the bar caught my eye. My stomach did a little dip. "Shit."

Adam turned and followed my gaze. "What's wrong?"

Crap. I hadn't meant to say that out loud.

"Oh, nothing." I shook my head. He'd already seen who caused my reaction so there was no use in lying. "Just surprised to see Slade. I thought he was still in California."

Adam shrugged. "Cinnamon said he got back this afternoon. It'll be interesting to hear what news he has about how Tanith's doing as Despina."

I nodded absently. As much as I wanted to know what was going on now that Tanith had taken over the leadership of the vamp race, I wasn't sure I was ready to hear it from

Slade. Ever since we'd returned to New York, I'd managed to avoid much contact with him.

My avoidance had less to do with his personality and more to do with our shared, very personal history. As far as Adam knew, that history was old news. I'd told him about how back in Los Angeles in the late '70s, Slade and I had partnered on a case that went south. And when I say "partnered," I mean in more ways than one. But what Adam didn't know was that Slade and I had repeated history just before Maisie was kidnapped. It was only one night and the mancy and I weren't together at that time, but I'd kept that mistake to myself because I knew it would hurt Adam. Okay, it would hurt me to tell him, too. Regardless, I tried to avoid Slade as a rule to avoid any chance the truth might come out.

Unfortunately, Slade hadn't gotten that memo. Because he saw me looking at him and headed our way. I tensed. I couldn't very well escape the booth with the show going on. Besides, I couldn't think of a way to justify avoiding Slade that blatantly to Adam. So I just sat there and prayed I didn't look as uncomfortable as I felt.

By that point, Pussy Willow had moved on to an acoustic version of "Papa Don't Preach." I glued my gaze to the stage, pretending I wasn't counting down the steps until Slade reached us. So when he tapped me on my shoulder, I performed a pretty convincing startle.

"Oh!" I said, jerking around like he'd caught me off guard. "Hey, Slade."

He grinned down at me. Damn him. He knew I saw him coming. "Can I talk to you?"

I cupped a hand to my ear. "Sorry, can't hear you over the—"

Just then, Adam leaned over, interrupting me. "Care to join us?"

Slade's grin widened. I wanted to scrape that smile off his face with a belt sander. "Actually, I was hoping to steal Sabina from you."

My fists clenched at his double entendre. Damn him.

Adam shrugged. "Fine by me."

Slade smirked and raised an eyebrow at me. I wanted to kick both him and the mancy. But instead of hitting either male, I leaned over and slapped a wet, sloppy kiss on Adam. "Be right back," I whispered, pulling away. He looked a little dazed by my enthusiasm, but managed a nod.

As I exited the booth, I took my frustration out on Slade's foot. He gave me the devil's own smile and stepped back with a slight limp.

Giguhl looked up to shoot us a nasty glare for disrupting his enjoyment of Pussy Willow's show. But when he saw me standing next to Slade, his eyebrows shot to his horns. He was the only one I had told about my indiscretion with Slade, so he had cause to speculate. Luckily, he covered his reaction smoothly and turned to engage Adam with some comment about the show.

$\mathcal{A}$s I climbed the metal stairs, Slade's presence loomed behind me. Even though I had no interest in him as a lover anymore, it was hard not to appreciate his hotness. Auburn hair combed into a carelessly expensive style. An easy smile backed up with steely confidence and charming opportunism. His white dress shirt was open at the neck, exposing corded muscles and a thick, blue vein. Looking at him was like being a kid presented with candy from a handsome stranger.

Luckily, I'd outgrown my sweet tooth for that particular confection. Plus, the lie I'd told Adam hung around my neck like a lead scarlet letter.

Once we reached the office, he closed the door behind us. The muffled strains of Pussy Willow's rendition of "Crazy for You" filtered into the room.

"I'm surprised to see you here," I said, leading the way into the office. "I thought you were still in California."

He leaned against the edge of his desk and crossed his arms. "Been keeping tabs on me, Bina?"

I narrowed my eyes. "Please. Everyone knows you're Tanith's man now."

Tanith was the new leader of the vampire race. She used to share that role with two other vampires, the three making up the triumvirate we called the Dominae. My grandmother, Lavinia Kane, had been the Alpha Domina until Tanith conspired with the mage Hekate Council to have her killed to prevent a war between the races. Now that Lavinia was dead, Tanith had maneuvered herself into being named Despina of the race. From what I'd heard, the third former-Domina, Persephone, had been demoted to little more than Tanith's lapdog.

As the leader of New York's vampire population, Slade was a good ally for the Despina to have in her pocket. It didn't hurt that he had good relations with the Hekate Council— or that his support for her new regime was easily bought.

"I just returned from Los Angeles last night," he said. "The Despina decided to come to the Big Apple early to finalize some of the finer points of the treaty with the Hekate Council."

My eyebrows shot up at this news. I hadn't heard Tanith was already in town. But then, it's not like the Hekate Council felt the need to keep me updated. Besides, I was hoping they'd keep the new Despina so busy I wouldn't have to see her at all until the night of the treaty signing. I just wanted to keep my head down and the drama out of my life until that damned thing was finalized.

But Slade hadn't called me to his office to discuss the Despina. "I need to talk to you about a delicate matter." Tension braided through his words like piano wire.

I crossed my arms and tilted my head. "Why do I sense I won't enjoy this conversation?"

"Now, now. Don't go getting all defensive."

"Who's defensive?" I said, unclenching.

He smiled knowingly. Then he went in for the kill. "See

anything interesting on your stroll through Central Park earlier tonight?"

Shock rippled through me. Slade's knowledge of my activities shouldn't have been a surprise. As the leader of New York's vampires and mob boss of the Black Light District, he had eyes all over the city. I forced a casual shrug. "Oh, you know, the usual. Joggers, muggers, a dead body." No point in denying I'd seen the murder scene. He already knew.

"You want to explain to me why you didn't come to me with the information?" His paternal tone set my fangs on edge.

"It's none of my business." Slade's face tightened into a disapproving frown, but before he could launch into a lecture, I had a question. "Who told you they saw me in the park?"

He crossed his arms. "One of Michael's packs was on patrol. They saw you."

Fucking werewolves. Slade's main duty was keeping the vamps in line, but he also had influence over the local fae and werewolf packs to keep peace in the city. To prevent territorial disputes, he'd divided the boroughs into separate feeding areas. A pack that called themselves The Lone Wolves got most of Central Park. The pack's Alpha, Michael Romulus, and I were friends, but this wasn't the first time The Lone Wolves had caused me trouble.

"Did they also tell you there was another vampire chick there?"

Slade frowned. "No, they didn't mention it. Who was she?"

"Never seen her before." I shook my head. "I only got a quick look from far away, but her red was lighter than mine, so she must have been young. You might ask the pack again. See if any of their guys spotted her."

Slade smiled. "Does this mean you're going to help after all?"

"No. That's as far as I'm going down this path. Just look for that chick and you'll probably find your killer."

Slade shifted on his desk and his face took on a devil's advocate slant. "You know, her presence at the scene is no more proof of her guilt than it is of yours."

"What the hell do you mean by that?"

He shrugged. "Some might speculate that you hung around to admire your own handiwork."

I choked out a laugh. "Give me a fucking break. Even if I was still feeding from humans—which we both know I'm not—I'm smart enough to clean up after myself."

His expression cleared and he pushed away from the desk. "I know that. Which is why I want you to help me find the idiot who did this."

"Why?" I didn't even try to hide the suspicion in my tone.

"Why do I need help? Or why you?"

"Why *everything*?"

I'd worked for him on a job months earlier—before Maisie was taken and shit went down in New Orleans. He'd asked me to rough up a strip club owner named Tiny Malone who owed Slade some money. I'd delivered the threats but then Tiny turned the tables on me and I barely escaped. The altercation had sparked off some emotional shit for me and I'd ended up calling Slade for help. Which is what led to us sleeping together. So needless to say, his request made all my warning bells shriek with alarm.

"Don't get me wrong. I'm not asking you to come on my payroll permanently or anything. I know you've got your own . . . stuff going on." The undertone in that one sentence was strong enough to give me pause, but he kept talking. "This is more of a favor that I'm willing to pay you for. But

I need you to promise you won't tell any of your mage buddies about it for now."

I swirled my hand through the air so he'd continue. I wasn't promising not to tell anyone about it until I knew everything. Slade was notorious for "forgetting" to mention important—and damning—details.

"It worries me that the cops are involved." He spat this out like a gunpoint confession. Like he hated admitting he worried about anything. "Usually we're able to clean up these messes and put the mortals off the scent of vampire involvement. But they're all over this. Right now they're calling it a murder, but once the press gets ahold of the details we could have trouble."

I leaned back and crossed my arms. "So you've got a vamp who sucks at covering her tracks. Why do you need my help?"

He hesitated. "It's complicated."

I rolled my eyes. Since when weren't things complicated with him? "Save your breath, Slade. I'm not looking for complications in my life right now."

"Hmm." He pursed his lips.

He was baiting me. I knew it. "Whatever." I started to rise. "I've given you my answer."

"I have a bad feeling about this, Sabina." He stepped forward, his eyes pleading. Something about his tone told me he wasn't bullshitting me this time. I paused and crossed my arms, ready to listen. "If word gets out that I can't control the local vamps, the Despina might find someone else to take over here."

Satisfied I wasn't about to walk out the door, he approached the bar and held up a decanter filled with amber liquid. I shook my head and took a swig of the drink I'd forgotten I had. "I know you want to stay out of this, but if the Despina appoints some West Coast vamp to take control of the local population, the results could be potentially explosive. Especially since most of the local vamps escaped L.A. because they didn't want to live under the Dominae's dictatorial laws anymore."

The words "potentially explosive" had been used on purpose. He knew me well enough to know that no matter how much I claimed to want peace in my life, part of me would never fully be out of the game. On the other hand, working with Slade again had its own potentially explosive ramifications. Ones I was determined to avoid at all costs.

"New York's vamps are right to be wary. I don't buy Tanith's new kinder, gentler vampire party line. But none of that's my business anymore. I'm done with vampire drama."

Slade snorted and dropped a piece of ice in his glass. "Sabina, please. Let's not bullshit each other. You might have everyone else convinced you're cool with domestic bliss, but I know you better than that. I left the assassin life behind once, too, remember? Even tried to live the straight life for a few years. But the boredom almost killed me. Luckily, I wised up and got into organized crime. Otherwise I'd probably be a serial killer by now." He chuckled at his own joke, but we both knew he wasn't far off the mark. He took a casual sip of his drink. "How long has it been since you killed anyone?"

I schooled my features. "Only a psychopath would keep track of something like that."

"A psychopath is just an assassin without pay." A slow smile spread across his lips. "You don't want to admit what you really are? Fine. But don't be surprised when that darkness inside you rises up and you're forced to deal with it."

"That's the difference between you and me, Slade." I set down my drink and rose with deliberate slowness. "I'm actually happy no one's tried to kill me in months. It's a nice change of pace. I'm done with that dark shit. I'm embracing the light now."

He laughed out loud. "Sweetheart, you might like to pretend you're a mage now, but you're still half vampire. And we all know what happens to vampires who embrace the light."

Our gazes locked. Sounds from the bar intruded into the tense silence between us. I was so intent on glaring at Slade that it took me a second to register what I was hearing. The music had cut off and had been replaced by screams. But they weren't the shouts of a happy audience. They were the shrieks of terrified patrons. Slade heard them, too. One second he was by the desk and the next he ran past me to the large one-way mirror that looked down on the bar.

"What the—" he breathed. Curious, I joined him. By the time I reached the window, beings were running around like spooked animals.

In the center of the chaos, Tansy was screaming and covered in blood. Slade ran to the door and threw it open. I followed him onto the landing.

"Tansy?" he shouted.

The nymph looked up with wide, spooked eyes. "Someone killed my client!"

*I*n the aftermath of Tansy's shocking announcement, my stomach dropped as if someone had pitched it from the Empire State Building. My head started to shake from side to side, as if the movement could somehow reverse time and make her a liar. Marty was dead? No way.

Slade stared at her for a split second before leaping down the stairs. As he ran to her, he barked orders. "Giguhl, help Earl seal all the exits. No one leaves until I clear them. Once that's done, call Michael Romulus and tell him to bring his pack down to help take statements from everyone. Got it?"

The demon jerked into action and took off across the bar. I stood numbly, unable to process anything or do much more than stare dumbly at the spot where Tansy sat. Slade turned and located Pussy Willow among the onlookers. "PW, take Tansy. Get her cleaned up."

Pussy Willow came forward and wrapped a comforting arm around the nymph. "Come on, *cherie*. I got a special bottle of hooch in my dressing room. We'll have a nip or two and fix you up right as rain." Despite her upbeat tone, PW's face had gone pale under all that makeup. As the pair passed, the changeling looked at me with real fear in her eyes.

"What can we do?" Adam asked. Thank the gods one of us was thinking clearly.

Slade's jaw clenched as if trying to keep his temper in check. Knowing the vampire, underneath that calm but determined façade, he was simmering with anger that someone dare do something like this under his own roof. "Both of you come with me."

Slade led us through the door at the back of the club and into a nondescript hallway. A clutch of nymphs huddled at the end, whispering to each other and crying pretty tears. The air hung heavy with the aftershocks of violence and the scent of blood. Too much blood.

He stopped outside a door halfway down and on the left. His solemn eyes met mine; our shared look held the weight of . . . too much knowledge. Judging from the strong odor of blood, there was no chance Tansy was mistaken about Marty's murder. "Brace yourselves," Slade said. "This is going to be messy."

He twisted the knob and pushed. The portal swung inside slowly but the air, heavy with the stench of death, slammed into us like a sucker punch.

I swallowed hard. It was one thing to see a crime scene when the victim was a stranger. Easy to compartmentalize. But knowing that the victim this time was someone I'd known and liked made me pause at the threshold. Almost as if I knew that once I crossed into that room, life would never be the same.

I licked my suddenly dry lips. "Let's get this over with."

Marty's body hung from hooks like a macabre mobile.

Pinned like a bloody butterfly. Displayed like a gruesome objet d'art.

A single, surgical line ran from his Adam's apple to his groin. Wounds ravaged his neck, his thighs. But his lips tilted up in a secret smile.

Whoever strung him over the bed hadn't worried about the mess. The formerly white sheets looked like Rorschach ink blots made from pools of blood and entrails. The air stunk of sex and fear.

Oxygen was suddenly too heavy for my lungs. Cold sweat coated my chest. And my mind turned into a sadistic time machine, forcing me back to a night thirty years earlier.

The virgin corpses hang from hooks like grisly angels. The Dominae stand below, their moonbeam skin bared to our eager eyes. Blood rains down, coating their hands, their lips, their breasts.

I tried to blink away the memory. Wanted to dig it out with those hooks. But it wouldn't budge.

"No," Lavinia's voice cracks through the temple. "Not her." My dreams disintegrate, choke me. Wet cement hits my lungs. My cheeks burn with shame. But Lavinia's smile is cold.

"Sabina?" Adam's voice sounded far away. But it somehow managed to break through the haze of remembered pain. I swallowed hard. My eyes focused again and they found the carnage that met them a relief. The blood and the gore and the thumbprint of violence were preferable to the bitter memories of that night long ago. The night Lavinia stole the future I wanted and replaced it with the one she needed. The night that left me fractured. Gave me the wounds that never fully healed. The night she made me an assassin.

"Red?" Adam said, closer now.

I blinked. Confusion on his handsome face and worry. Worry and love I never saw in Lavinia's cold mask.

"Sorry. You were saying?"

Adam watched me warily, as if he expected me to bolt. He placed a hand on my arm. The contact was my undoing. I saw his lips move but I couldn't hear him anymore. The overpowering scent of blood, the nauseating reek of decay, the biting sting of those black memories suffocated me. I clawed at the collar of my coat. I needed fresh air. I needed space.

"I need to go." I barely managed to force the words out over the rising tide of bile and shame. Adam didn't try to stop me. Bless him.

I groped past Slade, past the nymphs clogging the hall-way. Didn't bother with manners. Just pushed through them like a drowning woman straining for the sur-face. Soon but not soon enough, I burst through the wom-en's restroom door. I slammed it closed and clicked the dead bolt.

The stalls and walls were painted industrial gray. Dingy white tiles looked like decayed teeth with plaque for grout. One of the faucets dripped methodically, like a counter ticking down the seconds to my nervous break-down. I sucked in lungfuls of fetid air despite the scent of old mildew and wet cardboard and pine solvent. But what the restroom lacked in fresh oxygen it made up for with privacy.

Fluorescent bulbs overhead sputtered light like strobes, flashing in time with my heartbeat. The mirrors were little more than scraps of polished metal. Apparently, the clien-tele of Vein had little interest in using the mirrors as intended. Instead, they'd graffitied every inch of the surface with markers and lipstick. My mirror, for example, served as a canvas for a spurned lover who claimed that "Ben Charles is a fucking liar!" The last two words screamed across my face in harlot-red lipstick.

I turned on the tap and splashed water on my face. It stunk like rusty pipes, but it was as cold as a much-needed slap.

"Get it together, Sabina," I said aloud to my reflection. But that face with the wide eyes. That pale visage with its lips pulled back in fear. That face wasn't impressed by my bravado. That face knew things I hadn't been able to admit to myself. Not yet.

I focused on getting my hitching breaths under control. On convincing my heart to stop trying to claw through my chest cavity. For a few moments, I hovered on the knife's edge between sanity and hysteria. Then, thank the gods, I finally took my first painless breath. My neck muscles unclamped, leaving behind a dull ache in my jaw. I took another handful of water and rubbed my hands over my face. When I looked up again, the panic in my eyes had dulled. But the smoky gray shadows still lurked.

I released a long, slow breath. And with it, Lavinia's ghost. But I knew the relief would be short-lived. Demons like Lavinia Kane never stayed exorcised.

The door handle shook. I swiveled, automatically crouching into a fighting stance.

"Sabina?" Adam's muffled voice drifted through the door.

I blew out a breath. "One sec!" I used my shirt hem to wipe away the rest of the water. Checked my reflection one last time in the mirror. I glared at the strange chick staring back at me. "Suck it up."

With that, I turned and went to the door. My hands shook as I flipped the bolt. The door whipped open with more force than necessary. It slammed against the gray wall like a gunshot. Adam flinched and narrowed his eyes at me. "Everything okay?" The question was hesitant, the kind one would use with a woman on the edge.

"Yep. All good."

"What happened back there?" He jerked his head toward the door down the hall.

This was definitely not the time nor the place to have a heart-to-heart with him about how seeing Marty strung up like a virgin sacrifice had resurrected feelings I'd believed buried for good. Feelings of revenge and loss, guilt and victory, disappointment and pride about Lavinia's death. One of the shittiest parts about mourning is that just when you think you've moved on, someone else dies and all that grief rises up, resurrecting all the pain and anger and remorse. But, like I said, not the time or the place. Hell, if I had my way, no time or place would ever be right to talk about it again.

"The smell got to me." I shrugged and forced a self-deprecating laugh to hide the lie. "Guess I'm losing my edge."

"I don't think anyone has an edge sharp enough not to be affected by that."

True enough. Even Adam, who was normally unflappable, looked green around the gills. "Does Slade have any idea who did this?"

Adam shook his head. He turned to walk back down the hall. I froze, my feet glued to the grimy tiles. My gut twisted at the thought of going back into that room. But then I noticed someone had closed the door. Swallowing my resistance, I marched toward Slade, determined to ignore the fear and the memories and focus on the job of finding out who killed Marty.

When we reached Slade, Michael Romulus was by his

side, going over what they knew so far. Adam and I exchanged quick handshakes with the werewolf Alpha before we all got down to business.

"None of the girls saw anything," Slade said. "Cinnamon found Tansy knocked out in the supply closet. They found the body together."

"How many entrances and exits are there to this area?" I asked, switching to just-the-facts-ma'am mode.

"Just the one door. None of the rooms have windows either. Best bet is the killer did the job and slipped back into the club while Pussy Willow was playing. Looks like probably a fifteen- to thirty-minute window between his escape and Cinnamon finding Tansy."

In other words, he had fuck-all in the way of leads.

"From the looks of it," I said, "the culprit is almost definitely a vampire."

Michael frowned at me. "What makes you say that?"

I hesitated, not wanting to go down this path but knowing I had to. "The position of the body." I couldn't stand to say Marty's name right then if I was going to maintain my distance. "There's an old Dominae ritual where they string up virgins above an altar and bathe in the blood."

Adam's eyebrow raised to his hairline. Something in his eyes told me he was connecting the dots about my earlier reaction. Luckily, Michael jumped in before the mage could question me about it.

"Or someone wants us to think it was a vampire to throw us off their scent," Michael said. "Any number of beings could have done it. Several classifications of demons would be capable of this."

"Or a rogue werewolf," Slade said.

Michael tensed like he wanted to get defensive about that theory but thought better of it. "A rogue wolf wouldn't make it far without me picking up a scent, but it'd be foolish to rule any possibility out at this point."

"He's right," Adam said. "A mage could flash in and out unnoticed, which blows Slade's escape-through-the-club theory out of the water. Hell, even a faery with enough motivation could have pulled this off."

"There's something else," I said to the mancy. The other two males knew this already but it was time to fill Adam in on the truth about what I'd seen earlier that night. "Remember how I said there was a murder in Central Park earlier?" He frowned and nodded. "When Slade asked me to come to his office it was to discuss that killing. When I saw the body, it had bite marks and there wasn't enough blood at the scene to show for the extent of the male's injuries. That means vampire."

"She's right," Michael said. "My boys saw the body and believed the culprit was probably a vamp, too."

"So you think the two murders are connected?" Adam asked.

"I think it'd be a mistake to think two sadistic murders happening on dark-race territory on one night is a coincidence," I said. "The real question is, are we dealing with a garden-variety psycho or someone with more strategic reasons?"

"Do you think this is related to the peace negotiations?" Michael asked.

My stomach tightened at the possibility. "Like you said, we can't rule anything out yet. But for the record, I sure as hell pray this is just a psychotic vampire with a hard-on for drama." I didn't even want to contemplate the alternative. I'd worked too hard, sacrificed too much to face yet another roadblock to peace.

Slade ran a hand over his face. "Christ, what a clusterfuck. When the Despina finds out about this, she's going to rake me over the coals."

"Forget the Despina," Adam said. "When Orpheus finds out a mage was murdered—possibly by a vampire—he's going to shit bricks. With the peace treaty signing looming, he's going to lock this city down until the perpetrator is found."

Slade looked like he was going to be sick. "Speaking of, I'd better go call the High Councilman now so he hears this from me. In the meantime, Mike, I want you and your boys to get statements from everyone in the bar. Maybe we'll get lucky and someone will have seen something."

"And if they didn't?" I asked.

"Then I'm going to tear this city apart until I find the asshole responsible."

That morning I had the dream again. The same one I'd had at least once a week since that fateful night in New Orleans. The night everything changed.

I am tied to a cold marble slab.

"Look at what you've done to them," Lavinia whispers. I jerk my head, desperate to block out the sight of Maisie's red-and-black head bobbing against Adam's chest.

So much blood. Too much. Adam's face contorts into a grimace of pain. Lavinia's fingernails dig into the soft skin around my eyes, drawing blood. But I am too crazed with guilt and horror to register the pain. If anything, the red blurring my vision is a blessing. "Oh, no, you must watch and understand. Your existence brings pain to all unfortunate enough to meet you."

Here the dream deviates from memory. Instead of calling on the powers of Lilith and Hekate for aid as I did that night, I rise from the slab under my own power. The shackles fall away. I inhale Lavinia into me until she is me and I am her.

As I rise, the walls of the temple fall away and reveal a

dusty crossroads with Adam and Maisie in the center, locked in their bloody embrace.

"Sabina!" Adam shouts, but his voice shatters and disperses like blood mist. I run toward him, but it's like running through a deep tide. When I finally manage to reach them, Maisie looks up.

I still and my heart stops. It's not Maisie who looks up. It's me. My face is smeared with Adam's blood. I smile and flash my sharp, red fangs at myself.

Cain appears. His red hair flashes brighter than arterial blood and his green eyes glow with evil intent. "Finish him," the father of the vampire race says. "Finish him, Lamashtu, and we can finally be together."

For a moment, I inhabit my vampire half's mind and I look up at my mage self. I pity her with her tears and sickening vulnerability. I can't blame her for her weakness for the mage, though. His blood tastes like candy. Like a drug I can never quit. I raise an eyebrow and smile at my mage self. Once I'm sure she's looking, I go back for more.

I slam back into my mage self. The greedy slurping sounds make my stomach turn. "No! Stop! You're killing him."

"Why do you deny yourself?" Cain whispers in my ear. "You are a killer."

I shake my head. "Not anymore."

A sword appears in my hand, as if summoned. I white-knuckle the grip. Adam sags as my vampire drains his life away drop by drop. Tears wet my face. Indecision shatters me.

Adam's face is pale, too pale. His eyes burn into mine, pleading. "Kill her, Sabina. One last time and then you will be free."

I peer down at the bloodthirsty incarnation of myself. The self I'd known for fifty-four years. The one whose past was soaked in blood and anger. I barely recognize her now.

She's all fangs and hunger. A wild thing. Uncontrollable. Savage.

"Don't listen to him," Lavinia's voice comes from the vampire-me's lips. "Without me you'll fade to nothing."

"Sabina," Adam pleads. "I love you."

Those three words work on me like a spell. Like a sleeper awakened, I know what I must do. My vampire self is a cancer. And like all cancer, it must be excised before life can flourish. The blade glints on its downward path. Slices clean through the neck. I feel the impact severing the umbilical cord connecting my two halves. My vampire explodes in a cloud of black smoke and flame.

The instant she is dead, Lavinia's soul rises from the ashes like a phoenix—or an exorcized demon. Adam falls forward into my arms. I cling to him like he'd just saved me instead of the other way around. Cain towers over us. But when I look up at him, he's transparent.

I wake with Cain's parting words on my lips. "We aren't finished."

The summons came at the butt crack of dusk. Adam was already awake and had received the note from Orpheus's assistant. When he woke me up and showed it to me, I cursed.

"Please tell me this is about Giguhl peeing in the flower beds again," I groaned.

"We both know what it's about." Adam slapped my ass. "Come on, get up. It'll only be worse if we keep him waiting."

"Worse for you, maybe. He's not my boss." Adam was a Pythian Guard, sort of a mage version of the secret service and special forces rolled into one. Part of Orpheus's role as the leader of the Hekate Council was to be the commander in chief of the guards. But in addition to being his boss, the ancient mage was also a father figure and mentor to Adam.

"Stop it," Adam said, losing his patience. "He's as much your boss as mine now, Miss High Priestess of the Blood Moon."

I shot a sour look in his direction. "Technically, Rhea is in charge of the priestesses. Besides, it's not like that's my job." In fact, I didn't have a job at all, except for twice-weekly magic lessons, which didn't earn me anything other than some cool new party tricks.

"Let's make a deal, then. If you get up and into the shower, I'll bring you a huge mug of coffee."

With a martyred sigh, I made a production of hefting myself out of the bed. "Fine, but make sure to put a shot of whisky in it. If this is really about the murders, I'm going to need some liquid fortification."

Thirty minutes later, we walked into the office of High Councilman Orpheus—no last name, like Sting, only with less tantric sex—of the Ancient Venerable Hekate Council. But it wasn't Orpheus who drew my gaze and made me stop in my tracks.

Slade had mentioned she was in town, but I certainly hadn't expected to see her right then: Tanith Severinus, Exalted Despina of the Lilim. She'd given herself the fancy title when she became sole ruler of the vampire race two months earlier. I'm not sure how her closest friends referred to her now, but I still called her "the Bitch."

For an ancient vampiress with total power over an entire race, you'd figure she'd have enough money to do something about her unfortunate appearance. Between the rusty mess of curls on her head, the bulbous Roman nose, and the cleft chin that resembled a butt crack, she'd lost the beauty lottery and then been beaten with the ugly stick for good measure. I wish I could say her insides made up for the unfortunate outsides, but they didn't. I'm not sure if the doctors surgically inserted the bug up her ass or if she'd been born with it, but a less personable vampire I'd never met—with the exception of my own grandmother, but even she managed to crack a smile every now and then in between attempts on my life.

When she saw me enter, her lips puckered up like an

anus. "Mr. Lazarus." She nodded regally like she was balancing a tiara on her head instead of a mop of kinky frizz. "Sabina."

"Hey, *Tanith*." Her eyes narrowed at my use of her given name. Too damned bad. I wasn't her underling anymore. "I wish I could say it's been too long, but—you know."

The last time we'd seen each other was three months earlier just after we'd returned to the Seelie Court fresh from our victory over Lavinia and the Caste of Nod in Louisiana. Not long enough in my opinion.

"Orpheus tells me you've settled right into mage life," she said. "I wish I could say it's a surprise you shed your illustrious vampire heritage so easily but—you know."

The corner of my mouth twitched. As implied insults go, it wasn't half bad. Alluding to the shame of my mixed blood was a smooth move on her part, but I was beyond caring what any vampire thought of me, especially a former Domina.

"I was hoping to meet that twin of yours," Tanith continued. "I've been told she is your mirror image."

I opened my mouth to respond, but Orpheus interrupted. "Maisie has gone into seclusion to meditate and prepare for sharing a prophecy at the Imbolc festival."

I flinched in confusion. Why was he lying to Tanith?

"Ah, yes," the Despina said. "I understand. I must admit I'm quite eager to hear what the Oracle has to say about our new future as allies."

Orpheus cleared his throat. "As am I." He shifted and shot me a meaningful look. I wasn't sure if it was a warning to keep my mouth shut or a promise that he'd explain his reasoning later, but I held my tongue either way. I was no more eager to discuss Maisie's situation with Tanith than Orpheus was.

"Let's begin," Orpheus said. "We don't have much time before we have to get on a conference call with Queen Maeve."

"Why hasn't the Queen come to the city for the meetings?" Adam asked, taking a seat next to me.

"She refuses to leave the court unless it's absolutely necessary," Orpheus explained. "She'll be here for the treaty signing, of course, but all the negotiations are happening virtually."

I raised my eyebrows in relief. As much as I didn't enjoy seeing Tanith again, I thanked the gods for saving me from suffering the Queen's mercurial moods, too. Of the two evils, I preferred to take my chances with the former Domina over the fae monarch. While Tanith tolerated me because I was occasionally useful to her, the Queen hated me. Flat-out, unapologetic hatred. The grudge had something to do with a turncoat ambassador who'd tried to kill me but ended up faery flambé courtesy of my Chthonic magic. The Queen never forgave me for killing him, despite the proof that I'd only been defending myself against a traitor to her crown.

A movement behind Tanith caught my eye as a female approached her from behind. The same female I'd seen on the sidewalk outside Central Park. "Who's she?" I demanded, ignoring the stern look from Orpheus for my rudeness.

Tanith raised a pale hand. "This is Alexis Vega."

Alexis looked like something out of vampire discipline porn. She wore a long-sleeved black shirt and leather pants. A holster circled her hips, displaying two massive sidearms. I couldn't see the lower half of her, but I'd bet cash money she was wearing stiletto boots. This chick's entire getup was about intimidation, and if I hadn't used the same tactics myself, I might have been impressed.

She met my gaze across the table and nodded slightly.

"You two have a lot in common, Sabina." Tanith was oblivious to the tension zinging past her as the bodyguard and I sized each other up. "Alexis was an Enforcer before she was promoted to my personal guard."

"Oh, yeah?" I barely managed not to roll my eyes. "You look familiar," I said. "Have we met before?" I was testing her, wondering if she'd fess up to witnessing the murder scene the night before.

Although, to be honest, I also was curious whether we'd crossed paths back in Los Angeles at some point. Most likely, she'd graduated from the same Enforcer school that turned me out in the 1970s. But even if I hadn't met her before, I certainly knew her type.

"Miss Kane, you know very well you saw me last night outside Central Park." She smiled. "Just as I saw you."

The corner of my mouth lifted. "Touché."

I kept my eyes on the vampire, looking for signs of guilt. Honestly, now that I knew she was the Despina's guard, she'd fallen way down the suspect list. Plus, if she'd killed the human, wouldn't she deny being at the scene? However, I'd had enough experience with the last person on the list being the bad guy that I couldn't completely disregard her. But all the normal tells were absent—no tightening of the mouth, no fidgeting, no squinting or evasive glances. Either Alexis was telling the truth or she'd been trained very well. My guess was the former, but I planned on keeping an eye on her, just in case.

Orpheus cleared his throat, a not-so-subtle reminder that the clock was ticking down on our meeting. "We understand there was some excitement at Vein last night."

Shit. Right. I pulled my gaze from Alexis and shifted in my seat. Since this was mage business, I deferred to Adam out of habit. Plus, he always did a better job with the niceties of talking to leaders. I usually ended up kicked out or yelled at or worse.

"Yes, sir," Adam spoke when I didn't. "Sabina was meeting with Slade Corbin when it happened. I was watching Pussy Willow's performance with Giguhl. It wasn't until The Shade's nymph reported the murder that we became involved and went with him to survey the murder site."

"Yes, I was briefed by Mr. Corbin on the specifics." Orpheus grimaced. "Dreadful business." Tanith made the appropriate noises but her expression remained coldly detached.

"Does Slade have any leads yet?" Adam asked.

Orpheus and the Despina exchanged a look I couldn't read. "Actually, that's why we've brought you in. If Slade is correct and the culprit is a vampire, the ramifications for the peace treaty are potentially disastrous." He pressed a fist into his palm. "Swift, decisive action is crucial."

I shifted in my seat. "You said 'murders,'" I began. "I guess that means Slade filled you in on the park murder, too?"

"Alexis informed me of the crime last night and I shared the information with Orpheus," Tanith said. "Before we could call Mr. Corbin in to question his knowledge of the matter, he'd contacted us about the second killing. He told us everything he knew about both when he came here early this morning."

"Including the fact that you knew about the human murder and did nothing," Orpheus said, his tone accusing. "Why didn't you come to me about this, Sabina?"

"It's true that I saw the scene in Central Park and assumed that the killer was a vampire." I shifted uneasily in my chair. "However, in my defense, I didn't come to you with that information because I believed it was a vampire problem and should be handled by Slade."

The Despina leaned forward. "Yet, Mr. Corbin asked you to assist him in tracking down the killer and you refused. Isn't that also correct?"

Why was I suddenly on the hot seat? "Again, I didn't think it was my concern."

"You were correct on that account. I'd have preferred you told me, but I understand you were following proto-col," said Orpheus, surprising me. "But the mage murder is very much your concern."

Adam stiffened beside me. I frowned at Orpheus. "What?"

"You and Lazarus will take the lead on the investigation."

"Sir," Adam said, clearing his throat. "Forgive me, but shouldn't this still be Slade's responsibility?"

"Normally, yes," Orpheus said. "However, Mr. Corbin's failure to report the human murder and the fact that the second murder happened in his own club casts serious doubt on his ability to handle this sensitive matter. We have already informed him of our decision that you and Sabina will lead the investigation."

Oh, I bet that went over well. "Sir, no offense, but I think that's a really bad idea. Slade's got more contacts on the streets than Adam and I," I said. "Besides, he's done a damned good job for you for decades."

"Regardless, he failed to inform me when the first murder—"

I cut him off. "Dude, it was a human. They die all the time—*it's what they do.*" I raised my hands in a what-can-you-do gesture. Next to me, I felt Adam shoot me a hot, annoyed glance. Whether he felt I was being disrespectful or he believed I was overdoing the Slade defense, I didn't know. Frankly, it didn't matter. I was so focused on not

having to do this job I'd argue all night long in Slade's favor
if that would do the trick. "And Slade deserves more than
to be tossed aside because he didn't call you the minute he
found out. If the second killing hadn't happened, you
wouldn't have batted an eyelash at one dead boy in the
garbage."

"If Slade had told us about the garbage boy," Tanith
said, raising a single, rusty brow, "then we might have been
able to prevent the murder of a mage."

"She's right, Sabina," Orpheus said. "Look, I respect the
hell out of Slade but this is not a game. I want whoever did
this found and ended ASAP. And I want you to find him
for me. Got it?"

I blew out a long breath. Despite my plan to filibuster on
Slade's behalf, I knew when I'd been beaten. "Yes, sir," I
grumbled.

"In addition," Orpheus continued, "the Despina has graciously offered the assistance of her personal guard, Alexis."

I gritted my teeth. It was one thing to force me to head
an investigation I wanted no part of. It's not that I wasn't
sad Marty died, but I didn't necessarily have a burning
desire to declare a vendetta against his killer, either. However, one rarely won an argument with the leaders of not
just one dark race, but two of them. But forcing me to work
with Alexis? No fucking way. "No offense to Alexis," I
said, "but her assistance won't be necessary."

"On the contrary," Tanith said, her voice steely. "It is
quite necessary."

I looked up at Alexis. She raised a single mocking brow
in challenge. Bitch.

"I understand," I said, gritting my teeth.

Under the table, Adam squeezed my hand as a warning.
"With all due respect," he said, "if Sabina and I are to take

point on this investigation, we expect Miss Vega to follow our orders."

"Naturally." The Despina nodded. "However, I will remind you that the true chain of command begins with Orpheus and me."

"Of course," Adam said quickly.

"We'll expect daily reports on your progress," Orpheus said. "And I can't stress enough how important it is to settle this situation as soon as possible. We can't afford to have the peace process compromised."

"Not to be contrary," I began. Orpheus shot me an ironic look. I ignored it and soldiered on. "But how can we be sure this is all related to the treaty?"

"Mr. Corbin showed us pictures of the murder scene," Tanith said. "The way that body was staged was clearly a message."

I flinched. Ever since my freak-out at seeing the mage's body, I'd managed to not think about the chillingly familiar pose.

"Whoever did this," she continued, "was familiar with the Dominae's rituals and wanted us to know that. We'd be fools to not take it as a threat."

"Sabina," Orpheus said, his tone dripping with patronizing empathy. "I understand your reluctance to get involved. It's common knowledge you and Mr. Corbin are old friends and no doubt his ego has taken a hit over our decision. However, given all the trials you endured to stop the war, you of all people should want to ensure nothing stands in the way of getting that treaty signed."

I clenched my jaw. Normally, I would have argued with him, but it was clear the noose had already tightened. Arguing would only make things worse. "Of course I'm committed to peace."

Orpheus clapped his hands together. "Then it's settled."

Adam raised his hand. "Just to be clear, what exactly is our focus? The human or the mage?"

"The mage. At this point, the human death is low priority unless information comes to light connecting it to the other one. But for now you will follow the trail from Vein."

"And once we find the vampire responsible?" I asked.

The Despina smiled, flashing fang. "You bring them to us."

After the meeting, I stormed out of the room, leaving Adam to say his good-byes to the Despina and Orpheus. I'd just made it to the door of the outer office when a female voice called out. "Sabina?"

I turned to see Alexis hot on my trail. An impatient sigh rose in my chest. I knew it wasn't her fault we'd been saddled with her, but I disliked the Enforcer from the first moment I saw her. "Yes?"

"So what's our first move?" She moved toward me, her leather holster creaking with each step.

Adam walked out then. His gaze took in the vampire's eager posture and my grumpy expression. "Alexis?" She turned toward him. "We haven't been properly introduced. I'm Adam Lazarus."

She shook his hand, putting a little English on her grip. Adam wasn't fazed by the display and smiled.

"And that's Sabina—"

"Sabina Kane, I know," she said. "Your reputation precedes you."

I choked out a laugh. "Oh, I just bet it does."

"I meant that as a compliment," she said.

That brought me up short. Considering my checkered

past among the vampire community, I found it hard to buy her claim. "Really?"

She nodded eagerly. "Oh, yes. Everyone knows that without you two we'd be in the middle of a war right now. I've studied your track record as an Enforcer. You had an impressive career."

"Thanks," I said, uncomfortable with both the praise and her use of the past tense.

"So," Adam said to cover the uncomfortable silence. "What's the plan?"

I glanced at the wall clock. I opened my mouth to speak, but Orpheus stuck his head out of the door. "Sabina, Rhea asked me to remind you about your training session." He glanced at the clock. "It starts in five minutes."

I frowned at the mage leader, confused. "But I thought you wanted us to get started on finding the killer?"

"Adam and Alexis can begin without you. Rhea has something important to discuss with you. About the favor you asked of her last night." I assumed his vague cagey-ness was due to Alexis's presence. But I managed to put it all together and realize Rhea needed to discuss Maisie with me.

"Are you sure that can't wait?"

The leader met my eye, his expression solemn. "Positive."

I sighed. "Understood."

He nodded and disappeared back into his office.

"Okay," I said slowly. "Here's what we'll do. You and Alexis head to Vein and get a briefing from Slade. Maybe he's got some new information that will help us figure out where to start. We'll rendezvous back at the apartment after my training session and figure out next steps."

"Sounds good." Adam stepped forward and gave me a quick peck on the lips. "See you later."

I felt Alexis's eyes on us during the exchange, but I was trying very hard to ignore her existence.

I turned to go without a glance at the vampire. However, she wasn't going to let me get away that easily. "Miss Kane?"

Tamping down my frustration, I turned with raised brows.

"I look forward to working with you."

I paused. Maybe I was being unfair with her. After all, it's not like she had a choice about working with us on this case. I forced my shoulders to relax. "Me too," I lied.

After I left Adam and Alexis, I raced up to the gym to make my training session with Rhea. I walked in at exactly 7:59.

Rhea was already there, of course. "You're almost late," she joked.

I paused, dropping my backpack on one of the blue mats that covered half of the gym's hardwoods. "Almost late is the same thing as on time," I snapped.

She waved a hand to dismiss my logic and busied herself setting out props for that night's lesson—bundles of herbs, ceremonial daggers, the usual. "Sabina?"

"What?" I picked up a bundle of dried sage and lavender from the table. Normally the soothing scents would have helped me relax, but I was in no mood.

"What's the matter?"

I slammed a smudge stick on the table. Broken sage leaves scattered across the surface like aromatic confetti. "Nothing!"

Her brows snapped up.

I sighed, knowing she'd drag it out of me by force if

necessary. "It's Orpheus." My lips didn't form his name so much as expel it like a bad taste.

"Oh?" Rhea said. "What's he done now?"

"He's forcing Adam and me to take point on the murder investigation."

Her brows furrowed. "The mage who was killed last night?"

I nodded.

She shrugged. "Are you mad because you don't want to be involved or because he didn't ask you nicely?"

"Both!" My chest hurt. Pressure made my lungs tight. I hated it when she was so insightful. "Plus, they're insisting we let one of the Despina's guards tag along. You should see her, Rhea. She wears more leather than a fucking cow. She's a walking stereotype."

Rhea raised an eyebrow. "She's an Enforcer?"

"Was." I nodded. "Before she became Tanith's guard."

"So you two should have a lot in common."

That stopped me. Her observation was too close to the truth to be comfortable. "Hell no," I lied. "I was never that much of a cliché."

"Sabina." Judgment weighed her tone.

"What?"

"I'm sure Orpheus had good reasons for putting you and Adam in charge. Besides, maybe it's a good thing for you to have a mission. You've been a little restless lately."

I grimaced. "Maybe." I had been feeling at loose ends for a while. With the exception of my magical training, I didn't have much to do. Adam still had his duties as a Pythian Guard to keep him active, but I'd been feeling about as useful as a three-dollar bill. I'd tried to convince myself that I'd finally gotten the peace I'd dreamed of during all those months of disaster. But deep down I suspected that I wasn't the type of female who thrived in calm waters because I was always waiting for the next tidal wave.

She patted my hand. "Just focus on the mission and try to ignore the fact that Orpheus can be an incredible ass without even trying."

I couldn't help smiling. One of my favorite things about Rhea was her straight talk. Of course, I didn't like it so much when that laser-sharp tongue was aimed at me. "You're right. Thanks."

She sighed. "Speaking of Orpheus, I have to talk to you about something else you might not like."

I paused, bracing myself. "What's up?"

"It's your sister."

Gods, just when she'd gotten me to calm down about Orpheus she chose to bring up the only other subject guaranteed to upset me again. "Oh, yeah. Thanks for checking on her last night."

She waved a hand. "It wasn't a problem. By the time I got to her room, she was already asleep."

I frowned. "That's weird. She was pretty upset when she left. I'm surprised she was able to sleep."

"That's the thing. She's been sleeping a lot lately."

"Isn't that pretty normal for someone who's having problems like hers?"

"Of course, but the sleeping isn't the issue. It's the lack of dreams. Orpheus and I are concerned she may have permanently lost her abilities as an Oracle."

"Why now? She hasn't had a prophecy in months."

"Yes, but Imbolc is coming up. As the Oracle, she'll be expected to deliver a prophecy for the coming year. Especially with the treaty signing happening that night."

I recalled Orpheus's reaction earlier. "So that's why Orpheus changed the subject so quickly earlier when

Tanith asked about Maisie. He's worried she won't be able to deliver."

As an Oracle, Maisie took the images from her dreams and painted them to translate the symbols into prophecy. But for several months, she'd been totally blocked. The dry spell began before she'd been kidnapped, but Orpheus and the Council were worried that after the trauma she'd endured they might never return.

Rhea nodded. "That, and he's worried that if Tanith finds out how erratic Maisie's been lately that she'll delay the signing—or worse."

"I don't know how he'll manage to keep Maisie's state hidden from the Despina. It's not like her troubles are exactly a secret."

"Mages in our inner circle are aware of your sister's situation but it's not like anyone on the Council is going to run to Tanith to gossip about it. Beyond these walls, Maisie's situation isn't common knowledge. Orpheus is so determined for the ceremony to go off without a hitch he's controlling all the information going out to the mage masses. The annual prophecy is the centerpiece of the entire Imbolc ceremony. He's worried that without a positive prophecy some mages will take it as a bad omen for the peace process."

"That's silly," I scoffed. "If Orpheus just explained what happened to Maisie—"

"It's not that simple, Sabina," she interrupted. "Some mages are having problems adjusting to the idea that the vampires are our allies. They'll see Maisie's lack of prophecy as further evidence that we should not trust the vampires."

"But who wouldn't want peace between the races?"

"It's not that they don't want peace. It's that they don't

believe vampires are capable of it." She shrugged. "Centuries of animosity aren't easily overcome."

"I guess that's true. But I'm still not sure what Orpheus thinks I can do about Maisie."

"I just don't get it," Rhea said, absently, almost to herself. "She used to have them all the time. Her accuracy made her one of the most powerful Oracles in the world. But ever since—" She stopped short.

I filled in the words she'd been about to say. "Ever since I came to New York." Rhea looked ready to deny. To apologize for the truth. "Don't bother." I held up a hand to stop her. "We both know it's true."

"Regardless, I've done almost everything I can think to help her regain her visions."

"*Almost* everything?" I frowned.

"There's an ancient rite the Greeks used to use called 'dream incubation.' I mentioned it to Maisie, but she refuses to do it because it involves a tiny blood sacrifice and being given a potion to summon sleep."

Given Maisie's reaction to seeing a little pint of blood in my apartment, I couldn't imagine the words "blood sacrifice" had gone over much better. "Do you really think this incubation is the key to helping her?"

"I believe so. The Greeks used it to cure all sorts of ailments—both physical and mental. Besides, it's the only option we have left." Rhea peeked up at me between her lashes. "Orpheus and I were hoping to convince you to speak to Maisie about it."

I sucked down a deep breath. The air felt sharp in my lungs. On some level, I knew it was only a matter of time until I was asked to intervene more directly with the Maisie situation. Up until that point, I'd tried to stay on the periphery of the drama. It's not that I didn't care what happened to her. More like, I had no clue how to help her. And, frankly, my own internal conflict where Maisie was concerned held me back.

The truth, the deep-down-I'd-never-admit-this-to-anyone truth, is that I blamed myself for everything that happened in New Orleans. And Maisie served as a flesh-and-blood personification of my own failures both as her rescuer and as her sister.

It didn't help either that while Maisie was busy fading away, everything in my life was looking up. That's where the real guilt lies. I had an amazing partner, a great pad, my magic lessons were going well, and overall things pretty much were awesome. Sure, I had a few nagging complaints, but who didn't? I certainly didn't have the sort of challenges Maisie was facing. All of which added up to a massive case of survivor's guilt on my part.

So I should have wanted to help her. To make amends, if nothing else. But something held me back, which I suspect was tied to the fact I could barely stand to be in the same room as my sister.

Still, even I wasn't immune to the pleading look Rhea aimed at me. Plus, if I'd learned anything in the last twenty-four hours, it was that peace was not a sure thing. The cynical part of me was not shocked at all by the recent developments. That side always wondered when the other shoe would drop and we'd all wake up from this dream of peace. But the other part—the stubborn one—refused to allow a couple of stumbling blocks to ruin everything we'd worked for.

I didn't want to contemplate the alternative. But I knew one thing: I couldn't go back to that life of constant uncertainty and violence. I wanted—no, I needed that treaty signed so I could finally put the past behind me and relax into a safe, happy future with Adam and everyone else I cared about. So, yeah, I'd find the murderer despite my misgivings about Alexis and how Slade was being treated. And, yes, I'd do everything in my power to convince Maisie to try the dream incubation. To refuse either challenge would feel too much like surrender.

"Okay, I'll try. But don't get your hopes up. I doubt a simple conversation with me is going to magically fix her."

Rhea smiled and gave me a tight hug. "Thank you! I know it won't be easy, but I honestly believe it'll help. Besides, if nothing else, maybe it will help you two grow close again."

I didn't bother arguing with her. If Rhea wanted to believe that some girl talk could erase months of resentment and pain, who was I to disillusion her?

"Now, enough woolgathering." Rhea shook herself. "Are you ready to try some interspatial travel?"

I went still, as if sudden movement might scare off the opportunity. "Really?"

I'd been begging Rhea for months to teach me how to travel magically. But she'd insisted on going back and covering the basics of magic before we jumped into big magic. To me, it felt like taking about ten steps back after some of the magical feats I'd managed during battle, but she claimed that if I ever wanted to gain control over my powers, I'd need a stronger foundation in the fundamentals.

"I've been pleased with your progress lately." She smiled proudly. "You're ready."

"Awesome!" I said. "I can't wait to not have to ride the subway anymore."

She leveled me with a look. "Not so fast, missy. What's the first rule I taught you about magic?"

"Magic must always be used responsibly," I said in a monotone.

"Exactly. Having the ability to wield magic is no excuse for laziness." Her posture went schoolmarm erect as she paced before me. "You can't just flash around willy-nilly because you're too lazy to climb some stairs."

"Rhea, I might be stubborn and impatient, but I think I've proven by now that I'm not lazy."

She put a hand on my arm. "You're right. I'm sorry."

I smiled at her so she'd know I wasn't really offended. Then I clapped my hands and rubbed them together. "Okay, what's first?"

Thirty minutes later, she'd gone over the entire process verbally, walked me through it by flashing out and back again, and made me repeat the instructions from memory. So by the time she said I should try it myself I was impatient to get started.

"Now, let's try something easy. Pull up an image of the hallway in your mind. Make sure it's as detailed as possible or you may end up in some random hallway in gods-know-where."

I nodded and closed my eyes. Breathing in slowly through my nose and exhaling through my mouth, I pictured the hallway. The dove-gray walls, the Greek urns, the dark wooden floors, the window at the end of the hall.

"Can you see it?" Rhea whispered.

"Yes," I responded on the next exhale.

"Take your time. Now imagine the scent, feel the air."

I inhaled again, imagining the scent of the white roses I'd seen in a vase on the console table just outside the room. Drafty air from the cracked window prickled my skin.

"Say the words."

One more long breath. "*Daltu peta.*"

The wind rose around me, a vortex opening. As Rhea had instructed, I kept the image of myself standing in the hall in my mind. Cold air rushed in my ears. Static crawled over my skin. Power surged through my veins.

Then, as quickly as it came to life, the wind died. My ears popped. And the power settled to a low hum in my solar plexus. It was only a flash of time, but it felt longer.

Labored breathing. Heart thudding in my ears. I settled back into my skin. The air brushing my skin felt colder.

I'd done it. I had finally traveled through space without anyone's help. Smiling, I opened my eyes.

Shock hit me like a blast of magic.

Instead of looking at the hallway I'd been expecting, I was standing in a vast expanse of nothing. Well, not nothing exactly, but the landscape before me was little more than a barren field coated in gray ash—like pictures I'd seen of the surface of the moon. And despite the general dreariness, the light hurt my eyes, like a full moon's light reflecting off snowdrifts.

But there was no sun here. No moon. No stars. The sky was an oily black dome pressing down on me.

"Rhea!"

RheaRheaRhea.

The warped echo made my blood rush. Where the hell was I? I spun in a circle, my heart throbbing in my ears. Not far from where I stood, a crossroads of sorts spread out in a wagon-wheel pattern. In the center of the eight spokes, a bright red flag flapped in an unfelt breeze.

Now that my eyes had adjusted to the odd light, I could see farther. The horizons in either direction shimmered like the edges of a mirage. Whatever this place was, it clearly wasn't my world.

The howl clawed through the air and pierced my chest.

What was it? *Where* was it?

I fell back into my fighting stance. The distance was impossible to judge. Sound was both muted and amplified, like shouting underwater or screaming into sharp winter air.

I knew one thing with crystalline clarity: Whatever made that horrible sound was hunting me.

Despite my trembling limbs, I took a deep, calming breath. Despite the cold sweat coating my back and stomach, I closed my eyes and pictured the gym. Despite the fear clawing my throat, I smelled the sour, sweaty workout mats and Rhea's sandalwood scent. And when the howl came again, this time much closer—too close—I willed myself back to that safe room with every ounce of will in my being.

The wind rose. The vortex wrapped me in its frigid arms and rescued me from the nightmare realm.

9

When I woke, I didn't care how long I'd been out. Or about the cold sweat gluing my body to the floor. Never in my life had I enjoyed the pungent scent of old sweat and vinyl so much. Thank the gods—I'd made it back to the gym.

Rapid footsteps vibrated off the gym's hardwood floor. I groaned and peeled my face from the mat. I rolled over in time to see Rhea's face snap into focus.

"Sabina! Gods, what happened?" She knelt beside me. Worry aged the planes of her face.

"I don't know." I rubbed my eyes. "One minute I was focused on flashing to the hall and the next..." My voice trailed off. I tried to figure out how to describe the place I'd gone, the terror I'd felt there. "I went someplace else. Someplace...other."

She frowned and felt my forehead. "Are you okay?"

I swallowed the clump of remembered fear in my throat. "I think so. How long was I gone?"

"Just a few seconds. You disappeared as expected but when I ran to the hall you weren't there. By the time I made it back to the door, I heard a thud and there you were."

I shook my head. "That can't be right. I was there for at least five minutes, maybe longer." She hooked her hands under my arms to help me stand. "Physically, I feel fine, but my brain feels like I spent too much time on a Tilt-a-Whirl."

She clucked sympathetically and led me to a chair. She disappeared for a moment but when she returned, she pressed a glass of blood into my hand. "Praise the gods you badgered me into keeping blood stocked in the gym."

"Amen." I tilted the glass and gulped the liquid like someone who'd just stumbled out of the desert.

Once I'd finished, she crossed her arms. "Okay, tell me what you saw."

I rolled the glass between my palms. "It's hard to describe." I went on to tell her the details I recalled. I told her about the odd light, the barren landscape, the crossroads. When I got to that part, I paused. "Wait a second."

"What is it?"

"The crossroads. Remember that dream I keep having? The one about Cain?"

Rhea frowned and nodded. "Sure."

"There's this point in the dream where the setting changes and we're suddenly in a crossroads. The one in this place wasn't exactly like the one in my dreams, but I wonder if there's a connection."

Rhea pursed her lips and frowned. "Describe the one in the other realm."

"Eight spokes, a tall pole in the center with a red flag."

"I'll look into it. Chances are good it's a coincidence, but it never hurts to check it out." She dipped her chin at me to continue. "What else?"

I got to the howling part and I gripped the glass so tightly it cracked. She took it from me and nodded for me to continue. "Wherever I went, it wasn't of this world."

Rhea had gone very still. And too quiet. The kind of quiet a person gets when they're busy restraining their fear for you to respond. Finally, she arranged her features into her best academic poker face. "From your description, I'm tempted to agree you left our world. But before we jump to conclusions I'd like to do some research."

"What kind of research?"

"Everyone has different experiences when they do travel spells for the first time. It's not unheard of to end up in a completely different place than where you'd intended. I'd like to look back through the archives to see if anyone else has ever left this plane of existence."

"Isn't that the sort of thing you'd have heard about?"

"Not necessarily." Her eyes scanned the middle distance, as if the answer hung there waiting to be snatched. "But I've never trained a Chthonic before. Ameritat trained your father."

I tried not to be frustrated by her dropping the C bomb. By definition, a Chthonic mage was one who specialized in dark magic. Not black magic, exactly, but definitely not white either. If you needed a zombie raised or a spirit contacted or an enemy immolated from twenty paces, a Chthonic was the mage for the job. But good luck finding one when you needed them. My father was a Chthonic, but he was dead. Maybe there were a few others floating around the world, but I hadn't heard of them. As far as I knew, I was the only one.

"You know what?" I said. "Being a Chthonic is a pain in the ass. Every time I think I'm finally getting the hang of magic, my Chthonic power sweeps in and fucks it up."

Rhea dragged her attention from whatever theories were spinning in her headspace. "Now, now, Sabina. What happened is troublesome, but let's not go into martyr mode. This could end up being an opportunity."

"Right," I snorted. Despite my flippant response, I was remembering that howl and the sickening conviction I'd die if I didn't escape. Goose bumps spread on my forearms. "An opportunity to get my ass chewed up by some horrible netherworld beast."

Rhea ignored my dramatics. "I'll look in Ameritat's old journals. Maybe Tristan had a similar experience."

My head jerked up. "You have her journals?"

"I don't have them personally," she said. "They're kept in secured archives out at the Crossroads," she said, referring to the mage estate up near Sleepy Hollow. "I need to go out there tomorrow anyway to help finalize some things for the festival." She paused and gave me a thorough once-over. "Are you going to be all right? Should I call Adam?"

I shook my head. "Don't bother. I'm on my way to see him now anyway." I blew out a breath. "I'm fine though. But if it's all the same to you I think I'll stick to public transportation for the time being."

She patted my arm. "That's probably best. Let me smudge you before you head out."

I paused. "Why?"

She looked like she was considering lying but thought better of it. "It's just a precaution since we don't know where you were or what type of creature was coming for you."

"You think that thing followed me back?" My stomach dropped.

"No, nothing like that. A good cleanse will help dispel the negative energy that's clinging to you. Your aura is all wonky."

I frowned at her. "Define 'wonky.' "

She moved away to grab the sage and some matches.

"Your aura is normally bright red. And lately it's also had happy gold and purple streaks running through it."

I'd known about the red part but this was the first I'd heard of streaks. "What does that mean?"

"That you're in love." She smiled. "The gold means happiness and the purple is the result of Adam's blue aura melding with your red one."

I wasn't sure whether to feel all mushy or embarrassed. On the one hand, yes, being with Adam made me very happy. On the other, I didn't like the idea that I'd been wearing my heart on my aura for all to see.

"Anyway, that was before. Right now, the gold has been replaced by a smoky black." She paused and added, "That's bad."

"I figured as much," I said. "So the sage will clean that off?"

Rhea lit the sage bundle and blew on it until its fragrant smoke billowed. "Yep." She came back to me. "Now, try to think happy thoughts."

She circled me three times clockwise, chanting the whole time in Hekatian. Over the last few months, I'd picked up more of the ceremonial mage language. I was far from fluent, but I was able to pick out enough to recognize she was calling on Hekate to banish any bad energy from my being. I concentrated on breathing deep to allow the sweet smoke to do its magic inside as well as out. When she'd finished the third circle, she turned and went the other direction. This time I recognized the words "purify" and "protect."

By the time she finished her third lap, I was already feeling better. Like a heavy garment had been lifted from my body. Rhea stood back and squinted at me. "Well?" I asked.

She nodded. "I think we're good now. The darkness has

dissipated a bit and there are specks of gold around the edges. But you might want to try to avoid any negativity over the next few hours."

Since I was headed back to my apartment to work on a murder investigation, I was pretty sure she was asking for the impossible.

When I got back to my apartment, I was hoping to find it empty. After the meeting with Orpheus and my bizarro training session with Rhea, I craved quiet and privacy. What I found instead was even better—Adam.

I stopped inside the door, my eyes scanning the room for Alexis.

"Relax," he said. "She's still at Vein."

I let the tension drain from my shoulders and continued into the apartment.

"How'd training go?"

I groaned. "Let's just say my first attempt at interspatial travel was a massive fail." At his confused look, I briefly explained what had happened. I toned down the fear part so he wouldn't worry, and also because I didn't want to think about it anymore.

When I'd finished, Adam's eyes were wide. "Good gods, Red. Does Rhea have any idea where the hell you ended up?"

I shook my head. "No idea. She's going to do some research and get back to me. In the meantime, you're in charge of flashing us around town."

"No problem. I kind of like the way you press against me when we're zapping around." He smiled and pulled me in for a hug. "What did Rhea need to talk to you about?"

I hesitated. The subject of Maisie was even trickier for Adam than it was for me. He and Maisie had been best friends their whole lives. But even the strongest of friendships had a hard time weathering the aftermath of attempted murder. Even if Maisie's bloodlust wasn't her fault, I could see the distrust in Adam's eyes every time he was near her. Like he expected her to attack again at any moment.

"She and Orpheus want me to talk to Maisie about trying a rite Rhea thinks will help her dream again." His arms had been around me when I started talking. The minute the words left my mouth, every muscle in his torso tensed. Time to change the subject. "Anyway, how'd you manage to get away without your new shadow?" I said, referring to Alexis.

He shrugged, his posture relaxing a fraction. "I put her in charge of interviewing the nymphs. Figured you and I could use some unchaperoned time to wrap our heads around what's going on."

I smiled and threw myself at him. "Gods bless you."

He kissed me hard on the lips but pulled away too quickly. "As much as I'd love to explore the depth of your gratitude, we probably need to talk."

"What's there to talk about? Orpheus commands and we follow, right?"

"Don't be like that. I know you're unhappy about this but I think it's important."

"I don't disagree."

"But?"

I crossed my arms. "Why do you think there's a but?"

"Because I know you."

"Look, I'll admit I was pretty pissed with Orpheus's approach but I get why he asked us." I ran a hand through my hair. "It's just...I don't know. Everything has been going pretty well. Almost too well. I can't help feeling like this whole thing is the other shoe falling. Like maybe we were naive to think we could finally let our guards down and be happy."

Adam reached for me and pulled me against his chest. "Red, no matter what happens, we'll deal with it. Together." He lifted my chin with his finger. "Just like we always do. Besides, solving this murder is the best way to ensure that bigger drama doesn't come along, right?"

"I guess you're right."

He kissed me softly and smiled against my lips. "Of course I'm right."

I sighed and surrendered myself to the inevitable. "So what'd Slade say?"

Adam's face tightened. "Besides the tidal wave of obscenities?"

"I was afraid of that." I grimaced.

"Who can blame him? I mean the Black Light District has been his domain for decades. By rights, this should be his investigation. Plus, he's understandably pissed that someone dared commit this crime under his own roof."

"I just hope he doesn't plan on using his anger to stonewall us."

"Quite the opposite, actually." Adam rose. "He's not happy with the Despina or Orpheus, but he seemed pretty cool about you and me taking over." He paused. "Especially you."

I looked up quickly. "What's that supposed to mean?"

Adam shrugged and made his way to the bar separating the kitchen from the living room. "Oh, nothing. He just had lots of nice things to say about your . . . abilities. Actually, if I didn't know any better, I'd think that vampire has a crush on you."

I froze. Shit. If there was any time to tell Adam about

my past with Slade, now was definitely *not* it. The murder investigation didn't need the added complication of the two leads having a lover's spat. Plus, and I'm just being honest here, the very idea of coming clean to Adam scared the ever-loving crap out of me. So instead of sitting the mage down and having a nice long heart-to-heart, I forced a breathy laugh. "Don't be ridiculous. Slade probably wants to butter us up so we'll keep him in the loop."

Adam turned slowly, looking unconvinced. "I don't know, Red. I've seen the way he looks at you."

I rose quickly and went to him. My heart thumped against my ribs, but I forced a smile. "Adam, I told you. Slade and I were ancient history. Hell, half the time we argue more than anything." My laugh sounded forced to my own ears. Shit, was I talking too fast? Was that suspicion in Adam's eyes? Oh, gods. I reached for Adam's arms and pulled him toward me. "You have nothing to worry about from Slade. Even if he was interested, I'm not. As for his praise, well, we have worked together before and he asked me to help him before Orpheus took him off the job. He knows I'll find who did this for him."

Adam pulled away. Instead of the accusatory frown I'd been expecting, the corner of his mouth tilted up in his trademark Lazarus smile. "You mean 'we,' right?" My mouth fell open. I can't believe I'd forgotten to give Adam his due. I had tons of experience killing people, but Adam had more experience with investigations. Luckily, he laughed then and pulled me in for a quick hug. "This isn't all on your shoulders, Red. We'll find this bastard together."

I closed my eyes and tried to ignore the pain where my conscience bore a hole through my chest. "Old habits die hard, I guess." We stood there like that for a few minutes.

Finally, I relaxed enough to let out a relieved breath. I knew that soon I'd have to come clean to Adam. I just hoped it would happen later rather than sooner.

Adam pulled away first. "Speaking of Slade helping us..." He turned and lifted something from the bar. The item was a large zip-top baggie I hadn't seen before. "He gave us our first clue."

My eyebrows shot to my hairline. From what I could see, the thing in the baggie was nothing more than a black clump. "What is it?"

"See for yourself." He offered the bag to me.

When I took it, I realized the black thing was actually a glove. Leather, or a decent imitation. I turned it over to inspect the palm. Thin silver spikes covered the surface. "What are these for?"

"You've never seen a glove like that before?"

I shook my head. "No, why?"

He shrugged. "According to Slade, it's called a vampire glove. I figured you might have run across one once or twice in your former life."

I frowned down at it and gently fingered the spikes. "Can't say that I have. What's the deal?"

"Slade said they're commonly used in the S&M community," Adam explained. "The spikes mortals use usually aren't sharp enough to draw blood unless some intense pressure is applied. They're mostly for skin stimulation, I guess. But apparently, in the vamp S&M scene, they modify them to cause instantaneous bleeding for their blood-sport games."

"I had no idea." Not that I was a prude or anything, but I never considered such a thing existed. Sexual blood play wasn't something I'd really explored much. Too many control issues, I guess. In fact, Adam was the only sexual partner I'd ever fed from, and even that was just the once. "Well, this certainly supports my theory that the murderer was a vampire."

"Or someone who wanted us to think it was a vampire."

I looked up quickly. "You think this is a frame job?"

Adam shrugged. "Honestly, I don't know what I think. I just don't want to rule out any possibilities until we have more evidence."

"Obviously we need to track down the owner of this glove."

Adam shot me his trademark grin. "Already ahead of you. Slade graciously offered me a list of the top vampire sex shops in Manhattan. I figure we'll start there and see if we get any leads."

Rhea's warning to avoid anything stressful flashed through my head. Probably she wouldn't include visiting fetish shops as relaxing activity. But now that we had a lead, I could feel my old fire igniting in my belly. The one that loved a challenge. It'd been too long since I'd had one I'd almost forgotten the adrenaline rush. "Sounds like a plan."

Just then, the door to the apartment opened. Giguhl strolled in. He had a pair of roller skates hanging over his shoulder. "What up, playas?"

"Where have you been?" I asked.

"The girls and I were having some skating practice in the courtyard."

"How'd it go?" I asked.

He shook his head sadly, his horns swishing from side to side. "Pitiful. I need some more power on the team or we're never going to win our first match."

I cleared my throat meaningfully. Giguhl pursed his black lips and looked me up and down. "Don't be desperate, Red. It's beneath you."

My mouth fell open. "I am not desperate."

"Anyway." He rolled his goat-slit eyes. "What are you two up to?"

"We're just about to head out," Adam said. "Orpheus asked us to help find the asshole who killed Marty."

Giguhl's eyes lit up. "Really? Why didn't you tell me Team Awesome has a new case to solve?"

I tilted my head and shot him a look. "Team Awesome doesn't have a case—Adam and Sabina do."

He put a claw to his heart. "That hurts, Red."

"We figured you were too busy with your Roller Derby stuff to help out," Adam said to soften the rejection.

"Are you kidding? I'm never too busy to fight crime. Where are we going?"

Adam and I exchanged a look. The minute we told Giguhl where we were headed there'd be no stopping his involvement. While we silently debated whether to tell him, Giguhl spotted the glove. He grabbed it from my hand. "Oh, shit, is this one of those S&M gloves?"

I shot the demon an incredulous look. "How in the hell did you know that?"

He raised a scraggly black brow. "Bitch, please. I have all sorts of knowledge I haven't even begun to lay on your ass."

I raised my eyebrow and waited.

He grimaced. "Okay, fine. Cinnamon overheard Slade and Adam talking at Vein and called me. But still, I can totally help you guys. Can I pleeaaase go with you to the sex shops?"

I looked at Adam. He sighed and said, "All right, but you go in cat form and you behave yourself or else."

"Really?" The demon tilted his chin down to shoot Adam a blunt look. "Has that ever worked with me?"

"Promise, or you're not going," I said.

"Fine, geez." He crossed a claw over his heart. "I promise I'll *try* to behave."

"Fair enough," I said, knowing that was the best I could hope for from a Mischief demon. "Let's head out."

*T*wo hours and five shops later, we were running out of steam.

"Who knew there were this many sex shops in Manhattan," I observed as we approached the next store on the list.

"Are you kidding?" Adam said. "The list Slade gave me has twenty shops on it and he said that's just the ones vampires might frequent."

From inside the canvas tote, Giguhl added, "This would go a lot faster if you guys allowed me to sneak into the back rooms of these places."

"Dream on," I said. The last thing I needed was to let a hairless demon cat loose inside an S&M dungeon.

"Party pooper," he grumbled.

"Let's hope this next place offers some sort of clues. We're burning moonlight," Adam said.

I squinted up at the discreet sign over the door that read SPANK. According to the note Slade made on the list, this place catered to the wealthy kink connoisseur out front but in the back was a vamp-only dungeon.

We would have headed to Spank first, but we'd started

with the shops in Hell's Kitchen, close to the Black Light District. Since Spank was located on the Upper East Side, it got pushed down the priority list. And judging from the elegant hand-painted sign and the tasteful window displays, the place was by far the most upscale shop we'd been to thus far.

When we walked in, a tall female dressed in a severe black suit was refilling a display of mink-lined handcuffs with brisk efficiency. The conservative suit surprised me, but not the black fishnets and expensive stilettos on her feet. Her cherry-red hair hung in lush waves down her back. It might have been bottle dyed, but I doubted it. Besides the overpowering odor of latex in the air, the telltale copper-penny scent told me she was a vampire.

The vampinatrix paused, as if considering approaching us, but a group of WASPy human females approached her with questions. Instead of interrupting, Adam and I headed to the glass counter. To the naive eye, the strings of colorful beads inside might look like kitschy jewelry. They would have been mistaken.

The door behind the checkout was standard issue. But the black plastic tarp edging from beneath it was an ominous detail. What kind of activity required a waterproof drop cloth? In addition, the lemony-fresh scent of disinfectant hinted at some recent sanitizing. I'd bet cash money they weren't doing some spring cleaning or having a picnic back there. Suddenly, my imagination filled with images of a room lined with large metal kennels filled with trussed-up and gagged businessmen in gimp masks.

"Red?" Adam whispered.

"Yeah?" I said, my eyes still on the door to what I was now convinced was a sex dungeon.

"What the hell is that thing?" I looked up and saw him

pointing to a wall covered in sex toys of every shape, size, and color. The particular item he pointed out was called "The Fang Banger." From what I could tell, and granted I refused to get any closer for a better look, it consisted of a metal cylinder topped with a lifelike rubber mouth. The lips gaped open to reveal a set of ceramic fangs for the "lifelike scraping you crave."

I patted Adam's arm. "Don't ask."

At my side, the cat poked his head out of the bag for a look around. "Holy shit, this place is awesome," he whispered.

About that time, the saleslady finished up with the socialites who were buying gag gifts for a friend's bachelorette party. The vampire waved to get our attention. She jerked her head toward the black door. "Wait in there."

I frowned. "Um?"

Her eyes narrowed. "Get in there and strip or leave." Instead of shouting the command, she lowered her voice. "I do not enjoy repeating myself."

My hands flew to my hips. "And I do not enjoy kicking perfect strangers' asses—" Giguhl snorted. I ignored him even though he had every right to question the accuracy of that statement. "But if you keep talking to me like that, you're going to get a boot in yours."

The corner of her lip quirked. "I believe that's *my* job."

"Sabina," Adam whispered. "It's probably not wise to antagonize a dominatrix."

Hearing Adam despite his low tone, she frowned and moved forward, looking slightly abashed. "I'm sorry. I thought you were my next client."

"Do you always threaten your clients?"

She smiled fully then. "Honey, I'm a domme. People pay me good money to do all sorts of mean things to them."

My mouth pursed into an *Oh*. "Gotcha."

"I have to admit I'm disappointed though." She eyed Adam up and down. "Couples parties are always fun."

The corner of Adam's lips quirked up into a grin. But before any of us could respond, Giguhl's head popped up from inside the bag. "What's a domme?"

"Giguhl!" I scolded. "I told you to stay quiet."

The chick reached out and scratched the demon cat under his naked chin. "Aren't you precious?" She looked at Adam. "You must be a powerful mage if you can give your familiar the power to speak."

Part of me realized correcting her assumption that Giguhl belonged to Adam was silly. What did it really matter? But the territorial part of me needed her to understand that both the mage and the demon belonged to me. "Actually, he's not a familiar. He's my minion."

Her eyes crinkled with confusion.

Giguhl winked at her. "What she means is, I might look like a pussy but I'm really a badass demon."

She tossed back her long red velvet hair and laughed, a throaty sound not unlike that of a female pirate. She looked at me to join in her mirth but I merely raised my eyebrows. "Wait, he's really a demon?"

I nodded. "Yep. I'd have him change forms but it's a bit of a production. Especially in such a public place."

She nodded sagely. "I understand completely."

"Anyway," Giguhl butted in, "what's this domme thing all about?"

"Men pay her to beat the shit out of them for sexual gratification," I explained.

She raised a hand. "Women too. And not everyone wants to be beaten. Sometimes they just want to be humiliated."

The cat's eyes widened. "No shit?"

"No shit," she said, flashing the cat another smile. "I'd be happy to give you a demonstration sometime. In demon form, though. I don't do bestiality."

Nice to hear she had standards.

"Anyway, I'm Sabina and"—I pointed to the mancy—"this is Adam." I raised the bag. "And Giguhl."

"I'm Mistress Bianca." She didn't offer her hand. I got the impression this was a dominatrix trick of ensuring I didn't consider us on equal footing.

"Listen, Slade Corbin sent us," Adam said. "He believed you might be able to assist us with an investigation."

The corner of her mouth lifted. "If Slade said it, it must be true."

For the briefest of moments, I indulged a wayward curiosity about the nature of their acquaintance, but when I saw the same question in her eyes, I squashed it.

"Anyway," I said, pulling out the bagged glove, "we're looking for the owner of this."

She pursed her lips and lifted the baggy. The light caught the metal spikes. She flipped the bag over and ran a finger across the tooled leather through the plastic. I caught a flicker of recognition in her gaze, but she shuttered it quickly. With a businesslike smile she said, "Why don't you come back to my office?"

An image of a caged man wearing a gimp mask flashed into my head. But I wasn't about to let Mistress Bianca see my hesitation. I held out a hand. "Lead the way."

A few moments later, she opened the door. The base whispered across the plastic sheeting on the floor. I mentally held my breath, telling myself even as I did so that I was being ridiculous. But, as is often the case, my fears proved to be right on the fucking nose.

In addition to the masked gimp lying in the fetal position in the kennel in the corner, there was also a vampire male wearing a charming outfit that consisted of a pair of nipple clamps, some testicle weights, and a pained grimace. Without a word, Mistress Bianca snapped her fingers. Nipple Clamps jumped to do her bidding. As he minced across the room to the wet bar, the testicle weights clacked together disconcertingly. Adam, Giguhl, and I watched, slack-jawed. Bianca either didn't notice or didn't care about our shock. She just walked to her desk and plopped down in her chair.

Giguhl stood on my shoulder, his little body stiff with alarm. In my ear, he hissed, "What the fuck?"

I shook my head. "Act natural."

That earned me a bitch-please snort from the feline. Beside me, Adam shot me a wide-eyed stare.

"Sit," Mistress B's voice snapped like a whip.

The cat's ass hit my shoulder. Adam scrambled into a chair. Nipple Clamps dropped to the ground.

"Not you, worm. Stand up and get the drinks," she said quietly. Her volume might not have been loud, but her tone clearly promised retribution if he didn't comply. She looked up and noticed I was the only one who hadn't done her bidding. "Sabina?" She didn't say please, but a *now* was implied by her tone.

"I'll stand." I wasn't so much challenging her authority as trying to avoid touching anything.

The dominatrix's head snapped up and her eyes narrowed into razor-sharp slits. The newspaper lining the gimp's cage crinkled as he whimpered and curled into the fetal position. Nipple Clamps wrapped his arms protectively around his torso, as if he expected a beating for my impertinence.

"Oh, shit," the cat whispered under his breath.

I held the vamp's gaze steadily. After a few tense moments, she smiled. "As you wish."

"What can you tell us about the glove?" As an afterthought Adam added, "Ma'am."

She leaned back in her chair. "Well, it's not a simple glove, as I'm sure you've noticed." She ran a black-lacquered fingernail over the spikes on the glove's palm. "Vampire gloves are quite popular among blood-sport enthusiasts."

"Is that a politically correct term for vampires?" Giguhl asked. "Ma'am," he added at the last moment.

She shook her head. "No. Blood sport is not confined to vampires. Plenty of humans enjoy a little blood play. In fact, most vamps don't even bother with this type of accessory." She smiled widely to flash her fangs. Her pink tongue flicked against the sharp points. "May I ask how you came by it?"

I crossed my arms. "That was found in a murder scene."

Her red brows shot to her widow's peak. "Is this about the mage who was killed at Vein?"

Word certainly had spread quickly. No point in denying. "Yeah."

Nipple Clamps clanked his way back to the desk carrying a tray. He went to the mistress first and deposited a glass of blood near her hand. She didn't look at him but he bowed anyway. Then he came to me and handed me an identical glass without making eye contact. I wasn't sure of the etiquette. Was it a faux pas to thank another woman's slave?

In the end, I decided to take the mistress's example and ignored him. He offered a glass to Adam, but the mage grimaced and shook his head.

"What exactly do you need to know?" she asked.

"Where would someone buy vampire gloves?" Adam asked.

"Ah," she said. "That's simple. There's only one place in New York where someone could get a pair of gloves exactly like these."

"Just one?" Adam said. "That's surprising. Didn't you say it's a common item for blood fetishists?"

"That would be true if it were a generic vampire glove. Those you could get in dozens of shops and even online. But this level of craftsmanship?" She ran a finger over the intricate designs along the glove's knuckles. "There's only one vampire capable of making such a masterpiece."

I raised an eyebrow. "Well?"

She laughed, a deep throaty sound. Tossing the bag on the desk, she leaned forward with her chin on her hand. "Me."

Giguhl tensed, as if ready to run away. In front of me, Adam stiffened and I placed a hand on his shoulder. I kept my features calm, but my heart was thumping in my chest. "Are you saying that glove belongs to you?"

She leaned back with her hands folded neatly across her taut midsection. "I believe I said I made it, not that it is my personal glove."

"Where were you last night around midnight?" Adam asked.

"I was here. Had an appointment with a client."

"Can you prove that?" I said.

The corner of her lip lifted, but her eyes hardened. "In theory, yes. But since you're not an officer of the law and you have no warrant, I will not. My clients trust me to protect their privacy."

My eyes narrowed. "That excuse would work if this was a mortal criminal investigation. But we are here under the authority of Despina Tanith Severinus, High Councilman Orpheus of the Hekate Council, and The Shade. I'm sure all three would be very interested to know you aren't cooperating." Honestly, I didn't believe Mistress Bianca was the murderer. But I hoped putting her on the defensive would encourage her to open up about who bought the glove.

She raised an eyebrow. "Oh, Sabina, let's not let this polite conversation devolve into power plays and vague threats. It demeans us both." She leaned forward and flipped through a leather-bound agenda on the desk. "I won't give you the client's name, but the appointment lasted from midnight to one a.m."

"Can anyone verify that information?" Adam asked.

She waved a hand toward Nipple Clamps. "Francis will confirm it as truth." She snapped her fingers.

"I confirm it as truth," Francis said.

My face tightened into a fuck-you smile. "Yes, I'm sure the testimony of your slave is reliable."

"I'm not sure what to tell you." Her shrug made something squeak under her suit. I wondered if she had on some sort of crazy latex contraption under there. "But why would I admit to making the glove if I'd murdered this mage?"

"She makes a good point, Sabina," Adam said. I made a mental note to exclude him from interrogations with hot dominatrixes in the future.

"Fine. I still need to know who purchased the glove."

"Again, I protect my clients. If word got out that I opened my books to you, my credibility would be shot." She smiled smugly.

"Not as shot as it would be if Slade revoked your feeding rights."

Her smile faltered. "He wouldn't do that."

"Oh, I assure you that he would. The murder happened in his club. I'm sure you're aware how seriously The Shade takes his position in the vampire community. And even if he didn't, I'm fairly certain the Despina and the High Councilman would have an opinion. Your persistence in obstructing this investigation will not go without consequences."

She sat still for a few moments, thinking it over. The truth was I hoped she didn't call my bluff and get Slade on the phone. I had no idea if he'd agree to revoke her feeding rights over this. For all I knew, they were lovers and he'd be pissed I threatened her.

Mistress Bianca rose with as much dignity as she could muster. She walked stiffly to a filing cabinet and unlocked it with a key hanging from a chain around her neck. She pulled out a ledger and flipped through it. After a moment, she said, "According to my records, that item was sold four nights ago here in the store. The purchaser paid cash."

"Were you here? Do you remember the buyer?" Adam asked.

She shook her head. "No, I would have remembered selling that pair. Whoever bought it must have come in during daylight hours. I have human employees who run the shop while I'm sleeping."

"Who was working that day?" I asked.

She pursed her lips. "Let me check the time sheets."

Bianca rifled through some more file folders. When she found what she was looking for, she ran a black nail down the paper. The finger stopped on something and her face changed. "Shit," she whispered.

I rose and went to her. "What is it?"

She held up the sheet. "Liam worked that day." Her voice sounded different, strained.

"Can we talk to him?"

She shook her head. "I'm afraid that's not possible."

What the hell was this chick's problem? "Do we really

need to go through this again? It's imperative we speak to Liam to find out who bought the gloves."

"You don't understand," she said, her voice cracking. "You can't talk to Liam because he's dead."

My stomach did a triple backflip. I glanced at Adam, who looked as shocked as I felt. "What?"

Mistress Bianca's eyes sparkled wetly. "It was horrible. They found his body in Central Park just last night."

A chill crawled down my spine. "Holy shit."

"After I found out, I called Slade and he said he'd take care of it." Her eyes widened then. "Wait, does this mean Liam's death is related to the mage's murder?"

I swallowed the bad feeling rising in my throat. This shit just got a whole lot more complicated. Especially since our only witness to the glove's owner was in the morgue, which meant our one clue, like Liam, had just met a dead end.

"It's possible," Adam said. "As far as we know, Liam was the only one who could identify the owner of the gloves."

"Which means we're back to square one," Giguhl said.

"Maybe," I said. "Have you heard any talk lately of someone wanting to unseat Slade's power?" Ever since Slade asked me to help him, I'd wondered if a rival might be behind the murders. A male like Slade didn't run a dark-races underworld without collecting a few enemies. And now that he was working for the Despina, it stood to reason the rivals might resent his broadening influence.

Bianca frowned at the seemingly random question. "There are always vamps who talk big about wanting to be the one in power."

"But have you noticed any changes? Anyone talking bigger than the rest of late? Especially since Slade made his deal with the Despina?"

The domme's lips wrinkled in distaste. "Oh, sure. Lots of local vamps consider themselves enemies of the Dominae. When Slade agreed to work with the new bitch in charge, a lot of vampires said he couldn't be trusted anymore." She paused, as if remembering something. "You know, now that I think about it, I did hear that this one guy had a major hard-on for getting Slade out of the picture."

"Who?"

"I don't remember the name. The last name started with an 'M' maybe. But I do remember he owns a strip club in Alphabet City."

I closed my eyes and cursed. "Tiny Malone?" Before she confirmed it, I already knew I was right. I'd had a run-in with Tiny months earlier, the last time I worked for Slade. That slimeball triggered my gag reflex.

She snapped and smiled. "That's it. Apparently he's trying to unite some of the local vamp business owners against Slade."

Adam looked at me. I'd told him about my run-in with Tiny months ago so he recognized the name, too. "Did Tiny approach you?"

She grimaced. "He sent his goons to threaten me. I told them to go fuck themselves. Slade isn't an angel but he's always been fair. Plus, I think it's a good thing he's trying to mend fences between the exiled vamps of New York and the new leadership out West."

I grabbed a pen and paper from her desk. "This is my phone number. If you think of anything else that might help us, please call me."

She folded the sheet and stuck it in her cleavage. "Sure. Anything I can do to help find Liam's killer."

We turned to go, but I paused when something caught my eye. I pointed to a flag over the door. I hadn't seen it when we first walked in. It was a red triskelion set against a black background. "What's that?"

Mistress Bianca smiled. "That's the symbol for vampire S&M community. The mortal version is all black, but we vamps modified it with red for obvious reasons."

Those reasons being a vampire's preternatural bloodlust as well as the telltale red hair that marked every vampire in existence.

"Hmm." I made a mental note to keep an eye out for it. "Learn something new every day. Thanks for your time."

11

The next evening, I decided to make good on my promise to speak to Maisie. No point in putting off the inevitable. I had about an hour until Alexis was scheduled to come over so we could formulate next steps, which also happened to give me a handy excuse to extricate myself from my chat with Maisie if it went sour.

I found my sister on the rooftop terrace outside her apartment. She stood at the wrought-iron railing, looking up at the waxing moon. She hadn't heard me arrive, so I took a moment to watch her—and work up my courage. Here, far above the city's traffic, it was quiet. Quiet enough for me to hear that she was whispering to herself.

I wasn't sure if it was the white hand repeatedly tugging on the black clump of hair. Or how her lips moved in hushed conversation. Either way, chilly fingers danced up my spine. But I couldn't stand there forever, putting off the inevitable. Clearing my throat, I walked toward her.

As if someone had snapped their fingers under her nose, she jerked to attention. She turned slowly and her eyes narrowed a fraction for a moment before recognition lit her irises. She released the strands she'd been torturing and smiled.

I pasted a grin on my face. "Hi, Maze."

"Sabina!" Her arms wrapped around my neck. After a brief hesitation, I hugged her back, trying to ignore the urge to push her away instead.

Her enthusiasm made my stomach contract with guilt. She'd hugged me like this the first night we'd met. Despite fifty-some years and a chasm of issues to overcome, she'd welcomed me into mage life like she'd always known me. Like we'd been real sisters our whole lives. No one before that moment had ever been so accepting of me, so genuinely glad I was alive.

The memory made me regret my earlier uncharitable thoughts. After all, like Giguhl kept reminding me, it wasn't my sister's fault she had issues. He never said the next part of that thought, but I always filled in the missing words silently to myself: It was *my* fault she was so fucked up. And now I could finally do something to help her.

"I'm glad you came to see me." She was holding on longer than she should. I backed away smoothly, my hands still on her shoulders to soften the rejection.

"Really? I thought you might not want to see me."

She frowned. "Why?"

I paused, wondering if she'd forgotten about her freakout a couple of nights earlier. Instead of reminding her, I quickly said, "I know you like your privacy."

Despite being the same height, it seemed as if she looked up at me. Like a child. "It's not that I like to be alone; it's just easier than . . ." She trailed off with a shrug that felt like an accusation. I mentally filled in the rest: *Easier than watching you all pity me.*

"I'm sorry I haven't visited more often. It's just been

busy and Rhea said you weren't feeling well," I finished diplomatically.

Her mouth worked for a second. "I feel much better now."

I eyed her. Honestly, she did look good despite her general twitchiness. Maybe it was wishful thinking but her cheeks had more color. There was also an air about her, an energy that was missing before, I guess.

"What have you been doing different?"

She leaned in to whisper. "I stopped sleeping."

My face tightened into a frown. "I don't follow. Why would that make you healthier?"

"Don't tell Rhea. She'll make me take herbs so I'll sleep."

I picked through my thoughts, trying to avoid potential conversation land mines. "Don't you want to sleep?"

"No!" She shook her head so hard her hair fell into a limp curtain around her face. "When I don't sleep, the bad memories stay away."

I ran my hands down her arms to grab her hands. "Maisie? Look at me." She looked up until her hair parted to reveal two haunted eyes. "Bad memories? Or bad dreams?"

"I don't know," she whispered. "I think they might be flashbacks." She rubbed her face, as if she could scrub away the memories. "It's confusing."

According to Rhea, it was normal for people recovering from trauma to have nightmares about their ordeals. But as far as we'd known, Maisie wasn't having any dreams at all. If she was wrong and the flashbacks really were dreams, this was big news. "Have you told Rhea about this?"

"No, Sabina. Promise me you won't tell her either." Her voice was cold with fear. "Or Orpheus. No one can know."

"But why? Maybe Rhea can help you stop having the flashbacks. She said that the dream incubation might help—"

"No," she said, her voice panicked. "I don't want to do that."

I rubbed her arms, trying to comfort her obvious distress. I was torn about keeping this information from Orpheus and Rhea. But I put that issue aside for the moment. "Can you tell me what you saw in your dreams?"

She swallowed. "I—I can't speak of it."

I blew out a breath, trying to keep my patience in check. *Don't push her, Sabina.* "I still think you need to tell Orpheus about this. With the Imbolc festival coming up, he's pretty determined to make you have a prophecy again."

She was already shaking her head before I stopped speaking. "I can't. He'll make me sleep. I can't sleep again, Sabina. Don't make me."

Her whole body trembled now. Time to change tacks. "How long has it been since you slept?"

"Not long. A couple of nights." She moved closer. The fingers of her right hand weaved through the air like she was playing an invisible piano. "I have a system." While her right hand continued its air sonata, her left hand came up to tug on the lock of hair below her ear. Up close, I could see the stray hairs clinging to her fingers. "Have to trick the circadian rhythms. I stay up all day. At night I go to bed, but I set an alarm to wake me every thirty minutes." She smiled at her cleverness, revealing fangs gone gray. "That keeps me from entering the REM state."

My mouth fell open. As a half vampire, like me, Maisie's natural cycle was to sleep during the day and be awake all night. Also like me, she was immune to death by UV ray that plagued all other vampires, but our bodies had a hard time keeping up with the sun's weakening effects long term. It could be done, but only with massive infusions of fresh blood to repair the damage.

"Please tell me you're drinking plenty of blood." For someone in her weak physical state, her body definitely wouldn't be able to keep up with the sun, lack of sleep, and no blood.

She swallowed and looked away, like she was ashamed. "Rhea was making me take intravenous infusions twice weekly. But my thirst has increased since I stopped sleeping," she said. "I have been supplementing with bagged blood."

I let out a relieved breath. When we'd gotten back to New York, it had been a struggle for weeks to get her to take any blood at all. If she'd told me she'd shunned blood, too, I'd be forced to go directly to Rhea with this information. But knowing she was at least taking care of herself in that regard allowed me a few extra days to convince her myself without bringing in the big guns.

"Is Orpheus going to send me away?" she whispered.

I hesitated and considered talking to her about the peace treaty and the ramifications if she didn't have a prophecy. But even I wasn't so insensitive not to know that would cause more harm than good. Instead, I took another approach.

"Of course he isn't going to send you away. He's just worried about you. We all are." I moved my head until I captured her gaze and forced her to look into my eyes. "That's why you have to start sleeping again. It's not healthy to force your body to stay awake."

She shied away, her breath escaping through her teeth in a hiss. "No! I can't. I c-can't. Sleep is bad." She tugged at the hair with both hands. Large clumps pulled away between her knuckles. "Badbadbadbad."

I reached out and tried to halt her obsessive grooming. "Maisie, stop." For someone so emotionally fragile, she fought me off long enough to get a couple more handfuls. I finally managed to hold her against me and force her hands by her side. I turned to look at her and had a clear view of the bald spot just behind her ear. "You have to stop hurting yourself." I closed my eyes against the stinging tears that threatened to fall.

She shook her head. "I'll be better. I promise. Just don't make me sleep."

"Shh," I said, rocking her. "I promise." Fear for Maisie made my stomach turn. I'd rarely felt more impotent in my life.

"Sabina?" Maisie whispered, her face turned away from mine.

"Yeah?"

"I've missed you."

Well, if that wasn't just a knife to the gut. A flash of Maisie's head bent over Adam as she sucked the lifeblood from his veins flashed through my head. Then the look on her face after she'd ripped our grandmother's head from her body—her haunted eyes and blood-smeared mouth. I blinked away the memories and looked down at the broken wraith who used to be my happy sister. "I miss you, too."

12

After talking to Maisie, I headed back to the apartment to meet up with Adam and Alexis. Orpheus and the Despina needed an update on our progress, and Adam and I were hoping they'd give us leave to interrogate Tiny Malone. Granted, the information Mistress Bianca gave us about him trying to recruit vampires wasn't exactly the strongest lead, but it was better than sitting around waiting for Slade to find something else to share with us. Plus, after my talk with Maisie, I was kind of hoping things with Tiny went south. I needed an excuse to hit something. Hard.

When I entered, the scent of stewing meat and herbs wrapped around me like a shawl. I shook out the tension in my shoulders. "Honey, I'm home!"

"In the kitchen," Giguhl called.

Just inside the doorway, I stopped to admire the scene waiting for me. Giguhl loomed over a bubbling pot on the stove. He wore an apron that read ANGEL IN THE KITCHEN, DEMON IN THE SACK.

"What's for dinner?" I leaned around Giguhl's back to peek inside the pot. He shrugged me off.

"Oh, no, you don't. The last time you tried to help me cook you ended up ruining my *coq au vin*."

I nudged him in the side for the reminder. "I thought PW was going to help you cook tonight."

He stirred the pot with a little too much gusto. Red liquid splashed and sizzled on the burner. "She's working at Vein."

My eyes widened. "She's singing again?"

He shook his head. "Waitressing. The nymphs have gone on strike until the murderer is found so Slade's desperate for help. And Pussy's determined to save up enough for her own place."

The topic of PW moving out was a source of tension between Giguhl and me. When PW had first brought up the idea of renting an apartment in the Black Light District, she and Giguhl were determined to become roommates. But I'd had to put a kibosh on that plan. It's not that I didn't want him to live with PW. Honestly, part of me would love the chance for Adam and me to have the place to ourselves. But even though I'd love the demon to have more freedom, magic bound Giguhl to me as my minion. Not only did he need my permission to do almost everything, but he also had no income of his own. And I sure as hell couldn't afford to pay partial rent for two apartments in New York.

To avoid having that argument with the demon again, I downplayed the chance that PW would be moving anytime soon. "Don't worry, she won't make much in tips tonight. Everyone's probably still staying away from the scene of the crime until the killer's found."

He continued as if I hadn't spoken. "I told her she should tell him no. It's not safe."

"She'll be fine. Slade will keep an eye on her." I patted his arm. "Is Adam around?"

Giguhl perked up. "In the living room." A mischievous smile spread on his black lips. "With a surprise."

I rolled my eyes. A surprise was not something I needed. "Is it Alexis?"

"She's running late." Satisfied with the stew's progress, the demon tapped the spoon on the edge of the pot. "This is an even better surprise."

I grabbed a beer from the fridge and went to investigate. As I walked down the hall, the demon called after me, "Dinner will be ready in thirty!"

Closer to the door, the low, comforting rumble of Adam's voice reached me. Every few seconds a higher feminine response echoed down the hall. Recognizing the voice, I sped up and burst through the door.

Three faces looked up at my entrance. Adam rose with a smile. "Red, look who the cat dragged in!"

"Hey, Georgia!" I grinned at the redheaded female who stood gracefully. After a quick, hard hug with her, I glanced at the female werewolf slouching on the couch. "Mac."

The werewolf wore an artfully ragged jean jacket and a black tank top. Think Joan Jett only hairier around the full moon. Despite her petite frame, she could be intimidating when she wanted to be, which, unfortunately, was often.

Georgia, on the other hand, looked like something off a fashion magazine with her lithe frame and hair the color of a polished copper pot. They were complete opposites, but somehow they complemented each other.

I hadn't seen the couple since we'd left New Orleans. They'd helped us find Maisie and also fought with us against my grandmother and her goons. Georgia was awesome. And Mac? Well, let's just say the were and I had a complex relationship.

The were crossed her arms but deigned a terse nod in my general direction. Ignoring her surliness, I turned to Georgia. "What brings you to the Big Apple?"

Georgia looked to Mac expectantly, but the werewolf hunkered down. Finally, Georgia realized she'd be doing all the talking and explained. "Mac's uncle called her back."

Mac's uncle was Michael Romulus, Alpha of the New York werewolves. Since I'd just seen him a couple of nights earlier at Vein, I was surprised he hadn't mentioned Mac's imminent arrival. Although, to be fair, we had been discussing a brutal murder.

"Do you know why?" I went to join Adam on the sofa, while Georgia took her place next to Mac across the table from us.

Mac crossed her arms and scowled at the coffee table. "Yeah."

Adam put his arm around my shoulders. "Before you got here, Georgia said they have a favor to ask us."

I looked at the couple for confirmation. Georgia nodded, but Mac looked more miserable than ever. Finally, the vamp nudged her lover's side and wasn't subtle about it.

Mac sighed and sat up straighter. "Do you remember in New Orleans when you asked me to help you find your sister?"

"Of course," I said.

"And how you promised a favor in return?"

Heaviness settled in my center. Somehow I just knew this favor wasn't going to be something I liked. "Yeah."

"I'm calling it in now." Her tone was tight, like uttering the words cost her a chunk of pride.

Adam pulled his arm away and leaned forward. "What do you need?" His casual demeanor was gone now.

"I think Mike called me back because he wants me to

find a mate." She tipped her head toward her lover. "Obviously that's a problem."

I sucked in a breath. This wasn't good at all. Even if Michael could accept the fact his niece was a friend of Sappho, which was unlikely given werewolves' male-dominated culture, he probably wouldn't be too thrilled by the fact she'd fallen for a vampire. Mating between the races had been forbidden centuries earlier by the Black Covenant. Abolishing that provision was on the table for the peace talks, but it was also one of the big sticking points of the negotiations. Naturally, as the product of such a forbidden match and the participant in one now myself, I was also pretty invested in the outcome of that line item.

"So what are you going to do?" I asked.

"What choice do I have? I'm going to have to tell him about Georgia and me."

Adam and I exchanged a tense glance. "Well, it probably won't be easy, but Mike's a reasonable guy." Adam's tone was overly bright with false optimism.

"You have to understand. I'm an old maid by were standards. Most of my friends and cousins were married off by the age of twenty. I'm pushing forty."

Georgia patted her girlfriend's arm. "You're just a baby."

She was right. By vampire standards, forty was pretty young. Georgia had told me back in New Orleans that she was seventy-five—twenty years my senior. But werewolves had shorter life spans than the other dark races. No one really knew why. The average werewolf would live only about two hundred years. Compared to mages who lived to be two thousand and some vampires who'd literally been around since before antiquity, they were little more than violent puppies. That reputation also explained their lack of power at the negotiating table.

"Either way," Mac continued. "Michael's been on me for years to settle down. That's one of the reasons I went to New Orleans. I figured, out of sight, out of mind, you know? But I guess with everything going on he's decided to do something about his spinster niece. And with the Lupercalia mating rituals coming in a couple of weeks, well, I put it together." She rubbed her hands on her jeans. "Needless to say, I don't think he'll do a miraculous one-eighty and welcome Georgia into the pack."

I sighed and scooted closer to Adam. I'd certainly had my share of shitty family setups and betrayals, but at least I'd had a right to choose my own mate. Of course, it took killing my grandmother to achieve, but still. "So how exactly do you need our help?"

Mac leaned forward with her elbows on her knees. "You said you were friends with Uncle Mike, right?"

"Sure," I said slowly.

Mac grabbed Georgia's hand. "We were hoping you could talk to him for us. You know, open the door to ease the way and all."

I went still. "Um, Mac? Not that we're not totally supportive of your right to be with Georgia—"

"We are," Adam jumped in. "Totally."

"But?" Mac demanded, her eyes going all squinty.

"But don't you think it's best if he hears it from you?"

"If I believed that, I wouldn't have come to you." Mac's jaw went hard. I knew it was costing her a lot to ask me of all people for help, but she was asking the impossible. "You squelching on your promise?"

"You don't understand," Adam said. "It's not that we don't want to help you. But we've got some serious shit going on right now. Sabina and I are knee-deep in a murder investigation. We can't put that aside to play mediators for you and your uncle."

Mac jumped up. "I told you they wouldn't do it!" She raised her voice at Georgia. "We're out of here." She began to stalk off, but Georgia pulled her back.

"Mackenzie Romulus, sit your ass down!" she demanded. "Adam and Sabina have every right to have reservations." She turned to us. "Sorry, guys. We're both feeling pretty frustrated right now."

"Totally understandable," Adam said.

Mac dropped back onto the couch and crossed her arms. Georgia ignored her and soldiered on. "If you're unable to talk to Michael on our behalf, could I at least trouble you for a place to crash?"

"Wait, so you're not going to Michael's now?" I asked.

"No, Einstein," Mac said. "She means that she needs a place to stay until I have a chance to talk to Uncle Mike."

I glared at her for the insult. Lucky for the surly were-wolf, I really liked her partner. Otherwise I'd kick both their asses out of my apartment for Mac's attitude. "Of course Georgia can stay here."

"Thank you so much," Georgia said. "It shouldn't be more than a couple of nights, right, Mac?" When Mac didn't answer, Georgia elbowed her again. "*Right*, Mac?"

Her tone was too pointed for me not to raise a brow. The tension between the couple was palpable. If I had to guess, Georgia was annoyed Mac hadn't already told Michael about their forbidden love.

Mac sat up straighter. "Sure. A couple of nights. Two weeks at the most."

Adam's head whipped toward me. He mouthed, "Two weeks?"

"Um, that's quite a range," I said. "Why two weeks?"

Georgia's eyes had narrowed into thin slits. "Yeah, Mac, why two weeks?"

"Because, *honey*, that's when the Lupercalia mating rituals happen," she said in a patronizing tone. "Worse comes to worst, I'll just come out to the entire pack that night."

Adam was so shocked by this announcement, he jerked in his seat. "Uh, that's a really bad idea."

Mac's eyes went all flinty. "Why?"

"Don't you think announcing your forbidden love for a vampiress at a werewolf ritual might piss off a few of your kin?" I said.

Mac's chin came up. "So?"

"So it's fucking dangerous," Adam said. "The Lupercalia feast is one of the sacred nights where werewolves can change forms without the full moon, right?"

"Yeah."

"So you're going to just drop this bombshell and then expect dozens of werewolves in full wolf-berserker mode to just take it in stride? Especially your uncle, who's going to be embarrassed and angry," Adam said, his voice incredulous. "More than likely, you'll both be punished, if not killed, and then if you're still breathing, you'll be shunned."

"Let them shun me." Mac's chin came up. "I don't care."

Georgia squeezed Mac's hand in support.

"Pardon me, but if you really feel that strongly, why haven't you already declared your intentions to Michael?" I knew I was stirring the pot, but it had to be asked.

The were's eyes narrowed and a low growl rumbled in her chest. "What are you implying, mixed blood?"

I held up my hands. "Mac, stop it. I know we've had our issues but I'm not your enemy. I'm just saying maybe it's better to just go talk to Michael now instead of staging melodrama in front of the entire pack. He'd probably be more receptive to the idea that way."

Mac shot a glance at Georgia and sighed. "You're probably right." Georgia patted her arm.

"Whatever you decide, you know Sabina and I have your back. Giguhl and Pussy Willow, too. In the meantime, of course Georgia can stay with us."

Mac looked up quickly. "Really?"

We both nodded. "I should warn you, it gets a little crowded," I said. "Giguhl and Pussy Willow have the twin beds in the guest room. But you're welcome to the couch you're sitting on. The windows have blackout shades so you should be safe in here during the day."

Georgia patted the couch. "This'll be great. Thanks, guys."

"Yeah, well," I said, "we'll see if you're still thanking us after you've had to share a bathroom with a drag queen and a demon for a few nights."

I'll give Giguhl some credit. He managed to wait two seconds after we'd all emerged from the back room to launch his campaign.

"Seriously, you guys should consider it," he said, stabbing the air with his claw for emphasis. "You'd be awesome!!" He looked over at Alexis, who'd arrived while we were talking to Mac and Georgia. "You, too. Especially you."

Alexis crossed her arms. "No."

Giguhl's lips pursed into an offended pout. I covered my grimace with a sip of beer. I knew it was childish, but my ego skipped a beat. Alexis got an invite but not me?

Before the conversation had turned to Roller Derby, I'd been enjoying hanging out with old friends over a beer. But with the change in topic, every swallow tasted fuzzy and bitter, like wounded pride.

Luckily for Giguhl, Georgia and Mac weren't as closed to the idea. "I'll admit it sounds fun. What do you think, Mac?"

The werewolf shrugged. "I don't know."

"Actually," Adam offered, "it might be a great solution. Until you can sort things out with Michael, it'll give you two a chance to be together without raising any suspicions."

"Totally," Giguhl said. "We'll have two practices a week plus the bout, so you'll see each other all the time."

Mac paused and set her drink down slowly. "Hmm, that would give me a little more time to work up to telling Uncle Mike."

Georgia's face fell. I wanted to hit Mac for her insensitivity. I couldn't imagine what this was doing to Georgia's pride. But Mac didn't notice her partner's distress.

"And you say we'll get to hit people?" Mac continued.

"Oh, most definitely," Giguhl said. "In dark-races Roller Derby, violence is not only encouraged; it's also required."

A slow smile spread across the were's lips. "Awesome."

Alexis cleared her throat. "They're waiting for us."

I sighed and set down my beer. I wanted to stay and hang out with our friends, but duty called. "Giguhl, can you take Georgia to Vein and get her cleared with Slade for feeding?"

"Wait, what's that about?" Georgia asked.

"If you want to feed while you're in the city you have to pay the blood tax to Slade Corbin. Folks around here call him The Shade and he runs the nonmage dark-race business in the city."

"How much is the tax?"

"Two Gs."

"Ouch," she said.

"If that's too much, I can hook you up with bagged blood while you're here. But either way, it's still best if you introduce yourself to Slade to avoid any misunderstandings."

Georgia grimaced at the mention of bagged blood. "No offense, but I'd rather go into debt to this Shade than drink bagged blood."

My lips twitched. I remembered a time when I'd have agreed with her. "Suit yourself."

Giguhl raised his claws with a huff. "Wait, what about dinner?"

"Sorry, G." Adam grimaced. "We're going to have to take a rain check. Orpheus and the Despina are waiting for us."

"Well, that's just great," the demon said, crossing his arms. "I give and I give and I give. And what do I get in return? More orders! I don't exist just to do your bidding, you know. I have rights!"

"Give it a rest, Norma Rae," I said with an eye roll. Gods save me from demon diva fits. "This way you'll be able to check on Pussy Willow."

The demon stood straighter. "Hmm, you have a point." He turned to Mac. "You wanna come with? PW will be thrilled to see you."

Mac shook her head. "If I don't report to Uncle Mike's soon I'll have to spend the night listening to a lecture about punctuality and respect for one's Alpha."

"Okay, we really need to get going," Adam said. "Mac, let us know how your talk goes. Giguhl, behave yourself." He turned toward Alexis and me. "You guys ready?"

Just before I followed them out the door, I remembered Giguhl couldn't escort Georgia to Vein in his demon form. I stopped in the doorway and yelled, "Giguhl, change forms!"

A pop echoed through the apartment. A gasp and a curse followed. "That's not right," Mac growled.

"Oh, please," Giguhl hissed. "Like anyone's gonna believe you're disgusted by a little pussy."

"The pussy part's not the problem," Georgia responded, her tone positively arid. "It's the double entendre between your legs."

"Bitch, please," the demon cat responded, obviously enjoying the banter. "One night with this bad boy and you'll give up the poon forever."

Alexis shot me a confused look from the hall. "What the hell are they talking about?"

"Trust me." I shook my head and shut the door behind me. "You don't want to know."

*I*n conclusion," Adam was saying to Tanith and Orpheus half an hour later, "we now believe the two murders are connected."

Once again, we were sitting around the conference table in Orpheus's office. We'd had Alexis start with her findings, which frankly didn't amount to much. No one at Vein the night of the murder saw a damned thing. She also said when no witnesses turned up, she'd asked Slade if she could see the security footage. Naturally that was a dead end, too, because Slade didn't allow cameras in the back rooms, to protect his customers' privacy.

After Alexis finished her report, Adam took the lead on relaying what we'd learned from Mistress Bianca. His observation about the murders being connected grabbed the leaders' interest big-time.

"They certainly sound connected," Orpheus said. "Unfortunately, the human's death also means your trail has dried up."

"Not necessarily," I said. "Mistress Bianca told us that she'd been approached by some rough vampire elements about supporting a change in the Black Light District leadership."

The Despina perked up. "Oh?"

I nodded. "Apparently, Slade's alliance with the Despina shook up some old resentment among the city's vamps."

"Who's behind the movement to oust Slade?"

Adam looked to me to explain. "Tiny Malone." I grimaced. "He runs a strip club in Alphabet City. He's little more than a hustler. Hardly powerful enough to give Slade a direct challenge for power."

Adam stepped in. "Unless he could work behind the scenes, sowing discontent among the vamp population while also undermining Slade's authority by making it look like he's not in control."

Orpheus nodded. "Sounds like you need to go pay this Malone a visit."

Ugh. I knew it was inevitable, but the very idea left a bad taste in my mouth. Especially since I knew the minute I walked in his club, Tiny would recognize me.

Alexis had been mostly quiet during the discussion. I assumed she was allowing Adam and me to take the lead, as Orpheus had instructed us to do. But the scowl on her face indicated she was annoyed we'd been the ones to get the new lead. "What exactly is our objective when we approach him?"

I squinted at her, wondering if it was a trick question. "Obviously, we're going to talk to him to figure out if he's behind the murders."

"Talk," she snorted. "You ask me, we grab him off the street, take him to a remote location, and beat the truth out of him."

I had to bite my lip to keep from pointing out that, in fact, no one had asked her shit. Next to me, Adam opened his mouth to respond, but the Despina beat him to it. "I concur. Swift, decisive action is the best approach."

Adam shot them both a disbelieving look. "Pardon me, but at this point all we have to go on is hearsay. If we beat him, he'll maybe confess but only because he wants the pain to end."

"There's no maybe about it," the Despina said without a trace of concern. "Torturing confessions out of criminals is Alexis's specialty."

The vampire cracked her knuckles. "Back in Los Angeles they call me the Iron Maiden."

I closed my eyes and prayed for patience. When I opened them again, Adam was staring at the females like they'd grown two more heads. "Well, Iron Maiden, it's common knowledge that you can't trust confessions from torture victims. And since our goal is to find a killer, not just a random, forced confession, I think we'll skip the beatings for now."

Tanith narrowed her eyes at the mancy. "That's not your decision to make. Orpheus, what do you say?"

"I am committed to finding the murderer as quickly as possible." He cleared his throat and shifted in his chair, clear signs there was a "but" coming. "However, in this case, I don't believe we have enough evidence to justify such extreme measures with Mr. Malone." The Despina stiffened, but he continued. "Sabina, Adam, and Alexis will question Mr. Malone. If they feel that harsher measures are warranted based on that conversation, then I'll consider your suggestion."

"With all due respect, High Councilman, you're making a mistake," Tanith snapped.

"I welcome your participation in this investigation as an ally," Orpheus replied coolly. "But you would do well to remember that you are in mage territory."

The air was sucked out of the room. I wanted to pump my fist to support Orpheus's kick-ass display. But I refrained because at that moment the Despina looked like she was ready to jump across the table and, mage territory or no, show the High Councilman how vampires dealt with public shaming. Not very diplomatic of her, I must say.

However, she seemed to get herself under control quickly. Her nostrils flared as she sucked some air into her lungs and swallowed her pride. "Understood."

Orpheus acknowledged that with a dignified nod. "I applaud your dedication. Just as I know Sabina and Adam appreciate Alexis's assistance."

This was the part where Adam and I were supposed to eagerly nod and make appreciative noises. Only one of us managed to pull that feat off. I was too busy swallowing the bile that always rose when politicians tried to force saccharine platitudes down my gullet. However, no one seemed to notice my discomfort. Except Alexis, who glared at me so hard I think I felt my skin burn.

Needless to say, as we all rose to go find Tiny, I wasn't feeling very optimistic about the outcome of our upcoming chat.

The Fang Bang squatted between a liquor store and a brick tenement that escaped the 1990s Alphabet City gentrification. The facade of the two-story building was painted black. The only color at all was the red of the tufted vinyl door. The sign out front advertised the business as FB CLUB, MEMBERS ONLY.

Adam, Alexis, and I stood on the sidewalk outside the club discussing the plan. "Red, what can you tell us about the layout?" Adam asked.

"There are two exits—the front door and another at the rear of the hallway next to Tiny's office. I never went to the second floor, but I assume that in a pinch, we'll probably find a fire escape or two."

"Where does the back door lead?" Alexis asked.

"An alley runs along the back of the building."

She raised a brow. "You're sure?"

"Positive." I didn't mention that I'd escaped into that alley after my last visit to the club. Or that I'd puked my guts out next to the Dumpster after the scent of Tiny's singed skin made me physically ill. Or that Slade had to come pick me up because I'd been too out of it to make it home on my own.

"So how are we going to play this?" Alexis asked. "Since we're not ambushing." Her tone held lingering resentment. I ignored it. She didn't like not being in charge? Too damned bad.

"What do you think, mancy? Good vamp, bad mage?"

Adam's lip twitched. "Considering you kicked his ass last time you were here, I'm pretty sure Tiny won't buy you as the good vamp."

"Wait a second," Alexis said. "You mentioned you'd been here before, but not that you fought this guy. Do you really think he'll tell us anything if you're there?"

I pursed my lips. I didn't want to admit that she might be right. But in all honesty, I was expecting Tiny to take one look at me and sic his goons on us. "I'm hoping the three of us can talk some sense into him before he does anything stupid."

"Or you could stay out here and let the mage and me handle it."

I was already shaking my head halfway through her sentence. "Hell, no. I'm not freezing my ass off out here while you two get to have all the fun."

"Sabina," Adam said. "She may be right. We're here for answers, not a fight."

"Adam, this is a vampire club. They're just as likely to attack when you walk in as they would be if they saw me."

Adam frowned. "That would be the case in Los Angeles. This is New York. Even a slimeball like Tiny has to understand that pissing off the Hekate Council would be very bad for his health."

"You must be joking," I snorted. "Or did you forget the reason we're here? Tiny is a suspect in the murder of a mage, Adam."

Alexis raised a hand. "Guys, there's a simple solution here. I'll go in alone and find out what I can."

"Oh, hell no," Adam snapped. "You're the one who wanted to kidnap the guy and cut his fingers off."

She raised a brow. "Not his fingers."

I rolled my eyes. "Look, like it or not, we're all going in. Together."

"Wait," Adam said. He had that clever little gleam in his eye that always preceded an idea. "Sabina, why don't we just use a glamour spell on you? Then Tiny won't recognize you."

I snapped my fingers. "Perfect!"

"Wait, why does the mancy have to do the spell on you?" she asked. "I thought you were all magical and shit."

Her tone and her challenging glare tested my already thin patience. "I can't do every type of spell in existence, Alexis. But I'd be happy to perform a demonstration of one of my specialties if you'd like."

"What is it?" she asked.

"Well, we're not close enough to a cemetery for me to summon the dead," I said in a matter-of-fact tone, "so we'll just have to settle for me forcing your body to spontaneously combust."

Alexis pursed her lips and narrowed her eyes, as if trying to decide if I was bullshitting. "If it's all the same to you, I'd prefer to skip the showing off and just get this job done before I choke on the overpowering stench of sandalwood."

"Suit yourself." I shrugged. Turning to Adam, I said, "What's the plan?"

He noted the smirk on my lips and shook his head in that annoyed but amused way of his. "It's fairly simple. We don't need a complete transformation. Good thing, too, because I don't want to deplete my energy too much in case shit goes down in there. Since your hair is a dead giveaway, I'll just make it all red so Tiny believes you're a full-blooded vamp. That should be enough to throw him off. Sound good?"

"Go for it."

He mumbled something under his breath and waved his fingers around my head. The next instant my scalp crawled with magic. Alexis's soft gasp proved the spell had worked.

"There. All done," Adam said, brushing his hands together. "How do you feel?"

"The same." I shrugged. "What do you think, Alexis? Is it enough of a disguise?"

"I guess so. If I didn't know otherwise, I'd assume you were a pureblood." Her tone indicated that she found the very idea I was pretending to be a pedigreed vamp blasphemous.

I grimaced at the reminder of my mixed heritage. I'd lived among mages so long I had almost forgotten what it was like to constantly be reminded of my shameful beginnings. But for vampires like Alexis, the fact that my blood was tainted by my mage father was cause for suspicion and downright antagonism.

"Anyway, if we're all satisfied with the new look, I say

we get moving." I reached back to touch the gun in my waistband. I'd pulled it out of its storage case in the closet before we left. Funny. I'd spent so many years wearing it, I'd grown used to the heft tugging at my waist. But now it felt like it weighed twenty pounds. My fingers itched to fire it for old time's sake, but I reminded myself that bringing it was purely a precautionary measure.

"Once you're inside, keep your eyes sharp for unfriendlies, which will probably be everyone. But most of all, keep your weapons holstered and your fists to yourself unless directly challenged. Got it?"

Her eyes hardened into two glittered beads. "Yes, ma'am."

"Then let's give our regards to Tiny Malone."

When Alexis opened the door, a blast of hot air, cigarette smoke, and Lords of Acid's grinding synthesizers
assaulted us.

Adam wrinkled his nose and held out a hand. "After
you." I shot him a grimace and forged in after Alexis.

The main part of the club housed the typical strip club
accoutrements—a round bar in the center, a stage with
brass stripper poles, and lots of shadowy corners for lap
dances. Customers willing to spend a little more money for
some serious fun had two options. First, they could slip
their stripper a couple hundred bucks to pay a visit to
the "blood rooms." These were like the champagne rooms
at mortal strip joints, but the only liquids in these particular
rooms were blood and ejaculate. For those who preferred
their blow jobs fang-free, Tiny also offered nymph prostitutes, who serviced customers from second-story rooms.

Anyway, no one looked up when Alexis and I walked in.
After all, we were, as far as they knew, just two vampire
chicks. Nothing special, considering we were both fully
clothed—or mostly so, in Alexis's case. But when the

mancy stepped in behind me, it was like someone scratched a needle across vintage vinyl.

The music didn't literally stop, of course. But the air shifted and tightened. A few of the patrons stood, looking primed for action. The bartender stopped wiping down the bar and shot the mage an aggressive glare. "Can't you read?" he shouted over the music at Adam.

Adam tensed next to me. "Excuse me?"

The barkeep jerked his head toward the door. "Sign says vampires only."

"Actually," Adam responded, "it says members only."

"Oh, yeah, smart guy? You a fucking member?"

Adam shook his head. "No, but I'm not here as a customer. We need to see Tiny."

"Tiny's in a meeting. You and your two skanks need to get the fuck out of here."

Alexis lurched toward him. "Listen, asshole." I grabbed her arm and shook my head. Once she looked like she'd stay put, I turned and flashed my most charming smile at the bartender.

"We really need to speak with him," I said, my tone cajoling. "Do you know how long his meeting will take?"

His eyes narrowed. "I'm not his fucking social secretary."

Apparently, manners weren't going to work with this guy. "The mage is a Pythian Guard for the Hekate Council." I jerked my head toward Alexis. "My colleague and I are Enforcers for the Despina," I fibbed. "We have a few questions for Mr. Malone."

The dude's eyes widened. His hand moved under the counter. I grabbed his arm. "Ah, ah, ah." My voice promised deadly force. "Let's keep this nice and friendly. Hands where I can see them." Grimacing, the bartender slowly withdrew his hand and placed it flat on the wooden surface.

I didn't look behind me to confirm Adam's location. I knew he had my back covered. "Mancy, you and Alexis make sure things stay civil out here. I'm going back."

"Be careful," Adam said.

I nodded and moved toward the back hall. The strippers shot me surly looks as I passed. I ignored them and pushed through the velvet curtain separating the blood rooms from the club.

The hallways held four blood rooms with curtained doorways, one standard office door, and a reinforced steel exit. The latter's sign cast the darkened space in a bloody glow. I passed the curtains cautiously, but other than some moaning and the stink of illicit sex, nothing jumped out at me. Tiny's door was closed, but I didn't bother knocking. I pushed it open with my gun at the ready. The portal swung back and slammed into the interior wall.

I'd been expecting to find Tiny "auditioning" a girl on his office bed. Instead, he was sitting behind his desk with his hands raised. The male standing across the desk from him swiveled his gun from Tiny to me.

"What the fuck are you doing here?" I demanded, taking a step into the office.

"Sabina?" Slade lowered the gun and raised his eyebrows. "What's up with your hair?"

I waved a hand to dismiss my magical dye job. "Are you going to answer my question?"

"I'm interrogating this piece of shit," he said, tilting his head toward the obese vampire. Sweat beaded on his pasty brow.

"Why? You know damned well the Despina and Orpheus wanted you off the investigation."

"Yeah, thanks for defending me there." His tone dripped with resentment. "I'm here because I figure finding the killer is the only way to save my job."

Tiny lurched his bulk to the side. His ass was stuck in the chair, but he managed to hit a panic button next to his phone before Slade or I could stop him. "Freeze!" Slade yelled, pointing the gun at the vampire.

Tiny's rubbery lips spread into a fuck-you smile. "In five seconds your asses will be toast." To support his claim, the sounds of shouting and stomping footsteps reached us from the hall. I spun around just in time to see the first of Tiny's goons burst through the door. From the sounds of things, at least five other guys were behind him.

"Everyone freeze!" I yelled. "I'm not here for trouble. I just need a few words with the boss."

The males filling the doorway froze with their hands halfway to their sidearms. They looked to Tiny for instruction. Their boss, who was wedged into a large black executive chair, laughed. "Kill 'em, you fucking idiots!"

It all happened quickly. The goons started firing. Tiny dove under the desk, pulling the chair down with him. Cursing, I ducked behind the chair and returned fire. I took out the first two, who exploded in the doorway like Roman candles. The resulting smoke and flame slowed down those in the hall.

Slade had squatted behind the other end of the desk. Together, we fired through the smoke to deter any more uninvited guests. Between shots, the sounds of a scuffle came from the hallway. Sounded like Alexis and Adam were taking them out from the rear.

"Slade!" I yelled. "Enough!" I was worried about accidentally shooting Alexis or Adam. But Slade didn't listen. I finally leapt at him and forcibly pulled the gun from his hands. "I said stop! Adam and Alexis are out there."

Slade blinked and his eyes finally focused. "Sorry, I got a little carried away."

Considering my own hands were shaking with adrenaline rush, I couldn't blame him. It'd been a long time since I'd had the opportunity to have a good old-fashioned shoot-out with anyone.

"Adam," I called. "It's all clear!" Now that the gunplay had ceased, the sounds of a stampede in the club carried back to us. Funny how a shoot-out can clear a joint.

In the next instant, the mancy and Alexis entered the office, stepping over the smoking remains of several of Tiny's goons. "Holy shit," Adam said. "What the hell happened? And why is Slade here?"

I let out a shaky breath. "He was in here when I arrived. Looks like we weren't the only ones who thought Tiny was the perp."

Slade adjusted the cuffs of his white dress shirt. "Yes, thanks so much for fucking things up. Tiny was about to confess when you came barging in."

"No, I wasn't," a muted voice came from under the desk. We all ignored him for the moment.

"Excuse me?" I rounded on Slade. "You have a lot of nerve blaming this on me. You were the one sticking your gun where it didn't belong. Besides, if you'd been paying more attention, he wouldn't have pushed that panic button."

"All right," Adam said. "Both of you retreat to your corners so we can figure out what the hell's going on." He turned to Alexis, who stood by watching the scene with a disdainful scowl. "Will you help Mr. Malone out from his hiding place, please?"

I crossed my arms and slouched against the wall, shooting glares at Slade, who was returning them with a pretty intense glower of his own. Alexis ignored both of us and helped Tiny get unwedged from beneath the desk. A few grunts and curses later, Alexis yanked him up and pushed him toward the rumpled bed in the corner. On his way down, Tiny knocked over the cache of sex toys he kept within easy reach of his casting mattress.

"Now," Adam said, his tone overly patient. "Let's back up. Mr. Malone, we just have a few questions."

Tiny flailed on his back like a disoriented beetle. When he finally managed to heft his upper body up, he was red-faced. "You motherfuckers! I ain't telling you shit!"

Alexis lurched at him, a knife flashing in her hand with menace. "Stop!" Adam yelled, obviously annoyed. Turning toward Tiny, he softened his tone and said, "Mr. Malone, I must apologize for my colleagues. Things have gotten way out of hand. We just need a couple of things cleared up and then we'll be out of your hair."

"What's in it for me?" the fat vampire said. His spit a wad of saliva on the toe of Adam's boot.

At that point, Adam had reached the edge of his patience and diplomacy. He bent over and grabbed Tiny by the collar. "Listen to me, you fat fuck! We just killed all your men. Do you really think we'd hesitate to kill you, too?"

Tiny stuttered and a white globule of spit beaded on his lower lip. "What do you want?"

I stepped forward. Now that the first wave of adrenaline had worn off, I felt more steady. "For starters, where were you the night the mage was killed at Vein?"

Adam released the vampire but stayed close enough to loom over him. Slade remained where he was, looking like he was ready to shoot all of us for screwing up his chance to exonerate himself with the Despina.

Tiny's beady little porcine eyes widened. "Is that what this is about? I didn't have nothing to do with killing that mage."

"He's lying," Slade said. "He might not have done the deed himself, but he orchestrated it."

"No, I didn't!" Tiny said. "I swear!"

"Cut the shit, Tiny," I said. "We have a witness who claims you've been trying to undermine Slade's position as leader of the Black Light District."

Tiny ignored that statement and narrowed his eyes at me. "Wait a second. You look familiar. Who the hell are you?"

I crossed my arms. "I'm asking questions, not answering them. Now, do you deny you've been working against Slade?"

Tiny crossed his arms over his enormous belly and pursed his rubbery lips together like a recalcitrant toddler.

"All right, that's it," I said. "We're not going to get anywhere like this. I think it's time to unleash the Iron Maiden on you."

Adam shot me a warning look. I shook my head to let him know I hadn't changed my stance on torturing Tiny. But I'd never promised not to *threaten* him with torture.

Tiny forgot his silent act and stuttered, "W-what?"

Alexis came up next to me. With a quick, decisive slash downward, she embedded the knife in the mattress, right between Tiny's fleshy thighs. He yelped and jerked backward, hitting his head against the wall. "You crazy bitch!"

"Start talking or next time I won't miss on purpose," she said, her tone ice cold.

"Okay, okay!" he yelled. "I admit I tried to get some vampires together to unseat The Shade." He swallowed hard, making his Adam's apple bob beneath his many chins.

"Why?" I asked.

"Because he's gonna sell us out to the Despina!"

I glanced at Slade, whose face had gone hard. "What does he mean?"

Slade shook his head. "He's delusional."

"Ha! I know all about how that ugly Despina's gonna come in here and start calling the shots. You ask me, once a Domina, always a Domina. The vampires of New York won't take it, I tell ya. We all came here to escape those crazy bitches."

"Watch your fucking mouth," Alexis said, her voice low and deadly.

Tiny ignored her. "So yeah, I figured The Shade deserved to see what New York vamps do to traitors who sell us out."

I stilled. "So you admit you were behind the murders?"

Tiny stilled, his face hot and red. "No! That's not what I said."

"You just admitted you had motive," Adam pointed out.

"Motive isn't the same as doin' it."

"Okay, for argument's sake, let's assume you're telling the truth," I began.

"I am telling the truth." Tiny's voice took on a hysterical note.

I nodded. "Yeah, yeah. You already said that. So if you didn't do it, who did?"

He looked taken aback. "How the hell am I supposed to know?"

"Oh, come on, Tiny," I said. "Do you really expect me to believe that the murders haven't been a source of gossip among the vampire community? Surely you've heard something."

Tiny pulled at his collar, like he could feel the noose tightening. "All I heard is some rumors. Not facts."

"Enlighten us," Slade said.

Tiny shifted his ass on the mattress. "Some vamps think the Despina's behind them killings."

Before any of us could react to that bombshell, Alexis lurched forward and slammed her knife into Tiny's chest.

"Alexis! What the fuck!" I yelled, jumping forward to try to help Tiny. But it was too late. She'd struck so hard and fast that only the tip of the hilt showed from the wound. The instant the applewood handle pierced his skin, the forbidden fruit's toxic juice robbed him of his immortality so the blade in his heart could do its job.

The problem with killing an obese vampire is that the results are always messy. All the blubber acts like an accelerant. Thus, two seconds after Tiny ignited, his body exploded.

My body flew back and slammed into the opposite wall. My head took the brunt of the impact, knocking my brain around in my skull. I woke up a few seconds later in a lump on the floor. The scent of Tiny's charred flesh and burned silicone from the sex toys filled my nose. I groaned at the pain in my head and forced my eyes open.

As it turned out, I wasn't the only one scattered to the wind by the explosion. Alexis sat on her ass, looking dazed and lightly flambéed. Slade lay a few feet away. His eyes were closed and black smudges covered his face. But he was a vampire. Barring decapitation or being impaled by an applewood stake, he'd live.

Adam, however, was not immortal, and his limp body was draped over the desk, moaning. I pulled myself off the floor with a groan and went to check on him. Rolling him over, I felt for broken bones and shrapnel wounds. His body flinched and one eye snapped open. "Please tell me that didn't just happen."

Relief that he was okay warred with anger in my gut. "I'm having some trouble believing it myself." I helped him up and steadied him when he wobbled. We both turned to look at the smoldering mass that used to be Tiny Malone.

The bed was a swampy mess of blackened fluid, scorched bone, and glowing embers. The wall behind the bed had crumbled with the explosion. The resulting hole gave us a view of the blood room next door, where two frightened strippers huddled in the corner.

"Well," Alexis said behind us. "That's that, I guess."

I turned slowly, feeling my temper rise like mercury in August. Alexis stood behind me with her hands on her hips, looking quite pleased with herself.

"Care to explain to me what you were thinking?" If Alexis had known me better, she would have recognized that my preternaturally calm tone was a warning. As it was, she felt no need to tread carefully.

"He was guilty. I killed him. End of story." She ended in a careless shrug.

"End of story?" My tone was still deceptively quiet, but inside a tempest gathered strength in my stomach, waiting to be unleashed on the bitch. "Adam?"

"Yes?"

"Did you hear Tiny admit to killing a mage?"

"Nope."

I raised an eyebrow at Alexis.

She responded by crossing her arms and jutting out a hip. "Please, we all know he was guilty."

"Actually," I said, my voice finally rising, "we did not fucking know he was guilty. Which is why we were interrogating him. So again, I ask, what the fuck were you thinking?"

"Sabina, your ego is showing," she said.

I tilted my head. "Excuse me?"

"Oh, please," she said, her tone defensive. "I just bet it chafes your ass that a younger, full-blooded vampire got the kill."

Was this chick serious? I sighed the sigh of a woman who had outgrown such petty arguments. "I don't give two shits about getting credit for the kill. My concern is that the kill shouldn't have happened at all. Our job was to get either a confession or information that might lead to the real suspect. Now, thanks to you, we have neither. You were out of line and you know it."

We stared each other down like two gunslingers at the O.K. Corral. After a moment, Slade groaned from his spot on the floor. "I'll take care of it," Adam said, sounding relieved to get away from the cone of tension surrounding Alexis and me.

After he'd walked away to help Slade, Alexis pursed her lips and shrugged. "We'll just see what the Despina says about who was out of line."

My lips tightened into a fake smile. "I'm fairly sure Orpheus will also have plenty to say."

Instead of being intimidated, she smiled back, flashing some fang. *Bitch*.

15

Orpheus and Tanith received us at the Crossroads later that night. They'd moved their meetings out there to finalize details for the treaty signing, which was set to happen in one week. We walked into the Council chambers in the middle of a meeting. The entire Council, the Despina, and several other mages and vampires filled the room. And on the table in front of the mage and vampire leader, a speakerphone emitted the shrill voice of Her Benevolence, Queen Maeve of the Seelie Court.

We snuck in and took seats near the back, not wanting to disturb the proceedings. Our news was bad enough without interrupting not one, not two, but three dark-race leaders. I was struck by how much things had changed in the last six months. Back then, a gathering of the two races would have ended in magical fireworks and copious bloodshed. But now they all sat around as civilized as can be, discussing the agenda for peace.

Adam, Alexis, Slade, and I hadn't spoken much since leaving Tiny's club. Alexis and I shot each other occasional glares. Adam glowered at both of us. And Slade ignored everyone, choosing instead to remain stonily silent. We'd forced him to come along both as a witness to Tiny's demise and to answer to the Despina and Orpheus about his interference.

By the time Orpheus and the Despina hung up with the Queen and summoned us forward, our resentments simmered like a pungent stew. The pair behind the table were oblivious to this, of course. They still hadn't looked up from the paperwork they were going over.

"What news?" Orpheus said in the clipped tone of a man too busy to worry about niceties.

Alexis and I bookended the males. She posed with her arms at her sides like a good little solider. I chose a less formal posture with my arms crossed and my hip cocked at a rebellious angle. Beside me, Slade's resentment radiated off him in waves. Knowing that none of us wanted to be the first to speak, Adam stepped in. "We've just returned from Tiny Malone's club."

"And?" Tanith looked up. She saw me first and frowned. "Sabina, what happened to your hair?" Orpheus's gaze shot up then. My hand flew toward my head. I'd totally forgotten about the stupid glamour. But before I could answer, she saw Slade. "Mr. Corbin? What are you doing here?"

Slade cleared his throat and stepped forward. "Despina. High Councilman." He bowed slightly but offered no explanation.

Orpheus threw down his pen and sighed. "Gods, please tell me there hasn't been another murder."

"There hasn't been another murder. Not exactly."

"Explain yourself," Tanith snapped.

Alexis butted in. "We went to Mr. Malone's club as instructed," she said. "However, when we arrived, Mr. Corbin was already interrogating the suspect."

Orpheus's gaze zeroed in on Slade. "You were told to stay out of the investigation."

Slade nodded to acknowledge the truth of that statement. "I'd hoped that securing a confession from Tiny would help redeem my earlier missteps on this case."

"You hoped to redeem yourself by disobeying a direct order?" the Despina said, her tone cold. "I don't follow that logic."

Slade shrugged. "It seemed like a good idea at the time."

Orpheus's frown deepened. "Lazarus, what happened when you discovered Mr. Corbin at the club?"

I raised a hand. "Actually, I was the one who walked in on their meeting. Unfortunately, my arrival distracted Slade and Mr. Malone was able to push a panic button to alert his bouncers he was in trouble." Slade shot me a sharp look, as if he was surprised that I'd downplayed his screwup. "They shot first. Mr. Corbin and I returned fire. Adam and Alexis assisted and together we killed six of Tiny's men."

"Any innocents harmed?" Orpheus asked.

I shook my head. "No, sir. The damage was contained." I swallowed, knowing this next part was going to open Pandora's box. "We then proceeded to interrogate Mr. Malone. He denied any connection to the murders."

The Despina snorted. "Of course he did."

"However," Alexis said, cutting in, "he did admit to trying to incite rebellion against Mr. Corbin due to his connection to the Despina."

Tanith's eyebrow lifted. "Oh?"

"Yes, ma'am," she continued. "He was quite adamantly opposed to the idea of New York's vampires being under your control."

"So he was the one behind the murders," Tanith concluded.

"Not necessarily," I said, unable to help myself. "Having strong opinions doesn't make one a murderer."

Tanith arched a brow at me. "You disagree that his subversive opinions don't indicate a motive?"

I crossed my arms. "Oh, I think Tiny had plenty of motive. That's not the issue. My problem is that motive is not the same as proof."

Orpheus sat up straighter. "Do we need to bring Mr. Malone in for a more persuasive interrogation after all?"

"Unfortunately that's not possible." I jerked my head toward Alexis. "The Enforcer over there killed him."

"That's a bit of an oversimplification, isn't it?" Alexis replied. "He all but admitted he was behind the murders."

I rounded on her. "It's the 'all but' that concerns me. The only thing he admitted to was that he thought Tanith is a bitch, which wasn't exactly a shocking revelation."

Orpheus gasped. "Sabina! That is quite enough. You will apologize to the Despina immediately."

I glared at him and then at Tanith. It was no secret to anyone in the room that I was not her biggest fan. In fact, the only reason I helped her gain her position as Despina was that it happened to fit it with my plan of killing Lavinia Kane. Regardless, insulting her publicly wasn't going to encourage her to listen to my side of this argument. "Despina, I apologize if I offended you by repeating Mr. Malone's insult."

She nodded regally, but her eyes were hard. "I fail to see why you're so upset, Sabina. Alexis may have acted rashly, but that doesn't mean she didn't ultimately do the right thing."

"If I may, I'd like to point out that our objective was not to execute Mr. Malone, guilty or no," Adam said. "You and the Despina instructed us to gather information and, if we deemed he was the likely culprit, to bring him to you.

Regardless of whether he ultimately would have been executed, Miss Vega was out of line."

I shot the mancy a smile for taking my side. Adam wasn't a hothead like me. If he thought Alexis was justified he'd let me know.

Orpheus heaved a sigh. "Do you have any other suspects?"

Adam hesitated. "No, sir."

"And isn't it true that during your investigation, no additional evidence was found to indicate that another might be responsible?"

"Actually, sir," Adam said with great reluctance. "Just before Alexis shot Mr. Malone, he indicated he believed the Despina was behind the murders."

Silence. Then, after a few tense seconds, the air filled with a rusty-sounding screech. "Oh, that's priceless," Tanith said between chortles. "Orpheus, can you believe Mr. Malone had the nerve to say such a thing?"

Orpheus wasn't quite as amused as the Despina. "Well, it certainly does shed new light on Alexis's actions, doesn't it?"

Tanith's laughter cut off abruptly. "You aren't serious," she said, her voice hard. "What possible motive would I have to kill a human or a mage?"

"The human could have been a botched feeding," I offered.

Tanith's reptilian gaze glinted at me. "I assure you that if I were to lower myself to feed from a common human, I would not botch the job."

She had me there. I knew that the Dominae all refused to drink any but the finest blood from human virgins or genetically superior specimens. "You've got me there, but who's to say you didn't kill him just for fun?"

"I will admit I've killed humans for sport." She shrugged. "But that doesn't explain why I'd risk peace negotiations by killing a mage. How would that benefit me?"

Orpheus rubbed his lower lip thoughtfully. "She has a point. Tanith knows that screwing me over will result in me unleashing the full brunt of mage magic on her and every vampire in existence." He said the words conversationally, but the threat in them glowed like neon. "Besides, are we really going to believe the ravings of a known criminal over the Despina?"

"Plus," Alexis said, "the Despina was in a meeting with Orpheus the night the human was murdered."

Orpheus inclined his head to confirm Alexis's claim. "She's correct."

Adam nodded. "I apologize, Despina, but you yourself said we should explore every angle."

Tanith lowered her head regally. "Understood. Now that that's settled, I believe you were telling us you had found no other evidence."

"But that doesn't mean that evidence doesn't exist," I pointed out.

"Mr. Corbin?" Tanith said, ignoring me. "Did you find any additional clues in your club?"

He shook his head. "No, Despina."

"And should we assume by your presence at Mr. Malone's club earlier this evening that you also believed he was the culprit?"

"Yes. Of all the vampires under my jurisdiction, Tiny was the most vocal about his opposition. I had reports from more than one witness who heard Mr. Malone say that he wanted to take me down."

"Wait," I said. "Something's been bothering me about Tiny as a suspect. If all he wanted to do was make Slade look bad, why would he go to such lengths?"

Orpheus frowned. "What do you mean?"

"Think about it. The human in Central Park wasn't just

murdered. He was brutalized and dismembered. That level of violence was either orchestrated to make the cops freak out or it was done by a monster who couldn't control himself. And let's not forget the mage's murder was over the top on the violence scale with bonus Dominae symbolism thrown in for good measure."

"So?" Alexis said. "You know as well as I do that most hired killers aren't exactly the most stable beings. Maybe he decided to play with his food before carrying out Tiny's orders."

"Right, and now we're supposed to believe that if Tiny contracted this, the killer's just going to stop?"

"Sabina, please," Slade said. "You know how this works. When the money dries up, so does the blood. No more Tiny means no more cash."

I jerked my head toward Alexis. "Well, thanks to Stabby McStabberson over there we can't know for sure whether Tiny used a hired gun, can we?" I said. "Or if Tiny was even behind the murders. Has anyone considered all this has nothing to do with Slade and everything to do with the peace treaty?"

"Sabina—" Slade began.

I talked right over him, warming up to my new role as devil's advocate. "The timing can't be a coincidence. The signing is next week. What if someone is trying to stop the alliance? It's not a secret that some beings on both sides are opposed to the end of hostilities."

"You're making it sound like this is some conspiracy orchestrated by the Caste of Nod," Orpheus said. "But we all know that is impossible."

I went still. I hadn't been specifically thinking about the Caste or its leader, Cain. But now that Orpheus mentioned it, I started thinking about my dream. Was it just a coincidence that I had another Cain dream just after the first murder?

I knew that the next thing out of my mouth was going to cause a scene, but I had to put the theory out there. "But... we never caught Cain. What if he's behind this?"

The room went quiet. I looked around at the shocked faces, waiting for someone, anyone to say something. Adam had gone still and alert, as if just saying Cain's name would summon him to the room. Slade and Alexis stared at me with puzzled expressions, as if trying to decide if I was joking. Orpheus's frown deepened into an all-out scowl. Tanith looked nervous, like I'd said "Bloody Mary" three times into a mirror.

"Sabina," Orpheus began slowly, "that's simply not possible."

I knew it sounded crazy, but I also knew this was the best way to make my case. Playing devil's advocate was always more effective than trying to debate with people who wouldn't listen. "Just hear me out. The other night I had a dream about Cain. He said something like, 'We're not finished.'"

Adam blinked at me. "Red," he said carefully. "You've been having dreams about Cain for months now. Plus, no offense, but we both know seeing Marty's body strung up like that dredged up some issues for you about Lavinia."

A hot flash consumed my body. How could he bring that up here, in front of everyone?

Despite the lava-hot glare I shot in his direction, he soldiered on. "It's understandable you'd have some disturbing dreams with everything going on. But that's hardly proof Cain committed these murders."

My cheeks burned at the careful, pitying stares. "You don't understand. It's not just the dream. Think about it:

Who else would be more motivated to cause trouble than the man who tried to start the war between the dark races to begin with? Peace is the last thing Cain wants."

Cain, in his role as leader of the Caste, wanted to start a war between the races because he believed it would bring on the second coming of Lilith. No one knew why he was so determined for that prophecy to happen, but he'd caused a ton of problems for the leaders of both races in pursuit of that goal. He'd even recruited my grandmother to his side, a move that led to her death.

"I'll admit the timing might not be a coincidence, but Cain? You told us yourself the Caste tried to summon him and failed," Orpheus said. "That tells me that wherever he is, he's not free to move about on his own. He'd need help, and we've killed everyone we could find who owed him allegiance."

"I know it's a stretch," I said, raising my hands in a pleading gesture. "But it's not totally out of the realm of possibility."

"No," Orpheus snapped, finally losing patience. "But I am secure in the knowledge that every member of the Caste of Nod was rooted out and executed. I am secure in knowing that at the peace signing, we will have almost every mage, vampire, and faery guard in America in attendance." As he spoke, his voice rose with each point. "But most of all, I am secure in the knowledge that it's far more likely that a two-bit pimp with ambitions toward organized crime is behind these murders rather than the father of the vampire race, who no one has seen in the flesh in centuries!" He pounded the table with his fist like a gavel sealing a verdict.

Swallowing, I looked at the floor. Of course it was crazy. I knew that before I'd said one word. But Sabina's Law stated that not sharing wild theories virtually guaranteed they'd become fact and bite you in the ass later.

"I concur with Orpheus," Tanith said. "We must be careful right now. But we also must not allow fear and superstition to dictate our choices. Logic and reason must prevail."

My head snapped up at the word "superstition." She knew damned well Cain was more than some dark-races boogeyman. I'd seen the Caste of Nod attempt to summon Master Mahan—their title for Cain as the leader of their secret sect—to that cemetery. I'd seen his spectral form begin to coalesce into flesh. And I watched as the Caste members lost the connection when they were attacked by the revenants I'd summoned to kill their asses. Oh, yes, Cain was real. But whether he was behind the murders? Well, I wasn't convinced either, but their stubborn insistence that Tiny was the killer chapped my ass.

"Sorry, Red," Adam said, "but I have to agree with Tanith and Orpheus. Other than your dreams, we've seen no sign of him."

"You don't believe this is Cain's doing? Fine. But you have to admit that we don't have enough evidence to say without a shadow of a doubt that Tiny was behind those murders. We cannot afford to shut this case just because we all want the matter settled."

The High Councilman cleared his throat. "Granted, Miss Vega's actions were premature, but I have to wonder if in this case the ends justify the means."

"You can't be serious!" My voice rose and echoed through the chamber.

Orpheus's eyes narrowed to two sharp slits. "Sabina, I have tolerated your impertinence as far as I'm willing. I understand that you disagree with Miss Vega's methods, but unless you can show me evidence that proves Mr. Malone was not involved, I am going to trust that justice was served."

"By evidence, do you mean someone else dies? Because that's what's going to happen if she killed the wrong guy."

"Lazarus, I suggest you take your *partner* out of my sight before I lose my good humor." Orpheus refused to look at me. "Miss Vega, you are also dismissed."

I opened my mouth to argue, but Adam gave me his patented don't-do-anything-dumb look. Alexis turned to go and Slade turned, too, but Tanith spoke up. "Mr. Corbin? A word, please."

I shot Slade an apologetic glance. No doubt, my outburst had soured the leaders' dispositions and he'd pay the price. But Slade wouldn't look at me. So I had no choice but to follow Adam out like a dog with my tail between my legs.

The minute we reached the hallway outside the chamber, Alexis started in on me. "Nice try, mutt. Too bad you made yourself look like a jackass before you tried to throw me under the bus."

"Fuck you, Alexis."

She laughed. "That's the best you got? Oh, right. I forgot. You're nothing but a burned-out mage lover."

"All right, that's enough," Adam said.

I pushed him out of the way and got in Alexis's face. "You want to go?"

"Please don't embarrass yourself. You might have red hair now because your boyfriend performed a little spell, but it can't hide your greatest weakness, mixed blood." Her lips curled into a mocking smile that showed fang. "You've gone soft."

My vision blurred red. How dare this bitch accuse me of losing my edge. Before I stopped to consider the ramifications, I delivered my very hard fist to her very fat mouth. The impact of fang to knuckle hurt like hell, but I relished the pain. The adrenaline rush. The satisfaction of making her bleed.

"Sabina!" Adam grabbed me from behind.

Alexis recovered quickly. She wiped the back of her hand across her lips and her knuckles came away bloody. Her smile revealed teeth and fangs coated red. Her tongue ran over the enamel as if relishing the coppery taste. She took a step toward us.

"Back off, Alexis." Adam was struggling to hold me still. He's a strong guy, but I wanted more blood.

"Relax, mancy. I'm not going to ruin my victory with the Despina by beating your girlfriend's ass."

"What victory?" I demanded. "When the next body shows up she'll nail your ass to the wall."

"There won't be another body. Not on my watch." Alexis smiled then, totally sure of herself. "And as a reward for disposing of Tiny, she's going to put me in charge of New York's vampires."

My shock made me go slack in Adam's hold. Adam's shock made him loosen his grip. "Wait a second," he demanded. "You're angling for Slade's job?"

She nodded. "If my guess is correct, she's in there right now relieving him of his duties."

"What makes you so sure she'll give you the job?"

"Because she promised it to me."

The door opened then and Slade emerged, looking shell-shocked.

"Slade? What happened?" I asked, ignoring Alexis for the moment.

He ran a hand through his hair. His once-pristine white shirt was covered in blood and black smudges. I'd never seen him looking so disheveled. "They've relieved me of my duties."

"Did they say who your replacement is?" Miss Sensitivity demanded.

Slade looked through her when he answered, like he couldn't quite believe this was all real. "No. They said they need time to discuss who would be the best fit."

That gave Alexis pause. Obviously, she'd been expecting to be called back into the room to hear she got the job.

"Shit, Slade. I'm so sorry," I said, placing a hand on his arm. Adam noticed the move and stiffened. As naturally as I could, I withdrew the contact. "I can't believe this is happening."

He snorted a humorless laugh. "That makes two of us."

"What are you going to do?" Adam asked.

Slade blew out a deep breath that hinted at surrender. "I honestly don't know. I still have my businesses to run, so that's something. But I'm not sure I'll be sticking around the city once they appoint a new leader. In fact, I'm not so sure they didn't just do me a huge favor."

"Why?" Alexis asked.

"Because once the vampires here find out the Despina's appointing one of her flunkies to run things, all hell's going to break loose. I don't envy the poor bastard."

Before any of us could respond, Tanith swept out of the room. She didn't pause to acknowledge any of us. Alexis, who until that point had been bitchy but relaxed, snapped to attention. The Despina didn't pause as she passed her guard, but the look she shot Alexis brooked no delay in accompanying her to the elevator.

A few short seconds later, the female vamps exited the

hall, leaving the area quiet and blessedly bitch-free. Before we could enjoy the change, Orpheus's assistant stuck his head out the door. "The High Councilman would like a word," he said, his eyes on Adam and me.

Slade ran a hand through his hair. "That's my signal."

We said our good-byes to Slade and followed the assistant back into the chambers. Only Orpheus was no longer on the dais. The assistant passed the table and led us to a doorway at the back of the room. He knocked briskly before opening the door and shooing us in.

The new room was a greenroom of sorts used by the Hekate Council between meetings. Orpheus stood at the wet bar, pouring himself two fingers of Scotch. "Gods, what a night." He kept his eyes on the amber liquid and took a liberal gulp before finally turning his attention to us. "Are you certain Tanith isn't an energy vampire?"

I bit my lip to hide my smile. "Last I checked, she was the good old-fashioned blood-sucking kind."

He shook his head and went to sit in a large wingback chair. "I didn't bring you here to discuss the Despina or the murders. Although, I should probably issue the standard threats about how failure to comply with my demands won't go well for you, Sabina."

I shrugged. "Understood. Although, I should mention I think this is all going to bite us in the ass."

"Keep your eyes open, but don't do anything without consulting me first. Got it?"

I let out a breath. He was going way too easy on me given the way I'd spoken earlier. Now that I'd had some time to think about it, I realized how stupid I'd been to undermine him like that in front of Tanith. "Yes, sir."

"Lazarus? Now that this murder business appears to be settled, I want you back on the task force to prep security for the festival. I don't want any surprises. No one comes onto those grounds without us knowing every detail, from their race to their family background to their shoe size. Got it?"

"Yes, sir."

"Sabina, how'd your talk with Maisie go?" The mercurial change in topic caught me off guard.

"Uh, fine, I guess."

He rested his tumbler on his knee and pinned me with a stare. "You guess?"

"I meant, yes, it went well. Better than I expected." I hadn't had a chance to fill Adam in on the talk I'd had with my sister, but I was very aware of his stare as I spoke. "Maisie has some qualms about the incubation ritual, but I think if I keep talking to her she'll eventually agree."

Orpheus hit the armrest with the butt of his hand. "We don't have until eventually."

I chewed my lip, trying to find a way to convince him to let me continue handling this. "I just need a little more time. Now that I'm not running around the city looking for a murderer, I can spend more time with her. Wear her down."

He crossed his hands over his stomach. "See that you do. Getting her to try this ritual Rhea has planned needs to be your top priority now. I don't think I need to explain to either of you how important it is that we have a positive prophecy to share on Imbolc."

"Actually," I said, "I have a question about that. Even if Maisie starts having dreams again, there's no guarantee they'll be positive, right? What will you do if her visions reveal negative outcomes to the treaty?"

Orpheus lowered his chin. "Sabina, in no possible universe would ending centuries of hostilities between our races be a bad thing."

"Sometimes even good things have unintended consequences," Adam said softly.

I shot him a look. Something in his tone put me on edge. Well, more on edge. Lying about Maisie already had me feeling twitchy.

"True enough, son. True enough." Orpheus stood and put a hand on Adam's shoulder. "Look, you focus on securing the compound, and Sabina will make sure Maisie starts dreaming again. You can both let me worry about everything else, including what to do with the prophecy once it's been had. Okay?"

I nodded. "Fair enough."

"All right, it's been a long day and an even longer night." The High Councilman drained his Scotch. He looked like a man with the weight of an entire race's fate resting on his shoulders. Probably because that's exactly what he was. "Let's all gets some sleep. No doubt tomorrow will present us with a whole new set of disasters."

16

The next evening, I woke with a bitter taste on my tongue. The vague, uneasy feeling that settled into my stomach had less to do with dreams and more to do with the conviction that we'd missed something—some crucial bit of evidence about whether or not we'd found the real killer.

After we'd gotten back to the apartment the night before, Adam and I stayed up a long time talking about what had happened. In the end, he convinced me that my personal feelings about Alexis and my guilt over Slade's dismissal were coloring my opinions.

Because the truth was, I'd believed Tiny was guilty, too. Maybe Alexis was right to kill him.

Also, I'd never admit this to her, of course, but I was a tad jealous of her. It's not that I missed that Enforcer lifestyle, exactly. But I did sometimes long for more adventure. Hell, hadn't Slade said the same thing? What were his words? "But don't be surprised when that darkness inside you rises up and you're forced to deal with it."

I tossed back the covers and got out of bed. Outside the bedroom, I could hear voices in the kitchen. Laughter and the homey sounds of a meal being prepared. No doubt Adam was there with Giguhl and Georgia. Part of me longed to join them and relax. But I needed to get dressed and go talk to Maisie again.

My lie of omission to Orpheus about the Maisie situation meant I was on my own in convincing her to try the incubation. I couldn't even recruit Rhea because she'd have no choice but to tell Orpheus what was really happening. I couldn't risk that. Not yet. Maisie's fragile grip on reality didn't need Orpheus's ham-fisted dictates.

While Adam and I had discussed the Alexis issue at length, we'd pretty much avoided discussing the Maisie situation. We both knew at some point there'd be a reckoning. Issues as big as the ones between the three of us didn't stay ignored for long. But I suppose first the more immediate issue of Maisie's prophecies needed to be dealt with. Once the peace treaty was signed and we could all breathe a sigh of relief, then we could face the ever-present specters that followed us home from the Big Easy.

Needing to wash away those nasty thoughts, I stepped under the shower's hot spray. I emerged from the bedroom half an hour later, clean and dressed. On my way to the kitchen, I still felt conflicted and restless, but I pasted a smile on my face.

Giguhl and Georgia were cooking at the stove while Adam sat at the table reading the paper. I don't know, I guess the domestic scene should have felt warm and comforting. But the overpowering scent of sizzling meat and the expectant glances of my lover and friends suddenly felt stifling.

"Hey, Sabina!" Georgia called. "I hope you're hungry. Giguhl and I are cooking enough to feed an army."

I grimaced. "Thanks, guys, but I'm not really hungry." I looked at Adam. "I'm going to run out for a bit."

He frowned. "Where are you going?"

His question had been innocent, a casual query, but it felt invasive. "I'm going to go see my sister," I snapped. I knew my tone was unfair, but I couldn't help it. I resented having to handle this on my own. Not to mention the fact I couldn't even talk to him about it.

He rose from his chair and approached me. Taking my hands in his, he forced me to look at him. "Is everything okay?"

I sucked down a breath, trying to remind myself that he hadn't done anything wrong. "Everything's fine." But it wasn't. Not really. "I just want this all over with so everything can go back to normal."

Whatever normal is.

"Hey, it's all right. We're all a little edgy. But in a few days, the treaty will be signed and we can finally relax." He smiled and kissed me on the lips.

"Hey, Red," Giguhl said. "Be sure to be back early tonight."

"Why?" I asked, wondering if he was planning a makeup dinner party.

Giguhl waved a spatula in the air like a magic wand. "We're going to a concert," he announced in a singsong voice.

"What? I thought Pussy Willow didn't have another show for a while."

"Not Pussy Willow," Giguhl said, grinning like a child with a secret on his tongue. "You'll never guess who Georgia and I ran into at Vein last night!"

I'd heard Georgia and Giguhl come in just before dawn, so I figured they'd spent their night partying it up at Vein. But since I couldn't figure out who Giguhl would be so excited about seeing, I didn't bother guessing. "Who?"

"Erron Zorn!"

My head jerked back in shock. Talk about the last person I expected him to say. "You're kidding! I thought he was on tour in Europe?"

Giguhl nodded eagerly. "He was, but I guess the band's wrapping up the tour here in New York tonight."

The band in question was Necrospank 5000. Erron and his drummer, Ziggy, had pitched in with our battles in the Big Easy. "I'm surprised they're playing New York. I figured they'd want to steer clear of the Hekate Council."

"Wait, why?" Georgia asked. "I thought they were mages."

"Erron and Ziggy are Recreants," Adam explained. When Georgia raised her eyebrows to show she'd never heard of a Recreant, he went on. "That basically means they defected from the Council and its laws."

What Adam didn't mention was that they were stripped of their ability to cast healing spells as punishment for their defection from the Council.

Giguhl waved an impatient claw. "Anyway, they're playing the Jupiter Ballroom tonight." He pulled something from the pocket of his sweatpants. "And Erron gave us tickets and backstage passes!"

"How many tickets did he give you?" I asked.

Giguhl grimaced. "Five—that's enough for all of us and Pussy Willow."

"Where is PW?" Adam said.

Giguhl rolled his eyes. "She was so excited about being invited to the show, she decided she needed a new wig and a mani-pedi. She said she'd meet us here in time to head to the show."

"Well, you guys can go ahead," I said. "I'm sitting this one out."

It's not that I didn't want to see Erron and Ziggy again, but I couldn't work up any excitement about the show itself.

Necrospank 5000 specialized in industrial shock rock. I'm generally not opposed to angry music, but Erron's songs turned rage into a fetish. And the idea of sharing a club with hundreds of mortals who got off on that shit had about as much appeal as having my fangs yanked out with pliers.

"Oh, c'mon, Red!" Giguhl said. "Don't be a party pooper."

I glanced at Adam. He shrugged. "It might be fun."

"Are you kidding?" Giguhl interrupted. "It's going to be a total freak show. I can't wait. Do you think he'll have a gimp onstage?"

My lips twitched. The first time we'd met Erron we'd stumbled on an orgy his band was hosting in a mansion in the Garden District that involved midget strippers, golden showers, and males in gimp suits with exposed undercarriages.

"I don't know, guys. I was kind of hoping to take it easy tonight."

"Oh, wait, I almost forgot to give you this." Giguhl pulled a crumpled piece of paper from his pocket. "If this doesn't change your mind, nothing will."

I took it from him. Adam read the note over my shoulder. *Sabina and Adam, please come. I have some interesting news about M.M.*

A shiver passed through me, like someone walked over my grave. "M.M." stood for Master Mahan. That's what the members of the Caste of Nod called Cain.

Giguhl was right. Erron's note did change my mind. After voicing my suspicions about Cain and being dismissed, I couldn't help but wonder if Erron was about to alleviate my fears—or confirm them.

I glanced over my shoulder at Adam. His eyebrows shot up to his hairline.

"Okay, I'm in," I said, my pulse thrumming. "I'll be back in a couple of hours."

A cheer rose up in the kitchen. I left them to make plans while I went in search of Maisie.

As it turned out, Maisie was harder to find than I expected. I checked her rooms and the library down the hall from her apartment with no luck. Finally, I decided to check the rooftop greenhouse.

Since Prytania Place was basically a mage city within the city, they kept a greenhouse for easy access to herbs and plants for use in home remedies and spells. I'd spent many hours in there over the last couple of months taking notes while Rhea lectured me on the proper uses for each species of plant.

I'd never admit this to Rhea because she'd make me listen to more lectures, but I kind of liked it in there. The warm, damp air intensified the sharp, green scent of leaves and the dark, rich perfume of fertile soil. But most of all, it was my sanctuary from the expectations of mage life and the city's constant noise.

But, once again, no Maisie. However, I did find Rhea wrist deep in a patch of mugwort near the back of the structure. She looked up when I rounded a display of ferns at the end of the aisle.

"Fancy meeting you here," she said, sitting back on her heels. With the back of her hand, she smoothed a loose strand of silver hair from her face.

"Hey, have you seen Maisie?"

She pursed her lips. "She came by and had lunch with me in my apartment earlier. Why?"

"I just wanted to check on her, but she wasn't in her rooms or the library."

"Ah, yes, I think she's with Orpheus. She told me she

wanted to sit down with him and go over the plans for the Imbolc festival."

My eyebrows rose. "Really? That's new."

Rhea brushed her hands together and stood. "I know. You should have seen her this afternoon. She was more relaxed than I've seen her in weeks. I don't know what you said to her during your talk, but it must have worked." Her words were carefully casual, leading. She wanted to know what we'd spoken of, but I wasn't ready to tell her the truth.

"Not sure I can take the credit. We mostly chatted about the weather and Giguhl's latest exploits," I lied. "Nothing of substance, really."

She motioned toward the door of the greenhouse. "Yes, well, she's spent so much time alone lately, I'm sure she appreciated that you showed an interest in spending time with her."

We walked together through the aisles of frilly green ferns and rosehips and clusters of yellow and red witch hazel blooms. Once we were back in the chilly night air, we headed toward the pool of golden light spilling from the French doors that led into Rhea's workroom.

As we walked, I couldn't help feeling suspicious of her report about Maisie. When I'd last seen my twin, she hadn't shown any signs of progress. If anything, the lack of sleep seemed to make her regress. But I also worried that expressing my confusion over the change might cause Rhea to ask me questions I wasn't ready to answer. I'd promised Maisie I'd keep her secrets. And for now I intended on keeping that promise. "I'm glad Maze seemed to be doing better. Did she mention anything about the dream incubation?" I asked as we entered the workroom.

"No, actually. I tried to broach the subject, but she kept diverting the conversation." As Rhea spoke, she washed her hands in a copper basin set in one of the long soapstone counters bordering the room. "So, as promising as the change was, I'm afraid we still have some work ahead of us to convince her to try it."

I should have known better than to hope it'd be that easy. "I'll try again tomorrow night."

I sighed and dropped onto one of the wooden stools Rhea stored under the lip of the counters. With my free hand, I picked up a sprig of parsley. Several weeks earlier, Rhea and I had spent an entire evening discussing its medicinal properties. In addition to protecting food from contamination and promoting fertility and freshening the breath, it was also an herb of protection. I rubbed it between my fingers, releasing its fresh, green scent.

Rhea patted my arm. "Keep the faith, Sabina. The clock is ticking, but we're not out of time or options yet."

Not sure what to say to that, I just nodded. Optimism wasn't exactly one of my strengths.

"But enough of that," Rhea said. "I've got some news on your botched interspatial travel attempt."

I perked up. "Oh?"

"I was out at the Crossroads yesterday and tracked down Ameritat's journals." She moved toward a red chinoiserie armoire in the corner. Under her breath, she whispered some words and a magical tingle spread through the room. Once her wards dissolved, she used a key around her neck to unlock the latch and open the doors. Inside sat several leather-bound volumes, which I assumed were her special spell books. The ones she didn't want to leave just lying around. From the bottom shelf, she removed a large book—about the size of an unabridged dictionary.

She lugged it over to the worktable and set it down gently. "This is one of her volumes. It covers the years she spent training your father."

I scooted my chair closer for a better look. Rhea opened the massive book, revealing page after page of neat script. "Wow, how many other books are there?"

"Hundreds," Rhea said. When my mouth fell open in shock, she explained. "Ameritat lived to be almost two thousand years old. Her life was...eventful."

While I digested that, she found the page she was looking for. "Ah, here it is. As I suspected, your father also had trouble at first with interspatial travel." She pointed to a section of text. "See here? The description of the place he went matches the one you gave."

I scanned Ameritat's words. Rhea wasn't kidding. The details of the place Tristan had ended up in were almost identical to what I had seen. "He didn't say anything about howling, but otherwise, yeah, it sounds like the same place. Did they ever figure out what it was?"

Rhea nodded and flipped forward in the book. "The Liminal."

I frowned. "What's that?"

"It's the borderlands between our world and Irkalla." She shifted excitedly in her seat and thumbed through more pages. "Ah, here it is. Listen."

She leaned over the book and read directly from it. "'Tristan continued his exploration of the Liminal today. When he returned, he described finding the edge of the borderlands—a shimmering veil of magic. He attempted to pass through it but reported the contact disoriented him. He wandered around the in-between for what he said felt like hours before he regained his memory and returned to my workshop. It is my hope that continuing with his Chthonic training will increase his powers until he is able to access Irkalla through the Liminal.'"

Rhea looked up then. "Amazing!" She looked so

excited, like she'd discovered a new land. But I found it hard to share her enthusiasm.

"Did he ever figure out how to do it?"

She frowned. "No."

"Why not?"

She turned to the last page of the book. "This ends just before your father's disappearance. But before that, Ameritat said she was going to make him stop trying because it was getting too dangerous."

"Dangerous how?"

"The Liminal isn't just the borderlands between our world and Irkalla. It's also the place our subconscious connects to during our dreams. Tristan reported seeing confusing images and getting lost in serpentine labyrinths. She was afraid if he kept trying, he'd eventually get too lost to find his way back."

"Wait," I said. "That doesn't make sense. If this Liminal is where we go when we dream, how do we manage not to get lost there?"

"Ameritat's theory was that our bodies act as a tether to our subconscious. So dreaming is kind of like an out-of-body experience. Our spirits go to the Liminal and our bodies anchor us to the mundane world. But Tristan, and now you, accessed the Liminal in your physical bodies. That means there's nothing here to pull you back out. The only way to exit is through your will and magic. So if you get confused or lost, you could conceivably become stuck there."

I was silent for a few moments while that sunk in. If what she said was true, I was damned lucky I'd made it back the other night. "You said there were hundreds of journals. Did you go through the rest to see if she wrote more about the Liminal after he disappeared?"

Rhea frowned and shook her head. Her eyes were shadowed with old memories. "Ameritat was so devastated by his disappearance that she refused to record those events in her journals. Those were very dark days for all of us. And once she took custody of Maisie after your mother's death, Ameritat threw herself into raising your twin, as if Maisie could somehow fill the Tristan-sized hole in her life. All her journals after that are about raising Maisie and her work with the Council."

My stomach twisted. I didn't like to think about the events of more than fifty years earlier that led to my birth. "Well, at least we know what that place was."

Rhea frowned at me. "Sabina, why aren't you more excited?"

"Why should I be? You said it yourself: The place is too dangerous."

"There are risks, sure, but I don't think we shouldn't continue experimenting. You could be the first mage to access Irkalla without dying first."

"Rhea, just because I could do something doesn't mean I should."

"Don't be silly, of course you should try!"

"Why?"

"Maybe the problems Tristan had won't affect you, since you're the Chosen."

I slammed my hand down on the table. "Gods, not that again."

Rhea looked confused and hurt by my tone. "Why do you continue to deny it?"

"Yes, sure. The Chosen who can't get the leaders of the races to listen to reason. The Chosen who can't even control her own minion half the time. The Chosen who can't even get a simple interspatial travel spell right."

"Yes, you," Rhea said. "The Chosen who called on the powers of Hekate and Lilith to stop a war. The Chosen who united all the dark races in peace. *You.* Like it or not, Sabina, you *are* the Chosen."

"Look, all that might be true, but I don't know how you think it's related to this Liminal business."

"Well, according to Maisie's prophecy, the Chosen is actually the New Lilith."

"So?"

"So think about it: It's always bothered me why you would be the Chosen and not Maisie. I mean, you had the same parents, were born at the same time. I think your Chthonic powers have to be the key. The same Chthonic powers that allow you to access the Liminal. And the Liminal could be your doorway to Irkalla...and Lilith."

I crossed my arms and gave her a dubious frown.

"Your magic is special, Sabina. It gives you rare abilities. That has to be tied to the prophecy." She shrugged. "I'm just saying that nothing is a coincidence. Maybe accessing Irkalla through the Liminal is part of the prophecy."

I sighed and stood, choosing my words carefully. "No offense, Rhea, but I don't give a damn. I'm not about to start screwing around with dark magic and instigating contact with the underworld just for shits and giggles—or worse, because some ancient arcane prophecy can be twisted to fit any situation."

She held my gaze for a moment. I could see the gears moving behind her eyes, weighing the pros and cons of fighting me on this. I couldn't blame her for her excitement and curiosity, but I wasn't about to be a magical guinea pig. Not when there was a risk of getting trapped in the Liminal with that howling beast for all eternity.

Finally, her shoulders slumped as she surrendered hope

that I'd relent. "I can respect your hesitation. But I think you're making a mistake. Far better to pursue your destiny than to have it find you when you least expect it."

I crossed my arms. "The only thing I'm interested in pursuing right now is dinner."

She frowned at my lame attempt at humor. "Just think about it, okay?"

I'd already thought about it, but I didn't have the heart to put my foot down. Rhea had done so much for me, and she'd proven a wise mentor and dependable friend. "I will."

I said my good-byes—promising I'd let her know how my conversation with Maisie the next night went—and then promptly reneged on my promise about considering the Liminal experiments by pushing the entire issue from my mind.

By the time I made it back to the apartment, I'd totally forgotten about the concert. So when I walked in to find everyone waiting for me I paused.

"What's up?" I asked slowly, tensed for bad news.

Giguhl crossed his arms. "You're late. Again."

I closed my eyes and silently cursed to myself. "Right. The concert. Sorry, guys."

"Don't let him give you shit." Adam came forward and gave me a hug. "We're still waiting for Pussy Willow anyway."

As if his comment summoned her, the door to the apartment swept open and a vision in a black wig, leather pants, and a purple latex bustier sashayed in. "What's up, bitches?"

"Wow, PW," Adam said. "That's quite an outfit."

She blew a kiss at the mancy. "Thank you, darling!" She turned in an elaborate circle. "Are my pants too tight? I had to do my industrial strength tuck to fit in these babies." She patted her boyish hips with pride and shot Adam an expectant look.

Adam shot me a wild-eyed plea for help. "That depends," I said. "Did you intend for them to be tight enough for everyone to see your pulse?"

"Of course!" She threw back her head and emitted a throaty laugh. When she stopped laughing, she gave me a judgmental once-over. "Sabina, darling, can we talk about your ensemble?"

I frowned and looked down at the jeans and black T-shirt I'd thrown on earlier. "What about it?"

"You're not seriously wearing that to the concert."

"Um, yes, I am." Granted it wasn't the most glamorous outfit I owned, but who did I need to impress? Besides, I wasn't about to take fashion advice from a lady-man whose fashion motto was "the more rhinestones the better."

"Oh, honey. No, no, no." She looked at me like I was a misguided child. "Don't you want to look hot for your man?"

"Hey, don't pull me into this," Adam said. "She always looks hot to me."

I patted him on the arm. "Good answer." I shot PW a superior look, but she executed an exaggerated eye roll. I had to bite my tongue to keep from calling her out for her rudeness. Ever since she'd decided to be a full-time chick, her sense of humor had gone from sassy to bitchy. And not fun bitchy, either. All her jokes were as cutting as barbed wire and her dependence on passive aggression grated on my last nerve. So, yes, I bit my tongue. But the day was coming when Miss Thang was going to go too far.

"Can we go now?" Giguhl said into the tense silence following my exchange with the faery.

"Sure," I said. "Just as soon as you change into cat form."

A puff of green smoke erupted where he'd been standing. When it cleared, his little hairless body merged from the puddle of black sweatpants. "Bael's balls, Red! Give me some warning next time."

"Quit your bitching." I rolled my eyes. "You know you can't show up as a demon. There will be hundreds of mortals at the concert. Now go find your sweater and we'll head out."

He hissed in response and went to weave his way through Pussy Willow's legs. The fae bent down to pick up the bitchy cat. She petted his head with her recently manicured silver-tipped fingers. "Don't worry, Gigi. I have the perfect outfit for you. Some people might prefer to look frumpy"—she shot me a pointed look—"but you, at least, will show up in style."

The audience clogged the dance floor like arterial plaque. Humans, mostly. Kids dressed in black with multiple piercings and enough angst to power the Eastern Seaboard.

"Um," Giguhl hissed into my ear. "What the fuck are they doing?"

I turned my head to where he sat on my shoulder and had to squint. The club was dark, but the rhinestone skull on his knit cap reflected the stage's lights and nearly blinded me. I don't know where Pussy Willow managed to find Ed Hardy cat clothes, but she'd wasted her money. Instead of looking tough, he looked like a tiny, hairless douche bag.

In response to his question, I shrugged and watched the scene below with a grimace. For some reason, the fans of Necrospank 5000 enjoyed nothing more than taking a saliva shower with five hundred of their closest friends. Not that I was one to judge, given I'd consumed blood from hobos and rapists. But seriously, what kind of freak enjoys having strangers spit on them?

Adam stood next to me, his arm casually draped around my waist. "Just be glad Erron sent us balcony tickets."

"You've got to admit, there's something about that Erron Zorn," Pussy Willow purred. "I still can't believe y'all didn't introduce me to him in New Orleans."

"Yeah, sorry about that," I said. "What with the battle for our lives and all, there just wasn't time for proper introductions."

"They're certainly loud," Georgia yelled. Her fingers were stuck in her ears and she cringed to buffer herself from the pounding bass line. She'd been quiet on the way over and hadn't said much since we'd arrived. I wondered if part of her mood had to do with the fact she hadn't heard from Mac. I hoped that seeing the werewolf the next night at the first Roller Derby practice might improve her mood.

Erron stood onstage with his head thrown back and his arms spread wide to receive the spit shower. He wore tight leather pants and little else, except for a self-inflicted chest wound he'd scored into his skin with a razor. The song he sang was a ballad of sorts, and by that I mean it had a slow tempo. The lyrics weren't much different from all the others—lots of macabre symbolism accented with creative variations on the word "fuck."

I turned to Adam. "I think this is the last number. Let's head down."

On my shoulder, Giguhl growled. "Dammit! Already? We only got to see three songs!"

By the time we got Giguhl dressed in his outfit and found a cab to the club, we'd ended up arriving halfway through the concert. In my opinion, this was far from a tragedy. But I suspected Giguhl would have plenty to be excited about backstage if the after-party was anything like the other Necrospank shindig we'd witnessed.

Adam dragged his eyes from the flashing lights that

signaled the finale and blinked. "Maybe we should give Erron some time to grab a shower first."

"C'mon," I said. "It's going to get crowded if we wait too long. And I have no intention of acting like some groupie begging for a moment of his time."

Fifteen minutes later, we all stepped out of the elevator and directly into gridlock. I shot Adam an I-told-you-so glare. He grimaced and adjusted Giguhl on his shoulder.

"Lead on," he said. "But don't hurt anyone."

I rolled my eyes, but he was right to remind me. My first instinct was to bulldoze through them. Instead, I played fair and tried to be patient as my polite requests to scoot by were ignored. After five minutes, we'd made it only ten feet from the elevator.

Giguhl perked up on Adam's shoulder. "If you're not going to start punching them, at least let me change forms. That'll get 'em all moving."

"Judging from the looks of Erron's fan base, they wouldn't be shocked by a naked demon in their midst." As I said this, a chick with connect-the-dot piercings on her face turned to hiss at me. She'd had her tongue surgically split down the center and proceeded to waggle the forked thing at me.

"Bitch, please," Giguhl said. "I'll show you something forked."

The chick squinted at me. Her dilated pupils were the size of pennies. "Did your cat just talk?"

"Of course not." I laughed, the sound false and awkward to my own ears. "You might want to back off on the Special K, sweetie."

She was unimpressed. "Please. Cat tranqs are so 2007."

Unable to resist, I asked, "So what's the big thing now?"

She squinted at me. "Are you a narc or something?"

"Believe me when I say I am as far from a cop as you can get."

Her pupils were two black holes set into red-veined nebulas. "The newest thing is called Dry Humps."

"What's in it?"

Pin Cushion moved in closer. Her breath smelled of old cigarettes and daddy issues. "It's combination of Viagra, Ecstasy, and Benadryl. Plus a few other goodies."

"Jesus!" I looked over my shoulder at Adam. Judging from the way his mouth hung down to his clavicles, I figured he'd overheard. "Seriously?"

"It's invigorating, really," she said. "Especially once the stool softener hits. You should try it."

Adam ignored her and stood on his tiptoes, seeing the long corridor ahead and judging our chances of making it through the throng in anything resembling a reasonable amount of time. Behind him, Pussy Willow and Georgia were too busy gawking at the freaks to be much help. "Okay, screw civility. Barge through there, Red."

I smiled and kissed his cheek. "Yes, sir."

Thirty seconds, four bruised ribs, two "accidentally" bloodied noses, and bucket loads of cursing later, we stood in front of two burly human security guys. They wore earpieces and sidearms, but they had rent-a-cop written all over them.

If they noticed the carnage we'd left in our wake, they didn't react. Either they were used to Erron's fans getting rough with each other, which frankly was a major possibility, or they didn't care—the more likely option. "Passes?" the one on the right said in a bored tone.

I squinted at him, looking for some sign of life behind

his dark glasses. I flicked my wrist up to show the backstage passes Erron had sent over that afternoon.

The left guard gave the passes a cursory glance. Then he straightened and looked at Giguhl. "No pets allowed."

"Who, him?" I nodded toward the hairless cat on Adam's shoulder. "He's not a pet."

Leftie lowered his shades a fraction. "Do you really expect me to believe that hideous cat is a service animal?"

The cat in question tensed, ready to deliver a barbed retort, no doubt. Adam pulled Giguhl off his shoulder and squeezed him tight against his chest, just in case. My lip twitched. "As a matter of fact, he is a service animal, of sorts." It wasn't exactly a lie. As my minion, Giguhl performed all sorts of services. Granted, his specialty was lip service, but still.

The guards didn't look like they were buying it, so I soldiered on before they could refuse us entrance. "Listen, ask Erron. Tell him Giguhl the cat is out here. He'll let us in."

The right guy looked unconvinced. But since we had passes and seemed not the least bit nervous that he'd call my bluff, he spoke into the mouthpiece. "Ask Erron if he knows a cat named Giguhl." Pause. "Yes, a fucking cat. Just do it."

Adam crossed his arms and looked about ready to just flash us directly into the room. That was the problem with trying to fit into the mortal world. Having to ignore that we had the ability to circumvent their rules and little inconveniences at will.

The guard put his hand to his ear. He looked at me with a frown. "Is your name Sabina Kane?"

I paused, not liking his tone. "Maybe." It's not that any of us had reason to feel threatened by the dude. A couple of humans versus a mage, a vampire, a demon cat, a transsexual faery, and a former assassin with death magic skills? Please. No contest. But I'd had enough experience with people gunning for me that I knew better than to not be on guard.

He murmured something into the mouthpiece. "Hold on. Someone's coming to get you."

A few moments later, the door opened behind him and a familiar face peeked out. It was Ziggy, Necrospank 5000's drummer. Like Erron, he was a Recreant, or shunned, mage. Unlike Erron, he didn't go for the industrial aesthetic in his choice of hair or clothing. Instead, Ziggy sported his usual rockabilly look—black T-shirt with a pack of cigs rolled up in one sleeve, dark jeans with a silver chain at his hip, and ankle cuffs rolled up over red Converse. Both arms were tattooed up with pinups, swallows, and four-leaf clovers. A gigantic pompadour towered over his face like the prow of an ocean liner. He was also angry, judging from the flurry of signs jumping off his fingers.

"What?" the guard yelled.

"Dude, he's deaf," I said. "Screaming isn't going to help." I waved at Ziggy to get his attention. Shrugged to let him know we weren't following. He sighed and shot us an annoyed look. Finally, with exaggerated movements he pointed to Adam, Giguhl, PW, Georgia, and me and waved us toward the door. From behind the steel panel, the sounds of breaking furniture and more cursing than a group of horny sailors on shore leave echoed down the hallway.

"Let's go." With that, I pushed past the guards, high-fived Ziggy on my way by, and stormed straight into the eye of a Necrospank 5000 hurricane. We'd entered a dressing room, or at least it used to be one. The band members had broken most of the furniture. The things that hadn't been broken were covered in various liquor, foodstuffs, and body fluids. In the corner, a groupie gave the bassist oral pleasure. Another chick lay on her stomach on the coffee table, where the keyboardist snorted white lines off her ass.

I suppose they believed they were being shocking and edgy. But the whole thing was so stereotypical that it struck me as a little desperate and pedestrian. I looked over my shoulder at Ziggy. He shrugged and made a wanking gesture with his hand. With his free hand, he pointed to a doorway to the right. Adam nodded and made toward the door, looking as unimpressed as I felt. But Giguhl and the others were rubbernecking like crazy.

"But—" The demon strained to get a better view. "But—"

I looked at the three sets of eager gazes watching the party. Since Erron's information about Cain really affected only Adam and me, I decided it was probably best to leave the others there. "Okay, you three stay here and enjoy the party. Adam and I will be back in a few." I lifted the cat from my shoulder and handed him over to PW. "Behave."

The cat blinked his eyes at me. "Sabina, you wound me."

"Whatever. Just don't hump anyone. You don't know where these humans have been."

We left them and followed Ziggy into a dark hallway that led to another dressing room. This one was larger than the other. Instead of the moldy Berber and office furniture of the other room, this one had plush shag carpeting and velvet divans and a tufted ottoman. Clearly, we'd entered the sanctuary reserved for the real star.

But the star was nowhere in sight. Instead, the only inhabitant was a tiny woman dressed in a red vinyl mini-skirt, miniature fishnets, and a black-sequined halter top. I remembered her from New Orleans, but I'd never caught her name. However, I did remember she was Erron's full-time hairdresser as well as a part-time gimp equestrian. Long story.

If she noticed our arrival, she didn't show it. Instead, she busied herself painting her nails. Ziggy whistled to get her attention. She looked up then. "Hey, Zig."

He nodded toward us expectantly. Her eye roll did little for my ego. "Oh," she said in a bored tone. "It's you."

Before any of us could respond, Erron emerged from a side door. He wore the same leather pants he'd had onstage. But he'd thrown a black kimono over his torso, unbelted to show off his chest wound, I presumed.

When he saw us he stopped. "I wasn't sure you'd come."

"How could I resist after I read your note?" I said. "Great show, by the way."

He ran a hand through his hair. "Thanks." He turned toward Ziggy, speaking as he signed. "Remind me to tell MC Macabre that he's coming in too early on 'Fuck the Clowns.'"

Ziggy flashed a thumbs-up and signed something back I couldn't decipher. Erron merely nodded and collapsed with a groan onto the couch.

After that, Erron seemed to dismiss our presence altogether. The table in front of the couch was a mosaic of multi-colored pills, snack foods, and drug paraphernalia. Erron grabbed a handful of M&Ms—or at least I hoped that's what they were—and threw them into his mouth.

"Erron," Adam said, speaking with exaggerated patience. "Your note said you had new information for us?"

The singer swallowed a mouthful of liquor. "Oh, right, sorry. I'm always a little spaced out after a show. I just need a minute to chill, if you don't mind."

I glanced at the dressing table where the little person continued to paint her nails. If we were about to discuss dark-races business, it probably wasn't a good idea to do it in front of a mortal. "Um, maybe you should ask the midget to leave first."

Erron looked over at her. "Who? Goldie? She knows everything."

I choked. "Seriously? Your name's Goldie?" The first time I'd seen her, Erron's little friend had been peeing on his bassist during an orgy, so the name seemed too good to be true.

Goldie jumped down from the counter where she'd been perched. "That's right, bitch. Goldie Schwartz. And I'm not a fucking midget. I prefer the term 'fun sized.'"

I squinted at her for a moment, wondering if she was fucking with me. But she held my stare with the menace of a woman three times her size. "No offense intended," I muttered.

She ignored me and sidled up to Erron. Rubbed his arm with her nubby fingers. "You need anything, baby?"

He took her hand and kissed the knuckles. "No, I'm good. Why don't you go join the others?" After his initial stance that she was welcome to stay, she seemed shocked by his dismissal. But instead of challenging him on it, she strutted in her miniature stilettos toward Ziggy.

"Come on, doll," Goldie signed as she sashayed toward him. "Let's go get coked out of our minds and show those amateurs a real party."

Ziggy's eyebrows shot up to his pompadour. He nodded enthusiastically and saluted us as he followed her out the door. Once they were gone, the dressing room fell silent except for the muted beat of music from the party.

Adam and I exchanged a tense look. Erron had said he needed a few minutes, but I wasn't really in the mood to cater to his rock star ego. I cleared my throat. "Listen, if this isn't a good time—"

Erron set his bottle of Beam on the table and sighed. "No, it's fine. I'm just so fucking glad this tour's finally over. I was just savoring the silence. But I appreciate you guys coming." He scrubbed a hand across the bandage on his chest, as if the wound still hurt him.

If he'd been an Adherant mage, one who followed the dictates of the Hekate Council, he'd have been able to heal that wound no problem. But that cut and the scars left over from other such stunts bore testament to his Recreant status. The minute he'd broken from the Council, they'd stripped him of his ability to heal himself. Judging from the multitude of scars crisscrossing his chest, I had to wonder if Erron's little cutting hobby was really a "fuck you" to the Council. Sad, really, considering the Council paid no attention to his activities as far as I could tell.

"Do you guys remember what I told you about when I hunted down Cain?" Erron said suddenly.

"Yeah," Adam said, dropping onto the couch across from Erron. "You said you hunted him down after he killed your band, but when you figured out you couldn't kill him, you ran away."

"Right. I also told you that after six months of hell I finally realized he wasn't coming for me." He took another swig of bourbon. "The news is, I finally found out why."

"Well?" I demanded.

"For the last few months I've been on tour in Europe. While I was there, I tracked down that group I told you about."

"Yeah, I remember you mentioning them in New Orleans. The ones who helped you find Cain to begin with," Adam said. "Who are they exactly?"

"They're a small band made up mostly of mages and vampires. They're led by a male who calls himself Abel.

Not the original guy from the mortal Bible, obviously. I never met him when I worked with the group in the past because he's super secretive. But he's a mage and he's ... weird."

My eyebrows rose at the irony of hearing the leader of a shock-rock band with a penchant for midget strippers call anyone weird.

"He wears these robes like a monk and refuses to let anyone see his face. Still, his people helped me in the past, so I know he's solid."

"Any idea who he really is?" Adam asked.

Erron shook his head. "He may be weird but he's dead serious about stopping Cain. Anyway, when I was in Rome, I got in touch with one of his associates. Set up a meeting."

"Why?" Adam asked.

Erron leaned forward. Now that we'd gotten him talking, he'd dropped the weary rock star routine. Even his eyes had cleared, like he'd sobered up. "Because after my involvement in your mission in New Orleans, I wanted to be sure Cain wasn't going to start gunning for me again. Plus, I might be a Recreant, but I still give a shit about whether someone's planning on wiping all mages from the earth."

"Fair enough," Adam said. "What did this Abel tell you?"

Erron rubbed his hands on his legs, as if settling in for a long story. "Turns out he and his group finally made their move on Cain right after my encounter with him. This would be about ten years ago. There was some big showdown and they managed to bind Cain magically. He's been on ice in a secret location ever since."

Adam frowned. "Why didn't they just kill him?"

"Cain can't be killed," Erron said. "When God marked him after killing his brother, he decreed that anyone who killed Cain would reap punishment sevenfold. So Abel's only choice was to use a spell to put the asshole in a state of suspended animation, kind of like a permanent coma without the need for respirators."

"Wait," I said. "That doesn't make any sense. Lavinia's goons almost managed to summon Cain to that cemetery in New Orleans. If Abel's spell was so great, how did the Caste manage that?"

"Naturally, I asked Abel the same question. He said I must be mistaken. One of his people is with the body at all times and no one reported anything out of the ordinary. He also claims only his blood can break the spell."

"I've never met this Abel guy, but he sounds like an idiot." I huffed out a breath. "I saw Cain begin to materialize with my own eyes. Plus, he visited my dreams more than once."

"If Maisie had been dreaming about Cain, then we'd have a reason to worry," Adam said. "But yours are just probably your subconscious's way of dealing with everything that happened."

"I can't say whether that's true or not, but Abel seemed convinced there was no reason to worry." Erron shrugged. "Maybe the summoning was an illusion or a trick to make you think they had Cain on their side. Either way, Abel said he'd step up his wards around the body as a precaution."

"Did you see the body?" Adam asked.

"Not in person. Abel isn't messing around. He doesn't let anyone near Cain except for his own people. But he did show me a video feed from the surveillance cameras. The body I saw was Cain's. I'm sure of it."

I snorted. "No offense, Erron, but there are so many holes in that story that I'm actually less convinced we're safe."

"I don't know what to tell you. But if Abel is lying and

Cain actually is capable of escaping, why hasn't he come after you? Or me, for that matter?" He shook his head and took another swig.

"But if Cain has been imprisoned all these years, why did Lavinia claim she was working for him?" I asked.

"Just spit balling here," Adam said, "but maybe it was because your grandmother was a vindictive, scheming bitch?"

"True enough, but she also had the Caste working for her," I said. "Surely that suggests Cain's involvement."

"Or she convinced the Caste that Cain was communicating with her to get them to cooperate," Adam said, almost to himself.

I jerked my head to stare at him. "Look, I want to believe Cain isn't an issue anymore, too. But this is all a little too convenient, don't you think?"

"I know it's hard to believe, but I trust Abel," Erron said. "That guy's odd, sure, but I've never met anyone with more single-minded dedication. He eats, breathes, and sleeps keeping Cain imprisoned."

I leaned forward. "That's bugging me, too."

Adam looked at me. "What?"

"Why is Abel so obsessed with Cain?"

We both looked at Erron for the answer. "I don't know, but if I had to guess I'd say Cain probably caused some trouble in Abel's life along the way. Isn't that how all these stories start? Bad guy kills a man's lover or family and that man turns into a vigilante?"

I sucked a deep breath in through my nose and leaned back. Releasing it slowly, I said, "I wish I could believe that was all true. But something tells me we haven't seen the last of Cain."

"Maybe not. But until there's some reason to believe

otherwise, why not relax a little?" Erron leaned back, cradling the Jim Beam like a security blanket. "Lavinia's dead and the treaty is about to be signed. Even if Cain could somehow manage to escape Abel's bonds without being noticed, he'll still have a hell of a time trying to start a war now."

I wished I could share Erron's optimism. But my hands were clammy and a tickle at the base of my skull told me that letting my guard down would be a colossal mistake. I turned toward Adam, who looked pensive rather than skeptical. "What's your gut saying?"

He sighed and scrubbed a hand over his face. "That until Cain makes another move—if he makes one—there isn't much we can do." He leaned forward with his elbows on his knees. "All the leaders know what happened in New Orleans and are vigilantly working toward peace. They already rooted out any remaining Caste members they could find," he said. "They even killed several human members of the Brotherhood of the Eastern Mystery for their involvement with the Caste in New Orleans. Even if Cain was really a threat, he'd have a tough time trying to start a war now. I vote we move on until there's a concrete reason to worry."

It all sounded so reasonable, but I couldn't let down my guard that easily. "Does Abel have any plans beyond keeping Cain bound? I mean, they can't keep him like that forever."

Erron shrugged. "I honestly don't know. But he's a mage and mages live for a long time." He rubbed his wound absently. "Most of them do, anyway."

"I'd feel a lot better if I could talk to this Abel myself."

Erron smiled tightly. "Sabina, I understand your concerns, but I have as much—if not more—reason to want Cain out of the picture. He killed my old band and, before that, he almost killed Ziggy and left him permanently deaf. I've looked into Cain's face and seen the murder in his cold green eyes. If I had any reason to believe that sadistic bastard could get to me or anyone I gave a shit about, I'd tell you."

I sighed and leaned back into the cushions. For all his strange fetishes and his angry music, Erron was a good guy. I knew I could trust him. He'd proven himself more than once in New Orleans. But my stomach clenched anyway. Why was letting go so tough?

"If you hear anything new from Abel you let me know ASAP."

"Of course," he said. "If it's any consolation I understand how hard it is to relax. When you've spent so long waiting for an attack, it's hard to believe you're finally safe."

I swallowed the knot of emotion in my throat. His words conveyed what I was feeling exactly. "I guess I do need some practice with optimism."

"It just so happens I know the perfect way to start doing just that," Erron said. "How about we all go join the party?"

I grimaced. "No offense, but I've seen what you call a party. Not exactly my scene."

"Don't listen to her," Giguhl said from the doorway. "Give her five minutes in there and she'll be snorting coke off a whore's ass, too."

We all turned to see the demon cat cradled in the midget's arms. "Come on, you guys," he said, nestling into Goldie's tiny bosom. "MC Macabre is about to show everyone how he can blow himself."

Adam squinted at the demon. "Are you drunk?"

The cat hiccupped. "Don't be ridiskulous." He giggled.

"Where are Georgia and Pussy Willow?" I asked.

"The lady boy's trading fashion secrets with the groupies," Goldie said. "And the vampire has cornered Ziggy to tell him all about her problems with the werewolf. She's so drunk she doesn't realize he's deaf."

I frowned. "Georgia drunk?"

"Relax." Giguhl waved a paw. "She deserves to let loose a little."

"We'll round them up on our way out," I said.

I took Giguhl from Goldie. Loud music and laughter filtered into the room from down the hall. The party must have been picking up steam. Giguhl squirmed in my arms and rose to put his paws on my shoulder so he could look me in the eyes. "I wanna stay." His breath reeked of whisky fumes.

"How will you get home?" I didn't want Giguhl getting trapped in the middle of a groupie orgy in cat form. Not that he'd mind. But he also couldn't exactly ride the subway home. And from the sound of things, Pussy Willow and Georgia weren't in any state to navigate the city.

Erron shrugged and said, "I can have a car take them home later. It's no problem."

I shrugged. "Fine by me." I didn't argue for two reasons. One, he might be my minion, but I wasn't Giguhl's mother, thank the gods. And two, I wouldn't mind an evening without all our guests underfoot. Adam and I could definitely use some time to ourselves. I glanced at the mancy and raised a brow. A slow, promising smile spread across his lips. He was thinking the same thing.

Adam stood and went to shake Erron's hand. "Will you be in town long?"

"Leaving tomorrow morning. I'm gonna hit New Orleans for some R&R."

I approached Erron and gave him a big hug. "Thanks for everything. I know you didn't want to be involved in any of this."

He gave me a quick squeeze. "My pleasure. Just promise me you'll try to relax. You deserve to let loose, too."

I pulled back and smiled. From the corner of my eye, I saw Adam waiting impatiently to get me home. Alone. "You know what?" I winked at Erron. "You might be right."

I surrendered Giguhl to the ground and went to join the mancy. Just before the magic rose and we poofed out of there, I shot a look at Giguhl, a silent reminder to behave himself. Two seconds later, Adam and I were back in the apartment and all thoughts of Cain, the Recreant, and our drunk friends disappeared.

18

*N*ot wanting to waste any time, the mancy flashed us back to our bedroom, instead of the living areas. The apartment's silence enveloped us. The windows overlooking Central Park cast gray shadows across the wooden floors and bed.

Adam and I stared at each other, not quite trusting that we were alone. After weeks, maybe months, of never having the place to ourselves, the rare privacy felt decadent.

"Finally," Adam breathed, "I have you all to myself."

I smiled an impish smile. "Whatever will you do with me?"

Instead of telling me, he showed me. With his mouth on mine, with his hands. Instead of the feverish quickies we'd gotten used to sneaking in around Giguhl's schedule, we took it slow, savoring the rare luxury of time.

As he kissed me, he urged me back toward the bed. His hands were busy removing my shirt, unbuttoning my jeans. Mine were busy exploring the hard planes of his chest, teasing the ridges of his stomach under his shirt.

The backs of my knees bumped the mattress. I lowered myself slowly, not wanting to break the connection. He followed, his tongue exploring mine.

I ran a teasing finger along his waistband, dipping the tip lower to brush over his Hekate's Wheel birthmark. I unbuttoned the top snap of his jeans and placed my lips there, savoring the way his muscles jumped under my mouth.

Adam's fingers were busy, too. Soon, my bra joined the tank top on the floor and he lowered his head to lavish my breasts with his own form of worship. He grabbed my hands, held them over my head in playful bondage. But soon, the pull of his hot mouth against my sensitive skin had me writhing, yearning to touch him, too.

He pulled away only to allow me to lift his shirt over his head. As he returned for more, I ran my hands over his broad shoulders, enjoying the way his muscles danced. I wanted to push him over and climb atop him. To let my hands explore his skin while I watched his eyes glaze over with passion. But I knew better than to try to take control. Ever since New Orleans, he'd been skittish about the slightest bit of sexual dominance from me. It would be too easy to indulge my bloodlust if I had him pinned to the mattress.

Instead, I took his face and pulled him up for another kiss. While our tongues tangled, his fingers slid down my stomach, dipping into my navel, before continuing south. He caressed me gently at first, then faster, firmer. I pushed my hips toward him, needing more than his finger inside me. He recognized the signal and pulled back so I could help him out of his jeans. His sex sprang forward, eager for my touch. I wrapped my hand around the heat and guided it home.

The first thrust forced groans from both our throats. He bent over me, entering me with both his tongue and his sex. The dual sensations sparked a new need in me. One I knew better than to indulge. I pulled my mouth from his and bit my lip. He didn't seem to notice the withdrawal. Instead, he pushed up on his arms and thrust deeper, harder. Each movement brought me closer to the edge of both pleasure and pain. The pleasure of release. The pain of self-denial.

The need to taste his blood grew until my head rocked restlessly on the mattress. My fangs cut deep into my bottom lip. The taste of my own blood bloomed on my tongue. But it wasn't enough. The hunger would never be satisfied with anything less than Adam's sweet blood.

But the refusal to indulge my hunger heightened my other senses. The feel of pressure building in my core. The smell of Adam's sandalwood and hot male scent. The sight of Adam's face flushed and determined to bring us both to release. The sound of his panting breaths mingled with my moans.

Adam lowered himself to my chest, his hands wrapping my legs around his hips. I cradled him there, squeezing with my thighs and meeting his thrusts with my hips. He didn't try to kiss me. He knew the temptation to feed would be too strong to deny. Instead, he buried his lips on my throat, sucking and licking the sweat from my fevered skin. Harder now. Faster. Close, so close.

My stomach muscles ached with the exertion. My fingernails dug into his back. His slick skin glided against mine with delicious friction. Until...yes, yes, yes! The pressure reached its apex and I plunged into the void.

Adam thrust faster, faster until, finally, he joined me there. He reared up, every muscle taut, as he screamed his release.

I finally floated back into myself. Wrapping my arms around his sweat-slicked back, I held him to me, enjoying the weight. Yet, I kept my face averted from his until my fangs finally withdrew, unsatisfied.

*   *   *

The dream was different his time. His body fills the opening of a dark portal. In the small room, the blue light flickers against rough stone walls. I spin around, looking for another way out.

Even in the dim light, his green eyes shine like emeralds.

"Sabina." My name spills from his lips like a prayer. "I've been waiting for you."

Suddenly, I am afraid. I never should have come here. My mouth opens to scream for help, but the words clog in my throat like glass shards.

"Lamashtu," he breathes. "Do not fear me. We are meant for each other."

The cave swirls around us like a cyclone. The rocks dissolve and painted walls rise in their place. Now I am strung up, my arms tied over my head. Bruises throb on my cheeks. Blood coats my chest from the wounds at my wrists.

"Come to me," he demands. "Submit."

"Never." I raise my chin despite the pain. "I will never submit."

He moves closer, gliding across the floor like a specter, though he is flesh and bone. I can smell the rage on him. Feel the heat of his wrath on my skin. "Let me go!"

He smiles sadly. "I can't." He touches my face gently. "Why do you make me hurt you?"

"Let me go," I say again. This time the words are a plea. I hate him even more for making me beg.

Cain raises his gaze to mine. His eyes are unfocused, crazed. "You belong to me."

He lifts the dagger high. The metal flashes in the light. His hand swoops down. I wake gasping and covered in sweat.

19

The next evening, Adam had to report at the Crossroads for a meeting with the other Pythian Guards about security for the Imbolc festival. Meanwhile, Giguhl and Georgia were about to head out to Vein for a practice session. Since the first Roller Derby match was the next night, Giguhl wanted to be sure the Manhattan Marauders were ready for prime time.

Before they left, Georgia seemed more chipper than I'd seen her in days. When I asked her why, she smiled broadly. "Mac called last night and said she's made some progress with Michael."

My brows rose in shock. "Really? That's great."

"Yeah," she said, and nodded. "She didn't have too much time to talk but said she'd fill me in at practice."

"You better talk to her before," Giguhl corrected. "Because by the time I'm done with your asses, you won't have the energy to talk."

"In that case we better get there early." Georgia rolled her eyes and pushed the demon toward the door. "Let's go, coach!"

After everyone left, I decided to head to Maisie's apartment to check up on her and try to make some progress with her about the dream incubation. Time was running out before the festival, so I needed to step up my campaign.

When I reached the door to her apartment, I knocked twice but didn't hear an answer. Just when I was about to turn and go look for her elsewhere, a loud crash sounded inside the apartment. The door was unlocked and I didn't hesitate to rush inside.

Running through the apartment, I mentally prepared myself for anything. Probably the crash was nothing to worry about, but that didn't stop my heart from kicking up a couple of notches. Especially when the scent of blood reached me.

I skidded to a halt in the doorway of Maisie's bedroom. "Maisie," I called, pushing open the door. When I saw what waited for me on the other side, I froze.

Maisie was in the corner of the room with her back to me. Her head was bent over a squirming figure struggling in her grasp. It took a couple of seconds for my eyes and my mind to make sense of what I was seeing.

"Help!" a panicked voice whimpered.

Out of instinct, I ran across the room and grabbed Maisie's arm. Adrenaline and shock exaggerated my movements, and Maisie flew across the room.

I recognized my sister's victim now as her maid, Hannah. The young mage's dress was covered in blood and tears soaked her face. In her confusion, she didn't realize I wasn't my twin. She fought me, scratching and slapping at my face and chest. I managed to grab her arms and pin them to her sides. "Shh, it's okay. You're safe now."

Wide, haunted eyes looked up at me. I tried to smile

reassuringly. She blinked once or twice and collapsed against me. "Oh, Sabina, thank the gods."

"Haven't you heard of knocking?" a bored voice said behind me.

I turned slowly to face my sister. Her rebellious posture and bloody lips didn't disguise the fear and guilt in her eyes.

"What the hell were you thinking, Maisie?" I demanded. Behind me, I felt Hannah cringe like she wanted to disappear.

"Don't take that holier-than-thou tone with me, Sabina. You have no room to judge me."

"Like hell I don't. You could have killed her!"

Maisie rolled her eyes and crossed her arms like a rebellious child. I turned back to the maid. "Stand still and let me heal your wounds," I said, softening my voice. I raised a hand to place over the puncture marks. She cringed but didn't run away. Closing my eyes, I called up the Chthonic powers that allowed me to heal injuries. The energy zinged up through my body, making me gasp softly. It gathered in my fingertips, where it drew the pain from Hannah and into my body. My arm stung as if I'd been bitten myself. Gritting my teeth, I focused on reversing the energy and injecting her skin with healing energy. When her neck was whole again, I released the Chthonic magic back in a rush that left me light-headed.

The entire process took only a few seconds, but I was drained and panting like I'd run a race. My eyes blinked open and Hannah's face wavered for a moment before my eyes regained focus. "There," I said, breathless. "Good as new."

A slow, ironic clap echoed in the room. Looking over my shoulder, I saw my sister watching us with a scornful expression. "I was going to heal her when I was through."

"You shouldn't have had to heal her at all." I ran a hand through my hair, trying to gather my thoughts. "Since when do you feed from your servants, Maisie?"

She shrugged. "This was only the second time."

My mouth fell open. "Wait, you've done this before?"

"Yesterday was the first time," she said.

"But how—" I began, but my mind was having a hard time catching up. However, that certainly explained why she'd seemed so changed to Rhea when they'd had lunch together. I turned back to Hannah. "Why didn't you tell anyone?"

The maid frowned. "This is the first time."

I looked back at Maisie, who cocked a brow. She waved a hand. I felt the rise of magic an instant before it zinged past me and slammed into the maid. I flinched and ducked a second too late. But Maisie hadn't been attacking us. Instead, Hannah's expression had gone slack and her eyes vacant.

"Hannah, you've spent your morning cleaning my apartment and then left without seeing me."

The maid nodded. "Haven't seen Maisie," she said in a monotone.

"Go now," Maisie commanded.

The next instant, Hannah brushed past me as if I wasn't there and she walked out of the room in a trance.

"What the fuck, Maisie?"

"Please give me a little credit. I know better than to feed from someone without clearing their minds."

I scratched my forehead, trying to keep my temper under control. "Let's back up. Why exactly have you suddenly decided to feed from the help?"

Maisie grabbed a towel from the edge of the bed and took her time wiping the blood from her mouth and hands before answering. "I told you before. The lack of sleep is making my hunger grow. I tried to satisfy it with the bagged blood, but it wasn't enough. And now thanks to you I barely got more than a mouthful."

"Jesus, Maisie," I said. "Why didn't you tell me you were struggling this bad?" I waved my hand through the air to indicate the scene I'd walked in on. "If Orpheus found out you're feeding from mages, he'd go ape shit."

She rounded on me. "Orpheus won't find out. You heard her. She didn't remember the previous feeding. I covered my tracks. As long as you keep your mouth shut, no one has to know."

For a split second, the air shimmered around her, allowing me to see through the glamour she'd used to hide her true appearance. Her eyes were sunken and ringed with dark shadows. Her skin was sallow and her cheeks sunken in. Despite the blood she'd been consuming, the physical toll of no sleep and, frankly, her personal demons were too much for the blood to repair. So she'd resorted to using a glamour spell to convince everyone she was healthy.

I didn't mention the spell. In the grand scheme of things it was such a little detail compared to Maisie attacking an innocent and her continued mental decline. But seeing it made me change tactics. Yelling would only make her dig in her heels more. So I sucked in a deep breath and lassoed my anger. When I spoke again, my tone was even, reasonable.

"What exactly is your goal here?" I asked, and crossed my arms.

She frowned. "What do you mean?" Her free hand came up to tug the lock of hair beneath her ear.

"Let's say I agree to help hide your activities so you can heal the damage you're doing to your body. How long do you think you can keep it up? And for that matter, what are you going to do when the treaty signing gets here and you don't have a prophecy?"

She shrugged. "I'll just make one up. Orpheus has such a hard-on for a positive prophecy, he'll buy any vaguely optimistic symbolism I throw out."

My mouth fell open. "You're unbelievable!" My voice lowered into a deadly serious volume. "This ends tonight. Do you hear me? No more not sleeping, no more feeding from anyone. You're sick and you need help. I'm not going to stand by and let you destroy yourself anymore."

Silence crashed over the room. Maisie had gone totally still, her eyes blazing with anger. When she finally spoke again, her voice was low and mean. "And you're more of a hypocrite than I thought. How dare you judge me? You of all beings, who used to kill for a living. You who has fed from the necks of countless victims. How many lies have you told, Sabina? How many times have you justified hurting others because it served your own selfish needs?" Her face was red and her hands shook with rage. "You said you want to help me. But what you really meant is to manipulate me into doing what you want. Because that's why you're really here, isn't it? Orpheus and Rhea told you to talk me into doing the dream incubation."

Her words hit me like acid-tipped arrows. When I spoke, my voice shook with guilt and anger. "The reason I am saying no to you is not because I am selfish. It is because I have experienced the consequences of the life you just described. And more than anything, I don't want that kind of life for you. I'm sorry if you don't understand that, but I will not be helping you keep up this charade."

"Then I guess we have nothing more to say to each other." Her chin came up. "Leave now."

My mouth worked open and closed as I scrambled to figure out how to salvage the conversation and convince her to do the right thing. "Maisie—"

Her hand slashed through the air. "Good-bye, Sabina."

I went still, trying to give her the chance to change her mind, but she didn't. Deflated, I turned to go. But then I stopped and turned. "You know, you're not going to get better until you face what happened and deal with it."

"Is that what you think? That I'm not trying to get better?"

I crossed my arms. "Honestly, I don't know what the hell you're doing. But I do know your recent choices aren't doing anything for your sanity."

She huffed out a humorless laugh and shook her head. "Think what you want. You always do anyway."

With that, I turned on my heel and stormed out of the apartment. Obviously, I could no longer lie for Maisie. It was one thing for her to decide to stop sleeping for a while. It was something else altogether for her to think vein raping people and lying about prophecies were good life choices.

As much as it pained me, it looked like it was time to come clean to Rhea about what Maisie was up to. I just hoped that by the time we figured out how to help Maisie, she'd eventually forgive me for betraying her. Again.

20

*W*hen I found Rhea in her workshop, she was bent over a marble pestle on the worktable grinding seeds into a powder. Judging from the strong scent of licorice filling the air, I identified the mystery substance as dried anise pods.

I paused, realizing that six months ago I'd not even known what anise looked like, much less been able to identify it by scent alone. But under Rhea's tutelage, I knew all sorts of random tricks and uses for herbs and plants. Like how wrapping a small bit of skunk cabbage in a bay leaf on Sunday promotes good luck. And that coriander can be added to wine to make an effective lust potion.

But more than that, Rhea had helped me tap into a side of myself I never knew existed when I lived in Los Angeles. A deeper side that didn't rely on fists and threats to solve problems. It was a softer, more introspective part of me that understood words can be more powerful than bullets. The realization told me I was making the right decision in coming to her.

So why did the words feel like thorns in my throat?

She looked up with a smile, but the minute she saw the

look on my face, she frowned and set down her tools. "Sabina? Everything okay?"

I took a deep breath and walked farther into the room. I'd been in this place for lessons more times than I could count. When Rhea wasn't putting me through my paces in casting spells, she was lecturing me on all sorts of magical therapies here and overseeing my attempts at making my own potions. But that classroom was about to become a confessional.

"I need to talk to you about something."

"Okay." She slowly set down the mortar. "Does this have something to do with Adam?"

I waved my hand, dismissing her worried expression. "No, nothing like that. It's—" I blew out a deep breath. Now or never. "It's about Maisie."

Rhea came around the table, her interest immediately piqued. "Did she have another episode?"

"You could say that," I said. "I—I wasn't completely honest with you when I told you the talk with Maisie the other day had gone well."

Rhea sat down on one of the stools, as if she knew the news I was about to share wasn't the kind one should hear standing. She didn't say anything, obviously sensing that I needed to just get this out.

"She told me something that night that she made me promise not to share with you or Orpheus. But I realized I can't keep that promise anymore."

Rhea reached out and placed a papery palm over my hand. "Sabina, breaking confidences is a serious thing. Are you sure you want to do this?"

"The last thing I want to do is betray Maisie. But this is pretty serious and I think that not telling you would have worse consequences."

"I see," she said. "I'm listening." She gave my hand an encouraging squeeze.

"Maisie has been telling us she hasn't had any dreams, but she was lying."

Rhea pulled away slightly, as if it had been me telling lies instead of my sister. "You're certain?"

I nodded. "She's been having bad dreams."

"Nightmares?"

"She was fairly vague with the details but she seemed pretty upset. That's not the most troubling part, though. She told me the dreams were so horrible that she's stopped sleeping altogether."

Rhea gasped. "What? How?"

"Apparently, she's been setting an alarm to keep her from entering REM."

Rhea pulled her hand away. "Oh, my gods. But she's looked so healthy lately."

"She's been using a glamour to hide the effects." I wiped my hands on my jeans. I briefly considered telling Rhea about Maisie's new feeding habits, but I knew that would condemn Maisie totally. If Orpheus and Rhea found out what she'd done, they'd shun her—or worse. No, I needed to focus on making sure the incubation happened so Maisie could have a chance to redeem herself. "I don't know what to do. If she's not sleeping, there's no way she'll be able to deliver a prophecy at the treaty signing."

"Did she tell if the dreams she had were precognitions?"

I frowned and shook my head. "No. She thought they were more like flashbacks from New Orleans, but I'm not certain she'd tell if they really were visions."

Rhea went quiet as she pondered everything. I fidgeted with an anise pod and tried to ignore the acidic guilt churning in my stomach. This was the right thing to do. And

Rhea was the right person to go to. If anyone could help Maisie, it was her.

"So the way I see it, we have two issues," Rhea said finally. "First, we need to figure out how to convince Maisie to sleep again. Then we have to help her connect with the part of her subconscious that produces the prophecies."

"Can the dream incubation do that?"

"Just a sec." She pursed her lips and rose from her stool. Turning her back on me, she went to a tall bookcase along the wall. She ran her fingers over the spines of several books before pulling a small green one from the shelf. She opened it and flipped through a few pages.

While she read, I rose and went to the windows overlooking the terrace. Rhea's workroom was on the side of the building facing the park. It was fully dark by now and the city's lights dotted the skyline like a swarm of fireflies. Across town, Giguhl was hosting a practice for his Roller Derby team. And farther north, Adam was at the Crossroads meeting with the Pythian Knights to go over security for the Imbolc festival. And I was there, betraying my sister.

The fact that Maisie had been such an evil bitch earlier didn't matter. I didn't condone her behavior, of course, but some sick part of me understood. Rhea and Orpheus would never be able to forgive Maisie for feeding from a mage. But they'd never experienced bloodlust. They didn't know how it made your skin burn and your fangs throb and your mind empty of everything but the need to hunt and consume and kill.

But I'd been there. And I knew that Maisie's state was as much my fault as her own. If I hadn't hidden her secrets, if I hadn't convinced myself that doing nothing was easier than doing what was right, the scene I witnessed earlier never would have happened. So even though it pained me to go behind my sister's back, I knew that tough love was the only thing that would save my sister from herself.

Behind me, Rhea made a speculative sound. I turned to see her holding up the book. "This describes the ritual."

A picture on the page showed the Temple at Epidaurus around 450 B.C., which the caption described as the largest of the temples dedicated to the god Asclepius. Looking up from the book, I asked, "Who is Asclepius?"

"He's the god of medicine and healing. The incubation is a ritual to invite the god into an ill person's dreams so he can help heal the ailments."

"Is it dangerous?"

"Not in and of itself, no." She shook her head. "But if Maisie's so desperate to stop the dreams that she's given up sleep, we're not going to be able to cajole her into it." Rhea's face scrunched up like the words she was about to say tasted bitter. "We would have to slip her a sleeping potion."

My mouth fell open. "You mean drug her?"

"That's one way to put it. I'd prefer to think of it as hiding something that's good for her in her food."

I shot her a disbelieving look. "Rhea, that's so wrong."

"What other option do we have? Sit by and watch her waste away? Wait around until Orpheus gets so fed up he has her deposed?"

"Can he do that?"

"Sabina, mages take the Oracle's prophecies very seriously. He can and would depose her if he felt her lack of prophecy posed a threat to the race."

"Shit." I dropped heavily onto the stool. How had this gotten so complicated?

"She won't ever have to know. In fact ... hmm." Her eyes

went all squinty and her lips pressed together like she was hatching a plan. "Here's an idea. We'll suggest that she try moving out to the Crossroads until the Imbolc festival. Tell her that maybe a change of scenery and some quiet might help her. We'd need the ley line in the Sacred Grove for the dream incubation anyway." Rhea started pacing, warming up to her idea as she moved. "We can slip the potion in her food. She'll sleep through the ritual, so she won't know we were involved. Hopefully, she'll wake up with a prophecy and won't suspect we had a hand in it."

"What if she refuses to go?"

Rhea stopped pacing and looked up. "Then we'll have Orpheus make it an order. But hopefully we can convince her without it coming to that."

I shifted on my seat, not liking this plan at all. We both knew Maisie would refuse. Drugging her was the only option if we wanted to make it happen. But I hated to do it after everything she'd already been put through.

Rhea noticed my discomfort and approached, softening her tone. "Sabina, I know you don't want to hurt Maisie. Please believe I don't either. But this is serious. The Council has always relied on the Oracle for guidance. They've been sympathetic to Maisie's issues, but the time's coming when they'll grow tired of waiting. Maisie's pedigree offers her certain protections but that goes only so far. I don't want to contemplate what will happen to her if she's stripped of her position."

I didn't either. She was already so fragile that something like that would totally leave her shattered. I sighed and brushed flecks of dried herbs off my palms. "Fine. But this is between you and me. You can't tell Orpheus what I've told you."

"Sabina, I have to." Rhea looked me in the eye. "Maisie is too important to the entire race to keep him out of this."

"What if he says no?"

She smiled a small, cunning smile. "You leave Orpheus to me. By the time I'm done with him, he won't just agree, he'll give us his blessing."

I prayed she was right. Because if her potion didn't help my sister, nothing could.

After I left Rhea to go talk to Orpheus, I was alone and restless. I returned to the apartment, but no one was back yet. Probably for the best, since I wasn't exactly in the healthiest state of mind.

The normally comfortable space did little to soothe me. I felt itchy and restless. If I stayed there, I'd just end up sitting around and stewing over the Maisie situation. As I paced by the kitchen for the tenth time, my eye caught a Necrospank 5000 T-shirt Erron had given Giguhl the night before. Seeing it brought back the revelations he'd shared.

It's not that I didn't trust Erron. But his report made me curious to know more about the mysterious Master Mahan. If nothing else, maybe facing the situation would make the damned dreams stop.

Deciding I needed to do something productive, I headed to the library on the second floor. I didn't really expect to find a ton of earth-shattering exposés on the life of Cain in a mage book collection, but I was desperate for anything that would take my mind off Maisie.

After grabbing a few books from the shelves, I took a seat in a leather armchair next to an arched window. The

moon was high—three-quarters full—and loomed over
my shoulder like it wanted to read, too.

The first book I scanned was called *The Book of Moses*.
I'd never heard of it, but it sounded vaguely biblical. I was
surprised to find a book of mortal mythology in a mage
library, but I guess it wasn't all that strange. After all,
mages live in a world dominated by mortal culture. Not
being familiar with the mortal myths myself, I quickly ran
through the pages and stopped when I got to a quote about
Cain.

*And Cain said: Truly I am Mahan, the master of this
great secret, that I may murder and get gain. Wherefore
Cain was called Master Mahan, and he gloried in his
wickedness.*

That certainly sounded accurate since the Caste of Nod
referred to Cain as Master Mahan. But the book didn't give
any details about when or why Cain created the Caste, nor
did it shed any light on his reasons for wanting to bring on
Lilith's return to the mortal realm. I slammed that book
closed and grabbed the next. According to the introduction, it contained a collection of oral histories passed down
through vampire families.

I flipped to the chapter on Lilith and started reading.
When I got to the part about Lilith and Cain's first meeting,
I stopped scanning and read every word.

As far as love stories went, it was fairly typical. Ban-
ished boy meets bad girl. They cavort by the Red Sea for a
few decades. Create a new race of immortal, bloodthirsty
offspring. Then, predictably, boy loses girl to demon king
of the underworld.

That's where things got a little fuzzy. The vampire texts
chronicled how Lilith married Asmodeus and became
Queen of Irkalla. There was some talk of how she shunned

life on earth to make little demon babies. But Cain? I couldn't find any documentation about him after he fled the Land of Nod to nurse his broken heart. Not all that surprising since vampire society was matriarchal. They worshipped Lilith and pretty much ignored Cain's existence except as a sort of damned sperm donor.

Unfortunately, the other books didn't offer much more in the way of details. I slammed the last one shut with a sigh. Glancing at the clock, I realized I'd just wasted two hours and had not much to show for it. Maybe Erron had been right. Maybe worrying about Cain was a waste of time.

I laid my head back against the back of the chair with a sigh. When I opened my eyes, my gaze was drawn to the painting that hung over the library's fireplace.

"What are you looking at?" I said to my father, whose painted eyes seemed to watch me with judgment.

Cursing, I rose to approach the picture. I'd seen it several times since moving into Prytania Place. But now I noticed a framed photograph on the mantel under the painting. I'm not sure how it got there or who added it, but I'd never noticed it before.

Seeing an oil-and-canvas rendering of a face was one thing, but staring at a photograph was different, more intimate. The stark black-and-white image made him seem more real somehow. He was standing next to a river—probably the Hudson, which ran along the border of the estate in Sleepy Hollow. All around, bare trees and a light snow on the ground indicated it was winter. Despite the stark surroundings, he was laughing at whoever took the shot.

Flipping it over, I unlatched the rear of the frame and removed the cardboard backing. On the upper-right-hand corner, someone had written "Tristan, February 1954."

My stomach performed a triple backflip. The picture had been taken just fourteen months before I was born. Had he already met my mother? Vampires have a twelve-month gestation cycle, so he'd either just met her or was just about to.

My heart thudded loudly in my chest. I turned the shot back over and studied it. His eyes sparkled with mischief—or was it the look of a man in love? I couldn't tell. I guess it didn't matter. Not really. Because while that one moment had been frozen for me to see almost fifty-five years in the future, back then time had marched on for my father. He'd met and fallen in love with my vampire mother. And that fateful introduction had cost both of them their lives.

As long as I'd been among the mages, I'd done little to learn more about my father, except what Rhea and others insisted on telling me about his "heroic life and noble death"—their words, not mine. Maybe I should have made more of an effort since, after all, I'd inherited his magical specialty. But what was the point, really?

He'd died before I was born. Rumored to have been murdered by Lavinia's goons when she found out he'd knocked up her daughter. No one ever found the body, but there'd been blood in his rooms. Probably they'd dumped his body somewhere. Either way, he was never in my life, except as a . . . damned sperm donor.

If it hadn't been my own history, I might have been amused by the Shakespearian irony of it all. But I'd spent most of my life paying the debts from my parents' mistakes. So all I felt was resentful. And hollow.

I shoved the picture back into the frame and turned away. Looking back at the books, I made a decision. It was time to leave the past alone. Ancient history—Cain—and more modern history—my father—were just skeletons.

There was no real meat to them. What really mattered was the present. And the future. It was about time I embraced the former and took steps to ensure I was ready for the latter.

As for the past? It was time to let it rest in peace.

21

*W*alking into Vein the next night was like arriving home after a long day at the office. I'd fully intended to be at the bar sooner, but the New York subway system had other plans.

I normally would have flashed over to the club with Adam, but he'd spent another evening out at the Crossroads dealing with security, so I told him I'd just meet him there for Giguhl's first Roller Derby bout.

After three months of living in New York, I still hated public transportation with the fiery passion of a thousand suns. I hated the confusing schedules. Hated the crowds of people who didn't give a shit that in my old life I would have ripped out their jugular for bumping into me. And I definitely hated the smell, a charming perfume of sour trash, hobo piss, and body odor. Considering it was January, I wasn't looking forward to experiencing the tunnel funk during the hellfire summers.

Anyway. After that nightmare, walking into Vein was like entering an oasis. I might have a more generous attitude toward humans in general, but I preferred the company of vampire hustlers, prostitute nymphs, and mage drug dealers to being surrounded by dirt-nappers.

Speaking of vampires, Alexis sat in a booth across the bar with a few of Tanith's lackeys. She saw me come in and held up her beer in salute, but she made no move to approach me. Thank the gods. The last thing I needed was to endure that harpy's attention. Especially when she'd probably just use it as an excuse to gloat about the fact there'd been no more murders since she offed Tiny. She seemed the type who'd really enjoy delivering an aggressive I-told-you-so.

Earl stood at his usual station behind the bar. His ever-present dirty dishrag worked the same spot on the bar over and over, like he was trying to clean his way through the wood.

"Hey, Earl," I said, taking a seat on one of the stools.

He nodded, Earl's version of a warm greeting. A raised eyebrow indicated he was listening for my order.

"I'll take a Bloody Magdalene. Make it a double."

The other eyebrow came up to join its mate. Like all good bartenders, Earl was an excellent reader of body language. But it wouldn't have taken an expert in behavior to figure out I was in a bad mood. A conscientious bartender made it his business to remember the preferences and habits of his customers. The small gesture told me he was recalling that since I'd been back in New York I usually stuck with imported beer. That meant the change to blood and vodka was cause for speculation.

"What?" I snapped. I didn't mean to be bitchy, but my craving for blood made manners impossible. Ever since I'd denied my craving during sex with Adam, bagged blood wasn't cutting it. I'd had three bags before I left the apartment, but I was still hungry.

While he went off to get the drink, I distracted myself

from both my hunger and my guilt with a scan of the bar. I hadn't seen Vein this busy since the early days of Demon Fight Club. A good sign. Also not a surprising one. If the dark races enjoyed watching two demons kick the shit out of each other, chances were good they'd go crazy over chicks on wheels having catfights.

A few moments later, Earl slid the highball in front of me with a nod. "Thanks, Earl." I tried to infuse my tone with the apology for being short with him earlier. He didn't acknowledge me. Instead, he went back to scrubbing the bar with his gray rag.

The mix of blood, vodka, horseradish, and Tabasco hit my tongue like liquid fire. Earl's way of letting me know he wouldn't put up with being disrespected. I looked over to catch the bellicose vampire grinning at me like a crocodile. My eyes watered and my taste buds screamed, but I lifted my glass to acknowledge he'd won this round. Besides, once you got past the taste of burning, the drink was actually pretty delicious.

I spotted Adam making his way toward me before I'd taken my second bracing gulp. I called to Earl. "Put it on my tab, okay?"

Another eyebrow raise.

I glared back. "Slade knows I'm good for it."

He gave me an it's-your-funeral shrug. Then he drifted away to fill another order.

I turned to smile at Adam. With a mouthful of liquor and my hot mage filling my visual space, my mood improved considerably.

"Hey there, hottie," he said, sidling up. "Looking for a good time?"

I swallowed and flashed a little fang. "Watch yourself, mancy." I ran a finger down his chest. "I like to play rough."

"Thank gods." He leaned in and gave me a fast, hard kiss. But he pulled away quickly, a grimace tightening his full lips. Realizing he'd tasted the blood on my mouth, I quickly wiped it away.

"Sorry," I mumbled.

He took a long pull from his beer. "I don't know how you can drink that stuff."

I took a pointed sip and smacked my lips. "That's funny. I don't know how you can *not* drink it."

"Just be sure you brush your teeth tonight. Morning breath is a fresh sea breeze compared to the *hell*itosis of blood breath."

I decided it was time to change the subject before the conversation turned ugly. "Did you see Giguhl?"

He took a swig of his beer and nodded. "I believe his exact words were 'I'm as nervous as a nun at a porn convention.'"

I rolled my eyes and took another sip of my drink. I always enjoyed the quality of Slade's blood. The stuff I got from the bank did the trick nutritionally but was the bloody equivalent to eating gruel. Slade's blood, however, was top shelf and fresh. I preferred not to ask where he got it because ignorance allowed me to have a clean conscience.

"Anyway," he continued, "we better head down. He said if you didn't stop by to wish him luck he'd use your favorite boots as a litter box."

Adam reached back and grabbed my hand to pull me through the crowd. I accepted it not because I needed his help but because I loved the feeling of being connected. I'd spent too many years steamrolling through crowds on my own. Besides, with him leading the way, my eyes were free to admire his ass.

He bypassed the aluminum risers that ringed the raised track and led me toward the locker room. Just outside the steel door, Giguhl paced and chewed at his claws. He wore green sweat shorts and a ringer T-shirt that read DEMONS DIG VIOLENT CHICKS. A clipboard and a whistle rounded out the look.

"Well if it isn't Sporty Spice," I called.

Giguhl's head snapped up with a scowl. But when he saw it was us, his black lips spread into a smile. "Thank Asmodeus! I thought you weren't going to make it."

"Are you kidding? I wouldn't miss your coaching debut for anything."

"Thanks, Red."

"So how's it going?"

Giguhl shook his head, making his horns cut semicircles in the air. "I think I'm gonna throw up."

"You'll be great." I stepped in and put a hand on his huge green bicep.

"Oh, I know that." He waved a claw. "It's Pussy Willow. She's mad she can't play."

"What? I thought she was on the team?"

"It's the whole penis thing." He shrugged. "Somehow the league found out she was smuggling extra equipment in her skirt. They're refusing to bend about the whole 'only biological females are allowed to be on teams' thing. So I had to tell her she can't play."

"Uh-oh," I said. "How'd she take that?"

"She accused me of buckling under the league's phallocentric tyranny."

"Wait," Adam said. "How is it phallocentric tyranny if they're insisting on people *without* penises?"

The demon tilted his head down. "Really, mancy? Would you ever say something that logical to Red when she's emotional?"

I frowned at the males. "I never get that emotional."

Adam raised his eyebrows and pursed his lips. That earned him a light punch to the ribs. "Ouch!"

"Anyway," I said, getting back on topic, "where does she stand on all this now?"

The door to the locker room opened and a blond head poked out. "Gigi?" Pussy Willow noticed Adam and me. "Oh! Hi, guys!"

"Hey, P-Dub," I said. "What's shakin'?"

She laughed, the sound filled with too much bass for a female. "Didn't you hear? I'm about to make my debut as a color commentator." Instead of sounding bitter about the change, she seemed excited by the prospect. But before I could comment, she turned to Giguhl. "The refs said it's time to line up."

Giguhl snapped to attention. "Oh, gods! I'll be right there."

Pussy Willow waggled her fingers in farewell and ducked back inside.

"Um, Giguhl?" I said. "I hate to point out the obvious, but she didn't seem pissed at all." I looked at Adam, who shrugged and nodded.

Giguhl crossed his arms. "Don't let her fool you. She's all smiles now because I agreed to let her do color commentary for the bout, but later she'll probably poison my food."

"Now who's the drama queen?" I patted him on the shoulder. "Go get 'em, tiger!"

He wiped the sweat from his brow with a claw and disappeared inside the locker room. "Is it just me," Adam said, "or are those two sounding more and more like a married couple every time we see them?"

"Seriously," I said. As far as I knew, their friendship was as platonic as one can be between a Mischief demon and a gay faery transvestite. Still, there was a vein of codependency there that concerned me. "But I seriously do not have the energy to analyze their dynamic right now. Let's go find our seats."

A few minutes later, Adam and I located spots between two nymphs and a werewolf couple. We settled in to wait for the bout to begin.

By habit, Adam's arm came up around my shoulders. I leaned into his side and tried to enjoy my new, more optimistic attitude toward life. But I couldn't quite relax. Being happy felt like wearing someone else's shoes.

A few moments later, the lights fell. A cheer rose up from the crowd. "Ladies and gentlemen of the Black Light District," Slade's voice boomed through the arena. He stood in the announcer's booth next to Pussy Willow. "Vein is proud to present the first-ever Hell on Wheel's Roller Derby Night!" Cheers, clapping. "Show some love for our visiting team, the Brooklyn Bloodletters!"

Then the speakers came to life, blaring out "Roller Girls" by the Soviettes. Spotlights flashed back and forth across the rink as the Bloodletters exploded out of their locker room. They wore uniforms that resembled naughty nurse costumes. Only ripped and spattered with blood. The crowd booed the visiting team, which only seemed to egg on their antics as they lapped the track.

Once they'd reached their bench and their coach, a female vampire, the music cut off. Then, over the loudspeaker, Pussy Willow shouted: "Manhattan! Are you ready to fight?"

The audience went wild. Adam and I jumped to our feet along with everyone else to cheer on the home team.

"Stomp your feet for the queens of pain!" the faery screamed. "The mistresses of mayhem! The Manhattan Marauders!"

The hundreds of stomping feet pummeled the aluminum bleachers. AC/DC's "Thunderstruck" boomed from the speakers. The Manhattan Marauders exploded from the locker room. Since Giguhl was their coach, the theme for their uniforms was "slutty." Baby-doll shirts, pleather bandages masquerading as skirts, and ripped fishnets.

With Giguhl in the lead, the girls zoomed around the track, playing it up for the crowd. Even Mac, who usually accessorized her outfits with a scowl, seemed to be enjoying herself. She and Georgia skated next to each other, smiling and waving at the fans. Pussy Willow announced them by their Roller Derby names—Bitch N. Heat and Eva Fangoria.

When the team reached its bench, Pussy Willow did a quick spiel about the rules. While she spoke, Adam leaned in to me and said, "You seem more chipper tonight."

I dragged my eyes from the rink. "What do you mean?"

He shrugged. "Your shoulders are relaxed and you're actually smiling. It's nice."

I laid my head on his shoulder. "Sorry if I've been bitchy lately. It's just been a little stressful."

He ran a hand over my hair. "I wasn't complaining. We've all been stressed. But you seem . . . lighter somehow."

"I guess I just decided to try out optimism for a change."

He reared back in mock surprise. "You?"

I swatted his arm. "Stop."

"Just kidding." He chuckled and kissed my hair. "Seriously. It looks good on you."

My conscience gave a slight twinge. I'd filled Adam in on the plan to trick Maisie into a dream incubation, but I hadn't told him everything. Adam would freak if I told him Maisie tried to exsanguinate her maid—not only because it was forbidden by mage law but also because of the issues it would bring up about Adam's own experience as Maisie's unwilling blood donor

However, just to be safe, I had suggested he assign a Pythian Guard to her until the Imbolc festival. Adam thought the suggestion was just a better-safe-than-sorry measure. But I just hoped a potential witness might dissuade her from making any more stupid choices. Until we could get this shit settled.

In the meantime, I scooted closer to my man. Tonight was just for us, and I was determined not to let my sister's drama—or anyone else's for that matter—ruin it.

The shrill squeal of the whistle. On the track, the players who scored the points for each team lined up. Over the P.A. system, Pussy Willow identified the raven-haired faery for the Bloodletters as Scarlet O'Scare-a. The jammer for the Marauders was one of Slade's nymphs, Pepper, who skated under the name Stankerbell. The black stars on their helmets identified them as players whose goal was to score points by skating past the defenders from the opposite team. Several feet ahead of them, eight other players—four for each team—bunched up in a group, ready to block the jammers with their elbows, hips, and fists.

The ref blew the whistle again and the pack of eight took off like someone shocked them with cattle prods. Not content to docilely skate along until the jammers got their whistle, the pack threw elbows, punches, and insults.

We all rose to cheer on the teams. Groups of spectators collected along the raised edges of the track, hammering their hands on the boards. My eyes wandered to the other side of the amphitheater. About halfway up the stands, I recognized a familiar face among the crowd.

I pulled on Adam's sleeve. "Michael's here." I pointed to where I'd seen the werewolf Alpha.

"Hmm," Adam said. He paused to cringe at a particularly vicious hit on the track. "Ouch! Wonder if that's a good sign. Didn't Mac tell Georgia she'd made some progress on that front?"

"I didn't get a chance to ask her about it after their practice." Giguhl had made good on his promise to put the team through its paces at practice the night before. When Georgia walked in, she looked like she'd been ridden hard and put up wet.

Adam shrugged. "Guess we'll find out after the bout."

I dismissed Michael from my mind and tried to focus on the match. Scarlet O'Scare-a had already passed two of the Marauders' defenders. But Stankerbell was getting clobbered by the Bloodletters. Obviously, she'd been a last-minute substitution after Pussy Willow got banned from playing. Despite her extra padding, she already had a fat lip, a severe limp, and a vampire on her back. As they rounded the track, the vamp brought down her prey in a tangle of skates, limbs, and fangs. The ref's whistle screamed through the arena.

But instead of stopping, one of the Bloodletters' werewolves took a cheap shot at Georgia. She got an elbow to the nose and went down like a two-dollar whore. Mac burst into action before the ref could blow the whistle again. Mac jumped on the were with hands curled into claws. They rolled down the track in a flurry of fists and kicks. The benches cleared and the track broke out into an all-out brawl.

The crowd shrieked and strained for a better view. The air crackled with excitement and blood scented the air. Had this been a mortal fight, no doubt the violence would have been stopped fairly quickly. But the refs leaned against the guardrails, looking bored. I guess dark-races Roller Derby had a more liberal definition of unnecessary roughness.

I wish I could say things improved after that. But ten minutes later, the Bloodletters—yes, the entire team—were ejected from the fight. Where the refs could stand by during a fight, they couldn't ignore the team pulling spectators from the crowd and beating them up, too.

Instead of cowing them, the ejection only seemed to appeal to their need for rebellion. The Bloodletters skated off with heads held high and their middle fingers raised in a final fuck-you to the crowd. The ref went over to Giguhl and raised his claw. Pussy Willow yelled into the mic, "And the Manhattan Marauders win!"

Mac put an arm around Georgia. The werewolf had two black eyes, a broken arm, and somehow lost her shirt in the scuffle. But their eyes shined from the surges of adrenaline and the good old high of kicking some ass. Georgia threw her arms around Mac and planted a long, sloppy kiss on her lips.

My gaze went across the arena to where I'd seen Michael earlier. "Uh-oh," I said to Adam. I had to nudge him with an elbow to pull his attention from the lesbians.

"Huh?"

I pointed across to Michael. His face was purple with rage as he watched his sole female heir mugging down with a vampire in public. "Guess that answers our question."

Adam blinked and looked. "Oh, shit."

Oh, shit, indeed. Michael stalked toward the rink like a predator. Spectators who got in the way were shoved or thrown out of his path. The unsuspecting couple on the track had no idea they were about ten seconds from a confrontation with a severely pissed-off Alpha werewolf.

Adam and I exchanged a look. "Should we step in?" I asked.

His jaw clenched. "Shit. Let's go."

Michael reached them first. "What is the meaning of

this?" His gravelly shout cut through the festive atmosphere like shrapnel.

Dead silence from the audience as the air tightened with anticipation. Despite the fireworks of the bout, they were eager for more drama. Judging from the volume of Michael's ire and the veins bulging from his neck, they were about to get it in spades.

Mac jerked away from Georgia, flinching as if expecting attack. "Uncle Mike! What are you—"

He slashed a hand through the air. "I thought I'd surprise you and come support your new hobby." He turned a distasteful glare on Georgia. "Who is this vampire?"

"This is Georgia Rousseau." Mac stood straighter, her chin coming up. "My girlfriend."

Michael's hands curled into fists like he wanted to throttle his niece. By that point, Adam and I had skidded into the periphery of the circle forming around them. I took a step forward to intervene, but Adam grabbed my arm. Nearby, Slade and Pussy Willow finally reached the track. PW made a beeline for Giguhl. Slade looked torn about whether to intervene. Sure, this was his club and he'd spent years working to keep the packs in line, but he was no longer the official leader of the BLD. Besides, he knew better than to interfere in pack business. Everyone did.

"How dare you shame your pack like this!" Michael's voice was low, but angry. "And your future mate!"

Mac's voice shook with anger. "Logan Remus is not my mate."

Michael's eyes widened. "Of course he is. The paperwork has already been finalized with the Alpha of the New Jersey pack. According to werewolf law, you are already as good as married."

"I never agreed to that!"

"Lower your voice, girl," he snapped. My jaw clenched at his tone. I liked Michael, but the way he was speaking to Mac made me want to punch him. How dare he belittle her in public like that?

"I'm sorry," she said. "But you never asked me if I wanted a mate. The real reason I even came when you summoned me was to tell you about Georgia."

"Yet, I had to find out this way?" His eyes narrowed. "Why is that, Mackenzie?"

Mac flinched and cast a guilty glance at Georgia. The vampire had wrapped her arms around herself and refused to look her lover in the eye. I couldn't blame her. Mac had told her she'd already broached the subject with Michael.

"I was waiting for the right time. Look, I know I screwed up. I should have told you a long time ago. But I kept hoping you'd realize I had no interest in mating with a male."

Mike threw his head back and laughed. "Then you were living in a dream world. Your first responsibility is to your pack. You know that. And as the only female in my bloodline, a good match is even more critical. I let you get away with putting it off for years, hoping you'd find a worthy male on your own. But my patience can be stretched only so far." He crossed his arms and speared his niece with a stare. "Now, say good-bye to your friend. You won't be seeing her again."

Georgia's head snapped up. The look she shot at Michael was full of hatred that would have made a lesser male cower. But Michael Romulus was the Alpha of one of the largest packs in America for a reason. "I'm waiting, Mackenzie."

Everyone on that track held their breath. Mac's eyes went from her lover to her Alpha. Michael had just drawn a line in the sand. If she didn't bow to him now, she risked being shunned. But if she acquiesced, she'd lose Georgia for good.

Georgia watched her lover with an unreadable expression. "Just go."

Mac's mouth fell open. "Wha—"

"I've waited around for months for you to declare yourself to your uncle. If he hadn't caught us tonight, he'd still have no idea I even existed." Georgia's voice shook with betrayal. The were flinched. "So I'm going to make things real easy for you, Mac." She kissed Mac's cheek. Michael growled a warning, which the vampire ignored. "Have a good life."

With that, Georgia finally acknowledged the Alpha. "She's yours."

She skated off the track with her head held high. Pussy Willow ran after her, but the vampire shot her a look that made the faery's steps falter. For all her dignity and determination, Georgia needed to go break apart in private.

Michael watched the vampire's retreat with a solemn expression. However, Mac sobbed openly. I averted my eyes from her pain. Adam grabbed my hand and squeezed. Pussy Willow went to Giguhl and they stood, arm-in-arm, looking like they'd just watched their parents' divorce. The rest of the crowd dispersed then, slinking away as if embarrassed to have gawked at Mac's public shame.

Finally, Michael cleared his throat. "Let's go." He took Mac's uninjured arm and led her away. I'd never seen her looking so cowed and beaten. As she passed us, she looked up at me. I flinched at the pain in her liquid brown eyes. I looked away quickly, not wanting her to see the judgment in my own gaze. My chest hurt for her, but my rational side wondered if it had all worked out for the best. If Mac and Georgia had really been in love, how could they let it slip away without more of a fight?

I glanced up at Adam's handsome, dear face. My heart contracted in my chest at the thought of ever losing him. If anyone tried to take the mancy from me, there would be blood.

Giguhl stood nearby, looking like someone had ruined his birthday party. In the heavy silence following the drama, he raised his fists and yelled, "Oh, fuck it! Let's get drunk!"

22

While Giguhl and the rest of the Marauders partied like rock stars at Vein, Adam and I went to find Georgia. Since she knew almost no one in the city, we followed our hunch and returned to Prytania Place.

"Georgia!" I called when we walked into the apartment.

"Back here," came the muted reply.

Adam looked at me. "You want to take this one?"

"Why me?" I frowned at him.

He shrugged. "Just figured she might need some girl talk."

"Adam, in your history of knowing me, have you ever witnessed me having girl talk?" I shot him a get-real look.

"You might have a point." He waved toward the door. "We'll tag-team it then."

I nodded resolutely and marched down the hall. When I opened the door, Georgia's back was to us. She was shoving wrinkled clothes into a suitcase's yawning mouth.

"Georgia?" I whispered.

She looked over her shoulder, and I was surprised to see her eyes were bone dry. "Hey, guys."

"Why are you packing?" Adam came up to stand next to me. "You can't leave now."

She snorted. "Why not? I never should have come here in the first place."

"You don't mean that," I said. "I know you're upset but—"

"I appreciate what you're trying to do, but I'm not upset." Adam and I both shot her incredulous looks. She deflated a little. "Okay, I am upset." She sighed and dropped onto the couch. "But not for the reasons you think. I'm mad at myself for not realizing Mac was stringing me along. I can handle her temper and the chip on her shoulder. But I won't be lied to. Remember how I told you she said she made progress with her uncle?"

I nodded and took a seat across from her. Adam joined me, since it looked like this was going to take a while.

Georgia continued. "Well, last night before practice she told me that she'd told Michael all about us and he'd taken it really well. I was so happy and relieved that I didn't question her when she claimed she still needed some time before she introduced us." Georgia shook her head sadly. "I'm such an idiot."

"No, you're not," Adam said. "Why would you assume the person you love would lie about something that important? She's the one person you should be able to trust."

I squirmed in my seat a bit. The parallels between this conversation and my own mistakes were hitting a little too close to home.

"But maybe Mac felt like she had to lie to protect your feelings," I said. Two frowns greeted that statement. "I mean, she was wrong to, of course, but maybe she felt she had a good reason," I added quickly.

"Sabina," Georgia said. "Even if she hadn't lied to me last night, she had the perfect opportunity to stand up to Michael tonight and she didn't."

"That's true," I said. But I was conflicted. Obviously, Mac fucked up. Bad. But I didn't think the situation should be as black and white as Georgia was making it. "Listen, Mac loves you. But it's not easy to stand up to your family. Especially when that family is made up of beasts who howl at the moon and have zero tolerance for questioning the Alpha."

"So what? I'm supposed to sit here and hope that the Alpha changes his mind? Michael's not going to suddenly give Mac and me his blessing. Especially since he said the mating contract was already signed."

Clearly, I didn't have an argument against that. Adam seemed to concur with Georgia's assessment of the situation. "What will you do now?" he asked softly.

I shot him a glare. Why wasn't he encouraging Georgia to stay and fight for her woman? Surrender was never an option.

"I'm going back to New Orleans, of course," she said. "That's my home. Always will be."

"You could have a home here, too," I said.

Georgia shook her head sadly. "Not if Mac's here. I couldn't stand seeing her and her new mate everywhere. It would kill me."

I was starting to feel a little desperate. I'm sure a therapist would have plenty to say about how the urgency I felt about saving Mac and Georgia's relationship was connected to my own guilt and issues in my relationship with Adam. But frankly, I didn't care why. I just needed to do something, anything. "I'll go talk to Michael!" I blurted out before I realized it was coming.

Adam stilled and looked at me with his mouth hanging to his clavicles. Georgia's head snapped up. "I thought you said you didn't want to get in the middle."

"I know what I said. But I was wrong. We're involved

because you're both our friends. If talking to Michael can help, then I'll do it."

"Thanks, Sabina. It means a lot that you'd be willing to do that." Georgia's shoulders drooped. "But it's too late. I let Mac go. I need to go home and come to terms with that so I can move on."

My blood rushed. How could she just give up? "Maybe I'm not doing it for you. Maybe I'm doing it so Mac isn't doomed to be mated to someone she didn't choose."

Georgia's cheeks colored with some emotion—shame? Anger? "Do what you want. It's not really my business any-more." She slapped her hands on her thighs and rose. "Now, if you'll excuse me I need to finish packing."

Adam and I looked at each other. Obviously the conversation was finished. I stood to go, but I had one more thing to say. "Georgia, I know you're hurting right now. But I hope you won't give up on Mac."

"I didn't give up on Mac, Sabina." For the first time that night, tears sprang to the vampire's eyes. "She gave up on us."

Adam and I left Georgia to finish packing and reconvened in the living room for a postmortem. He turned on me the minute we reached the couch. "How could you defend Mac like that?"

I stilled, surprised by the anger in his tone. "Adam, I wasn't defending her. I just think Georgia isn't being sensitive to the position Michael put Mac in tonight."

"*Georgia's* not being sensitive?" he repeated, his voice rising. "Seems to me Mac wasn't being very sensitive when she lied. Maybe Michael did Georgia a favor tonight."

I flinched. "Regardless, Georgia's not the only victim in

this scenario. And I meant what I said. I'm going to talk to Michael. Despite her poor choices, Mac shouldn't be forced to mate anyone she didn't choose."

"Yeah, good luck with that," he said. "You ask me, Mac's getting what's coming to her."

My mouth fell open. Where was this coming from? "How can you say that?"

He crossed his arms. "Mac had her chance to make things right with Georgia. She knew what was at stake and she chose the coward's way out."

My conscience was sparking like a Roman candle. "Sometimes lies are more about protection than deception, Adam."

Just then, the front door burst open and Giguhl and Pussy Willow marched in. They were laughing about something, but when they saw Adam and me facing off they fell silent.

"What the hell does that even mean?" He started pacing in front of me like a jungle cat. "Jesus, Red, what would you do if you found out I'd lied to you?"

I forced a casual shrug. "It would depend on the situation."

He stopped and laughed, a harsh, cold sound. "Bullshit. You'd castrate me and then force me to wear my balls like a necklace. Love can't survive lies."

From the corner of my eye, I saw Giguhl freeze.

"Not necessarily," I said. "Not if I thought you had a good reason for doing it." The look he shot me was heavy with irony. "I mean, yes, sure I'd be hurt at first, but I like to think that our relationship is strong enough that you—I mean I—would eventually get over it."

"Oh, shit!" Giguhl rushed forward. Adam swung around to look at him. "I told you not to mention the Slade thing!"

I froze as my gut clenched and cold acid shot through my veins. With wide eyes, I turned on the demon and tried to shoot him cease-and-desist semaphore.

But my efforts were in vain because Adam rounded on me. His face as hard as one of those Easter Island statues. "What Slade thing?"

I recovered a fraction of a second too late. "What? Nothing."

"Fuck me," Giguhl whispered, realizing his mistake. "Sorry, Red."

Adam stiffened but kept his eyes on me. "Sabina?" His voice was unnervingly quiet.

I blew out a breath. The kind that signals surrender to the inevitable. "Remember when I told you Slade and I hadn't been together since that time we worked together in Los Angeles?"

Adam's eyes narrowed to sharp slits. He didn't say anything, didn't move.

My stomach sunk like it was tied to a cinder block tossed into a freezing river. "Back in October—before you and I were together, mind you—I...Slade and I—"

I looked around frantically for help. For someone to finish the sentence so I didn't have to say it out loud. PW's eyes darted from side to side like she wanted to run but was worried about drawing any impending wrath in her direction. And Giguhl, the traitor, slinked away guiltily and dropped into a chair with his head in his claws, as if giving himself the time-out he deserved.

"I'm waiting," Adam said in that same deadened voice. His eyes told me he'd already figured it out, but he wasn't about to let me off easy. Part of my punishment was having to admit the betrayal out loud.

I licked my lips. Then words just tumbled out of me. "We slept together."

Adam's fists tightened into boulders. A vein pulsed in his neck.

"Adam, I—"

He slashed a hand through the air as if he couldn't stomach the sound of my voice. "Save it. I can't even stand to look at you right now."

My head throbbed and my vision went static. My chest felt like it would collapse under the pressure. My heart shriveled and blackened like a piece of coal.

Before I could react, Adam spun around and slammed out of the apartment. The ensuing silence felt like a verdict. Pussy Willow and Georgia wouldn't meet my gaze. And Giguhl moaned and rocked with guilt in the corner.

All the fight left me. I collapsed into a nearby chair. Numb shock descended to protect me from reality. I suppose I should have seen this coming. Who had I been kidding to think I could hide a lie of that magnitude from Adam?

"Sabina?" Georgia said softly. She knelt by my side. "What can I do?"

I couldn't speak. If I opened my mouth I'd start screaming and never stop.

Giguhl rushed over to join the vampire. "Red, I'm so fucking sorry."

I swallowed the panic rising in my throat. Pussy Willow answered for me. "It's not your fault, Gigi. Sabina should have told him herself months ago."

Giguhl shot the faery a hateful look. "Hey! She doesn't need to hear that right now."

PW crossed her arms and glared at the demon. "You always take her side!"

"I do not," he argued. "Besides, I'm the one who told her not to tell him. Then I went and opened my big mouth." He hit his head with the heel of his claw. "Idiot!"

Georgia stood and addressed both of them. "That's enough, you guys. Pointing fingers is a waste of time."

"I'm not pointing fingers." PW shrugged. "Simply stating facts."

"You can take your facts and shove them up your ass!" Giguhl said. "If you can't be supportive to Sabina, maybe you should leave!"

PW gasped and started yelling at the demon. Giguhl, naturally, yelled back. But I was so lost in my shock I couldn't understand them. Their words hit the air and then scattered like black confetti.

Finally, Georgia put her fingers to her lips and executed an eardrum-shattering whistle. It jerked me out of my trance and shocked PW and Giguhl into silence.

"Now that I have your attention," the vampire said, "I have a couple of things to say. First, Giguhl and PW, get a hold of yourselves. Right now we need to be supporting Sabina." She turned to me. "As for you, snap out of it. You're the one always saying surrender is never an option. If you want Adam, you have to go after him."

I sighed deeply. The air stabbed my lungs like shards of glass. "What's the point? You heard him. He can't even stomach being in the same room as me right now. Even if I knew what to say, he wouldn't listen." I sat up straighter. "Besides, aren't you being a little hypocritical?"

She tensed. "What?"

"You could have fought for Mac, but instead you gave up and are planning on running back to New Orleans."

She crossed her arms. "That isn't the same thing at all—"

"Bullshit," Giguhl coughed into his claw.

"Hey!" she protested. "Mac chose her kin over me. I know when I'm beat. But you have a chance to make this right."

"So do you," I countered. I knew I was harping on Georgia, but it was a lot easier than talking about my issues.

"Maybe once Michael calms down he'll listen to reason, too. Despite his Alpha ways, he cares about Mac. If we can talk to him and convince him that marrying her off will make her unhappy, maybe he'll listen."

She hesitated. "I don't know—"

"Listen, forget the lie for a moment. She doesn't deserve what Michael's planning. If you love her, you'll help her. She doesn't have anyone else right now."

Georgia's face fell. She didn't speak, but I got the feeling I was wearing her down. "How about we make a deal? You promise to go with me to talk to Michael, and I'll promise I'll try with Adam."

Her eyebrow went up. "When?"

"Tomorrow night. You and I can go see Michael just after sundown. That should give him enough time to calm down."

"And Adam?" she asked.

I sighed and sat back in the chair. "I don't know."

"He has to come back here at some point." Giguhl shrugged.

"I guess." I honestly wasn't sure what I'd say if he walked back through that door in a couple of hours. But Georgia was right. I couldn't let everything we had together dissolve because I made a dumb mistake. We were supposed to be stronger than that.

"What if they won't listen?" Pussy Willow asked. "What will you both do then?"

The promise of a challenge made Georgia's vampire instincts flare to life. A small smile lifted her lips, flashing a little fang. "We'll make them listen."

Adam didn't come home that night.

I lay alone in our bed staring at the ceiling well past

sunrise. I guess I was naive to hope he'd return to the scene of the crime so soon.

Probably, he'd crashed at Rhea's. The idea of my mentor finding out what I'd done made my already tight stomach knot painfully. Even if I could somehow manage to make things right with Adam, Rhea wouldn't be so easily won over. She was protective of her blood. The fact that we'd grown so close over the last several months wouldn't matter more than her connection with Adam.

I sighed and turned over. The movement ruffled the sheets and stirred up Adam's sandalwood scent. I grabbed his pillow and hugged it to me. Closing my eyes, I let the tears fall. I'd put on a brave front for everyone earlier. But the truth was, I didn't know how to fix this.

Since the first time I met Adam, I knew our relationship would end badly. With me involved, how could it go any other way? I'd fought being with him for so long because I knew I'd never be good enough for him. And if I were being honest with myself, maybe on some level I held this secret close to my vest, knowing that it would come back eventually. Maybe in some sick way it was my way of controlling how the end happened.

But even though I'd been expecting this all along, it still hurt like hellfire.

However, I'd always believed pain was my friend. In a fight, it told me I was still alive. And in love, it told me I still cared. Which meant I'd swallow my pride and beg him to forgive me, if that's what it took.

My fatalism about love might have turned into a self-fulfilling prophecy, but I'd never put too much stock in prophecies anyway.

23

The next evening, I decided to hit the gym for a workout. I hadn't slept at all, but my body strained for action. My pent-up emotions and worries needed a release.

The headphones on my ears blocked out the world and filled my head with angry music. All my energy was focused on knocking the stuffing out of the punching bag. My skin dripped sweat and my muscles screamed from exertion. It felt good to be back in the zone.

I was so focused on my punishing workout that I didn't notice the person coming up behind me. Not until a hand landed on my shoulder. On autopilot, I spun and swung my fist into a jaw.

"Oof!" My target fell to the hardwood with a crash.

Panting, I looked down and cursed. "Shit. Orpheus, I'm so sorry!"

I threw off my headphones and bent down to help him off the ground. His eyes were unfocused and he was so disoriented he didn't fight my assistance. When I finally had him upright again, he wobbled. His hand flew to his jaw and he worked it back and forth with a grimace. "That'll teach me to sneak up on a former assassin."

"Sorry." I grimaced. "You caught me off guard."

He waved a hand. "My fault. I should have made more noise."

I wiped the back of my arm across my forehead, suddenly self-conscious. "Did you need something?"

He shook his head, as if clearing out cobwebs. I bit my lip, as guilt warred with amusement. Over the last few months, I'd wanted to clean Orpheus's clock more than once after he'd done some asshole thing. But the truth was I never would have landed that punch if he'd seen it coming.

"It's about Maisie," he said. "Rhea came to me last night and told me about your talk."

I schooled my features at his mention of my mentor because it reminded me of my problems with Adam. Did Rhea know what happened? Did she tell Orpheus? But obviously, the leader of the mage race had more important issues to worry about than my relationship troubles.

"I wish you had come to us sooner," he continued. "But I suppose I understand how your desire to be loyal to Maisie made you hesitate."

I nodded. "Thanks for understanding. What did you two decide?"

"We agreed that immediate action must be taken. Obviously, refusing to sleep is dangerous to Maisie's health."

I raised a brow. "Yes, her health."

He paused and shot me a sharp look. "Save your judgment, Sabina. Yes, I am also concerned about what this development means for the treaty signing. But as much as you'd like to believe I am just a cold politician, I've known that girl longer than you. Hell, I practically raised her alongside Ameritat. Seeing her in pain hurts me as much as, if not more than, it hurts you."

I sighed and softened my expression. "I know. I just wish we didn't have this treaty deadline looming. She needs time to heal."

"If wishes solved problems, the world would be a very different place."

"I hear that," I said. "So what's the next step?"

"I've given Rhea leave to move forward with the plan to trick Maisie into doing the incubation."

"Really?" My eyebrows rose. "I figured you'd be against it."

He grimaced. "Let's just say Rhea can be quite persuasive when she wants to be." He rubbed his head as if comforting an old wound. "She convinced me that this is the only way to help Maisie."

"So where do I come in?" I asked. I figured I was the last person Rhea would want help from now.

"You're going to assist in the ritual." He frowned as if I'd asked a trick question. "Rhea said she'd already discussed it with you."

My eyebrows shot up to my hairline. "Of course. Sorry." I was shocked Rhea would allow me to help. That meant she was either desperate for help...or she didn't know about Adam and me.

He frowned. "Is that a problem?"

I shook my head. "Not at all."

"Good. Rhea is going to invite Maisie to go to the Crossroads this evening under the guise of getting away from the city for a couple of days. It'll give Rhea a chance to do the necessary cleansing rituals without tipping Maisie off to their real purpose. Plus, being close to the ley line in the Sacred Grove for twenty-four hours will help prepare Maisie for the incubation. Tomorrow night, you'll go out there for dinner. Rhea will slip a sedative into Maisie's food and then you will proceed with the ritual."

He noticed my grimace at his mention of the sedative.

"Don't get squeamish on us now, Sabina," he said, his tone rueful. "You've committed far more heinous crimes for far less noble causes. Don't let your conscience get in the way of what needs to be done. Not when so much is at stake. This may be our last chance to get Maisie back."

I swallowed the bile rising in my throat. I didn't like the idea of tricking Maisie, but Orpheus was right. I'd murdered people for looking at me the wrong way. This betrayal, at least, might have a positive outcome. And gods knew, where Maisie was concerned, we needed some good news.

"I'll be there."

"Good. Thank you."

I hesitated, wondering if now was a good time to bring up the other issue I wanted to speak to him about. It'd been so long since Orpheus and I had a positive conversation, I hated to ruin it. On the other hand, I didn't want to miss this opportunity to find out if Alexis was really taking over control of the BLD.

"Listen, have you and the Despina made a decision about Slade's position yet?"

He took a deep breath. "Sabina, I know Slade's your friend—"

"No, that's not why I'm asking. I mean, sure, I think Slade got the shaft—" He raised a warning eyebrow. "Sorry but it's the truth. Anyway, I ask because Alexis seemed pretty sure she'd be taking over that role."

Orpheus crossed his arms. "No final decisions have been made," he said, evading the question. "Should I take it you doubt Alexis's suitability?"

"Look, it's not that I think she's unskilled. She's clearly

well trained and strong. But does she have the judgment and patience a leader needs for such a politically sensitive role?" I shrugged. "I honestly don't know. Not after she killed Tiny."

Orpheus stiffened, as if preparing to argue, but I cut off his objections.

"Relax. I'm not going to argue that Tiny wasn't the killer. There haven't been any more killings, so it appears my objections might have been...reactionary." His eyebrows rose, his expression heavy with irony. But I'd be staked before I admitted to being wrong. "Anyway, my concerns about Alexis have more to do with her impulsivity and lack of knowledge about the workings of New York vampire culture. Is that really who you want in such a strategically critical and politically sensitive position?"

Instead of arguing with me or telling me I was overreacting, like he normally did, Orpheus put a hand on my arm and shot me a smile. "I appreciate you sharing your concerns. But let me ask you this: If you don't approve of Alexis, whom would you suggest?"

I raised my chin. "Slade."

"Sabina—"

I held up a hand. "No, hear me out. If we all agree that Tiny was the culprit, then we also have to admit that Slade was set up. Punishing him for Tiny's manipulations is unfair."

"Sabina, I understand what you're saying. I've worked with The Shade for years and have always found him capable. But like it or not, his ability to lead effectively was compromised by Tiny's scheme. We need a strong, competent leader to guide the city's vampires into the new era." He smiled to soften the unfairness of the situation. "And I'm afraid Slade Corbin isn't the man for that job."

"But you think Alexis is?"

"I didn't say that." Orpheus's expression became shuttered. "Look, the Despina went home to Los Angeles for a few days to handle some pressing business. No decision will be made until she returns in time for the Imbolc festival. In the meantime, I'm afraid you're going to just have to trust me on this."

Trust? How could I trust him when he'd proven himself so easily swayed in the past? But what choice did I have? Throwing a fit and starting a fight would only make his mind more closed to other possibilities. Plus, like his decisions or not, Orpheus always tried to do what was in the best interest for the entire race. I might not always like the results, but I couldn't fault his intentions. So instead of arguing with him, I sighed. "Okay, since you trusted Rhea and me to take care of Maisie, I'll trust you to not fuck up in choosing a good leader."

His lip twitched. "Thanks so much for that vote of confidence."

After my discussion with Orpheus, I returned to the apartment for a quick shower before Georgia and I headed out to find Michael. She sat on the couch, dressed and ready to go when I walked in.

"There you are," she said, sounding nervous. "I was worried you'd bailed."

"Just grabbed a quick workout. I need to change and then we can go," I said. "Where are Giguhl and Pussy Willow?"

"They had to go audition some new girls for the Roller Derby team. They have another bout in a couple of nights."

I frowned. "Why do they need new girls?"

Georgia looked uncomfortable. "If our talk with Michael doesn't go well, they'll be down two players."

I nodded but didn't comment. I didn't want to entertain the possibility of the talk not having a positive outcome. "I'll be right back."

When I reached my room, I noticed right away something was off. I couldn't put my finger on it, but I knew Adam had been there. I stepped back into the hall. "Hey, Georgia?"

"Yeah?"

"Was Adam here?"

A beat. "Yes. He came to get some clothes while you were gone. I'm sorry I didn't mention it but I didn't want to upset you."

It was a good thing she couldn't see me from the living room because her news made me slump against the wall in defeat. Had Adam been watching the apartment, hoping I'd leave so he could sneak in? Was he really that determined not to be near me?

"Sabina?" Georgia called, waiting for an answer.

Forcing a casual tone, I called back, "Did he say where he's staying?"

"No," she admitted. "He didn't say much at all, actually."

"Okay, thanks."

I escaped into my room and headed to the bathroom. Next to the sink, a glaring blank spot where Adam's toothbrush normally sat flashed like neon. It was such a small thing, the absence, but it felt huge.

I forced myself to turn away before I took an inventory of everything else he'd taken. Soon, the shower's hot spray eased my tense muscles. The soap scrubbed off the stink and sweat, like a baptism. Too bad it couldn't wash away the regret.

24

Georgia and I walked into Vein an hour later. I'd made a few calls after my shower and tracked Michael down to the club. Apparently, he had a weekly meeting with The Shade to report on pack business. With the Despina back in Los Angeles and the new leader not being announced for a few days, Slade was still unofficially in charge of the Black Light District.

I didn't have mixed feelings about seeing Slade. No, I felt very strongly that he was the last person I wanted to see. But I'd promised Georgia we'd talk to Michael, so I didn't have a choice.

When we arrived, Michael and Slade stood at the bar, talking over a couple of beers. Across the bar, I spotted Giguhl and Pussy Willow near the stage. Judging from their stiff postures and jerky movements, they were arguing about something and didn't notice our arrival. Seeing my minion helped me relax a fraction. If this conversation didn't go well, it was nice to know he'd have my back.

"Oh, gods," Georgia groaned. "I don't know if I can do this. I thought Mac would be here."

I grabbed her hand. "Michael's probably keeping her out of the public so she won't do anything dumb." I turned to Georgia and made her look at me. "Remember why we're here. Keep a hold of yourself and we'll get through this, okay?"

Michael had his back to us and hadn't seen us come in yet. However, Slade and Rex, Michael's Beta, spotted us immediately. If the Beta had a reaction to seeing us, he didn't show it except for a slight tensing around his eyes. Rex knew me so he wouldn't stop me from approaching the Alpha, but one look from Michael and the Beta wouldn't hesitate to intervene. Which might happen the instant Michael got an eyeful of the vampire by my side.

"How are we going to play this?" Georgia whispered to me as we made our way over.

"Michael doesn't like games. Our best bet is a direct approach," I said. "Direct but diplomatic."

"Okay," she breathed out. "Here goes nothing."

I tapped the Alpha on the shoulder. "Michael?"

He turned then, his eyebrows raised. But when he saw Georgia and me standing there, those same brows slammed down. "Oh, it's you," he said, his voice dripping scorn. "Back to cause more trouble?"

"Don't be like that, Mike. We just want a couple of moments of your time."

"Well, you can't have them. I have nothing more to say to you." He started to turn around and dismiss us altogether. I slammed a hand on the bar in front of him. The club went silent as the patrons perked up at the first sign of confrontation.

"I'm not asking you to talk," I said. "Just to listen."

"What makes you think I want to hear anything you'd have to say?" he countered.

"Maybe you should move this conversation to my office," Slade said, his voice tense.

Michael threw back his beer and shook his head. "Thank you for the offer, but we won't be needing it." He slammed his beer down and turned to glare at me. "Listen, Sabina, I know we've got some history. You probably thought our friendship might soften me toward your pleas on behalf of your vampire friend there. But this isn't about friendship. It's pack business."

"I understand that," I said. "But—"

His casual tone disappeared. "I said no," he snapped. "Now, if you have other business to discuss, say your piece. Otherwise, I'll bid you a good night and ask you to be on your way."

That did it: I understood Michael was Alpha and all, but no one dismissed me like that. Especially someone who was being a stubborn ass. I stepped forward and, keeping my voice low, said, "Will you stop being such a blind fool for a moment and think about what you're doing?"

Georgia groaned. "So much for diplomatic."

I ignored her and stared down the were. I knew I was taking a big risk challenging him publicly, but if I let him walk away, Mac's fate was sealed. "I respect the hell out of you, Michael. Usually. But you're letting your pride get in the way here. Mac doesn't want to mate with anyone but Georgia."

The Alpha moved toward me. I held my ground. He'd never raise a hand to me. He knew I had the skills to back up my talk and wouldn't hesitate to take him down. Besides, he might be the Alpha of his pack, but I was a member of the highest-ranking mage and vampire families and had a badass demon for a sidekick.

"You listen to me, now," Michael said, his tone hard and

low. "Our ways may seem unfair to you, but there is a good reason we arrange mates for our females. Werewolf numbers are small compared to the other races. To ensure the health and future of our kind, we must be careful to avoid inbreeding, which is why matings are arranged between packs. Doing so keeps the bloodlines clean and also strengthens the race as a whole." He crossed his arms and looked me dead in the eye. "What kind of example would I be setting if I allowed my own kin to mate with a vampire? You of all beings should also be aware that interracial mixing is against the Black Covenant."

The dig against my own tarnished lineage hit home. I gritted my teeth and struggled to maintain my calm. "I'm sympathetic to your reasons. But forcing Mac into a mating scenario with a male she doesn't want is as good as selling her into slavery. On top of that, you know damned well she doesn't want to lie with men, period."

Michael's fists clenched into rocks. "You're lucky you're surrounded by beings who would protect you tonight, mixed blood. Otherwise that duel we fought four months ago would look like a play date compared to what I want to do to you right now."

I raised my chin. "You mean the duel that you couldn't win? Don't flatter yourself, werepuppy. If we threw down now, I'd own your fucking pack by dawn."

Michael's growl made the hair on my neck prickle. Too late, I realized I'd gone too far challenging him in public. But I couldn't help it. I sent a prayer of thanks to the Goddess that it wasn't a full moon.

Beside the were, Slade tensed to intervene. From across the bar, Giguhl started in our direction, ready to get my back. A firm shake of my head told them both to stand down.

"Fucking werewolves," I spat. "Using females like broodmares so your mighty patriarchy can continue uninterrupted. Well, guess what? One of these days, those females you use will rise up and take over your power. But then I guess that's why you're so set on selling Mac to the highest bidder. She dared to shun the potent werewolf cock."

"Sabina." Slade's quiet warning sounded loud in the tense silence. "That's enough."

I slashed a hand through the air. "I'm done. Let's go, Georgia."

I marched off with my head held high. But I quickly realized that Georgia had not followed. When I turned back around, I saw the vampire standing in front of Michael like an Amazon.

"Georgia!" I called. "Come on."

"No!" she said, her voice high and clear. "Not until I've said what I came here to say."

I frowned. After my brilliant oration, I couldn't imagine there was much she could say to salvage the discussion. Still, she had the right to speak her mind.

"Mr. Romulus, my name is Georgia Rousseau. For the last year, I have had the honor of loving your niece. I have never met a more loyal female in my life. But you have betrayed that loyalty."

Michael crossed his arms. "Correct me if I'm wrong, but didn't you renounce your relationship to Mac last night?"

Georgia opened her arms to signal her vulnerability. I winced at the move, which would only been seen as weakness by the Alpha. "Last night I was hurt and angry. Mac promised me she'd already told you about us. So when you showed up and it was clear she'd lied, I was heartbroken. I thought that removing myself from her life would make Mac's choice easier." She lifted a shaking finger and pointed it at Michael's chest. "But now I realize that instead of helping her, I doomed her to live under a tyrant. Sabina helped me realize that as a werewolf, Mac's loyalty to her pack was as ingrained as her body's reaction to the full moon. But you've taken advantage of that loyalty and turned it into something ugly.

"I love Mac. However, I am willing to step aside if she chooses to do as her Alpha wishes. But she deserves a real choice. Not this blackmail disguised as duty. You don't want her to be with me? I can accept that. But let her choose her own were mate."

Michael's expression became harder, if possible. "I would never expect a vampire to understand the meaning of duty. You take what you want and damn the consequences for anyone else."

"I understand something stronger than duty," she said, her voice trembling with earnest conviction. "I understand love."

Michael tossed back his head and laughed. "You're a fool. Duty is love. Love is duty. What you're talking about is lust. And I'm not about to let my niece throw her family away because she's going through some sort of rebellious sexual experimentation phase."

Michael crossed his arms and looked Georgia right in the eye. "Whether you like it or not, Mac and Logan are already legally mated. I was going to wait until the Lupercalia rites to consecrate their union, but I see now that waiting would be a mistake. Their union will be made sacred on the full moon two nights from now." Georgia gasped and opened her mouth to argue, but Michael held up a hand. "I've tolerated your pleas because I believe in giving a person their say. But you've had it and that's that. If you try to contact Mac, I will consider it an aggressive act and have my men take action against you. Am I clear?"

Georgia's mouth opened and closed in shock, but she managed to nod.

Dismissing her, Michael slapped Slade on the shoulder. "Thanks for the beer, Slade, but if you'll excuse me I've had quite enough socializing for one evening." He motioned to his Beta. "Let's go."

He brushed past Georgia and walked toward me. My eyes narrowed into slits and I braced to deliver my last word. Instead, Michael made a preemptive strike. "You're one hell of a fighter, Sabina, but you suck at matchmaking. Stay the hell out of my pack's business."

Michael and Rex stormed out of the bar, leaving the rest of us behind to wallow in their wakes.

"That went well," Slade observed in a droll tone. "All things considered."

"How can you say that?" I demanded. From the corner of my eyes, I saw Giguhl and PW approaching. They looked like two bloodhounds hot on the trail of drama.

"Sabina, you publicly challenged an Alpha werewolf's authority and ability to lead his pack. You're lucky you're not short a couple of limbs."

I shot him a piss-off look and went to check on Georgia. Giguhl had an arm around her and PW rubbed her shoulder. Her head was down so I couldn't see her expression.

"Georgia?" I said, finally reaching them. "How are you doing?"

She looked up then. Instead of shining with tears, her eyes glinted with rage. I pulled back a fraction, shocked. "Georgia?"

"You!" she spat. "This is all your fault!"

My head tilted in confusion. Granted, I probably didn't help matters by calling Michael out, but the entire situation was hardly my doing. "Georgia—"

"Shut up!" she said. "If I hadn't listened to you, I would already be back in New Orleans and on my way to getting over Mac instead of embarrassing myself in public!" She wilted then, tears spilling from her eyes like acid rain, destroying her eye makeup and leaving black trails down her face. PW took the vampire from Giguhl and led her away.

Giguhl had the same look most males get once things go emotional and the tears start falling. "I guess now's not the best time to ask if you've talked to Adam?"

I glared at my minion with the ridiculously bad timing. "Bite me, demon."

"What's this?" Slade said, shit-eating grin locked firmly in place. "Trouble in paradise already?"

Oh, shit. The last thing I wanted was for Slade to find out he'd been the cause of my argument with the mancy. Luckily—or unluckily, depending on how you looked at it—Alexis Vega chose that moment to sashay into the bar.

"Sabina!" she called when she spotted me. Slade groaned. Good, I shouldn't be the only one uncomfortable.

"Oh, look, it's Vampira." Giguhl's tone was as dry as an Alcoholics Anonymous meeting.

I swallowed the bitter taste that sprang on my tongue the minute she'd walked in. "Shouldn't you be in L.A. with the Despina?" I asked, trying not to sound too disappointed to see her.

"She asked me to stay here to monitor things." Her tone implied I was one of the "things" she was monitoring. "Slade, how about a drink?"

Slade tensed beside me. "I'm not the bartender."

She grinned. "With that kind of attitude you're likely to fail as a bar owner almost as spectacularly as you failed as the leader of the Black Light District."

Slade tensed to strike. I grabbed his arm. "What do you want, Alexis?"

She shrugged and plopped on a stool. Her latex-covered ass squeaked against the vinyl seat. "Oh, nothing. Just wanted to gloat a little."

"About what?" I asked. But I already knew. She'd come to deliver that I-told-you-so I'd been dreading.

"It's been five nights without another murder. You know what that means, don't you?"

"No, but I doubt you're going to leave me in the dark for long."

"It means we got the right guy," she said.

"Oh, that's right. Does that also mean the Despina's already given you Slade's old job?" I knew Tanith had done no such thing. But I couldn't help digging at her massive ego.

Alexis's face tightened. "Not yet. I'm sure she's just planning on announcing it at the treaty signing. You know Tanith—she loves to make a big deal."

I cocked a brow. Actually, of all three of the Dominae, Tanith was the least enthusiastic about...well, everything. She was far more likely to call a business meeting than to make a fuss. "Or maybe she's decided you aren't the best woman for the job after all."

"Please," Alexis said. "Who else would they choose?"

I shrugged. "I don't know, but surely there are other beings who'd do a better job. Hell, even Giguhl would do a better job."

"Thanks, I think," Giguhl said.

Alexis shrugged. "Whatever. You're just in a bad mood because your boyfriend's sleeping at the Crossroads."

I stilled as shock froze my bloodstream.

"I ran into him there earlier. He looked terrible," she said with false casualness. "What happened, Sabina? He finally get tired of you?"

Giguhl grabbed my shoulder when I tensed. He stabbed the vampiress with an icy glare.

"If I were you I'd stop talking now."

Her lips curled up into a feline smile. Luckily, she wasn't as much of an idiot as I thought because she didn't respond. Instead, she snapped her fingers in Earl's direction. He was standing at the other end of the bar, reading the newspaper. "What's a vampire gotta do to get some blood around here?" she called.

Earl looked up slowly. Alexis spread her arms in a what's-taking-so-long gesture. Earl rolled his eyes and sauntered toward her. While she took her time choosing her poison, Slade pulled me away. "What's up with you and Adam?"

"As much as I'm sure you'd love to know so you can make jokes," I said, crossing my arms, "it's none of your business."

He had the audacity to look wounded. "Sabina, please. It's true I enjoy poking fun at the two of you, but it sounds like this is serious. If you need to talk about it, I'm here."

I eased up on my glare. It wasn't Slade's fault I'd screwed up. "Don't worry about it. We're just going through a rough patch. All couples do, I hear."

"If you say so." He looked skeptical.

At that point, PW and Georgia emerged from the ladies' room they'd disappeared into earlier. Georgia's face was scrubbed clean of makeup. Her eyes were red-rimmed and puffy. She looked young, vulnerable. But Pussy Willow looked like a mama bear protecting her cub. "We're leaving," she announced, her head held high.

"Okay, we'll see you back at the apartment," Giguhl said.

"No. You don't understand," she said. "We're not just leaving Vein. We're leaving this godsforsaken city."

I'd kind of expected Georgia to leave. After all, until I'd intervened, that'd been her plan. But this was the first I'd heard of PW wanting to go. Before I could question her, though, Giguhl did it for me. "What do you mean 'we're'?"

She raised her chin. "I'm leaving, too. I don't belong in New York. I thought coming here would be an adventure. A chance for a fresh start." She cocked a hip and crossed her arms. "Boy, was I an idiot."

"I had no idea you were unhappy here, PW," I said.

"I wasn't at first. But I have some things to work out." She glanced toward Giguhl. Something heavy passed between them in that moment. Regret, maybe? "Anyway, I called Zen and she said my old job is waiting for me."

Zen's full name was Madame Zenobia Foucher. In addition to being a voodoo priestess, she owned a voodoo store and apothecary in the French Quarter. Madame Z was as New Orleans as Mardi Gras and gumbo. We'd butted heads a bit, but I respected the hell out of her.

I glanced at Giguhl, knowing that of all of us he'd have the most important opinion on the subject of PW's departure. His posture was stiff and guarded, like he worried one false move might make her disappear. "Why can't you work it out here?"

"You know I can't do that. Not anymore. Besides, I miss N'Awlins like a phantom limb." She approached G and put a hand on his green cheek. "Plus, you've got your own stuff to work out here." She nodded toward me. "One day you'll be free, little Gigi."

My eyebrows slammed down. There was so much wrong with what she just said I wasn't sure where to begin. "Hold on," I said. "What the hell does that mean?"

PW turned on me, her red lips crumpled into a harsh pout. "Giguhl will never be truly happy until you release him from slavery."

I put my hands on my hips. I'd been getting attitude from the faery for weeks and never understood what I'd done to piss her off. I had no idea she believed I was being unfair to Giguhl. It was freakin' ridiculous. Unfortunately for the changeling, I'd had just about enough of everyone's shit to last the rest of my immortal life.

"Listen, Pussy, I'm not sure what kind of diva hormones made you lose your damned mind, but Giguhl is nobody's slave." I stepped closer to her. She crossed her arms and glared up at me. "I have never pretended to understand your special friendship, but I have done nothing to get in the middle of it. Nor have I done anything to restrict his freedom beyond the natural limitations of our arrangement that I have no control over. If you're having problems, don't lay them on my doorstep."

"Oh, really? You haven't restricted his freedom?" she challenged. Then she ticked off all my sins on her red-tipped fingers. "He can't go anywhere without your permission. He isn't allowed to make any choices without your input. And every time you force him to switch between his magnificent and sexy demon form into that embarrassing hairless carcass he dies a little more inside."

My eyes shifted toward Giguhl. He wouldn't look at me. Instead, his arms were crossed and a red flush spread across his cheek scales. "Giguhl? Is that true?"

"It doesn't really matter, does it?" he said, sidestepping that minefield. "This is about Pussy Willow running away."

He pointed a claw at her. "Right, babe? Shit got real and now you're booking."

I raised my eyebrows. What the hell was up with these two?

PW pursed her lips but wouldn't meet his eyes.

Georgia, who until this point had stood by looking miserable, plugged back into the conversation. "Let's go, PW."

Giguhl, realizing this was his last chance to have his say, marched over to PW and grabbed her arm. "Can I speak to you alone?"

Without waiting for her answer, he pulled her toward the shadows under the stairs leading to Slade's office. I tried to pretend I didn't want to eavesdrop on their conversation, but who was I kidding? I started to sidle in their direction, but Slade stopped me. "Do you need a place to stay?"

"Excuse me?"

He shrugged. "I just figured if you and the mancy were on the skids, maybe you'd need a place to crash." The look in his eyes told me that sleeping was the last item on his to-do list.

"Slade, not now." I started to dismiss him altogether, but paused. On second thought, maybe it was time I laid this out for him in clear language. "Actually, scratch that. I need you to understand something. I won't be 'crashing' with you ever again. Am I clear?"

His jaw went hard. "I was just trying to help."

"Yeah, help me out of my pants," I shot back. "Look, we had some fun. It's over now. I thought we'd discussed this already."

"Sabina, I don't know what the hell is going on with you, but I have no intention of making a move on you. You made your feelings quite clear on that score months ago."

I grimaced. He was right. I'd set him straight back in

October just before we'd left New York to go find Maisie. "I'm sorry. I didn't mean to insult you."

"That said, if you change your mind, I make an excellent fuck buddy."

My lips twitched. "Dude, why don't you try that shit on Alexis? She's totally your type."

"Now I really am offended." He tried to sound mad, but an undertone of interest filled the spaces between the words. "That bitch wants my job."

"Slade, do you really expect me to believe you wouldn't fuck her anyway?"

He fanged his lip and looked over at the bitchinatrix. "I didn't say that."

Males, I thought. "Go for it, stud."

He looked back at me quickly, his expression unsure. "You wouldn't be mad?"

"Hell no. Maybe a good lay will improve her disposition." *And keep both of you out of my hair*, I silently added.

He pursed his lips. "I'll think about it." Then he made a beeline toward her. That taken care of, I turned back to see Giguhl and Pussy Willow coming toward me. The demon's shoulders slumped. Not a good sign.

I raised my brows in question. "Well?"

PW raised her chin. "You win this time, Sabina. He's yours."

I rolled my eyes. "I'm sorry you're leaving. Give my best to Zen. Maybe we'll come down for a visit soon."

She hesitated, like she felt guilty for being so bitchy. Then she tossed her wigged head back and strutted away like a he-woman on a mission. Giguhl sidled up to me, his shoulders slumping. I patted his arm as we both watched the vampire and faery take their leave. "Sorry, G."

He sighed forlornly and shrugged. "Not your fault. She's punishing me."

Frowning, I looked up at him. "Why?"

He pressed his lips together firmly, like he wasn't going to tell. Then, he blew out a breath. "I told her she needed to stop hiding behind that broke-down wig and deal with her shit."

My mouth fell open. "Really?"

He nodded solemnly. "Don't get me wrong. Pussy Willow is fun. But I miss Brooks sometimes. He was nicer and more real, you know?" He crossed his arms. "Anyway, that's what we were arguing about when you got here tonight. I told her it was time to get over what happened in New Orleans and move on. She needs to figure out how to find synergy between both sides of herself so she can live her truth."

Hearing the word "synergy" come from a seven-foot-tall demon threw me off for a moment. "Let me guess," I said. "Oprah?"

"She's pretty wise...for a mortal." Giguhl shrugged. "But it wasn't just Oprah. I care about that fae bitch too much to let her keep fooling herself".

My memory flashed back to the night when the faery decided to leave Brooks behind and adopt his drag queen persona full time. The decision came after a particularly vicious attack that almost killed the faery. At the time, I understood why the changeling felt that wearing the wigs and dresses made him feel insulated from harsh reality. But the longer Brooks maintained the illusion of Pussy Willow, the less likable he became. "Wow, G, I have no idea what to say. You were a good friend to be so honest with her."

The demon huffed out an ironic laugh. "Right. If I'm such a good friend, why did she just kick me to the curb?"

"Maybe she's not ready to face her figurative demons so she decided to get rid of a literal one."

Giguhl shook his horned head sadly. "Denial ain't just a river in Egypt, Red."

"Amen, Gigi."

25

The next evening, I woke on the couch with a spoon stuck to my cheek. Following the dramatic exit of the faery and vampire from our lives, Giguhl and I had retired back at the apartment to drown our sorrows in gallons of ice cream and a couple of bottles of tequila we'd stolen from Slade's bar.

My head pounded like a bass drum and my eyes burned in the dusk's unholy light. A groan to my right had me turning over to peer at the floor. Giguhl had one leg propped up on the coffee table and the rest of his large body sprawled on the kilim rug in front of the couch. "Red?" he hissed.

"Mrrph," I replied.

"Am I dead?"

"Maybe," I said with a groan. "If so, we were sent to the Pit of Despair."

His eyes popped open. He smacked his black lips together and grimaced. "I think a feral cat broke in while we were sleeping and shat in my mouth."

I couldn't argue with that sentiment, so instead I moaned

and sat up. Immediately, regret set in. "Why did we think mixing tequila with triple chocolate heartbreak crunch would be a good idea?"

Giguhl hoisted himself into a sitting position, his knees pulled up against his chest. "I'm never drinking again."

I shot him a look.

"Okay, I'm never drinking again *today*."

I scrubbed my face and stood up. "I've got to get moving. Rhea is expecting me at the Crossroads in an hour."

"What's going on there?" Giguhl asked. I realized then that we'd both been so wrapped up in personal dramas that I hadn't filled him in on the Maisie situation. I gave him a quick rundown on the plan. His bloodshot eyes widened. "Holy crap! You're drugging her?"

I cringed both from the guilt and the effect his shriek had on my fragile cranium. "Not exactly. Just giving her a mild sedative."

"Sabina, please. You're totally drugging her."

"Okay, fine. We're drugging her. But it's for her own good."

"Well, I'll give you this. If Rhea thinks it's for the best, then it probably is."

"Yeah."

Giguhl squinted at me. "Why don't you sound convinced."

"I am. It's just that I haven't seen Rhea since my fight with Adam. I'm worried she's going to read me the riot act."

"Maybe he hasn't told her what happened?" His tone was heavy with skepticism.

"Who knows? I haven't seen him." But Alexis had—at the Crossroads. Would he be there that night when I went to help Rhea? The thought made me even more nauseous.

Giguhl rose and came to pat me on the shoulder. "He'll

come to you when he's ready. You hurt him, Red. He needs time to get a handle on his feelings. In the meantime, focus on helping Maisie. I know you feel guilty about the means, but like you said, it's for her own good."

I didn't want to keep talking about all this. I needed to keep busy or I'd end up right back on that couch with tequila. Instead, I busied myself making coffee.

"So what's your plan tonight?" I said, changing the subject.

Giguhl groaned and came to lean his elbows on the counter separating the kitchen from the living area. "I've got to find some warm bodies for the Marauders. We've got another bout the night after tomorrow."

I paused in the process of scooping grounds into the coffee filter. "Another one so soon? I'm surprised."

The demon shrugged. "I guess getting canned by Orpheus lit a fire under Slade. He's filling Vein's event schedule to try to make up for the income he's gonna lose running drugs for the Hekate Council."

Even though Slade's main job for the Council was peacekeeping among the nonmage races in the city, he also made a pretty penny running the mages' "herbal remedies" through the Black Light District. Made sense that he'd be looking to make Vein more lucrative now. "So you need to find two girls to replace Mac and Georgia?"

He shook his head. "I wouldn't have needed any but the next bout happens the night after the full moon. The league requires no werewolves play during the four-day window on either side of the full moon. That means the other were I had on the bench as a sub for the last bout is out of the picture, too. I'd like to find a few new players so we have substitutions, but with such short notice I'll be lucky to find the one player I have to have to meet the requirements for a full roster."

I closed the lid on the pot and hit the start button. "What about the nymphs?"

"No dice," he said. "Slade's short-staffed as it is and said he can't afford to take another nymph off rotation for the night. Besides, I need someone stronger than a faery." He paused dramatically. "I need a vampire."

The heavenly scent of coffee drifted from the machine. I took a deep breath, wishing I could inhale the caffeine directly into my bloodstream.

"It's too bad Alexis said no," Giguhl said, his tone baiting. "From what you've told me, she'd be ruthless on wheels."

I tilted my head and waited for Giguhl to look up. Finally, his eyes peeked up and he laughed. "Don't give me that look, trampire. You know I love stirring your shit." He bit his lip. "What do you say?"

I pursed my lips and played dumb. "Say about what?"

"Gods, you're such a diva. Pretty please, Sabina, will you join my Roller Derby team?"

I turned away to hide my smile and grab two mugs from the cupboard. "Correct me if I'm wrong, but aren't you the one who said I'm not a team player?"

"C'mon," he groaned. "Don't make me beg."

I set the mugs on the counter and pretended to think it over as I poured the coffee. "I suppose I could drag this out and make you suffer, but if your hangover is as bad as mine, you're already in enough pain." I took a deep breath. "Yes, I will join the team."

"Yes!" He pumped a fist.

"But just until you find someone else."

"Sure, whatever." He nodded distractedly. "We're going to have to think of a good name for you."

Remembering the silly names all the girls adopted, I grimaced. "Really?"

He pulled back, surprised. "Of course. It's tradition." He looked me up and down, tapping a claw on his lips. "How about Madam Menace?"

"Lame," I said over the steaming cup.

"Buffy the Roller Slayer Girl?"

I rolled my eyes. "How about Bloody Mary?"

"Sabina, please," Giguhl said. "This is serious."

I shrugged. "Fine, you figure it out and let me know what you decide. I've got to get going."

He waved a claw to indicate he'd already dismissed me. I polished off my coffee and grabbed a bag of blood on the way to my room for a quick shower. By the time I emerged a little while later, I felt like a new woman.

Just in time to go drug my sister and face my estranged lover's overprotective aunt.

Thirty minutes later, I turned Adam's SUV off the highway and onto the dirt road leading to the mage estate. I hadn't hesitated to take his car. Until I heard otherwise, I assumed I still had the right to use it. Besides, he had the ability to travel magically and I did not.

But honestly, on the drive up, I had plenty of time to stew about the situation and embrace my anger about his continued avoidance of me. It's not that I didn't accept my responsibility in the matter. I knew I was wrong and I felt guilty as hell. But I also felt that after everything we'd been through together and shared, I deserved the opportunity to explain my side of things. Part of me was even hoping he'd be at the manor when I arrived. I just wanted to get the fight over with so we could start picking up the pieces.

I pulled the gas guzzler up to the huge black gates set about a mile into the forest. The two iron gates met in the middle to form a Hekate's Wheel design. As usual, the magical wards protecting the entrance made the hairs on my neck stand at attention. I rolled down the window and punched the code to gain entrance. A surveillance camera above the box whirred to life as the mage on the other end focused on my face to verify my identity. I wiggled my fingers at it. A few seconds later, the gates creaked open.

As I drove through the grounds, I ignored the butterfly fight club in my gut. I hadn't seen Maisie since our argument in the greenhouse. I wondered if Rhea warned her I was coming or if I was going to be the first in a night full of nasty surprises. I sucked a deep breath through my nose and repeated my new mantra: "It's for her own good."

Soon, the forest opened to reveal the estate itself. It glowed like a mirage from some old-time fairy tale. With its spires and turrets and mix of architectural styles, it looked like schizophrenia translated into architecture. I pulled the car into the wide circular drive out front and cut the engine.

Before I could pause to collect my thoughts, the front door opened wide and Rhea emerged. Seeing me sitting in the dark car, she waved an impatient hand to hurry me on. Left with no choice but to comply, I got out.

"You're late," she called.

This time I really was. "Sorry. Did you start without me?" I said, climbing the steps.

"No, the chef is just laying out the first course now." She pushed me toward the door, chattering as we walked. "I'll slip the sedative into her drink during the main course. By dessert, she'll be out."

I blew out a breath. "Okay. What do you need me to do?"

"Just act natural. You'll come in later, once we move her to the *abaton*."

I paused. "What's that?"

She urged me forward, obviously not wanting any more delays. "It's the official name for a space used for dream incubation. In this case, the old chapel on the east end of the grounds."

I'd never seen an old chapel on the grounds, but as large as they were, that didn't surprise me. "Sounds good," I said for lack of anything clever. I couldn't help feeling on edge. Not just because of what we were about to do, but also because I was waiting for her to mention the Adam thing. As it turned out, I didn't have to wait long. But first, I had to get through seeing Maisie.

Rhea pushed me through the dining room doors. "Look who decided to join us," the elder mage called, her tone overly jovial.

Maisie looked up in surprise. Her brow knitted into a frown and she didn't say anything. Obviously, I wasn't the only one recalling our last conversation.

Rhea brushed past me, shooting me a look to remind me to act natural. I wanted to remind her that I used to be an assassin not an actress. But that didn't really matter because it was obviously up to me to get the ball rolling with Maisie.

"Hey, Maze," I said.

She rolled her tongue into her cheek. "I didn't know you were coming."

I cleared my throat. So much for warm greetings. Taking my seat, I flashed her a smile. "Rhea invited me."

Maisie shot Rhea a look, clearly believing the mage had set up the dinner as some sort of sisterly reconciliation. Rhea, a much better actress than yours truly, shrugged and looked abashed. "I thought it might be nice for all of us to sit down to a nice meal together. It's been too long, don't you think?"

Maisie shrugged. "Whatever." She busied herself by fussing with her napkin.

I grabbed my glass of water and took a drink to cover a visual inventory of my twin. Judging from the look of her, my idea of sticking a guard on her had prevented her from feeding from anyone. But the lack of blood also meant she couldn't maintain the glamour she'd been using to hide her physical deterioration. The circles under her eyes had darkened into bruises, like she'd been punched. Her cheeks had hollowed out and her hand shook when she lifted it to smooth a stray hair. I was surprised she managed to sit upright given how exhausted she looked.

"So, Sabina," Rhea said into the tense silence. "Is something wrong with Adam?"

The innocent question caught me off guard. I accidentally sucked down an ice cube and immediately choked. A violent coughing fit followed. Rhea jumped from her chair and pounded my back until I managed to swallow the frozen shard.

"Are you all right?" Rhea said, forcing me to look at her.

I swallowed against the pain in my throat and nodded. "Wrong pipe," I gasped.

"Hmmph." She gave my back one more pat for good measure and took her seat. "Well?"

"What?" I said, my voice hoarse.

"Adam?"

I shifted uneasily in my seat. Obviously, she hadn't seen Adam. Rhea might be a good actress, but if she knew what had happened, she wouldn't bother digging for info. She would have come out and asked me what the hell I'd been thinking treating her nephew like that. "Not sure," I said, evading. "He's been so busy we haven't seen much of each other lately. Probably, he's just stressed about keeping everyone safe at the festival." It wasn't exactly a lie, but it was much easier than the full truth.

Luckily, I was saved from further questioning when the door to the kitchen opened and servants entered with trays of food.

"So, Maisie," I said, "what did you do today?"

She stabbed at her food with her fork. "Rhea made me meditate in the Sacred Grove." Her tone was petulant.

"Who wants wine?" Rhea asked quickly. Obviously, the meditation had been a part of the covert prep for the incubation.

Before we could answer, Rhea rose and went to the side-board. Behind my sister's back, Rhea looked at me and gestured for me to make conversation. So with one eye on the vial Rhea produced to drug my sister's drink and the other on my unsuspecting sibling, I tried to mend fences. "I'm sorry, Maze," I said quietly.

She looked up. Her expression uncertain. "For what?"

I heaved a deep sigh. Good question. Was I apologizing for our fight or for betraying her? Probably both, I decided. But for now, I'd focus on past sins. "For our argument the other day. I know you've been going through a lot. Maybe I haven't been there for you as much as I could have."

Her cheeks turned pink. "Forget about it."

Rhea poured white powder into one of the wineglasses. I watched the granules fall and felt my conscience rise.

"I can't forget about it," I said, my voice tinged with remorse. "I can't imagine how hard it's been for you. And I know that I could have done more to protect you."

"Sabina—" she began, but I shook my head.

"Don't say it's okay. It's not." Behind Maisie, Rhea paused and turned to shoot me a concerned look. I ignored her and continued. "But I'm going to make it right."

Rhea came forward then and set Maisie's wine by her hand. "Here you go!" Her tone was overly bright.

Ignoring Rhea, Maisie snorted, a harsh sound. "Sabina, believe it or not, everything that happens isn't about you."

I pulled back, stung. "That's not what I meant. I—"

She lifted the wineglass and took a long drink. When she'd swallowed it, she glared at me. "You think the world revolves around you? Well, it doesn't. My problems are just that—my problems. I don't need you or anyone else to save me."

Rhea, quiet as a ghost, came around the table and handed me a glass of wine. "Careful," she whispered.

I looked up at her. Her eyes pleaded with me to let the matter drop. But I couldn't. Not now. If Maisie woke up in a few hours and realized what we'd done, she might never speak to me again. This was my chance to lay it on the table. "Listen to me, Maisie," I said. "Like it or not, I was involved with what happened to you. Lavinia kidnapped you to get to me. She unleashed you on Adam when you were blood crazed to punish me."

"Stop," Maisie whispered brokenly. "Stop it."

"No. This has to be said." I swallowed against the bitter guilt clogging my throat. "I'm sorry. I'm sorry that my coming here led to your being hurt. I'm sorry that I didn't kill Lavinia in California when I had the chance. If I had, then none of this would have happened to you. I'm sorry that I didn't find you sooner in New Orleans." My voice cracked. "But most of all, I'm sorry that being my sister has caused you so much pain."

"Enough!" Maisie roared. She stood so fast her chair crashed back into the sideboard. She opened her mouth to yell at me again, but her body swayed. She grabbed the tablecloth to steady herself.

"Maisie?" Rhea said.

"I—I feel weird." She put a hand to her head.

I jumped up. "You said it would take longer than this," I said to Rhea.

Maisie looked up sharply. "What?"

"She's so weak it must have acted faster than I intended," Rhea said. She moved quickly to Maisie's side.

But my sister ignored the aid Rhea offered. Instead, she glared at me, her eyes hot despite being unfocused. "What have you done?"

With that, Maisie collapsed into Rhea's arms.

26

I followed Rhea through the snow to a section of the mage grounds I'd never visited. Tree limbs tangled overhead, blocking out the almost-full moon's light. We trudged through the stark landscape in silence for what felt like miles. When my toes went numb, I asked Rhea why she didn't just flash us to our destination.

"It's part of the ritual," she said. "The extra effort signals our dedication to the outcome we desire." Her boots crunched in the snow and her cheeks were pink with chill. "The gods are never impressed by those who take the path of least resistance."

Ten minutes later, I wondered if the trek through the ankle-deep snow was really some sort of punishment. But then the moon's rays sparked off a roof's frosted peak.

"What is this place?" I wasn't sure why I was whispering. But something about the dense trees and the deep cold and the weight of our mission demanded a respectful volume.

"The family who built the manor used it as a chapel," Rhea said, stepping over a fallen branch jutting from the snow like a pleading skeletal hand. "When the Hekate Council bought the place, we deconsecrated it and turned it into a meditation retreat."

The building itself was made of old stones. The arched windows were dark but shadows hinted at stained glass. A small spire rose from the roof, but instead of a Christian cross at the top, there was a simple spiral circle forged from black iron. From my studies with Rhea, I remembered the symbol represented the cycles of life and spiritual journeys. Fitting, I thought, for both the building and our purpose.

Rhea opened the large red doors with a large metal key. "Quickly." She waved me in.

Hugging Maisie's limp body to my chest, I ducked through the dark doorway. The air inside was stale and cold, hinting that the space was rarely used. Rhea whispered something behind me. The air shimmered and static crawled across my skin. An instant later, several torches around the room flared to life. I blinked against the sudden illumination.

Once my eyes adjusted, I caught my breath at the beauty of the chapel. Dozens of candle flames flickered in large, wrought-iron candelabras. Set high in three of the walls, large stained-glass windows sparkled in the candlelight. Patches of glass in blues, greens, and purples formed images of gods and magical symbols.

I generally avoided churches as a rule. It wasn't that sacred spaces were dangerous or anything, no matter what mortal vampire lore claimed. It was just the principle of the matter, seeing as how the Big Dude turned his back on all the dark races in favor of his golden children, the mortals. But, like Rhea said, this place wasn't a church anymore. All Christian symbolism had been stripped away and replaced with more familiar and comforting mage and pagan accessories.

Speaking of pagan things, a stone altar squatted under a huge wall sculpture of a snake wrapped around a staff. Rhea waved me toward a space next to the altar. As she spread a pelt of some sort on the ground, she explained the symbol.

"It's the staff of Asclepius. Since he's the god of medicine and healing, the mortals borrowed the symbol for their medical professionals." She motioned me to lay Maisie on the pelt.

"Why aren't we setting her on the altar?"

"We need her as close to the earth as possible for this to work," she said vaguely. "Asclepius is a Chthonic deity, which means his energy is more powerful closer to the earth."

I arranged Maisie on her back with her hands crossed on her chest. Then, looking down at her, I realized the position resembled that of a dead woman. I quickly lowered her hands to her sides. Then I brushed her hair back from her face. Her face had softened in sleep. Gone was the betrayed expression, the anger, she'd had just before the sedative took effect. My stomach cramped with guilt.

It's for her own good.

Rhea set a large black bag on the altar and began removing items. Needing something to do, I went to look them over. Cakes of some sort wrapped in parchment came first.

"Honey cakes," Rhea explained. "To sweeten the god's disposition so he'll listen to our pleas."

She then removed some candles, wooden matches, and bundles of sage. "For cleansing," Rhea explained.

"What can I do?" I said, lifting a smudge stick to my nose. The soothing scent of sage and lavender calmed my nerves.

"You're going into the Liminal with her to make sure she's safe."

My skin went cold. "Jesus, Rhea."

"Look, I know it's scary. I know that you haven't had time to figure out the Liminal or how your powers work there. But we've run out of time here."

"How exactly am I supposed to protect her?"

"Just watch over her. Make sure she's safe until Asclepius arrives to heal her."

"Gods, I wish you had given me a little more warning."

She looked up sharply. "Why? So you could have tried to talk me out of it?" She shrugged. "This way saved time. There's no point in arguing now."

Normally, I eventually came around to Rhea's way of thinking on these matters. But this was some serious shit. The limited experience I'd had in the Liminal was enough to scare me. Add calling on gods and you had a recipe for a clusterfuck. All my experiences with the gods thus far had left me drained and a little freaked out.

"No dice. I've been to the Liminal only once. The only thing we know about it is from a decades-old journal. And that alone was enough to tell me it's too dangerous. You said it yourself: Ameritat was afraid Tristan might not come back." I raised my hands in a pleading gesture, hoping she'd see reason. "I want Maisie cured as much as you do, but toying with powers I can't control yet all but insures disaster. I've failed Maisie too many times to fuck around anymore. There has to be another option besides me going in with her."

Rhea sighed and chewed her lip. "The only other option is to make a larger sacrifice to Asclepius to ensure he'll fulfill our request. More than just honey cakes and a few gold coins."

"What then?"

"A blood sacrifice."

"Why do I get the feeling you're not talking about killing a chicken?"

"Because in this case, the blood sacrifice has to be from the one asking for aid. You're going to have to shed blood on the altar."

"Why me? Maisie's the one doing the incubation."

"Normally it would be her, but since she's unconscious, we're acting as her agents. And since you're tied to her by blood, the offering will mean more coming from you."

The idea of shedding a little blood for my sister didn't bother me that much. After all, it's not like the stuff made me squeamish. And a cut would heal almost as quickly as it split the skin. But I'd been around magic long enough to know there had to be a catch. "What aren't you telling me?"

Rhea grimaced at how easily I'd figured that one out. "Gods are fickle beings, Sabina. If you offer him your blood, it'll bind you to him."

"Bind me how?"

"He'll be able to call on you for a repayment of the favor whenever it suits him."

I sighed. I didn't exactly love the idea of being beholden to a god, but it beat another trip to that fucked-up in-between place. Besides, Asclepius was a god of healing. How bad could any favor he asked be? "I'll do it."

Rhea's eyebrows went up. "You're sure?"

I nodded resolutely. I was tired of talking. It was time to get this done.

"What's first?"

Rhea shot me an approving look. "Set these candles around her body. While you do that, cleanse the athame you'll use in the offering."

I busied myself forming a circle around Maisie with the votives. "How long until she reaches the dreaming stage?"

Rhea lit the smudge stick and paused to check her watch. "Not long now. We need to hurry." She waved the sage over the ceremonial dagger.

I placed the last candle. "Done."

"Okay, I'm going to smudge her now." Rhea's tone was all business now. "Go kneel before the symbol of the god and offer the cakes and the gold pieces. When that's done, use the athame to cut your palm and let three drops of blood fall on the altar. As you do that, ask the god to accept the offerings in return for aid. And, Sabina?"

I stopped and looked up. "Yeah?"

"Try to be humble. The gods know when you're patronizing them."

"I can do humble." I tried not to sound offended but failed, judging from the shake of Rhea's head.

"Sure you can."

I grabbed the cakes and the coins and approached the altar. Kneeling before it, I looked up at the symbol. "Asclepius, please accept these *humble* offerings," I said loud enough for both the god and Rhea to hear me. Then I pulled the dagger across my right palm. The sting was slight and blood welled up instantly. "God of healing, I implore you to aid your servant, Maisie Graecus, this night. Protect her on her journey through the dreamlands. Help her find her visions. Return her to us whole. In exchange for this boon, I, Sabina Kane, offer you my service at a time of your choosing." I squeezed my hand into a fist and squeezed three drops onto the stone.

The instant the third drop hit the altar it sizzled against the stone. The air shimmered and magical static skittered down my spine. The message had apparently been received.

I opened my eyes and stood. When I turned around, Rhea was watching me. Her eyes shone with a light I didn't recognize. "What?" I asked.

Rhea smiled. "Well done."

Suddenly self-conscious, I averted my eyes to Maisie's still form. "Now what?"

Rhea rubbed her hands together. "Now we wait."

Ten minutes later, I sat at Maisie's feet and Rhea behind her head. We'd remained silent but I knew Rhea's head was filled with silent prayers similar to my own.

Lilith, Great Mother of the dark races, protect your daughter and give her strength. Hekate, bringer of light, guide her back to us safely.

By then, it had been almost an hour and a half since Rhea had slipped Maisie the sedative. As if on cue, my sister moaned. My eyes shot to her face. Behind her pale lids, her eyes rolled back and forth in their sockets. I glanced up at Rhea, who nodded to confirm my suspicion—Maisie had entered the dream state.

I tensed, waiting for the first sign of a nightmare. If she cried out or flailed or anything else that indicated distress, I was prepared to force Rhea to rouse her. But other than a couple of eye flutters, she remained peaceful.

The first REM cycle lasted about two minutes and passed uneventfully. When her body relaxed again into deeper sleep, Rhea let out a breath. "So far so good," she whispered. "Hopefully the longer REM cycles will go just as smoothly."

"How many will she have?"

"Three or four, each longer than the last, with ninety minutes between. My guess is that if she's going to have a prophecy dream, it will be in the final cycle, closest to waking."

"How exactly does Asclepius heal people through their dreams?"

"The legends say he appears in the form of a black dog that leads the ill to a sacred spring in the Liminal. Apparently, drinking from this spring can heal even the most grievous wound—physical or mental. But first, the supplicant must be deemed worthy by Asclepius."

"Deemed worthy? How?"

"Purity of heart and intention. But the offerings help, too." She winked. "The gods love presents."

I blew out a breath and adjusted my sitting position to ease the numb spot on my ass from the cold stone floor. "Here's hoping the blood sacrifice will soften his disposition."

Here's the thing: Watching someone sleep isn't exactly the most exciting activity. Sure, every time Maisie hit a REM cycle, we both tensed and watched her like hawks. But my sister hadn't gotten the memo that she was expected to put on a display that we could observe and dissect for clues. Mostly, her dream state involved lots of eye twitching and the occasional shift of position. Eventually, Rhea and I took turns grabbing some sleep of our own. Which is how, six hours into our vigil, I was asleep on the floor.

At first, I wasn't sure what woke me. My first thought was that the sun's ascent roused me. My vampire instincts were fine-tuned for detecting the evil orb's arrival. When it rose, I felt a twinge in my gut, almost like a cramp. My second thought was that it was a mistake to sleep on a hard stone floor. My spine felt like it had been compressed by an industrial vise. I rolled over, trying to ease the kinks out.

That's when I heard the laughter. Opening my eyes, I

realized that sound—so foreign after all these months—is what had really woken me. I sat up slowly, hope blooming in my chest.

Rhea stood over the pallet, her body frozen in shock. Out of the corner of her eye, she saw me rise. She put a finger to her lips. I nodded and padded across the floor to the dais. Closer now, I finally saw the wide smile on my sister's lips. Her eyes were still closed, but whatever she was dreaming was making her happy.

Tears sprung to my eyes. We'd done it. Or rather, Maisie had done it with a little divine intervention.

A few moments later, Maisie's smile faded and she rolled to her side, a move that signaled her exit from the dream world and into a state of deep sleep once more. The move exposed the star on her left shoulder, so like my own. A symbol of our mixed heritage and the bond we shared as twins.

Rhea pulled my sleeve and we retreated to the far end of the altar.

"That was amazing," I whispered.

Rhea reached for me and pulled me into a tight hug. Against my ear, she whispered, "Praise be to the gods."

When she pulled away, her eyes shone with relief and happiness. "We need to move her back to her room before she wakes."

"Why?"

"If she wakes here, she'll realize she was manipulated and it will undo all the progress we've made. It's better for her to believe she did it on her own."

"But surely she'll remember drinking the wine and passing out," I argued.

Rhea shook her head and glanced over to make sure Maisie was still sleeping. "Not necessarily. The sedative is strong. She might remember being in the dining room but not the passing out part. We'll just tell her exhaustion finally caught up with her and we moved her to her rooms."

I sighed. "Okay. Let's do it quickly though. It would really suck if she woke up midtransport."

Two hours later, Maisie found Rhea and me sitting at the breakfast table in the kitchen. She wore a pink silk robe and her hair stood up in odd tufts. She yawned as she entered but stopped when she saw us.

"Good morning," she said, sounding dazed.

"You look like you slept well," Rhea said.

"You know, I think I did." Maisie's eyes squinted as if she was trying to figure out how that was possible. "What happened last night? The last thing I remember is Sabina getting here."

My eyebrows rose. Rhea wasn't kidding about the power of that sedative. But it was fine by me if Maisie didn't remember our argument. "You gave us a bit of a scare," I said. "One minute you were talking and the next you nose-dived into your soup bowl."

Maisie's cheeks turned pink. "Really?"

Rhea rose and put an arm around her shoulders, guiding her to a chair. "And it's no surprise. You looked like death warmed over. You must have been exhausted."

Blue eyes shot to mine. As far as she knew, her lack of

sleep was our secret. "I haven't been sleeping well," she evaded.

Rhea forced an awkward laugh. "Looks like that isn't a problem anymore."

I poured my sister a cup of coffee. "Must be something about the beds here," I said. "I haven't slept that hard in days. I don't even think I had one dream."

Maisie took a sip of coffee, totally unaware she was being played. "Not me. I had this really strange dream."

Rhea and I both spoke at once. "Oh?"

She nodded. "I was alone in a dark forest. A white stag with red horns jumped out at me." Her body shuddered like someone walked over her grave. "But all of a sudden this big black dog jumped out of the shadows and attacked the stag." Maisie busied herself buttering a piece of toast as she spoke, so she missed the look that passed between Rhea and me. "At first, I thought the dog meant me harm, too, but then it scared the stag away."

"That's weird," I said, trying to sound casual. "What happened next?"

"The dog got hurt in the battle but managed to limp over to me. Then it—" She paused and shook her head like she was embarrassed to go on.

"It what?" Rhea prompted; her hand clasped her mug so hard her knuckles were white.

Maisie smiled sheepishly. "It talked to me. Said it was there to help me." She shrugged. "It led me to this underground cavern with a large lake. The dog told me that if I drank from the water I'd feel better. When I knelt at the edge, the water turned to blood. I was scared at first, but for some reason I trusted the dog. And suddenly I realized I was thirstier than I'd ever been. I drank and drank until my stomach was so full I thought I'd burst."

I blew out a breath. "Wow, Maze."

She nodded. "But that's not the weirdest part. After I finished and thanked the dog, he said, 'Tell your sister she owes me big-time.'"

My knife clattered to my plate. As happy as I was that our experiment seemed to be a success, I wasn't looking forward to my comeuppance from Asclepius.

"Sounds like a positive dream," Rhea said quickly to cover my reaction. Then she shot me a keep-it-together look.

"It was," Maisie said. "That stag always scared me."

Rhea put her hand over Maisie's. "From the sound of things, it won't be returning."

Maisie bit her lip. "I hope not." She polished off her toast. "I think I'm going to grab a shower and head to my studio."

"Oh?" Excitement and hope rose in my chest. "Does that mean you had a prophecy?"

"Maybe." Maisie sighed. "It's been so long, it's hard to tell. I'm hoping some time alone with my paints and canvas will help."

"I think spending an afternoon painting will do you some good," Rhea said. "Even if you didn't have a vision last night, maybe the door is open for them now."

Maisie made a noncommittal sound and rose. "Will you be around today, Sabina?"

I looked up, surprised at the interest. "Actually, I'm beat. I might crash in one of the bedrooms until the sun goes down."

Maisie frowned. "I thought you said you slept hard last night."

Shit. "I um." My brain scrambled for a way to cover my slipup. "I did but Rhea had me up at the butt crack of dawn for training. She wore me out again." What was one more lie?

"Oh, okay. Well, come find me when you wake up. Maybe we can hang out, if that's okay with you."

I stifled a yawn and tried to smile. "I'd like that."

When Maisie left, Rhea blew out a breath. "That was close."

"Sorry. I'm so tired my brain feels like oatmeal."

"She bought it, I think." Rhea rose and took her mug to the sink. "Listen, before we both crash, we need to talk. What are we going to do if she didn't have a prophecy?"

I stretched my arms up, trying to stay awake. "You said yourself that the ritual may have opened the door, right? We still have a couple of nights."

"That's the problem. We can't be sure she'll actually sleep. After all, she managed to hide her sleep strike from us before."

I lowered my arms and crossed them. "So what do you suggest?"

Rhea turned and leaned back against the counter. "I think we need to keep drugging her." I opened my mouth to argue but she raised a hand. "It's the only way to ensure she keeps sleeping."

"No offense, Rhea, but I'm already in debt to Asclepius. I can't afford to keep racking up points with him."

"I'm not suggesting we keep doing the incubations. Just adding a little valerian to her food each night should do the trick."

"Oh," I said. "Will taking it that often harm her?"

Rhea shook her head. "No, it's perfectly safe. She'll just be so sleepy she won't be able to keep her eyes open. I wouldn't suggest it if I thought it would damage her."

My limbs felt so heavy that I felt like I'd taken valerian myself. "Whatever you think is best. Just promise me that if it looks like she might be having the nightmares again, you'll stop."

Rhea itched her nose. "Of course."

"All right. I'm going to go grab some sleep before I pass out. I'll check in with you this evening before I head back to the city."

"I'll probably be busy. It's the full moon tonight so I have some rituals to perform."

I paused. I'd totally forgotten that the full moon was that night. That meant that Mac would be officially mated to the Jersey wolf once the sun went down. Honestly, I was torn about going after my confrontation with Michael. On the other hand, I felt Mac deserved to have at least one ally in attendance. Besides, I knew Adam had been invited. And it was way past time my man and I had a little talk.

The Full Hunger Moon was a pale face in the eastern sky. In front of the stage, two young werewolves knelt in the snow at the feet of their Alphas. The ritual prepared the two males for the process of accepting their promised mates.

From what I could tell, the one on the right was Logan Remus, the New Jersey werewolf Mac had been promised to. He had long black hair with a single white streak that fell to the right of his face. Judging from the coy smiles and longing glances sent his way from the young females in the audience, he was considered quite a catch. But I doubted Mac agreed.

The crowd held its collective breath as the Alphas smeared goat blood on the foreheads of the young males. The goat that had involuntarily donated the blood roasted over a spit in the large bonfire along with a dozen others.

I stamped my boots into the hardpacked snow and

wished I'd chosen a spot closer to the bonfire. I made a mental note to listen to Giguhl next time he suggested I not wear stiletto boots to an outdoor werewolf wedding in the middle of winter. But in my defense, I'd worn them because I wanted to look my best in case I ran into Adam.

When I'd left the mage compound earlier, I'd totally forgotten to check in with Maisie. But I'd seen Rhea on her way to perform the full moon rites. She'd reported that Maisie stayed in her studio all day. As promised, Rhea had slipped some valerian in the meal Maisie had requested be brought to her. The last time Rhea had seen my sister, she was smiling and on her way to bed.

Before I left, Rhea promised to tell Maisie where I'd gone and let her know I'd check in with her as soon as I could. She also confirmed that Adam planned on attending the mating ritual. I hadn't seen him in the clearing yet, but I could feel his presence like a pulse among the crowd.

Not for the first time, I wished I could have convinced Giguhl to come with me. But after giving me the unsolicited fashion advice, he'd left for a last-minute practice planned with the Marauders. He'd been annoyed when I told him I wouldn't be able to make it, but once I explained why, he'd relented on his shit talk.

"Be careful, Red," he said. "It's one thing to confront a werewolf in a bar full of friends during the waxing moon. It's something totally different to walk into a werewolf ritual on the full moon."

I'd tamped down the nerves crawling in my belly. "Don't worry, G. I'm not looking for a fight. I know I can't stop the mating from happening. I just…I don't know. I need to be there for Mac."

The demon tilted his head down and looked up at me. "Still, if you run into trouble, summon me, okay?"

At the front of the crowd, the Alphas cleansed the blood off the foreheads of the young champions with bits of wool soaked in milk. "What a waste of perfectly good blood," I said to myself.

A female werewolf standing in front of me in the crowd turned to scowl. I bowed my head in apology. Then I checked my cell phone to see the time. In another fifteen minutes, the entire clearing was going to be filled with hundreds of mooned-out wolves. Not a good time to call attention to myself.

Just then, the two males onstage stood. Given the snow and the frigid February breeze, I wondered what kind of sadist insisted they wear nothing but loincloths made from goat hide. But instead of shivering from the cold, they threw their heads back and laughed at the moon.

A chill ran down my spine at the sound. "What the—"

"It's a show of strength to prove they're capable of protecting their future mates," a deep voice said just behind me. I whipped around to see Adam staring down at me. The breath escaped my lungs in a plume of steam. I hadn't heard him approach and the surprise caught me off guard. All this time I'd been looking for a chance to talk to him, but now that he stood right next to me, my mind went blank.

It felt like I hadn't seen him in years, instead of just days. He looked so good it hurt to gaze directly at him. The only sign he was hurting, too, was the guarded shadows in his eyes. I knew I'd put them there and it made my chest contract.

"Hey," I whispered, brilliant as usual. "Where have you been?"

He shrugged. "Around. Orpheus has been keeping me busy with security issues."

The prim werebitch turned again to shush us. I left out a frustrated breath. We both turned our eyes back to the stage, but tension zinged between our bodies like lightning. The need to touch him was a physical ache.

The wolf warriors stood proudly, their muscles straining and their nipples as sharp as glass shards. If things had been different, I would have leaned into Adam's side and teased him about getting him one of those loincloths. Instead, I clenched my fists tight and struggled not to grab him and drag him away to a secluded place where I could show him how damned sorry I was. How much I'd missed him.

"Have you seen Mac?" he leaned down to whisper. His hot breath on my ear made me close my eyes. Unable to speak, I shook my head.

Needing a distraction, I opened my eyes and stood on my tiptoes. I couldn't spot her among the crowd, but I knew it was only a matter of time before Michael paraded her out for the big event.

"You came alone?" Again with the hot whisper.

I shrugged. "Giguhl had practice."

"I heard PW left," he said.

I jerked my head up to look at him. "Who told you?"

His face was solemn, like he was about to admit a secret. "Slade."

Hearing that name on Adam's lips made my blood go cold. Had Adam gone to confront Slade? Did they fight? I immediately rejected that idea. Why would Slade tell Adam about Pussy Willow and Georgia's departure if Adam went there to beat him up? Besides, it wasn't Adam's style. I yearned to ask questions about their chat, but a ripple of excitement spread through the crowd.

Now that the preparatory rituals were done, Michael

and another male climbed onstage. Judging from the silver at the other male's temples and his regal bearing, this was the Alpha of the New Jersey pack. The crowd erupted into hoots and applause at the arrival of the Alphas. "We shall now draw the names of the females who shall be mated with these two warriors," Michael called.

Michael motioned to a female, who I assumed was the mother of his champion, judging from her age and the proud look she shot her son. She handed Michael a leather sack. Michael drew a name and called, "Calliope McShane."

Applause rose from the crowd. A young female with sable hair emerged from the crowd and climbed to the stage. The New Jersey Alpha hugged her before surrendering her to her grinning mate.

Adam leaned in. "That's the Jersey Alpha's daughter."

The New Jersey Alpha stepped forward then. He repeated the same process of drawing a name from a bowl offered by his champion's mother. "The mate for Logan Remus, New Jersey's champion, is Mackenzie Romulus!"

The crowd went wild. I tensed and grabbed Adam's hand without thinking. Only after our skin touched did I realize my error. I froze, waiting for him to reject it. Instead, he squeezed my cold fingers between his warm ones. We might have problems, but right then we were united in our concern for our friend.

Two large males "escorted" Mac onstage. She hadn't changed much since I saw her after the Roller Derby bout. Same petite frame, same brunette hair, same fierce scowl. Michael stared her down with a stern look that clearly indicated any outburst on her part would result in severe repercussions.

My stomach cramped for her. It was bad enough her

uncle had just decided she was going to marry a stranger against her will in the name of pack diplomacy. It was even worse that she was in love with Georgia and believed the vampire had rejected her. It was a good bet that Michael didn't mention that Georgia tried to fight for her.

Of course, Mac being Mac, she didn't pay heed to her uncle's warning look. The pair commenced with a whispered argument in front of the entire audience of werewolves. I couldn't help admiring her spirit. Most females would have been cowed by everything happening. But Mac faced her uncle like an Amazon, all clenched fists and chin held high.

"Is Sabina here?" Mac said suddenly, turning toward the crowd. My stomach dropped. Oh, shit, this wouldn't be good. "Sabina!"

I looked up at Adam. "What should I do?"

Already, werewolves were turning this way and that, trying to locate the person Mac was searching for. With my red-and-black hair, I stuck out like a sore thumb among the brunettes and blondes in the crowd.

"Come on," Adam urged. "I'll go with you."

If I wasn't so unsure of what was coming, I might have considered his offer a sign of hope. But as it was, I was too busy trying to ignore the stares of hundred of werewolves, who in about five minutes were going to morph into slathering hell beasts.

Adam and I surged through the crowd at the same instant Mac stepped forward.

"I'm surprised you showed your face, mixed blood," Michael called.

I shrugged. "You know me—I hate to miss a party." I might have been nervous, but any sign of fear would make me a target in this group of predators.

Michael turned his angry gaze on Mac. She raised her chin. "I'll do what you want, Uncle. But first I need to speak with Sabina."

The weres holding her tensed for the Alpha's order. Finally, Michael succumbed to the pleading in his niece's eyes. "Make it fast. The moon is almost at its apex."

Mac didn't waste time. She pulled away from her captors and jumped off the stage. Grabbing me, she dragged me to the edge of the stage, where there was a tad more privacy. By the time we stopped, she was panting, out of fear or urgency, I didn't know.

"When this is all over, I need you to do me another favor. I don't know when I'll ever be able to repay—"

I waved a hand to interrupt. "Don't worry about it. Anything I can do to help."

She nodded solemnly. Her eyes glistened with tears like a woman about to face execution. "I need you to find Georgia and give her this letter." From the bodice of her gown, she removed a small envelope. "I know I can't stop what's happening. I know it's my fault. But I can't do my duty without knowing she'll get this."

My own eyes stung with the weight of the responsibility. I considered telling Mac then about how Georgia had fought for her. But in the end, I held my tongue. I worried that if I told Mac how Georgia's heart had broken in the end, she'd have a harder time facing her own bleak but inevitable future.

"I promise I'll get it to her, no matter what." I clasped the envelope gently and held it against my chest.

"Thanks, Sabina." She paused, biting her lip. "I know you and I have had our problems, but I just want you to know that I respect the hell out of you."

I swallowed the lump of emotion in my throat. Praises

of my own rose to my tongue, but I knew it cost Mac a lot of pride to say what she had. Adding to the lovefest would only make her more uncomfortable. So instead, I just smiled. "Ditto, werebitch."

Something shifted in the air. I looked around. Every were I saw looked up toward the moon. Crap. They were all about to change. "Mackenzie!" Michael growled.

Mac grabbed me in a hard, impulsive hug. I squeezed her back, hoping to lend her some of my own strength. "Take care of yourself," I whispered. "Don't let them break you."

A round of growls emerged from somewhere within the crowd. Every were in sight was already in the throes of the change. "Get out of here," Mac said. "I can't do this if you're watching." With that, she ran back to the stage and jumped up.

I rushed over and grabbed Adam by the arm. "Let's go."

All around us, the werewolves growled as their bodies contorted. The sickening sound of joints popping to accommodate their new forms echoed like gunshots. Onstage, Mac had fallen to her knees. Her face stretched grotesquely as a muzzle grew where her mouth used to be. She howled, lifting her misshapen face to the moon. Unlike the joyful shouts of her brethren, hers was filled with mourning.

Adam wrapped his arms around me and began whispering the spell. Over his shoulder, I couldn't help but stare at Mac.

Her eyes glowed gold. She rose to her new height, topping six feet easily. Her body had expanded to twice its normal size. She raised her arms to the sky and howled her anger. She started to run toward the edge of the stage. She was about to leap off like she intended to run, but an impossibly large male with a skunk streak grabbed her from behind. Logan. He sunk his huge teeth into her neck and bent her over.

The magic rose just as Mac's terrible growl ripped through the night. I closed my eyes. Hot tears leaked from my clenched lids. The air popped and the wind rose. Finally, we escaped.

28

*A*dam flashed us back to our apartment. After the turmoil of the scene we had just left, the silence smothered us. The only sounds were our panting breaths and the pounding of my heart in my ears. I was pressed against Adam's chest, clinging to him like a drowning woman on a buoy.

The winds of interspatial travel had dried my tears into stinging tracks on my cheeks. Adam's heart thumped against my ear. My own chest felt tight, oxygen hard to come by. Rage and pain rose inside me like a tempest. The feelings overwhelmed me until I felt I needed to hit something or burst.

Adam tipped my chin up. "You okay?" he whispered.

I shook my head, unable to speak. Part of me wanted to run from him, to find someone to punch. He must have recognized the need in my eyes. He'd seen it there countless times before during battles and heartache. I tensed to pull away from the intimacy. I felt too raw and exposed. Too unpredictable.

Sensing I was about to retreat, he tightened his hold. I looked up into his eyes and stilled. His irises glowed with strong feelings of his own. Just as he'd recognized the emotions in me, I knew his, too. We stood there like that, the weight of our feelings and regrets hovering in the slim space between our faces.

I'm not sure who moved first. But two seconds later, we slammed into each other like a head-on collision. Need prevented the reunion from being sweet or gentle. Our hands groped for fastenings, ripping at buttons and zippers. The room filled with our harsh, mingled breaths and the sounds of ripping fabric.

We were wild things, unleashed. Alternately pleasuring and punishing each other. I wasn't sure which I preferred but it didn't really matter. All I cared about was the release and the miracle of being close to Adam again. I couldn't get close enough, though. I needed more.

Somehow we ended up on the floor, even though the couch was only a few steps away. We couldn't wait for comfort. Didn't need it. Our skin slicked with sweat, we glided against each other with fevered movements. Soon, but not soon enough, he reared up over me and drove into my core. My back arched to meet his punishing thrusts. Nails dug half-moons into his back, drawing blood. He groaned and strained to go deeper, as if he could fill me with his whole self.

I wanted him to.

But I wasn't content to lie submissive. Not this time. Wrapping a leg around his flank, I flipped him over. His back hit the hardwood with a slap. I clasped him between my thighs and rode him hard. His eyes glowed with an emotion so strong it burned me—love, hate, both?

I bent over him and kissed his mouth. His whiskers rubbed my skin raw but his tongue was soft and hot. I sucked on him, nipped his lip with my fang. The taste of his mouth and the metallic flavor of his blood nearly sent me over the edge. Hunger rose in me like a beast, demanding to be sated.

I wasn't thinking. Instinct ruled now. And the need to feed from my lover was stronger than I'd ever experienced. It had been months since I'd fed from Adam in that cramped bedroom in New Orleans the first time we'd made love. But now I took the bridle off the hunger I thought I'd tamed.

My tongue lapped the hot skin over his jugular. The taste of his salty skin and the scent of fresh blood made my eyes cross. I slammed my fangs into his throat like a snake strike. Adam's sweet, hot blood flooded my mouth. I was so drunk on him that I didn't realize he'd gone still.

"No!" His hips bucked and his hands pushed me off him. I fell to the floor, dazed. Cold air hit me like a slap in the face.

His sudden anger stunned me. "Wha—"

He jumped up and loomed over me, naked and furious. "What the fuck, Sabina?"

I licked my lips. They were wet with his blood. Suddenly ashamed, I wiped the damning evidence away. "I just—" I was confused and the haze of hunger and desire addled my brain. "I wanted you."

"You were feeding from me like an animal!"

My mouth fell open. What the hell just happened? "What? Why are you so angry? I've fed from you before."

He ran a hand through his hair. He was so tense, his biceps bulged. "Before, you asked first. Besides, you haven't done it in months."

"I'm sorry, I didn't think—"

"No, you didn't think. Gods, Sabina, I'm not a fucking blood dispenser."

I pulled my knees up to my chest. "I wouldn't have done it if I thought you'd be angry."

"Bullshit," he said. "You were out of control and you know it."

I rose slowly, my hands shaking with anger. How dare he act like I was the only one carried away? He'd been rough with me, too. "Look, I apologize for biting you. But you know damned well that sex and blood go together for me. I haven't bitten you in months and I resent the implication that I'm some sort of monster. You were as into that as I was. The only difference is you don't have fangs."

He crossed his arms. "Here we go again. Sabina's using her vampire nature as an excuse for poor decisions."

I reared back, stung by his tone and his attitude. "What the fuck is that supposed to mean?"

He laughed, a hard, cold sound. "Let's just acknowledge the demon in the room, shall we? We both know you believe your little escapade with Slade was a result of your struggle to control your vampire side."

My mouth fell open. "Don't put words in my mouth, Adam. If you'd given me a chance to discuss this like two rational adults, you'd know that had nothing to do with it."

He raised a challenging brow. "Enlighten me, then."

If I hadn't been so hurt and angry, I would have found the fact that we were arguing naked humorous. But considering how exposed I felt emotionally, the nudity seemed somehow fitting.

Memories of that week in October flooded my mind. I'd gone over and over my reasons for turning to Slade. At first, sure, I'd justified my actions, claiming I'd been emotional and confused. But eventually, the ugly truth became apparent. I'd stuffed it down, believing it didn't really matter anymore, since Adam and I were happy now. Or were happy before the truth came out. But now I couldn't avoid opening that secret box and exposing my true motivations and let the cards fall where they may.

"Where were you, Adam?" I said, my voice cracking. "Why didn't you come find me after Maisie helped me out of that cell? Or for that matter, why didn't you step in when Orpheus accused me of killing Hawthorne Banathsheh in cold blood?"

Hawthorne Banathsheh was an ambassador for Queen Maeve, sent to the mage Council to oversee negotiating an alliance against the vampires when war seemed inevitable. Unknown to the Queen and the Council, Banathsheh also belonged to the Caste of Nod. He'd attacked me and almost managed to end me before I used my Chthonic magic to turn him into a faery briquette. At first, given my violent background, Orpheus believed I'd murdered the fae in cold blood and thus ruined any chance of the Queen upholding the alliance. Adam tried to defend me, but in the end, he backed down when Orpheus threatened to kick him out of the Pythian Guard.

Adam's mouth snapped shut and his cheeks went red. "What does that have to do with this?"

My hands shook as I gave voice to the resentment I'd ignored for all this time. "You let Orpheus call me a murderer and stick me in that fucking prison cell. Maisie freed me and sent me to Slade for help since I had no other options. I waited for you to show up, but you didn't. And don't tell me Maisie didn't tell you where I was. You had to know."

"I fought for you! I told Orpheus there had to be an explanation—"

"I saw the doubt in your eyes," I interrupted, my voice shaking. "Knew that you believed I'd really killed the faery for my own selfish reasons. And then you backed down just like you always do where Orpheus is concerned."

"You wanted me to choose you over the man who raised me?" he roared. "We weren't even together then!"

I tilted my head. "Exactly. We weren't together. A fact made more apparent when you didn't come find me. When I turned to Slade, I honestly felt I had no one else in the world. He was there for me. You weren't."

Adam came up short. The room was silent and tense for a moment while that sank in. "I did what I thought was best at the time," he began slowly. "I knew that once Orpheus calmed down, he'd listen to reason. And I didn't come for you because Maisie said you needed some time to sort through everything that had happened." He blew out a breath. "You can build my mistakes up as justification for your own. You can claim you were upset and turned to the closest warm body. But we both know the truth, Sabina. You didn't sleep with Slade because you needed comfort. You slept with him because you needed an excuse to run."

"But I didn't!" I yelled. "I didn't run. I came back and helped fight."

"I wasn't talking about running from the mages. I was talking about running from *this* mage." He hit his chest with a thumb. "You were running because you were too scared to let yourself be happy with me."

I looked the man I loved in the eyes. "But that was months ago, Adam. I'm with you now. That has to mean more than a stupid mistake I made before we were together. I have no interest in Slade."

"I know. He told me as much when I talked to him last night."

"So you believe Slade but not me?" My mouth fell open. "Why was my word not enough?"

"That's the thing, Red. I would have gotten over you fucking Slade eventually. I know you don't love him."

"So what's the problem?" I cried, throwing my hands up in frustration.

"The problem is that you lied to me. Back then, I would have understood because I knew you were struggling to overcome your dark side. But now?" He ran a frustrated hand over his face and tried to get a handle on his temper. "You had a chance to come clean less than a week ago. Instead, you lied to my face. If our time together had really changed you, you would have told me the truth."

I paused as what he said sunk in. "That's the real problem, isn't it?" I shook my head as everything finally clicked. He raised a brow, waiting for me to continue. "Ever since we met, you've wanted me to change. To become some sort of Stepford mage. You like to pretend that my vampire side is a shameful part of me that I can flip on and off like a switch. But guess what, Adam? Like it or not, I am a vampire. My past really happened and it's as part of me as my fangs."

"You're not just a vampire, Sabina. You're also a mage. And for the most part, you've managed to be more mage than vamp over the last several months. That's why I got so upset when you bit me. You lost control."

I shook my head sadly. "You don't get it. The more I've pushed down that side of me, the less me I've become. The more I try to ignore the bloodlust and the darker sides of myself, the more they rear up and demand to be noticed. Just like when I ignored my mage side in L.A. and I was so out of balance. It's not about choosing one part of me over the other. I am both light and dark." My heart kicked up as the truth of that statement sunk in. "I have made mistakes. And I should have told you about Slade earlier. But the real issue here is that you can't accept me for who I really am. Fangs, magic, and all."

A muscle worked in his jaw. "Fangs, magic, and *lies*, you mean. You can try to make this about poor little Sabina being misunderstood because she's a mixed blood, but this is really about you not being able to be honest with me—or yourself."

"That's not fair. After everything we've been through together, I deserve more credit than that. I have never lied to you except about Slade. And I wouldn't have done that if I wasn't worried about hurting you. I love you, Adam." He shied away, as if the words stung. But I forged ahead. "Do you love me?"

His eyes hardened. "How can you ask me that? Of course I love you."

I looked into his green eyes. The same eyes that used to wink at me and crinkle at the corners when he'd laugh with me. Now they just looked tired. "I'm the first to admit I don't have a lot of experience with love. But it seems that if you love someone, then you should love all of them. If you can't love all of me"—my voice cracked—"then I don't know if we can be together."

He looked like I'd struck him. "Nice. You lie to me but I'm the asshole."

I took a step toward him and put out a hand to touch his cheek. He reared back like he expected a slap. I paused and pulled back. "I'm just asking you to love me without demanding I ignore half of my nature."

With that, I walked away and took refuge in the bedroom we used to share. When the door closed, I leaned against it and closed my eyes. I started counting, willing him to come after me.

One, two, three . . .

To walk through that door and tell me that I was enough.
Four, five, six...

That I'd misunderstood and that of course he loved me,
all of me.

Seven, eight, nine—

The front door slammed. The sound echoed in my
head like a judge's gavel condemning our relationship to
death.

I didn't come back out of my room until the next evening.
And then only because Giguhl threatened to break the door
down if I didn't open up.

He took one look at my red-rimmed eyes and held up a
claw. "Get dressed first and then you can tell me all about
it on the way to Vein."

Thirty minutes later, we were in a cab on the way to the
club. In cat form now, Giguhl sat in my lap and listened to
my sordid and sad tale. The cabdriver shot me worried
looks in the rearview but spent most of the ride chattering
to someone on his cell phone. When I finished, Giguhl
stood and put his paws on my shoulder. He looked me in
the eyes and blasted me with his rank cat breath. "I know
you're hurting right now, but you did the right thing. I
respect the hell out of Adam, but you haven't been yourself
for months."

"So if I did the right thing, why do I feel like I ruined my
life?"

"Stop being a drama queen," he said. "Of course it's
going to hurt. You love Adam and he loves you. But sometimes that's not enough."

The cab pulled up in front of the Chinese restaurant then.
I was so busy getting my gear and juggling Giguhl and

making my way through the restaurant to the secret entrance that I couldn't respond to the cat's insightful comment. But I thought about it all the way through the restaurant and down into the tunnel, as we made our way through the club to the dressing rooms. I pondered it while I changed into my ridiculous costume and laced up my skates.

Was the demon right? Was love not enough? I'd not known love before Adam. Lust, sure. Passion, definitely. But loving someone? Never. Not before Adam barged into my life. I'd fought my feelings for him for a long time, but in the end, he'd gotten to me. I lowered my defenses and let him in because he'd proven I could trust him. Yet all along, I was blind to what was really happening. To the price I had to pay personally to live up to his image of who he thought I could become.

From the start, Adam had encouraged me to get in touch with my mage side. Until he showed up, my mage blood had been a source of shame, something to ignore and hide. Because of him, I realized I had power I'd never conceived of before. Because of him, I found my sister and an extended family made up of both relatives and friends.

But all of those wonderful things had a darker side. Because even as he was pushing me to get in touch with my magic, he was also pulling me away from my vampire side. And the more I thought about it, the more I realized I'd missed her. She didn't let anyone push her around. She went after goals with the stubbornness of a mule. She was strong and brave and confident. All things I'd lost when I left her behind on that battlefield in the Big Easy.

What had Slade said about vampires who embraced the light? As much as I hated to admit it, he'd called this inevitable implosion between me and my darker nature. He'd been through it himself to some extent.

I sat on a bench, thinking all this over, when Giguhl blew his whistle. "All right, Marauders. It's time to go kick some ass. Who's ready?"

When the ladies around me shouted, I stood and joined them. I was looking forward to getting on the track and unleashing my dark side. It'd been far too long since I'd let her play.

As I skated out of the room, something else Slade had said popped into my mind: *How long has it been since you killed anyone?*

29

The elbow smacked me in the nose. A painful crunch. Wetness on my lips. The taste of my own blood.

"Oops," Merry Machete said, shooting an evil smile over her shoulder. The vampire wore boy shorts, fishnets, and a tank top with a skull bedazzled on the back. I smiled at her retreating back. Finally, an excuse to get serious.

My legs pumped harder, faster. I caught up with the vampire. Delivered a jab to Merry's ribs as I passed.

Her fist slammed into my kidneys with the force of a sledgehammer. Spine-bending pain almost sent me to my knees. My skates scrambled for purchase, but I somehow managed to dig in and right myself.

Rounding the corner, I scooted ahead. Adrenaline buzzed through my veins. Giguhl screamed something. I looked over my shoulder and spied my real prey. The black star on her helmet acted like a bull's eye.

What's it been, three months?

The jammer for the Jersey Devils was a mage who went by the name Ima Cutchoo. She was tough for a mage, but she lacked my vampiric stamina and speed. In a real battle, her magic skills might have made her a contender, but the brass armbands we were required to wear put the kibosh on that option. They dampened my magic, but I didn't need spells to defeat the bitch. I had fists and the need to make someone bleed urging me on.

I slowed so she could catch up, dug in, and bent my knees. Muscles bunched, waiting to strike. Ima fought off bumps from my teammates but passed them easily, earning two more points. On her left, the Marauders' jammer, Stankerbell, struggled to make it through the gang of Jersey Devils defenders.

The scent of blood filled the arena. Heightened my predatory instincts, made my fangs throb. I turned to glare at Ima. She made eye contact, her eyes sparkling with confidence. My own eyes narrowed with deadly determination.

All around me, my teammates were taking out Jersey Devils to clear a path for Stankerbell. A faery slammed to the floor and rolled into my path. My leg muscles screaming, I jumped her writhing form.

The crowd went insane. Hands and fists pounded wood, urging us on. In the chaos, some fingers might have been rolled over, but it was hard to tell screams of pain from screams for blood.

She was gaining on me. Almost there.

No, that can't be right. Ninety days?

Ima rode my ass. Her breaths coming out in harsh pants. I could feel her indecision, her brain working to decide the safest path around me. I held myself in check, luring her into a false sense of security. Then, just as she drew up on my right, I threw out my arm like a snake's strike. Ulna to windpipe—a satisfying crunch.

The force of the blow knocked her feet into the air. She

hovered there for a moment like someone hit the pause button for a better view of the action. Gravity kicked in and *bam*! Her back slammed into the wooden floor with a loud crack as her spine broke.

Whistles screamed. Boos and cheers from the audience.

I skated away. Raised a fist and extended the universal finger salute.

No, wait, ninety-one days. Three months and a day.

Ignoring the threats coming from the Devils' bench, I allowed my speed to drop and aimed for the center of the round track and Giguhl. He wore his usual green shorts with knee-high tube socks and a T-shirt that advertised the Manhattan Marauders logo. A clipboard and a scowl accessorized his coach's uniform.

"Seriously, Red?" he demanded. "This isn't Thunderdome."

I waved off his judgey tone and bent over with my palms on my knees. I wasn't really winded. But the adrenaline was already evaporating and in its wake, the now-familiar lethargy pulling at my shoulders.

I glanced up to see the ref point at me and then jerk a thumb, damning me to the penalty box. Heaving a sigh, I stood and put my hands on my hips. I should have been pissed. Put on a show for the audience. But I was too bored to care.

"Nice going, Betty Bloodshed!" This from Stankerbell, the nymph jammer for my team. I cringed at the ridiculous nickname Giguhl insisted I use. In fact, this whole charade was ridiculous.

I looked past Stankerbell to the crowd surrounding the ring. Their mouths stretched to scream, demanding more thrown elbows, more tripping, more pain. Watching their bloodlust, I was overcome with disgust. These mages, vampires, and faeries were nothing more than armchair warriors. They only wanted vicarious violence. But put them in a dark alley with a Vengeance demon and they'd all crap their pants.

I glanced up as the electronic scoreboard flashed the time—one a.m. *Scratch that, it's been ninety-two days now.*

From the clock my gaze landed on a familiar face among a crowd. Alexis sat three rows up. Seeing me notice her, she raised his chin and saluted me.

How long had it been for her? Probably hours.

Up in the announcer's box, Slade stood with his arms crossed. The corner of his lips lifted in a knowing smile.

I looked away from the weight of his stare and took off my helmet. "I'm out of here." I wasn't sure if those words were for Giguhl's benefit or my own.

"Wait, you're leaving?" Giguhl grabbed my arm.

"This is lame, G. I'm not cut out for Roller Derby." And by Roller Derby, I really meant Roller Derby and everything else my life had become.

"Well, excuse me, Miss Thang. I thought you were the one begging to join the team. Besides, you of all people should enjoy the violence."

"Skating in a circle wearing fishnets and a helmet isn't violence, Giguhl. It's a game. And I've had enough of those to last me a lifetime."

The demon's eyes narrowed. "Is this about Adam?"

My stomach dropped. I crossed my arms and glared at my best friend. "It's about everything."

I don't know who I am anymore.

The disappointed glare he shot me sent me over the edge. I threw up my hands. "Gods! Can't I just have an off night?"

"Okay," he said. "But if you need to talk, I'm here."

I looked around the huge room and our audience. Already the refs were preparing to blow the whistle to restart the action. Not the time or the place to get into a discussion about my existential crisis. Not that I was ready to discuss it with anyone. I was done talking.

"Forget it," I said. "I'm fine." With that, I took off my helmet and went into the locker room. I could feel Giguhl's and Alexis's eyes on me as I skated away.

It's been ninety-two days since I felt alive.

After I'd showered and changed, I left the locker room. The water hadn't calmed my itchy nerve endings or my restless muscles. Pent-up emotion and adrenaline mixed to form a dangerous cocktail in my veins.

The hallway echoed with chants from the audience and the rumble of wheels pounding wood. Instead of going through the club's front door, I slipped out a back entrance. It dumped me into an alley behind the Chinese joint.

I should have gone home. But the idea of spending a night alone with my thoughts held as much appeal as stabbing myself in the eye. Rhea and Maisie were at the Crossroads. But I couldn't face them right now, either. Not with my head so screwed up. Not with their inevitable questions. Slade was back in Vein. He'd be more than willing to help me work off my excess energy. But I wasn't looking to repeat that mistake again.

The alley smelled of sour garbage and stale urine. It had started to snow while I was in the club, but the minute the city streets got ahold of them, the pristine white flakes turned into gray slush. I trudged to the end of the alley and stopped. Traffic sped by, kicking up brackish water and soggy cigarette butts. Neon lights flashed like spastic fire-flies. I blinked, feeling disoriented as the world spun around me like a gritty kaleidoscope.

I'd never liked New York. It always felt like Los Ange-les's bitchy cousin with the gray teeth and the abrasive accent. The one who never wore makeup and refused to apologize for smelling like piss.

Surrounded by the snow and the traffic and the concrete and the cold steel, I had a sudden intense longing for Cali-fornia. My life there hadn't been perfect either, but at least I understood my place there. I had a job and a home of my own and a life. A shitty life, but a life nonetheless. It was easy to forget that I'd also been lonely. Easy to gloss over the fact that my life had been in constant danger.

Someone bumped into me. "Watch it, bitch," the man spat. He wore brown polyester pants and an ill-fitting sports coat.

I swiveled my head and glared at his back. Suddenly, that one mortal male became the breathing embodiment of everything I hated about New York in general and mortal New Yorkers specifically. Without putting too much thought into what I was doing, I followed him. I didn't make it obvious. Just hung back half a block, tracking his progress.

My heart rate picked up. It had been far too long since I had hunted. As far as prey went, this tubby asshole wasn't much of a challenge. He strutted along with his flabby beer belly hanging over his cheap pants. As he passed pretty women, he'd rake his eyes over their bodies like they existed purely for his viewing pleasure.

Eventually, he made his way to a subway entrance. He waddled down the steps, totally unaware he was being tracked. Adrenaline coursed through me like a drug. I was a junky looking to leap off the wagon. With each step down into the tunnels, my need grew. There was no turning back now. After my aborted feeding on Adam the night before, that brief taste of fresh blood, my body yearned for a fix.

On the C train, I sat on the opposite side of the car. Every now and then, the bodies in front of me would shift and I'd get a glimpse of him sprawled on the bench. Directly in front of him, an elderly woman and a pregnant mother with a tearful toddler clung to the bars. I added his lack of chivalry to my list of justifications.

My vampire whispered seductively. *An asshole like that? He deserves it. No one will miss him. No one will ever know.*

Several stops later, he hoisted his body from the bench and pushed his way toward the doors. He didn't see me rise and follow him. Moments later, the train's wheels squealed in protest and the doors opened. People spilled out like blood cells escaping a slashed vein. I rode the wave onto the platform and took my time following my prey up the steps. We emerged onto 8th Avenue in Bay Ridge.

Mr. Polyester was whistling tunelessly as he marched his way a couple of blocks and turned onto 7th Avenue before disappearing into a three-story building. I stayed across the street and waited.

A few minutes later, a light clicked on the second floor. Bingo.

It was already late—close to three in the morning. I was betting he'd turn in soon. Then I'd pay a visit to his shitty apartment and teach him what happens to mortals who don't know their place in the food chain.

Just then, the window blinds opened. Polyester stood outlined by the lights in the apartment, like Alfred Hitchcock. I narrowed my eyes and clung to my indignation and my hunger. I'd come too far now to allow my conscience to intercede. Still, it knocked against the steel door I'd erected, demanding to be noticed.

The man turned and a woman joined him at the window. She had something in her arms. He took it from her and lifted it. The blankets fell away to reveal a squalling infant.

I froze. At that moment, the enormity of what I'd almost done hit me like a cartoon anvil. The guy might be an asshole, but on my worst night—which might be that particular night—I wasn't capable of slaughtering an entire family. I sagged against the wall and let the fight drain out of me. In its place, shame rolled in like the tide.

"What are you doing?"

I whipped around, dropping into a fighting stance out of instinct. Alexis stood a dozen feet away, watching me. "Did you follow me?" Stupid question. Of course she had.

She crossed her arms and leaned against the wall, casual as can be. "You were so focused on your dinner you didn't even notice me." She grinned, showing fang. "I've been trailing you ever since you left Vein."

I closed my eyes and cursed. Gods, I needed to pull myself together.

"So you gonna do this or what?"

I opened my eyes and frowned at her. "What?"

She nodded toward the now-empty window. "You came all this way. Don't tell me you're planning on leaving hungry."

I ran a hand through my hair. "Alexis, I'm not killing a family."

She crossed her arms and leaned into the wall. "Jesus, you sound just like a mage."

I pulled away from the wall. "Look, I made a mistake, okay? I thought I wanted to feed, but I changed my mind. Let's go."

I tried to pull her away, but her eyes were on the window. "I'm gonna hang here."

"Bullshit. I'm not going to let you kill them."

Her eyebrows rose. "You're such a fucking hypocrite, you know that? Five minutes ago you were licking your chops at the chance of sinking your fangs into that guy."

"Five minutes ago I was an idiot. Let's go."

"Aren't you going to ask why I followed you?"

I sighed. "Would you tell me if I did?"

"Try me." She shrugged.

"Well?"

"At first, I was going to just congratulate you on that spectacular takedown during the bout. But then I saw you trailing that mortal." She tilted her head. "What can I say? I've heard the stories about you. I wanted to see if the rumors were true."

She was baiting me and I knew it. "Which rumors?"

Her eyes sparkled with humor. "That you are ruthless." She laughed. "Maybe you were once, but now?" She shook her head sadly. "Pathetic."

"You've got no room to call anyone pathetic, Alexis," I said. "You're a fucking cliché, with your tight leather and your attitude. Jesus, I bet you even sleep with your knives under your pillow."

Two red spots on her cheeks revealed my accusation as truth. She tightened her jaw and took a menacing step forward. "You got a problem with me, mixed blood?"

"As a matter of fact, I do." I raised my chin. "But you're not worth it. I was kicking ass before your milk fangs fell out. I don't need to prove myself to anyone, but especially not to some walking cliché who thinks a bad attitude can compensate for lack of substance."

She sneered at me. "You won't be talking to me like that

after Tanith names me leader of New York's vamps tomorrow night."

Jesus, was tomorrow already the treaty signing? You'd think I'd remember something that huge, but I guess all my fires lately had created enough smoke to screw up my memory. "Oh, right. Your big promotion." I snorted. "Do yourself a favor and spend more time brushing up on New York's dark-races politics and less time picking fights with potential allies." With that, I turned away and walked back toward the subway stop.

As expected, she took the bait and followed me. "What's that supposed to mean?"

I didn't slow my pace or look at her. "The shit's gonna hit the fan the minute New York's vamps find out that they're going to be under a Domina's thumb again. Once the signing is over, Tanith will go back to California and leave the governor to deal with the fallout. Don't fool yourself—that role won't be glamorous or easy."

She snorted. "It's got to be better than being an Enforcer. Don't get me wrong, killing people is fun and all, but I need a new challenge."

I rolled my eyes at her naiveté. "You want a challenge, tough chick? Go read a book."

We'd reached the subway station at that point. "Where are you headed?" I asked, hoping she wasn't planning on following me back to Prytania Place.

She looked up at the map of the city's routes. When she used her finger to trace the lines, the cuff of her jacket fell back to reveal a tattoo. I couldn't tell what it was, but judging from what I'd seen so far, I was guessing a dagger or something else equally ridiculous. "I need to get out to the Crossroads. The Despina wants me to do a run-through of the security with your boyfriend before tomorrow night."

Such a casual mention of Adam. But it felt like a punch to the gut. Luckily, she was so busy reading the map, she didn't notice.

"Well, I guess I'll leave you to it, then. I'll see you tomorrow."

She nodded absently. "Oh, and, Sabina?"

I paused and looked back at her. "What?"

"Thanks for encouraging Slade to make a move." She turned her head slowly to look at me. "He's a shitty leader"—her lips curled into a catty smile—"but a magnificent lay."

I held her triumphant gaze for a moment. She looked so pleased with herself, like she'd somehow bested me by sleeping with my leftovers. I couldn't help it—I laughed in her face. Finally, shaking my head, I turned on my heel and walked away.

30

Back in the fall, the drive out to Sleepy Hollow was always a treat. The tree line dripped with autumn's gems. The crisp, smoky air invited open windows so the wind could dance through my hair.

But now, February's skeletal trees curled their pointy bones over the road like claws. And the frigid breeze pounded at the windows like an intruder. After almost three months of the New York winter, I'd had more than enough of the cold. Which is why, when Giguhl reminded me that the mage ritual would involve standing outside for most of the night, I was far from thrilled.

"Suck it up, trampire," the demon cat said from the passenger seat. "At least your shorn testicles won't be swaying in the frigid breeze."

"You wouldn't have the problem if you'd worn the snowsuit I bought you."

"It was pink!"

I bit my lip to keep from laughing out loud. "Real males wear pink, G. It's a sign of confidence in your masculinity."

"The only thing I'm confident of is that you're a sadistic hose beast."

I shot the demon a look that had him easing back into his seat with his claws raised. "Jeez, sorry. You're so touchy."

"Bite me, demon."

He grew so quiet that I dragged my eyes off the road to see what was wrong. Silence and Giguhl usually meant trouble. But when I looked over, his feline lips were spread into a wide smile.

"What's wrong?"

"I've missed this."

"Missed what?"

"This. Us. It's been so long since we've hung out, just the two of us."

"You're crazy." I shifted my eyes back to the road. "We're together all the time."

"That's not the same and you know it." His paw touched my hand on the armrest. "It's been too long since we've spent quality time together."

"Dude, stop. You're freaking me out."

He laughed. "Oh, c'mon. Can't a magepire and her demon minion share a tender moment of intimacy without it being weird?"

I shot him a look.

"Okay, that sounded wrong. But you know what I mean. You're my best friend, Sabina."

I cleared my throat against the sudden emotion welling there. Maybe it was the stress catching up with me. Or maybe, just maybe, I couldn't believe my luck. Who knew that the same demon who tried to kill me the first time we met would become my best friend. "Back at ya, Mr. Giggles."

At that point, I pulled the Escalade off from the main

road and onto the dirt track leading to the Crossroad's massive gates. I jumped through the security hoops, which took an extra five minutes because of the heightened alert everyone was on for the festival.

Soon, we rolled through the gates and wound our way through the forest to the manor house. Now that we were there, all of the qualms I'd been ignoring rushed up like bile.

Rhea had left an excited message on my cell that afternoon, reporting that Maisie had spent another day locked in her studio. Even better, she'd informed Rhea she would be ready to share a prophecy at the Imbolc rites. I'd tried to call her back to get details, but I guess she was too busy with last-minute tasks to take the call. Regardless, knowing Maisie was prepared to offer a prophecy went a long way toward easing my worries. There were other issues, of course, but I was happy to have one less crisis to worry about.

Up ahead, the Crossroads manor glowed warmly against the dark wintry sky. Dozens of cars crammed the front drive, so we parked in the grass. As we approached, I pulled my coat tighter around me, both against the cold and the feeling of dread. Not only was I about to see Adam for the first time since our blowup, but also too many things could go wrong once the festival began.

"Relax," Giguhl said from my arms. "In a few hours, the dark races will finally be at peace. You should be happy."

He was right. That night was supposed to be a celebration. However, I couldn't shake the feeling that we were all fooling ourselves. But I reminded myself that was just habit talking. I'd spent so long expecting nasty surprises that it was hard to break the habit. I forced myself to relax.

"Peace," I said, testing the sound of it. The word felt foreign and sticky on my tongue.

*   *   *

We'd just made it inside the house when Rhea ran by. When she saw us, she skidded to a halt and doubled back. "Orpheus and Tanith are looking for you."

I tensed. "Is everything okay?"

"I think so." She nodded. "But they wanted to see you before the rites began."

"Okay," I said, relaxing. "How's Maisie?"

"All good, as far as I can tell. She spent the last two days up in her studio painting, so…" She crossed her fingers. "But listen, I've got to go deal with a minor crisis with Queen Maeve."

"What's up with her?" I shot Rhea a sympathetic glance, but really, better her deal with the Queen than me.

Rhea waved a hand. "She probably just wants to be sure the pen she signs the treaty with is filled with the blood of a virgin unicorn." She winked. "You know, standard stuff."

I laughed as I watched her go. If Rhea of all people wasn't worried about the night, then I felt I could relax, too. After all, like Giguhl said, it was a party.

I hefted the cat higher. "All right, let's go see what Orpheus and the Ice Vamp want."

We found them in Orpheus's office on the second floor. The two leaders stood in front of the massive bay window behind his desk, looking out over the festival. Already, hundreds of dark-race beings wandered the grounds. Light from the huge bonfire and dozens of torches formed a golden dome over the revelers.

Orpheus looked every inch the distinguished leader of a magical race. He wore a white chiton, the ceremonial uniform of all members of the Hekate Council. The golden staff in his right hand identified him as the High Councilman.

Even Tanith had shed her matronly suit in favor of a more festive ensemble. She'd donned a black satin gown with a high-necked collar. Her frizzy, dark auburn hair had been tamed into soft curls around her face. She'd obviously invested in some image consulting since I'd last seen her because her expertly applied makeup toned down the harsh, mannish features until they looked—dare I say it?—handsome with soft feminine edges.

I cleared my throat to alert them of my presence. They both turned. Tanith snapped her fingers and another figure stepped out of the corner of the room. I went still. It had been almost half a year since I'd seen Persephone. Still a beauty, she wore a satin gown in dove gray. I couldn't help but think the color choice symbolized her position as the Despina's shadow. She had not been allowed to take part in the treaty negotiations and I assumed her presence at the signing was only a formality.

"Sabina," she said, her voice quiet.

I dipped my head. I had to catch myself before I knelt before the two ancient vampires. I owed them no allegiance. Not anymore. "Persephone, you look well." It wasn't exactly a lie. Technically, her features were as perfect as ever. But something about her submissive posture and the shadows behind her eyes dulled the shine of her beauty.

While I was surprised to see Persephone, Alexis's presence wasn't a shock. Instead of her normal leather-and-latex fashion disaster, she wore a simple black velvet gown. The choice was both tasteful and surprising. But if I had to guess, her thighs were so strapped with weaponry she'd practically clank when she walked. She met my eyes across the room and raised an eyebrow. I responded with a bitch-please expression I'd learned from Giguhl.

Orpheus stepped forward. "Sabina, thank you for seeing us. I know holding a business meeting right before a ritual is quite unconventional but we needed to finalize this one last detail before the signing could proceed."

I frowned. "Okay," I said slowly. Why the hell did they need me here for a business meeting?

The Despina took over then. "As you know, we have relieved Mr. Corbin of his duties as the leader of New York's nonmage races. He will remain active in the Black Light District, but he will not have the authority to negotiate policy or mediate disputes. Orpheus will take a more active role in the werewolf and fae populations, but the vampires will fall directly under my leadership going forward."

I nodded but said nothing. We'd been over this before. What I wanted to know was why they invited me here to watch them give Slade's job to Alexis.

"I am restructuring my government so all the states will have a vampire governor. Because New York is a special case, given the dominance of mages in this region, my choice of governor here is especially important. The candidate needs to not only be familiar with vampire culture and political issues, but also be sympathetic to the needs and culture of the mages."

"So where do I come in?" Gods help me, I knew. I knew what she was going to say before her mouth tilted up in a let's-make-a-deal smile.

Orpheus smiled broadly and rushed to speak over the Despina. "We'd like you to become the governor of New York."

I went totally still. So still that Giguhl shifted restlessly in worry. I released my hold so he could jump to the ground. Whether he wanted down because he wanted to get out of the way in case I went ballistic or because he wanted to watch the fireworks from a better vantage point, I didn't know. Dumbfounded, I looked around the room, from Orpheus's and Tanith's self-satisfied smiles to Persephone's pained grimace to... Alexis's red-faced rage.

"Despina!" she said. "You promised that position to me!"

Tanith's head whipped around so fast I was surprised it didn't fly off her neck. "Silence!"

Alexis blanched. She shot me a look so full of venom the air shimmered green around her. But the Despina's barked order made her back down like a good little soldier.

I couldn't help it. The irony was too delicious. The first laugh escaped before I could stop it. And then I was doubled over with deep belly laughs.

"Sabina!" Orpheus scolded.

I held up a finger and tried to catch my breath. My stomach cramped and my jaw ached.

"I believe once you have a moment to think it over, you'll recognize you're the perfect candidate," Tanith said in her all-business tone. "Your experience with both the Council and my own government gives you insight into the special situation that exists for New York's vampires."

I waved a hand in the air, a silent plea for her to stop before I peed my pants. She and Orpheus shared a look that implied they worried about my sanity. Through the tears running down my cheeks, I saw Giguhl crouched on the floor in front of me. He looked like he wasn't sure whether to join me or go get help.

"I'm okay," I gasped. "Woo! Thanks for that. I haven't laughed that hard in a long time."

"I assure you, this is not a joke, Sabina," Tanith said.

Could have fooled me, I thought. Her offer was so absurd it made my brain explode. I finally got a hold of myself and wiped the mirth from my eyes. "Oh, I know you're serious. You've never had a good enough sense of humor to be this intentionally hilarious."

Tanith gasped. "I never."

"Dude, I *know*." I was being disrespectful and knew it. But I couldn't help myself. I should have seen this coming, but they'd caught me off guard and had me cornered. That left me with two choices, violence or sarcasm.

"Sabina, that's quite enough," Orpheus said. "The Despina just offered you a prestigious position based on my own recommendation."

That sobered me right up. "Wait, you suggested me for this? Why?"

He straightened his shoulders. "Believe me, it came as a surprise to me, too." His tone was disconcerted. "But once it became clear that other candidates might not be a good fit," he said, alluding to our talk about Alexis's temper, "I realized that you were the perfect choice."

"Okay, I'll play along," I said with a sigh. "First of all, my personal connections to the Council would make it impossible to be an unbiased advocate for vampires." I ticked off the reasons on my fingers. "Second, as far as I'm concerned, my ties to vampire politics were severed when Lavinia died. The mere idea that I'd even want to advocate for the race that treated me like an outcast my entire life is preposterous. And third, Slade is my friend and, despite his faults, he's a good leader. I'm not going to screw him over for a position I have no interest in."

"Are you saying your answer is no?" Tanith said, raising a brow.

My mouth fell open at her obtuseness. "Not just no, Tanith. Hell no. I'd rather French-kiss a rattlesnake than work for you."

Alexis jumped forward then. She must have had some sort of hidden pocket in her dress, because in a split second she had a dagger in her hand. "Show some respect, mutt!"

"Miss Vega!" Orpheus snapped. "Sabina is High Priestess of the Blood Moon and a member of noble bloodlines for both the mage and vampire races. How dare you draw a weapon on her!"

"I don't care who she is. No one disrespects the Despina like that."

"Alexis!" Tanith's voice cracked through the air like a bullwhip. "Stand down. This is precisely the behavior that prevented us from taking you seriously as a candidate for the governorship. You are excused."

Alexis jerked back as if Tanith had struck her. "Despina?" she whispered. "I'm sorry, I—"

Tanith pointed to the door. "Go!"

The Enforcer's cheeks turned as red as her hair. Ducking her head, she stalked out of the room, looking wounded and unpredictable, like an injured animal. Even though I could barely stand the bitch, I felt bad for her. I'd been on the receiving end of public shaming by the Dominae on several occasions myself. And from what I knew of Alexis, her greatest flaw was a need to prove herself to the Despina. Just like another naive vampire I used to know. She'd not recover soon from the humiliation.

After Alexis slammed out of the room, Tanith sighed. "Sabina, I understand that my offer is not an easy one for you to accept. But Orpheus and I had several long discussions about this and we both believe you are the only choice."

"I've already refused it," I said, raising my chin.

"Then I'm afraid we're going to have to insist."

My eyes narrowed into slits. "Are you saying I don't have a choice?"

Orpheus saw the warning signs that hurricane Sabina was about to blow. "Er, no, that's not what we're saying. But perhaps you should take a few days to consider—"

"I don't need a few days. I had fifty-four years of experience with the Dominae's very special approach to leadership."

"Things have changed, Sabina. The Dominae died with your grandmother. I am ushering in a more democratic form of government."

I snorted. "Forgive me, but isn't Despina the feminine form of the word 'despot'? Last time I checked, democracies weren't led by dictators."

Tanith's jaw hardened. "Why must you make this so difficult?"

"Why must you refuse to take no for an answer?" I shot back.

"Because she doesn't have another choice!" Orpheus said, his voice rising in frustration. "Part of our agreement is that I have the power to veto her candidates for the New York governor. After Alexis killed Tiny, I knew she was a poor choice for the position and I refused to accept her as a candidate. That leaves you, Sabina. There is no other vampire I trust more."

His grudging admission brought me up short. "Really?"

He grimaced and nodded. "Please do this. For me."

Orpheus and I had had our problems. But at that moment, I felt like I'd somehow achieved some impossible feat. He hadn't come right out and said he respected me, but trust was close enough. "Gods, Orpheus," I said. "You really know how to play hardball."

The corner of his mouth lifted. "So you'll do it?"

I sucked a deep breath in through my nose. "I'll *think* about it." I paused, as it occurred to me that Slade was going to be pissed when he found out they'd asked me to take his job. "In the meantime, please don't mention this to Slade."

"You have until the end of the night to accept." Tanith looked annoyed that I hadn't fallen at her feet and kissed her hem for this once-in-a-lifetime opportunity. "Don't worry about Mr. Corbin. He was not invited to attend tonight's festivities."

I rolled my eyes. I bet Slade's reaction to being excluded wasn't pretty. He'd served the Hekate Council for decades and now he was tossed aside like trash. I wished I could say I was surprised, but part of me wondered if all of this was Tanith's sick way of punishing Slade for abandoning the Dominae three decades earlier. More proof that the Despina's grudges had a long shelf life. "And you wonder why I have qualms about working for you."

"We really need to head down to the festival and get the rituals started," Orpheus said. "Sabina, we'll discuss this matter later. But I'll urge you in the meantime to really think about the opportunity. I really do think you'd be an excellent leader."

I nodded and crossed my arms. "We'll see."

31

A gauntlet of vampire, fae, and mage security guarded the entrance to the Sacred Grove. No weapons, magical or mundane, were allowed.

The vampires had argued that mages should be required to wear brass bands, but Orpheus had held firm. Vampires without weapons still had fangs and preternatural abilities. Therefore, he argued, mages should not be handicapped by magic-dampening brass. The Despina agreed only because enough guards were around so that if any fights broke out someone could step in quickly. In addition, the leaders sat behind a table inlaid with brass. Not only would this prevent any spells from reaching them but it also assured the Despina that the mages couldn't alter the peace treaty with any last-minute spells.

Because of my position as High Priestess of the Blood Moon, I was allowed to sit in the front row on the mage side. I sat next to the rest of the Council and Rhea. As my minion, Giguhl was allowed to sit with me but I'd insisted he stay in cat form to avoid making the security nervous. After all, a hairless cat in a black fleece sweater and hat was far less imposing than a seven-foot-tall demon with black horns.

Adam was on guard duty so he stood up on the dais behind Orpheus and Maisie. He wore the ceremonial black chiton that identified him as a Pythian Guard. He looked so handsome and proud that my chest tightened. It was the first time I'd seen him since our nasty fight and it was more difficult than I'd anticipated. It was easy to build myself up as the injured party when I wasn't looking at him. But now? Now I had to face the fact that our problems were as much—if not more—my fault as his.

The fact we'd both been through hell together to make this night possible made the moment even more bittersweet. We should be standing side by side, enjoying this victory together. Instead, we were separated by both physical and emotional distance. Distance I wasn't sure we'd ever be able to breach.

Tanith sat between Orpheus and Queen Maeve. Persephone cowered in the background, flanked by guards. It could have been my own prejudice talking but it seemed like they were holding her captive as much as protecting her.

Alexis stood behind Tanith's other shoulder. Her eyes scanned the crowd like a sentinel, searching for any hint of a threat. On one of her passes, her eyes landed on me. A slight tightening of her jaw was the only indication of emotion. Alexis might be a hothead, but she'd been trained well. Once the job was done, she'd probably vent her anger on some unsuspecting mortal. But in the meantime, she'd do the job.

Queen Maeve looked...confusing. Her tunic was winter white. Winterberry-red embroidery danced along the high tab collar and wide cuffs at her wrists. Rubies twinkled from her Celtic scrollwork crown. But it wasn't her outfit that confused me. It was her aged appearance. Last time I'd seen her she looked like she'd done more than fifty hard years of living. Now, her pale, gnarled hand gripped a wooden cane adorned with bay leaves, white flowers, and blackberry vine, and her face had taken on the translucent, papery cast of an octogenarian.

I leaned over to Rhea. "Is the Queen ill?" I whispered.

Rhea frowned at me. "No, why?"

"She looks like she's aged twenty or thirty years since I saw her in November."

Rhea snorted before she could stop herself. A couple of tight-assed fae courtiers shot nasty glares in our direction. Rhea nodded to them and schooled her features. Leaning in, she whispered, "Remind me to give you a lesson in the Queen's quadruple nature."

"Mind giving me a quick overview in the meantime?"

"She ages twenty-one years every season, which takes her through all the stages of a female's life—child, maiden, mother, crone. It's winter, so right now she's in her crone stage. Just before the spring equinox, she'll die and come back as a child and start the whole cycle over again."

I pulled back, giving Rhea a no-shit look. My mentor nodded to assure me she wasn't kidding. "That's fucked up."

I turned my gaze back on the Queen, looking at her with new eyes.

"Each new equinox and solstice takes the Queen into a new stage of life. That's why the courtiers' costumes and customs always correspond to the seasons. They're honoring each new stage of her life."

"I always wondered about that. I guess it makes sense, though."

Rhea nodded. "That's also why they wanted to get the

treaty signed now," Rhea continued. "The closer she gets to spring, the weaker she becomes."

I nodded, my eyes still on the regent. She had to be thousands of years old. And each of those years she'd sped through a complete life cycle. No wonder she was so bitchy. I would be, too, if I had to go through puberty again every year for millennia.

Onstage, Orpheus rose and clacked his gavel on the table. Normally, the beginning of diplomatic speeches would have me sighing and preparing for hours of boredom. But Rhea had told me the leaders all decided to keep the long speeches to a minimum. Everyone, it seemed, just wanted the peace treaty signed, sealed, and sanctified.

After brief opening remarks where he welcomed everyone, Orpheus surrendered the stage to Maisie. "And now, Maisie Graecus, High Priestess of the Chaste Moon and the Oracle of New York, will offer the traditional Imbolc prophecy for the coming year."

I crossed my arms and braced myself for the moment of truth. Even though Rhea claimed Maisie was ready to deliver a prophecy, I knew better than to relax. After everything we'd been through with my twin, I couldn't quite trust that one dream incubation miraculously cured her.

Maisie rose from her seat. She wore a white chiton that skimmed her curves. Her hair was wrapped into a chignon at the nape of her slender neck and her skin glowed in the torchlight. I couldn't tell if her improved appearance was the result of a glamour or if the incubation had improved her overall health, but she looked beautiful and every inch the High Priestess.

I held my breath as she gathered herself to speak. This was her first public appearance since she'd returned to New York. She'd been in the Council meetings, of course, but a room full of allies is a world of difference from an official gathering where everyone was depending on her to predict a peaceful resolution to centuries of hostilities.

"The Goddess has blessed me with a vision," Maisie said without preamble. A gasp rippled through the crowd from the assembled mages. Despite Orpheus's best efforts to keep her struggles under wraps, I found it hard to believe that the wider mage community hadn't speculated about the Oracle's lack of visions over the last several months. Even if they hadn't known, Maisie finally sharing a vision was an auspicious sign for the proceedings. But for me it was a sign that there was still hope for my sister. "The gods have spoken and the drums of war have been silenced. The white stag stands in the crossroads, ready to lead all the dark races to a different future."

I stilled. The white stag? Surely she didn't mean the same one that scared her in her dreams. I knew from past conversations that Maisie's prophecies were often difficult to take at face value. Often, the complex symbolism of the dreams had several layers of meanings. Still, it seemed too much of a coincidence. I looked at Rhea, who leaned toward me and said, "In many folk traditions, the white stag leads people to their destiny." She patted my leg and looked back at the stage.

Maisie continued in a tone I didn't recognize. Almost as if she were speaking in a trance. Figuring she was just playing up the Oracle role, I leaned forward to hear more. "The blue and the red will finally unite. As one, they will soar over vast seas and dine on olive leaves. The Great Mother will hold them close to her bosom and her blessings will shine upon them." She paused for that to sink in. "The Goddess has spoken. So mote it be."

With that, the sacred grove fell into reverential silence. I

let out the breath I'd been holding. I wasn't sure exactly
what the prophecy meant, but it certainly sounded positive.
Blue and red could easily symbolize mages and vampires,
respectively. And olive leaves? Weren't they a symbol of
peace? There was no mistaking that the blessings of the
Great Mother were auspicious. Yeah, I decided. The vision
was definitely positive.

Others must have agreed because applause rippled
through the crowd. Slowly at first, and then gaining energy.
Soon the night sky was filled with praises to Hekate and
Diana and Lilith. Everyone, it seemed, let out a collective
sigh of relief.

Onstage, Orpheus rose and embraced Maisie. She
sagged in his hold, as if delivering the prophecy had weak-
ened her. Over his shoulder, her eyes met mine. I don't
know if it was a twin thing or if some magical energy was
at work, but the look in her eyes made me shudder. She
looked away then, as if she couldn't stand the scrutiny.

That's when I knew my sister had lied. Whether she'd
made up the whole thing or left something important out,
I didn't know. But something was definitely wrong.

Out of habit, my gaze sought Adam. He stood still
behind Orpheus, surrounded by cheering beings. But his
eyes were on Maisie, watching her with a look I knew well.
It was the same one he directed at me when he suspected I
was up to something. I willed him to look at me. Finally,
his gaze shifted, seeking me out as if summoned. Our eyes
locked. A question passed between us, but no answers. He
broke the contact first, and I felt the loss of connection vis-
cerally, like he'd withdrawn physical contact, as well.

But before I could figure out what had happened,
Orpheus spoke again and yielded the podium to Tanith.
She rose regally, like she had been born to the purple

instead of earning her title through trickery and back-stabbing. All around, the mages in the audience tensed, as if expecting Tanith to call her vampire compatriots to fangs. After all, the last time vampires had stepped foot on this sacred ground it had been to murder their family members.

The Despina smiled at the crowd like a polished politician. "High Councilman Orpheus, thank you for the warm welcome. I speak for all vampires when I say we have eagerly awaited this auspicious moment in history. Thank you also to my good friend Queen Maeve"—she turned to smile at the fae regent—"for your hospitality and support through the rough weeks leading up to and following my predecessor's defeat."

I noticed she didn't actually say Lavinia's name. Smart.

"My advisors tell me that Imbolc is a time of new beginnings for both mage- and fae-kind. The perfect time, then, for all the dark races to finally rise above centuries of animosity to join together in peace." She paused to let the audience know they were expected to clap. And they did, just as she knew they would. "I am delighted by the Oracle's fortuitous augury this evening. It answers all our prayers for a peaceful future."

Another round of applause. "And in the spirit of new beginnings, I have an exciting announcement to make." She paused, drawing out the suspense. "Earlier this evening, Sabina Kane, High Priestess of the Blood Moon and beloved daughter of one of the most noble vampire families in the history of our race, agreed to accept the position of the vampire governor of New York."

"Oh, shit!" Giguhl hissed. I jumped out of my chair before I realized what I was doing. Rhea's hands grabbed at me, making me sit down. "Not now," she said, her tone firm.

If Tanith noticed my outrage, she covered it smoothly.

"As both vampire and mage, Sabina is the perfect symbol of the new spirit of cooperation between both our races."

All those years of yearning to be accepted by my vampire side. All that energy wasted on wanting to be acknowledged as more than just the bastard child of a forbidden love affair. All of those times when I'd felt the sting of rejection from my own blood kin. All that history had coalesced into this crystalline moment. I should have felt triumphant, fulfilled.

Instead, I felt betrayed and used. I'd become nothing more than a convenient symbol in a public relations campaign. It didn't matter that I'd thrown their offer in their faces. Or that they both knew that even given time to consider, I'd refuse again.

I was so angry, my vision filled with red static. But worse than the anger was the helplessness, the fucking impotence. I couldn't renounce the Despina of the vampire race two seconds before she and the other leaders signed the peace treaty. No, I couldn't call Tanith out. And I couldn't kill her. But at that moment, I certainly felt capable of it. Luckily, Rhea maintained her grip on my arm, a not-so-subtle reminder to keep it together long enough for the treaty to be signed.

Orpheus sat still, his eyes averted from mine. His expression stoic, resolved. And standing behind him, Adam looked as if he'd been sucker punched. He looked right at me, his expression a mix of betrayal and shock. Clearly, he believed I'd known all about this and hadn't told him. Considering our last argument had been about my vampire nature, he probably felt this was some sort of sick move on my part to embrace that side of my nature. After all, the position would make me one of the most powerful vampires on the East Coast. I tried to shake my head, to show him this wasn't my fault, but his eyes skittered away as if he couldn't bear to look at me any longer.

As if that wasn't bad enough, I felt Alexis's glare on my forehead like a target. I ignored her. Her wounded pride was the least of my worries.

"I am also told it is customary at Imbolc feasts to offer toasts with spiced wine," Tanith continued. She nodded to a servant bearing a tray of goblets offstage. The female rushed up the stairs and proceeded to set the goblets in front of Orpheus, Tanith, and the Queen. "So before we sit down to sign the treaty that will unite us all, let me be the first." Tanith lifted her goblet and waited for the other leaders to raise theirs as well. "To a future filled with tolerance, cooperation, and, most of all, friendship for all the dark races." She looked up to the sky. "Great Goddess Lilith, mother of all the dark races, bless all your children on this sacred night. To peace!"

The other leaders raised their glasses and echoed, "To peace!" Then, as one—as though they'd choreographed this moment—they each raised the goblets to their lips and took simultaneous sips.

Cheers rose like startled birds taking flight. Numb, I sat glued to my chair even when the standing ovation rose around me. Since I was in the front row, my lack of enthusiasm was apparent to all onstage. Tanith's gaze landed on me and narrowed. I glared back. The fire in my eyes promised a reckoning.

Her eyes widened. At first, I thought she'd read the hatred in my eyes and was afraid. But then her body started shaking uncontrollably. Black veins crawled across her pupils. More black crept down her neck, her chest, like spiderwebs. Fear was a cold fist around my throat, a dagger scraping down my spine.

I looked around for someone, anyone who could help her. But everyone else was too busy cheering and congratulating each other that they didn't notice the Despina's distress.

My blood went hot and cold at the same time. "Giguhl, switch forms!" I yelled. Leaping from my chair, I ran toward the stage. Behind me, a pop and the scent of brimstone filled the air. The demon's appearance caused a minor panic. This time, I assumed it was not his nudity but his sudden appearance that caused the shocked reaction. Mages, faeries, and vampires scattered, screaming.

It all happened so fast that only flashes of sensation and sound registered. Two vampire guards grabbed me. Giguhl ran up and tried to help, but it only made things worse. The guards thought we were attacking. My eyes scanned the stage, trying to find Alexis and warn her. But I couldn't locate her bright red hair among all the bodies onstage.

The guards dragged me backward, away from the stage and Tanith. "No! You've got to help her!" I shouted, struggling to get free. The noise of the crowd swallowed my words. My eyes stayed on Tanith. Steam began billowing out of her ears, her nose, her mouth.

Adam stood on the other end of the stage from the Despina and hadn't noticed the ruckus I was causing. "Adam!"

His head jerked in my direction. Seeing me struggling against the guards, he frowned. "Tanith!" I pointed to the struggling leader. "Help her!"

He looked over and his eyes widened. But at that moment, Orpheus groped for Adam's sleeve. His face had gone purple and his hands flew to his throat. Adam whirled around to catch his mentor. "Rhea!" he shouted. From the corner of my eye, I saw Adam's silver-haired aunt running toward her old friend, her expression both determined and terrified.

The fae guards finally noticed that both the mage and vampire leaders were in distress and leapt to protect the Queen. But from my vantage point, she seemed fine, if confused.

Just then, Alexis reappeared at the Despina's side. When Tanith slumped over, Alexis caught her limp body. "Oh, gods! She's burning up!"

Finally, Alexis's shout mobilized the guards. They dropped my arms and ran toward the dais. Before they reached her, Tanith's tortured scream cut through the noise like a shard of glass.

As I watched in horror, Orpheus gurgled and vomited black bile. All over the unsigned peace treaty. His eyes rolled back in his head and he crashed face-first into the table.

"No!" Adam's tortured yell made my chest constrict. Rhea pulled Orpheus's body from the table and tried to revive the leader.

Tanith let loose a belch that seemed to come from the bowels of Hades. Her eyes bulged and her tongue rolled out of her mouth bloated and blackened.

In the next instant, Tanith Severinus, Exalted Despina of the Lilim, exploded.

32

For a split second after Tanith's body went up in flames, the clearing went silent and still. Then, as if someone pushed the cosmic fast-forward button, people scattered and screamed.

Chaos.

Tanith's guards shot into action, scrambling to surround Persephone. Her expression pale and terrified, she stared in open-mouthed shock at Tanith's smoldering remains. The Pythian Guards formed a phalanx around Orpheus's body, too. The fae guards gathered up the Queen and scurried her off, presumably to a more secure area.

In the sea of panicked bodies, I stared at the scene unfolding. Shock numbed my limbs but my heart galloped. Giguhl grabbed my hand and held on. "Gods protect us," he breathed.

I wished I could share his conceit that we even deserved protection. The last nail had just been pounded into peace's coffin. The dark races, it seemed, were beyond salvation.

"Sabina!" Adam stood on the dais with other Pythian Guards, who'd surrounded the Council. I pulled my hand from Giguhl's grasp.

"Come on," I yelled, and ran to the platform. Now that I was closer, I finally saw Maisie lying on the ground. My heart lurched. I took the steps in one leap and reached her side.

"What happened?" My hands fumbled to find her pulse. When the steady beat pulsed against my fingers, I relaxed a fraction. Adam knelt down.

"She passed out. We need to get her out of here."

Behind him, I saw Giguhl go to Rhea, who wept silently over Orpheus's body. The demon grabbed a discarded cloak from the ground and wrapped it modestly around his hips before kneeling next to the elder mage.

"Do you want me to do it?" I asked, thinking Adam might need to help the other guards.

"Mage law dictates that if the High Councilman dies," he said, his voice cracking, "the Oracle steps in as leader of the Council until new elections can be held. Pythian Guards must remain with her at all times now."

I nodded. "What can I do?"

"Stay with Rhea," he said. "And, Sabina?" I looked up. His gaze was so intense I wanted to shy away from it. "Be careful. None of us are safe until we find the monster who did this."

I wanted to grab him and kiss and demand that he be careful, too. Tell him I didn't care if he could accept all of me or not because I needed all of him. But he was already gathering my sister into his arms and running off, followed by four other Pythian Guards. He'd not soon recover from Orpheus's death. None of us would. But in the meantime, we all had to focus on staying alive.

I allowed myself a moment to watch his retreating back. His broad shoulders tensed with Maisie's weight. I'd always admired those shoulders, so strong and capable. But I

didn't have the luxury of mooning over my personal heartache. The murders of Orpheus and Tanith were a crisis of
epic proportions, and until it got sorted out, everything else
had to get shoved down.

I turned toward Giguhl, who stood in front of Rhea like
a bodyguard, all shoulders and claws ready to defend. "We
need to get Rhea out of here."

Giguhl's eyes widened when he saw my burden. "What
happened with Maisie?"

"She passed out. Adam's going to take her to her rooms."

"I can't leave him," Rhea said. "I won't."

I knelt down beside her. "The Guards will take care of
him. But it's not safe for you here."

Tears rolled down her face. "Who did this, Sabina?"

Fighting my own urge to cry, I said, "I don't know." I
gently helped her rise. "We have to find the Queen and
Persephone. They'll be in charge until Maisie recovers."

Just then, a fae guard ran up, panting. "The Queen and
the Council are convening in chambers. All ranking members of the races need to report there."

"We're right behind you."

He nodded and ran off to spread the word to the others.

I turned to Rhea. "I need to get some weapons."

She nodded. "Let's stop by my rooms, too. I'd better
pick up some healing supplies while we're there."

I hesitated. "We'll drop you off at chambers. Give
Giguhl a list and he'll gather—"

She shook her head. "Absolutely not. Whoever did this
killed my best friend. I will not hide like a mouse when I
could be helping."

I knew better than to argue. Rhea was one of the toughest females I knew—hell, she was one of the toughest
beings period.

Just before we set off, Alexis ran by. All the other guards were busy trying to calm everyone down, but she was running in the other direction.

"Alexis," I called.

She stopped and shot me a venomous glare. "What?"

"We're supposed to report to chambers."

"I've got to do something else first."

I frowned at her. "What?"

"That's none of your fucking business," she spat out. In her hand, a dagger glinted in the torchlight. I looked down at it and saw the tattoo on her arm.

I grabbed it for a better look.

"Get off me," she yelled, and tried to push me away. But I held on tight.

"What's this?" I demanded. The tattoo I'd barely glimpsed the other night hadn't been a dagger at all. Instead, her wrist bore a red triskelion. Just like the one I'd seen at Spank. The one Mistress Bianca said indicated the bearer was a vampire who partook of blood-sport games. The kind of being who'd own vampire gloves like the pair found near Marty's body at Vein.

She glared at me as if I'd lost my mind. "It's a fucking tattoo." She jerked her hand way. "I don't have time for this shit." She ran off without another word.

In shock, I watched her go. The world seemed to spin and my mind filled with a dozen damning memories that supported my new suspicion.

"What was that all about?" Giguhl asked. He'd seen the tattoo, too, but hadn't put the pieces together.

"Remember the symbol we saw at Mistress Bianca's dungeon?" I said. Giguhl went still and stared after the running vampire.

"Oh, shit," he breathed.

Rhea came up, frowning with worry. "What's wrong?"

"Come on, I'll fill you in on our way to the Council chambers."

Fifteen minutes later, I had two guns, three knives, and a mission. I'd gone over my suspicions about Alexis with Rhea while she gathered her own supplies—potions, amulets, herbs. Giguhl listened, too, adding his own damning details to my list of evidence. By the time I finished telling Rhea everything, she stopped and nodded. "If Alexis is really the killer, we need to warn the Queen and Persephone in case she tries to take them out, too."

Instead of winding our way back through the massive mansion, Rhea flashed up directly into the Council chambers. Since everyone was already on edge, our arrival was greeted with the unholstering of guns and the static of defensive magic. Luckily, the Queen realized it was just us and yelled for everyone to stand down.

We ran over to her makeshift mission control at the front of the room. Aides and Council members rushed around. Vampire and mage guards eyed each other as potential enemies instead of the allies they believed they were just an hour earlier. The faery security watched with intense expressions and weapons at the ready should hostilities break out.

"Any news?" Rhea asked the Queen.

She looked like she'd aged another decade in the last ten minutes. "We tested the goblets. It appears the killer added apple juice and strychnine to the wine."

"Jesus," Giguhl breathed. "Just Tanith's and Orpheus's?"

"Mine as well." The Queen shook her head. "But I'm . . . difficult to kill."

My eyebrows rose. Supposedly, Orpheus and Tanith were pretty hard to kill, too, but they were dead. What was it about the Queen that made her so invincible? I would have asked but there were bigger mysteries to solve right then.

"I've got Pythian Guards and Tanith's security detail questioning the servants," Maeve continued.

"Not to be disrespectful," I began, "but shouldn't Persephone be involved in running this investigation?"

The Queen's frosty brow rose. "Persephone has disappeared."

"What?" Shock sharpened my tone. "How is that possible? Where's her security detail?"

Luckily for me, being in crisis mode had softened the Queen's normally tight-assed insistence on protocol. "I can't get a straight answer from anyone. The vamp guards claim that Persephone became someone named Alexis Vega's responsibility once Tanith died, since Persephone is now officially the leader of the vampire race. But no one can find this Alexis either."

My stomach tightened. "Last time I saw Persephone, her other guards were rushing her away. I saw Alexis seconds later running toward the manor."

"It's not a stretch that watching Tanith and Orpheus die spooked Persephone," Rhea offered. "She might have run, thinking her life was in danger, too."

"At this point, all we have are theories." The Queen pounded a jeweled fist on the table. Despite her aged appearance, her strength and power were impossible to dismiss. "I need evidence!"

Rhea looked at me, a cue to share my theories about Alexis's guilt. I took a deep breath. "Your Benevolence, I think I know who did this," I began.

She gripped her cane harder with a gnarled hand. "Enlighten me."

I told her everything. How I saw Alexis in Central Park the night the mortal was killed. About how she would have had knowledge of the Dominae's rituals and would have been capable of posing the murdered mage in the bar. "I should have questioned Tiny's connection then," I said. "There's no way he would have seen that ritual."

I went on to report that after she'd killed Tiny, Alexis admitted she wanted Slade's job.

"That's motive, right there," Giguhl cut in. "If she wanted that job bad enough, she might have thought killing the human and the mage would be enough to discredit Slade."

"And," I said, "once Tiny was dead and she was sure Slade was out of the picture, she stopped killing. That is until she found out tonight that I'd been given the job."

The Queen pursed her lips. "Why would Alexis kill Tanith instead of you, in that case?"

"Because Tanith promised her the job," I said. "She clearly felt betrayed by the female she'd pledged to protect."

"Besides, Alexis was up on that dais," Rhea said. "It wouldn't have been difficult to slip the poison into the goblets."

The Queen rubbed her temples and squeezed her eyes shut. When she opened them again, she called out, "Pull every guard off whatever they're doing and tell them to find Alexis Vega. Bring her to me. Now!"

The doors to the chamber burst open like they were kicked in. Everyone was still feeling twitchy, so every weapon in the joint turned on the new arrival. Alexis stood on the threshold, her chest heaving and her cheeks flushed. Her wide stance and raised hands made her look like an avenging angel.

"Who is that?" the Queen demanded.

"Alexis," I growled, glaring at the vampire.

The Queen's brows shot up to her crown. "Guards, restrain her!"

Alexis's expression dropped in shock. "What? No! I'm not the one you want." She raised a trembling finger in my direction. "The real murderer is Sabina Kane!"

If I wasn't so pissed that she'd managed to fool me for so long, I might have laughed at her pathetic attempt to frame me for the murders. But as it turned out, Alexis wasn't the only one with a short fuse.

The sight of her treacherous ass combined with her ridiculous accusation made every drop of rage rise in me like a black wave. She'd killed Orpheus. She'd killed her own Despina, a female she claimed to worship. And for what? Some sort of vendetta over a fucking bureaucratic post? She'd also killed an innocent human male and a mage by means so unnecessarily vile it made me want to vomit. Such a fucking waste.

I rode that rage like a missile aimed at Alexis Vega's heart. My vampiric speed made me little more than a blur in front of the mages' eyes. But Alexis saw me coming and crouched into a fighting stance. Her lips curled into an anticipatory smile. She'd been waiting for this confrontation.

I body-slammed her into the hall. We crashed to the floor and rolled, fists and fangs flying. I grabbed her red hair in my clawed hands and banged her head into the ground. Her own nails found my cheek and slashed. My skin ripped and hot blood dripped down my cheeks.

"Bitch!" I backhanded her. Blood bloomed on her lips. She grinned, showing red-tinged fangs.

Like a rabid dog, she found my hand and chomped down.

Bones snapped under the pressure. Hot lightning shot through my hand, up my arm. She took advantage of my pain and flipped me over, pinning my hips with her legs.

"Who's the bitch now, mutt?" Her hands closed around my throat, crushing my windpipe. I choked and clawed and kicked like a wild thing. In her rush to punish me, she neglected to remember the first rule of strangulation: Always tuck your thumbs. I grabbed the offending digits and snapped them like matchsticks. She reared back and screamed, cradling her broken hands to her chest.

I was about to follow up with the heel of my palm to her windpipe when her weight suddenly lifted. She screamed in frustration. Her legs flailed and her fists swatted the air, desperate to get in one more punishing blow. But the vampire guard made quick work of subduing her.

But no one was holding me. I leapt to my feet and rocketed toward Alexis.

It happened fast. One second I was running. Then next, the air sizzled and thunder rolled. The spell slammed into me like a wrecking ball. Knocked me off my feet before my body crashed into the wall. Stomach cramping with nausea and my vision doubled, I slid slowly down the dented drywall to land on my ass.

I shook myself, trying to get my bearings. The figure standing over me was blurry, but there was no mistaking the authority in her posture.

"Enough!" the Queen yelled. She snapped her fingers at a nearby fae knight. "Help her up."

Hands grabbed me under my arms and jerked me upright. Whatever spell the Queen had used on me, it had cleaned my clock. So much for faeries being the weaker race. I had to lean on my handler until the vertigo passed.

"Now," the Queen continued, her voice calmer but no

less threatening, "we're going to sit down and get to the bottom of this. Bring them both!"

The room was silent as Alexis and I were led to the front of the chamber. Already, I could feel my cells knitting my wounds back together. I glared over at Alexis. Her lip was still bloody but the cut had sealed into a dark line on her lip.

That's the problem with fighting vampires: Permanent damage was hard to inflict. A pity. I hadn't been trying to kill her, exactly. If I'd wanted to do that, I could have used my handy Chthonic trick of lighting her on fire with my eyes. But I wasn't Alexis's judge and jury. That was the Queen's job. However, I wouldn't have minded giving the bitch a permanent limp.

We were deposited into seats on opposite sides of the aisle bisecting the room. I stared straight ahead. From the corner of my eye, I saw Giguhl standing off to the side with Rhea. The demon gave me two claws-up and mouthed, "Awesome!" Rhea, however, looked unimpressed. Probably disappointed I didn't use my magic.

The Queen, her color high from anger, leaned heavily on her cane at the front of the room. "It seems we have ourselves a bit of a quandary. Sabina, you claim Alexis was responsible for four murders—"

"What?" Alexis jumped out of her chair, looking like she was ready to rumble again.

The Queen's head snapped around to glare at her. "Sit down or I will have you thrown in a cell, guilty or no!" Alexis narrowed her eyes and blew out a hard breath. But she dropped back in her chair and settled for shooting me venomous glares.

"As I was saying," the Queen said in an overly patient tone. "Sabina believes Alexis is the killer. However, other than hearsay, I have seen no physical evidence of her guilt."

"I—" I began.

Suddenly, I was on the receiving end of the same look she'd given Alexis. "Let me finish!" She slammed her cane against the floor like a gavel. I muttered an apology and slumped down in my chair. "Then Alexis arrives and accuses Sabina of the same murders. Since Sabina was given the chance to share her evidence, I feel it is only fair to allow Miss Vega to present hers."

Alexis shot me a superior look. Since I wasn't guilty, I shrugged. "Fine by me." Then I crossed my arms and settled in for the show.

"Miss Vega, you have the floor," the Queen said, pointing to the front of the room with her cane. At this point, most of the guards and staff had now taken their seats like a jury.

Alexis walked to the front of the room, her head high despite her ripped and soiled gown. Her cherry-red hair stood in odd tufts and angles. I would have been amused but I was pretty sure I wasn't looking any better.

"Thank you, Your Benevolence," Alexis began. "I'll need a computer." She removed a small black cartridge from the bodice of her gown.

The Queen frowned at the request, but she nodded at a nearby mage to retrieve a laptop. While the young male ran off, Alexis cleared her throat and began pacing like Perry Fucking Mason.

"As you know, I believed that Tiny Malone was the party responsible for the murder of both the human and the mage. But over the last few days, new information has come to light that leads me to believe we killed the wrong party."

"There was no 'we'—*you* killed Tiny Malone," I couldn't help pointing out.

"Sabina," the Queen said in a warning tone. "My patience for interruptions is wearing thin."

Alexis shot me a shit-eating grin. I pursed my lips and took my frustration out on the armrest of my chair.

"Regardless, I didn't want to believe Sabina might be responsible for such senseless acts of violence. But the more I put the pieces together, the more I realized she was the most likely culprit." She spun around and walked in the other direction, ticking off allegations on her fingers. "First, I saw Sabina leaving Central Park the night the human was murdered. When I had a chance to meet her, I disregarded her as a suspect because of her ties to the Council. But then the mage died. Like others, I believed the murderer was most likely a vampire."

I frowned. Hadn't I used similar arguments when I tried to convince the Queen that Alexis was the murderer?

"Sabina, as a former acolyte to the Temple of Lilith and granddaughter of the Alpha Domina Lavinia Kane, saw the virgin bloodletting ritual in person." She turned to the Queen. "As you said, though, hard evidence is needed to prove such a serious allegation. So I started digging into Sabina's life. It was only after Tiny had been killed and we believed the case closed that I realized Sabina had a motive for discrediting Slade Corbin." She paused dramatically.

My heart kicked into a rapid staccato. Surely she didn't know about—

"Sabina wanted Slade Corbin out of the picture because she was terrified that her mage lover, Adam Lazarus, would discover Sabina's secret affair with Mr. Corbin."

Gasps rippled through the crowd. I jumped out of my seat. "That's a fucking lie!"

The Queen's eyes narrowed. "You deny you slept with Slade Corbin?"

My guilty gaze flew toward Rhea. Her hand went to her lips in shock, but she refused to look at me. I didn't want to admit the truth in front of her. But I knew that lying now would only damn me further. I squeezed my eyes closed. When I opened them, I whispered, "No, I can't deny it."

Dozens of pairs of damning gazes burned into me. The Queen's scathing judgment didn't bode well for my immediate future. Giguhl looked like he wanted to jump to my defense, but I shook my head. I had to deal with this on my own. "But I didn't kill anyone. The night the mage was murdered I was with Sl—" I stopped, realizing that claiming Slade as an alibi wouldn't do me any favors. I cleared my throat and changed tactics. "I'd have to be a complete psychopath to murder innocents to cover up a stupid one-night stand."

"I'm glad you brought that up," Alexis said. To the room she called, "Last evening, I personally witnessed Sabina maim an innocent faery during a Roller Derby match. Sabina broke the faery's spine without one sign of remorse."

I rounded on her. "You're twisting the truth!"

"Oh, really? How about this for truth: After Sabina was ejected from the Roller Derby match, she proceeded to stalk an innocent human male to his home. If I hadn't stopped her, she would have murdered the man along with his wife and baby."

Outraged shouts came from the mages assembled. My stomach sank. This was bad. Really, really bad.

"She's lying," I cried. "She didn't stop me. I changed my mind!" Oh gods, that didn't sound any better.

The Queen raised a brow. I could practically see her adding this evidence to her own memories of how I killed one of her favorite ambassadors. She looked ready to declare me guilty.

"You don't understand," I cried. "She's twisting the truth to frame me for murders she committed!"

Just then, the young mage returned with a laptop. Alexis whispered instructions to him.

While he went to do what she'd asked of him, she turned back to the audience. "Of course, none of my accusations are hard evidence of Sabina's guilt. However, after my beloved leader, the Despina, was murdered, I ran back to the manor to check security tapes."

My eyebrows slammed down. What kind of game was she playing now? My stomach felt like I'd swallowed an iceberg.

While Alexis did her grandstanding, the young mage busied himself with setting up the projection system. He punched a button on a hidden console and a large white screen descended. He hooked the computer up to the projector and plugged in the thumb drive Alexis had provided.

"You see, I figured out someone had to have poisoned both the High Councilman and the Despina's wine. It seemed to me, we just had to find the correct camera and presto! We'd catch a killer."

She turned to the young mage. "Play the video."

The screen blinked to life. The video didn't have any sound, but we saw a couple of servants rushing around the kitchen, preparing food and drink for the festivities. A young female servant, the one who'd handed the leaders their cups at the ritual, came into view and loaded three goblets onto her tray.

The image flashed, like it was cutting from one reel to another. Now the hallway outside the kitchen came into view. The girl was still carrying the tray, her front to the hidden camera. A mage male strutted past and engaged her in conversation. She set the tray down on a table and flirted back. A few seconds later, he made his move and the two began tongue jousting. Soon, he backed her into a room off the hall and closed the door behind them. The tray stood unguarded on the table.

"This is ridiculous!" I called.

Alexis snapped her gaze in my direction. "But we're just getting to the money shot, Sabina."

A few moments later, I strutted into view.

"What the fuck?" I shouted. "That's not me!" But no one was listening. All eyes were on the damning evidence that I'd been alone with that tray.

Whoever the impostor was, she'd done an admirable job with her glamour spell. She even copied my outfit down to the tank top and boots. The only detail missing was the long winter coat I'd worn in deference to the cold.

But there was no mistaking the red-and-black hair. She even had my walk down.

Bitter bile rose in my throat. It tasted like fear. "No," I whispered.

"Keep watching," Alexis said.

Just then, the other me turned her back to the camera. Turning her head side to side to check for company, she pulled a vial out of her back pocket and poured its contents—presumably the apple cider and poison—into each of the goblets.

I clenched my eyes tight, trying to block out the damning image. How the hell was I going to prove that wasn't me? At that point, figuring why someone was trying to frame me wasn't as important as convincing them that Sabina-doppelganger wasn't me. Because if the Queen could be convinced I'd been the one to kill Tanith and

Orpheus, my life was forfeit. Permanently. With no hope of twelfth-hour clemency.

"Your Benevolence, please," I pleaded. "I swear on everything I hold sacred that female isn't me."

But the Queen's eyes were focused on the screen. Alexis paused the video on an image of the impostor turned halfway to the camera, vial in hand. The vampire rewound the tape frame-by-frame. Onscreen and in reverse, the impostor turned back, poured the poison, looked around for witnesses, and approached the table. Alexis hit play then and let it play through in real time again.

The air in the chamber was heavy and thick. The weight of dozens of accusing stares pulled on me like gravity. Ignoring the damning silence and the sweat dampening my palms, I forced myself to watch the video again, my eyes sharp for any speck of evidence that might exonerate me. But the longer I watched, the harder it was to fight the fear.

Finally, I swallowed hard and rose. If evidence wouldn't save me, I'd have to try to talk my way out of this. I turned to face the Queen. Every nerve ending in my body sizzled with adrenaline.

"Your Benevolence?" Her head turned slowly to look at me. Her eyes were hot with accusation. I pointed to the still image on the screen. Alexis had paused it with the female's back to the camera. "I don't know who it is or why they are trying to frame me for the murders, but I swear upon the Great Mother that I did not kill anyone."

Alexis laughed. "Says the former assassin. Correct me if I'm wrong, Sabina, but didn't you also murder one of the Queen's ambassadors last year?"

"Shut your mouth!" Giguhl yelled. I shot him a sharp look. He looked ready to keep arguing, but eventually he deflated and retreated to his corner.

"Queen, please," I pleaded. "You can't believe I did this."

She rose from her perch, using her cane as leverage. "The evidence is right there, Sabina. How can I not believe it?"

"Because I had no reason to kill anyone!" I yelled. "I was the one who made sure Lavinia was out of the picture so Tanith could become the Despina, remember? Why would I try to destroy any chance of peace when I worked so hard to achieve it in the first place? And if that's not enough to make you doubt Alexis's claims, ask yourself this: What possible reason would I have to kill Orpheus? It doesn't make any sense."

The Queen's chin came up. "So you weren't angry when the High Councilman sided with me regarding your mission in New Orleans?" My stomach sank, knowing exactly what she was referring to. The fucking past would never stop coming back to haunt me. "Surely you recall your reaction when I gave the order to let your sister die if it meant you had a chance to kill Lavinia Kane."

The decision she referred to happened the night before we attacked the Caste of Nod and Lavinia. Adam and I had two objectives: save Maisie and kill Lavinia—in that order. But the Queen stepped in and ordered us to reverse our priorities. Obviously, Adam and I argued and claimed that Maisie was more important. We'd thought Orpheus would agree, but the Queen pressured him with vague threats about withdrawing her support if he countermanded her. The fallout when he caved wasn't pretty. But in the end, I was the one who talked Adam down when his anger toward Orpheus almost derailed our plans altogether.

Gods, why did my judge have to be the Queen? She'd had it out for me for months. "I was angry that night, yes, but everyone's emotions were running high. Once I had a chance to calm down, I understood Orpheus felt he had no other choice. Besides, that was a long time ago. Orpheus and I had moved beyond all that. I would never kill him."

Alexis crossed her arms. "You would if you believed he was going to side with the Despina and force you to become governor of New York."

The Queen's eyes narrowed.

"I didn't—"

"I saw how angry you were when the Despina announced your new position," the Queen said. "Everyone on that stage saw the way you looked at her."

I threw up my hands. "According to that video, I would have had to leave our meeting and poison the wine before the ritual started and she took the choice away from me. The timing doesn't make sense!"

"Play it again," the Queen demanded.

She pointed to the screen. "Stop there." Alexis paused it on a shot of the imposter's back. I knew it wasn't me, but looking at the image, even I had a hard time believing it. My eyes scanned the still frame again, desperate for some clue, something that would prove the impostor was not me.

My eyes jumped to the tiny mark on the shoulder of the female on the screen. "Wait! The birthmark."

"What about it?" Alexis said.

"It's on the wrong shoulder." I stood and pulled my shirt to the side to show my eight-point-star birthmark on my right shoulder. In the video, the mark was on the left.

Alexis waved that away. "You could have used a glamour."

"Give me a break," I said. "Even if I could perform a glamour—which you know I can't—I would have done a hell of a lot more than move my fucking birthmark to the opposite shoulder—"

The truth slammed into me like a Mack truck. My knees gave out, and I slid into the chair, my limbs shaking.

"Sabina?" Giguhl called.

"Leave her!" the Queen yelled. "Sabina, what is it?"

I couldn't pull my gaze from the screen. To the female who looked just like me except for the reversed birthmark. The female who had the ability to perform a glamour. The truth exploded inside me like an electric shock. I closed my eyes as every remaining illusion I possessed drained from me like a rush of blood. "Fuck me."

"Explain yourself, mixed blood," the Queen snapped.

I opened my eyes. "I can't do glamour spells." I lifted a trembling finger toward the screen. They all turned skeptical gazes back to the screen and then back to me. "And my birthmark is on the right." I swallowed hard against the tears of denial that threatened to blind me.

"That proves nothing," the Queen said. "The damning evidence Alexis has presented combined with your notorious history of violence and your record of aggression toward both the Despina and the High Councilman..."

She trailed off as Rhea came forward, as if in a trance. My mentor's eyes were glued to the exact same space on the picture as my own. She pointed slowly to the screen. "It can't be," she whispered. Her eyes moved restlessly between the image and me as her mind pulled all the pieces together. Then, suddenly, she looked at me. The same horrible conclusion I'd already come to darkened her gaze.

"Rhea?" the Queen said, her voice shrill.

She turned slowly to the Queen. "Your Benevolence, Sabina is telling the truth. She is not the culprit of any of the crimes for which she's been accused this night."

"Sabina," Giguhl said, running up to me. "Is it really possible?"

I took a deep breath and grabbed his claw for support. "We need to find her."

Alexis snorted. "What scheme are you concocting now—"

"Shut the fuck up, Alexis," Giguhl snapped. "Sabina is not the killer."

"Who—" the Queen began, but Rhea cut her off, completely disregarding all protocol.

"Tell them," Rhea said to me, as if she couldn't stomach being the one to say it out loud.

I took a deep breath, but it did little to ease the pressure building in my chest, threatening to consume me. "The real killer is my sister, Maisie Graecus."

33

$\mathcal{W}$hile the chaos exploded around us, Rhea, Giguhl, and I stared at each other, trying to wrap our minds around the horrible rift the revelation ripped through our lives.

I tried to piece everything together. Tried to sort through my scattered memories of the last few weeks. To look for clues I should have seen. But I couldn't figure out what would cause Maisie to perform such uncharacteristic violence. She'd not been herself for months, but she never showed any signs that she was capable of murder. Or had she?

Obviously, she must have. No one makes such a one-eighty personality reversal without some signs. So I guess the real question was, how could I have missed something this huge?

But I knew if I allowed myself to ponder the whys, I'd never have the nerve to see this through to the end. So I sucked in a breath, shoved my feelings way deep down into the shadowy place where I kept my fears, and started barking orders.

"Alexis, you go with a few guards and make sure the grounds are secure. Rhea, we're going to her studio."

"Wait just a min—" the Queen began, offended that she wasn't the one calling the shots.

"Look, I don't have time to argue with you," I said, my tone hard. "We're going to find Maisie. You can punish me later."

Rhea threw her arms around Giguhl and me. "I'll flash us up there."

The magic rose quickly, surrounding us in a wall of static. The last thing I saw before we flashed out was the Queen turning to tell her guards to follow us on foot. Two seconds later, we rematerialized in the hallway outside the Star Chamber.

"Be careful," Rhea warned. "It might be warded."

I nodded and stepped forward to test the wooden panel. But when my fingers brushed it and nothing happened, I pressed my ear to the door. Frowning, I turned to the others. "It's quiet."

I reached down to turn the knob but found it locked. Since this was Maisie's private studio, she'd had a dead bolt installed to keep unwanted guests out. I'd kicked in my share of doors in the past, but I needed to be ready for anything once it burst open. Luckily, I had my very own demonic battering ram.

I turned to Giguhl. "All right, tough guy," I said, patting him on his massive bicep. "Break it down."

The demon smiled in anticipation and cracked the knuckles of his claws. "Stand back, ladies." He ran at the door with his head down like a charging bull. Before I could warn him that method was a great way to dislocate his shoulder, he slammed into the wood. The frame splintered and cracked off its hinges. His momentum carried him into the room. Two seconds later a loud crash echoed into the hall, followed by a groan.

"Giguhl," I called, running after him. I skidded to a halt when I saw the demon tangled up in pile of wood shards and canvas.

"Oops," he said, rubbing his shoulder. "Guess I underestimated my own power."

I held out a hand to help him up, my eyes doing a quick scan of the space. Because the Star Chamber was built in one of the manor's round towers, the room had curved walls. High above, the ceiling was painted blue with silver leaf constellations. In the center of the floor, a large worktable was scattered with paint tubes, brushes of every size, and cans of turpentine. The solvent's sharp, penetrating odor permeated the air.

But it didn't disguise the scent of blood.

I rounded the large table and froze. Behind me, Giguhl cursed and Rhea gasped. The bodies lay in thick, oily pools of blood and gore. My head swam from the overpowering stench of dirty, coppery blood and sandalwood. Counting the bodies took three tries. I didn't breathe again until I was sure there were only four. I hated to feel relieved not to see Adam among the carnage. I knew each of those Pythian Guards. They had families and friends who would mourn them. I would mourn them, too, once I was sure my sister hadn't also murdered the man I loved.

Rhea rushed forward to check for signs of life. I didn't say anything, but I knew she wouldn't find a pulse among them. Finally, she stood, her expression stoic and her skin pale. "Dead. All of them."

I acknowledged this with a curt nod. "Spread out."

"What exactly are we looking for?" Giguhl asked.

"Evidence that will lead us to Adam. And anything that can explain why the fuck she's suddenly turned into Lizzie Borden."

We dispersed, each heading to a different area. The last time I'd been in the Star Chamber was when I found the canvas left by Lavinia with the word "checkmate" written in blood. She'd left it for me to find after she'd kidnapped Maisie. Now, just a few months later, Lavinia was dead and Maisie was a killer.

Lavinia's canvas was gone, but other works of art filled the space. Ranging in size from small pieces of painted paper to huge canvases on easels, they represented the manifestations of my sister's subconscious.

Before Maisie had lost her mind, the paintings had a sort of Chagall dreaminess to them—lots of swirling colors and fantastical images. But now, every canvas I saw looked like evidence one might gather for a commitment hearing. Monstrous forms with sharp teeth and claws. Daggers and guns and other weapons. Lots of red slashing through every picture like blood spatter at a crime scene. No wonder Maisie hadn't allowed anyone in the room. One look at these canvases and there'd have been little doubt my sister had completely lost her fragile grip on sanity.

A small canvas near the window caught my eye. I frowned and approached it, my palms sweaty. Giguhl came up next to me, his claw on my arm, as if the contact would protect both of us from whatever dark magic waited on the canvas.

The image was about the size of a hardback book. It took my eyes a moment to adjust to the odd technique Maisie had used to render the image. From far away, the shapes came together to form something resembling a male face. The features seemed to be carelessly tossed across the bone structure, leaving individual elements to lie in unorthodox spots. The nose, for example, appeared where an ear should be. The eyes and mouth were reversed.

I moved closer and noticed that in addition to the decidedly Picassoesque composition, the image was composed of thousands of tiny dots. I wracked my brain for the art term for the technique. Pointillism? Yes, only creepier than any Seurat I'd ever seen. In the eyes, the dots of blue and yellow butted against each other so that when you backed up they combined to form vibrant green.

Despite the unorthodox composition that fractured the features, the green eyes and the thousands of bloodred dots that formed the hair told me whose face this was.

But it was a detail higher up on the image that made clammy fear spread across my skin. On top of Cain's head, Maisie had painted two large, red antlers.

I looked up slowly, my heart thudding in my chest. "It's Cain."

Rhea frowned. "How do you know that?"

"He's visited me in my dreams, remember?" Pointing a finger to the horns, I said, "Just as I suspect he's visited Maisie's."

Rhea frowned and came in for a closer look. "Cain is the white stag?"

I started to respond, but another grouping of canvases across the room caught my eyes. "Shit," I breathed. Raising a hand, I pointed them out to Rhea and Giguhl. It appeared my sister was building herself quite the themed art show. The title of these particular images might be something like *Murder: A Retrospective*.

They were all there. The human's broken body hanging out of the garbage. The mage suspended from hooks like a side of beef. The twin to the glove we'd found at the Vein crime scene was pinned to the canvas's upper corner.

But it was the last piece of art that made bile rise. It was a triptych. On the left, Orpheus bent over the table in a puddle of black. On the right, Tanith exploding like a super-nova. And in the center...

I wiped the sting from my eyes and forced myself to look at it. Really look. Because in the center, my twin had painted Adam. His golden head hung low over his chest, but there was no mistaking the Hekate's Wheel just under his navel. Worse, his body was strung up and covered in angry red slashes and bite marks.

"Gods, Sabina," Giguhl said. "We've got to find him."

"If it's not already too late," Rhea said in a dead tone.

"It's not too late. We'll find him." But tears sprung to my eyes even as the denial burst from my lips.

In the next instant, magic rippled through the room. I ducked down, prepared for attack. Giguhl and Rhea put their backs to mine, forming a defensive circle. But no blows—magical or mundane—came at us.

Instead, a female voice began humming from some-where across the room. My gut went cold. The sound seemed to come from behind a massive canvas. The position of the easel it rested on blocked our view of the person standing behind it. But I knew it was *her*.

My sister had finally decided to join the party.

"Maisie?" The humming continued as if I hadn't called out.

I flagged down Giguhl and pointed for him to approach from one side while I would take the other. To Rhea, I held out a palm, telling her to stay put.

"Maze?" With careful steps, I picked my way across the floor, past the bodies of the four dead mages, and toward the right-hand side of the canvas. When I came around it, I gasped.

Maisie was nude. Her right hand gripped a large paint-brush soaked with crimson, which she methodically scraped back and forth across the painting. More red—paint or blood?—streaked like wounds across her torso.

To distract myself from the panic rising like vomit in my throat, I looked up at the image she was defacing. The painting was one of the few left over from Maisie's pre-trauma days. She'd originally shown it to me just after my vision quest. The one where I found out I was a Chthonic.

The image showed a female that Maisie claimed was me flying through the night above a garden. The painting was supposed to prove I was the prophesized "New Lilith" who would unite all the dark races. Rhea believed that our victory in New Orleans, where members of all the dark races fought with me to defeat Lavinia and the Caste of Nod, was proof of that prophecy but I still wasn't convinced. After all, tonight's drama had thoroughly destroyed any chance at peace.

"Maisie, honey?" I said, taking a cautious step toward her. Her eyes stayed on her task; her mouth continued to hum. "What are you doing?"

No answer.

"Adam?" Rhea called, her voice panicked.

"Adam isn't invited to this party," Maisie said in a voice that chilled me to my marrow. If monotone can sound evil, this did. "He's been a bad boy."

My heart thumped like a fist against a door. "What did you do to him?"

The brush went back and forth, back and forth. "He needed to be punished for touching what belongs to another," she said in the same dead tone. "It's part of the plan."

My mouth went dry with fear. "If you hurt him, I'll—"

"Shh," she said. "It's the plan." Back. Forth. Back. Forth. Faster now, harder. "He said I had to follow the plan."

"Who did?" But I already knew.

"He who kills to get gain."

"Maisie? Look at me." Her eyes stayed glued to the

canvas. Now her restless side-to-side brushstrokes were harder, bowing the canvas in on itself. "Did you kill Orpheus and Tanith?"

The brush stilled. Her breathing went shallow until she was panting. Her body began rocking back and forth now. She lifted the brush like a dagger. With a hard downward stroke, she stabbed the brush into the female figure flying through the night sky. Her arm reared back and stabbed again, again, again. Each thrust stronger than the last until, finally, the brush broke through the canvas with a loud rip.

But still, the hand stabbed. Still, my twin rocked. Still, she panted like an animal.

I leapt at her, grabbing her wrist in a punishing grip and forcing her to stop. "Stop," I said, my voice cracking. "Please stop, Maisie."

As she fought me, my sister looked up at me with dark, haunted eyes. When she spoke, her voice was no longer her own. It was deeper, echoed, sinister. "Maisie's not here anymore."

Magic slammed through the room. It sizzled past my skin, followed by a hot wind. Maisie's body collapsed in my arms like someone had flipped her off switch.

I looked up, trying to figure out what the hell had happened. Rhea stood just on the other side of the canvas. She rubbed her hands together, as if to release excess energy. Her expression was as solemn as a dirge.

"Thanks," I said quietly.

I was so scared I wanted to vomit. Scared for Maisie. Scared for Adam. Scared for all of us. Whatever magic Cain had woven around my sister's fragile mind was blacker than midnight. I could feel it on her skin. Smell it in the sour sweat coating her body. Hear it echoing in the words she'd spoken.

I looked up and met Giguhl's eyes over Maisie's head. He looked as terrified as I felt. "Find Adam. He's probably close."

While Giguhl started stalking the room, I juggled Maisie's weight in my arms. "How long will she be out?" I asked Rhea.

"She'll sleep until I release the spell. But we have to hurry. She'll enter the Liminal soon," she said, her tone brisk and efficient. "Let's find my nephew."

I gently laid Maisie's body on the floor. She didn't stir, but underneath her lids, her pupils moved restlessly like she was dreaming.

From across the room, Giguhl cursed. "Guys! Something's behind this door." He pointed to a wooden panel set into the far wall. Another large canvas partially blocked the door, but I knew it was just a supply closet. One large enough to hide a body.

The thought made the blood in my veins freeze into ice floes. But if Giguhl had heard something moving, then that meant there was a chance Adam was alive.

"Open it," I said.

Gods, please let him be okay.

"Adam?" he called. He pushed the canvas out of the way, tearing it in the process. Giguhl threw the door open. Light flooded the closet. The beam of light illuminated Adam's back. He didn't move.

"No!" I screamed, running so fast the breeze blew my hair back. "Adam!"

34

*J*ust like in Maisie's painting, Adam's hands were bound to a low-hanging rafter. His head hung down, the muscles of his neck straining. The upper half of his chiton drooped around his waist, exposing his broad back. Red slashes ravaged his skin.

"Giguhl, help me get him down."

I wrapped my arms around Adam's midsection, easing his weight off the floor. The demon slashed the ropes binding his wrists. The mancy's body collapsed into my arms. I lowered him carefully to the floor, laying him on his side to prevent hurting the wounds on his back. He lay still with his eyes closed.

Rhea rushed forward, her face pale. She set the bag she'd filled with supplies next to us. Despite her obvious fear for her nephew, her movements were economical and swift. She removed a vial from the bag, popped the cork, and waved it under his nose. The ammonia scent of hartshorn filled the small room.

Adam's head turned away from the vial, trying to escape the strong smell. I held him still so he couldn't roll over and fall on his back wounds.

"Adam?" Rhea said, bending over his face. His eyelids fluttered and his mouth worked to make sound. Then, like someone had poked him with a cattle prod, he reared up with a gasp. His eyes were wide and he looked around like he didn't recognize us. Then his eyes shifted into focus and he grabbed my arms. "Sabina, something's wrong with Maisie. I think she—" He swallowed hard. When he spoke again his voice was hoarse with emotion. "I think she killed Orpheus."

"Shh. It's okay. We know." I untied the brass bindings on his wrists while Giguhl went to work on his ankles. "Tell us what happened."

He ignored my question and looked around wildly. "Where is she?"

"She's contained," Rhea said, relief making her voice tremor. "Where are you hurt?"

He grimaced. "My back is on fire, but otherwise I'm okay."

"Turn around so I can apply a salve," she commanded, her tone implying that no arguments would be tolerated. "And you can tell us how this happened."

He did as instructed. I had to stifle a curse when I saw his back again. Now that my vision wasn't blurred by fear, I noticed the bite marks mixed in with whip gashes. My stomach turned. It must have been agony for him. Not just the physical pain, but also the confusion and the fear as his best friend turned on him. Again.

Rhea made quick work of finding the appropriate salve to spread over the wounds. She used her fingers to spread the grease over each individual cut and bite. Adam's back muscles went rock hard and sweat bloomed on his shoulders. But he didn't complain. Instead, he spoke slowly, reliving the nightmare for our benefit.

"She woke once we reached the manor. She seemed...

dazed, but I figured she was just upset and confused over what had happened." His broad shoulders shrugged. "She demanded we take her to the studio. I argued with her, saying it was safer in her rooms. But she started pulling her hair and scratching her face. I didn't know what to do. She wouldn't listen to me or calm down. So I gave in, desperate to just make her stop hurting herself.

"Once we were up here, she said the other guards made her too nervous. When I offered to go in alone with her, she finally seemed to relax. The other guards stayed in the hall to patrol the area. Once we were in here alone, she was like a different person. Lighter, I guess. Not so brittle. That should have been my first sign. How could she joke around when she'd just watched Orpheus die?" He shook his head and wiped his brow with the back of his trembling hand.

"Don't be so hard on yourself," Giguhl said. "None of us saw this coming."

The mage sent the demon a small, forced smile. "Anyway, she said she wanted to paint. I figured that might help her stay calm so I helped her set up a canvas on an easel. While she painted happily in the corner, I started looking around at the paintings she'd done recently." He paused as if to collect himself. "Did you see the ones she did of the murders? The one she did of me?"

I nodded and pushed a stray hair off his damp forehead. "Yeah," I whispered.

"At first I couldn't figure it out. I wondered if she'd seen them all in her visions and just hadn't told us. I turned to ask Maisie about it, and she was standing directly behind me." His whole body shuddered. "Her eyes were wild. Like that night in the cemetery." He looked over his shoulder. "When we pulled her out of the crypt. Remember?"

I swallowed hard and nodded. I couldn't speak for fear

of screaming. Hearing him tell the story made my gut twist. I should have known something was wrong with Maisie. Should have insisted on going with Adam when he'd taken her from the Sacred Grove.

"She pointed a finger at me and said, 'You're in the way.' At first, I thought she meant I needed to leave the studio. I tried to tell her I needed to stay and protect her, but she laughed. Said I was the one who needed protection. That I needed to be punished for soiling you."

My eyebrows slammed down. What the hell?

"I should have subdued her right then," he continued, laughing bitterly. "But I was worried I might hurt her. She blasted me with a spell that paralyzed me. She must have hit me, too, because I lost consciousness for a while."

He paused to gasp as Rhea applied medicine to a particularly deep bite wound. "Sorry," she mumbled. I looked down and saw that her hands were shaking. With rage or fear, I didn't know. Probably both.

"Next thing I knew," he continued, his voice tight, "I woke up hanging from the ceiling. The ropes must have had brass woven into them because I couldn't use magic to defend myself. She whipped me with something that stung like a scorpion's tail. In between lashes, she'd lick the blood away." He started shivering uncontrollably. "Sometimes, she'd bite me, growling like an animal. Then she'd speak in this voice that scared me more than the pain." He paused, as if he didn't have the strength to continue.

I placed a gentle hand on his shoulder. "What did she say?"

He shook himself and wrapped his arms around his torso. "Mostly it was unintelligible rants. Maybe it was some arcane language. Every now and then, she'd fall back into English and say things like 'She's mine' and 'Must

punish him.' Then the whipping would start all over again."
He frowned. "I was having trouble following because the
blood loss and pain kept making me lose consciousness.
Before I finally passed out altogether, I heard her whisper
to herself, 'They're coming.' Then she stopped."

"That must have been when we arrived," Giguhl said.
He rubbed his claws over his arms, as if to warm himself.
"Gods, this is some fucked-up shit."

Adam let out a shuddering chuckle. "Amen."

Rhea finally finished coating all the gashes and bites.
She paused and looked over her work. "That should do it,"
she said in an overly bright tone. I knew she was trying to
be strong for Adam's benefit, but her expression was
tortured.

"Giguhl," I said. "See if you can find a blanket." The
demon nodded solemnly and ran off.

Adam turned around to look at us. "How bad is it?"

Rhea sniffed and sat up straighter. "A couple of these
probably need stitches, but you'll live."

He nodded, seeming to process the information. Then
he looked up at me. His eyes were like liquid shadows.
"What's wrong with her?"

I swallowed hard, gathering my courage. It's not that I
didn't think Adam should hear this, more that I wasn't sure
I could actually say it out loud and maintain my toehold on
sanity. "I think Cain had been visiting Maisie's dreams and
controlling her in some way."

Adam frowned. "But you said Maisie stopped sleeping."

I went still. My memory flashed back to the night I'd
talked to my sister about the dream ritual for the first time.
Back then, she'd said she'd not slept for two nights. I did the
math quickly in my head. "I'll be damned," I breathed.
Pieces started clicking in place. "Remember the night of

the first two murders? Maisie came by our apartment and freaked out?"

Everyone nodded.

"I thought she flipped out because I offered her blood. But when I did that, I'd been telling you guys I'd seen that crime scene in the park. What if that's what set her off? She was upset I'd seen her first kill."

Giguhl crossed his arms. "I don't get how that ties into her not sleeping."

I chewed my lip, trying to reason my way through memory and fact to piece it together. "The night Maisie admitted she stopped sleeping she said it had been two nights. Meaning she hadn't slept since the night of the murders." I leaned forward, warming up to the idea. "What if Maisie was somehow conscious of what Cain was making her do and believed the only solution was to go on a sleep strike?"

Rhea's head tilted as she thought it through. "That would explain why no other murders happened between that night and now."

A troubling thought hit me then. "Oh, gods! The dream incubation. None of this would have happened if we'd left her alone."

Rhea shook her head. "Don't go there, Sabina. Eventually Maisie would have had to sleep again. Besides, you heard her the next day. Asclepius fought off Cain in the form of the white stag that night."

"Which means Cain must have come back to her last night." I ran my hands through my hair, like it might somehow make my brain work better. None of this made sense. "Gods! I wish I knew what game he was playing."

"What do you mean? He achieved his goal. Maisie killed Tanith and Orpheus. Peace will never happen now."

I shook my head. "I'm not so sure. If she'd killed one or

the other, maybe that would be true. But both? Sure, the treaty didn't get signed but it's not like we're back on the brink of war. No. Cain had an ulterior motive."

Adam sighed, grimacing as the move pinched his wounds. "So what are we going to do?"

"You are going to rest," Rhea interrupted. "Between the blood loss and the risk of infection, you're in no state to do much of anything."

"Bullshit," he said. "I'm not going to take a nap like a fucking infant. We've got to stop Cain."

"And save Maisie," I added. He looked at me then, his eyes telling me what he didn't want to say out loud: He believed Maisie was beyond salvation. "Whatever she's done, no matter how horrible, this is not her fault. Cain is a master manipulator. Maisie is as much a victim—maybe more—as any of us right now."

Adam's eyes skittered away from my gaze, like he felt ashamed. I suppose I couldn't blame him for his feelings, especially given everything he'd suffered at Maisie's hands. But I wasn't ready to give up on her. Not yet.

Giguhl came back in and handed Rhea a blanket. She carefully wrapped it around his front. "Don't cover the wounds. They need air to heal." She turned to me. "Can I speak with you for a moment?"

I nodded. Before I rose, I looked at Adam. Despite the blanket, he was still shaking. I rose to my knees and put my hands on his cheeks. His eyes were red-rimmed and shining. I bit my lip and tried to fight my own need to fall apart. So much needed to be said between us. So much regret and sadness hovered between us like a ghost. But we didn't have the luxury of indulging our need to talk or find solace in each other.

So I simply leaned forward and kissed his forehead. I

closed my eyes and inhaled the sandalwood scent of him. But it didn't bring me the comfort it normally did because of the added stench of blood and fear.

I pulled away quickly before I could give in to the urge to wrap myself around him and make promises I wasn't sure I could keep. That we'd get Cain. That he was safe now. That Maisie wouldn't be a threat to him anymore. That everything would be okay between us.

"Giguhl, stay with him," I said, my tone clipped. Then I turned my back on Adam and followed Rhea into the studio.

She didn't shut the door. Instead, she pulled me to the other side, where we could keep one eye on Maisie's limp form and the other on Adam and his demonic nursemaid. "You know what comes next, right?"

I wished I didn't. I wished I could just turn away and disappear into the night, my memory wiped clean. But wishes were for children and fools.

Of course I knew what I had to do. The problem was, unlike conventional battles, I felt totally unprepared to fight Cain in the Liminal. Sure, I could get there. Sure, I could probably find Maisie's dream form. And then what? I couldn't kill Cain. But even if killing him didn't have horrible repercussions, how did one defeat a dream?

Rhea looked at me with those we're-counting-on-you pleading stares. It's funny. I'd spent so much time declaring myself a lone wolf. Shouting to the world that I didn't need anyone. But I'd learned a lot about working as a team over the last several months. I'd finally begun to rely on my mentor, my mage, and my demon more than I ever expected. Beyond just friendship and love. As allies. Warriors who had my back no matter the foe. As friends and champions.

But this was one battle I had to fight alone. One I might

not be able to return from even if I somehow managed to win. But I didn't have a choice. Again. Fucking fate had screwed me again.

"Yeah," I said finally. "Do we need to go back to the chapel?"

"Yes." She rubbed her lip for a moment, thinking it over. "It'll go better if we make another offering to Asclepius. He might be able to help once you're in the Liminal."

The false optimism in her tone told me she already expected to be mourning me too soon. But she also knew I would go through with the plan despite both our fears. If I was going to be trapped in the Liminal forever, fine. I'd just spend eternity kicking Cain's ass and making sure he never tormented anyone I loved again.

Giguhl emerged from the closet. "What's going on?"

I turned and frowned at him. "I thought you were staying with Adam?"

The demon shrugged. "He said he needed a minute alone."

"We're talking about Sabina going into the Liminal to hunt down Cain," Rhea said.

The demon's scraggly brows rose. "Since when can you access the in-between?"

I paused. How had I not told him about this earlier? Guess he'd been right when he said it'd been too long since we'd really hung out. I'd allowed us to drift too far apart. But now was not the time for sentimentality or regrets. Now was the time for action.

"It's a long story," I said. Then I paused. "Wait, how do you know about the Liminal?"

"Are you kidding?" he said, waving a claw. "It's like the rest stop between your world and Irkalla. I've been there lots of times."

"You've never gotten lost?"

He frowned. "Of course not. You know as well as I do that whoever summons me controls me. Even if I wanted to hang out there for a while, I couldn't if you told me to leave."

My mouth fell open. I slowly turned to look at Rhea. "Are you thinking what I'm thinking?"

A slow smile spread across the elder's face. "Let's get moving."

The three of us turned to grab Adam and head to the chapel, but the doors to the studio burst open. The Queen's knights rushed in like commandos storming a hostage situation. When they saw the three of us standing there frowning at them, they skittered to a halt. "Hold it right there," their leader demanded.

I didn't have time to argue, so I raised my hands. My companions followed suit.

The shout of "all clear" echoed back through the ranks until they parted to allow the Queen through. Alexis was by her side, looking shell-shocked to see the scene in the studio. Their eyes took in the four dead mages, the canvases filled with murder, and my bloody, naked twin unconscious on the ground.

Adam came out of the closet to see what the racket was and stopped just beyond the doorway. "What the hell's going on?"

The Queen raised a ringed finger. "What happened to you?"

Adam shook his head and blew out an annoyed breath. "If it's all the same to you, I really don't have the energy to explain it again."

"And we definitely don't have the time," Rhea said.

The Queen's eyes narrowed. "Mind your tone, Rhea."

"No, you mind yours, *Maeve*." The silver-haired mage

rose up to her full height and infused her tone with dignity. "Now, you can get your crown in a twist and throw a tantrum because we'd rather stop a murderer than bow and scrape before you. Or you can shut the hell up and let us do what needs to be done. Either way, you will not stop us. However, if you go with plan B we will explain what's happening on our way to the chapel."

The Queen's mouth fell open so wide a small family of birds could have taken nest in her maw. "Well, I never."

"That much is clear," Rhea said. "So what will it be?"

The Queen's eyes narrowed. But instead of calling for Rhea's head or whatever it is monarchs do, she scanned the room. Whatever she saw, which frankly could have been one of a thousand different damning details, must have convinced her we were more than prepared to handle the situation. Finally, she cleared her throat and nodded her head regally. "Lead the way."

35

A chill seeped from the stone floor and up through the thin cotton pallet. Maisie's still form lay a few feet away. Our positions brought on a wave of *déjà vu*. My memory flew back to another ritual space, in another town. To another night when both our lives had hung in the balance.

In New Orleans, our grandmother had chained Maisie and me to altars and then forced me to watch as Maisie fed from Adam. That moment wasn't the beginning of our issues, but it certainly took them to a new level. The image of my sister feeding off the mage I loved was the one that haunted me every night when I closed my eyes. It was the one I dreamed about. The one that made me wake up covered in sweat and grasping desperately for Adam to reassure myself he was still alive.

And there we were, months later, lying in almost the exact same position. Only this time, there were no physical bodies to fight. Only nightmares.

My willingness to fight this battle didn't prevent the cold sweat on my chest or the urge to jump up and run away. Gods only knew what horrors waited for me in the dreams that had become my sister's prison.

"Are you sure you want to do this?" Adam's color was better, thanks to a potion Rhea mixed up for him. But his eyes still had shadows that I worried might never go away.

"No." I forced a wobbly smile. "But I'm going to do it anyway."

He caressed my cheek with his palm. "Do you remember when you said I didn't love all of you?"

I swallowed hard against the knot of regret in my throat. "Adam—"

"Hush, let me finish." He placed a finger over my lips. "It's not that I don't love the reckless, dark parts of you. They're what make you brave and I love that about you. But the truth is they also scare the hell out of me."

"Why?" I whispered.

"Because deep down I've always known the day would come when they would take you away from me." He paused. "I thought that if I could get you to leave that part of yourself behind, you'd stay forever. But I see now I only managed to push you away sooner."

I sat up and pressed my lips to his. My hands twined up into his hair. I tried to put a lifetime into that kiss. Just in case. "You listen to me, Adam Lazarus," I whispered against his lips. "When I return, we'll have plenty of adventures. Together."

"I'm holding you to that." He grabbed me by the chin and forced me to look in his eyes. "Come back to me."

Emotion gathered in my throat like bile. My dry eyes stung. This wasn't new, this sinking feeling. It was so familiar now that I knew better than to indulge it. "It's a deal."

Too soon, he pulled away. Retreated to the rear of the temple. His gaze held mine as Rhea moved in to begin the ritual. I was so tired of saying good-bye, maybe forever, to him. Used to be that pain involved fist to flesh or snapped bones. Physical pain. Easy pain. But now? It had been a long time since I'd had even so much as a hangnail. But the emotional pain I endured since I'd left my violent life behind hurt worse than any fist, blade, or bullet.

In the back of my brain, a faint, echoed voice—the ghostly remains of the Old Sabina—whispered insults. Old Sabina never cried. She would never be scared of a fucking dream. And she sure as shit wouldn't volunteer to put herself in the path of a madman who knew all her secret weaknesses. Not for her sister. Not for anyone.

Rhea bent over me, bringing with her a calming herbal scent. "Try to relax."

A shaky laugh escaped me. "Easy for you to say." My fists wouldn't unclench. The spot where I'd cut my palm a few moments earlier to make another blood sacrifice to Asclepius had already healed, but the skin there still burned.

"Do it anyway," she said.

To distract myself from my fear, I focused on identifying the ingredients of the fragrant oil she dabbed on my forehead, temples, and wrists. Six months earlier, I couldn't tell the difference between a cannabis plant and a fern. But now I called up the name and purpose of each herb in the oil by scent alone. Sharp, woody rosemary for focus and purity. Helichrysum, with its musty-sweet straw and honey scent, for unblocking the subconscious and healing old emotional wounds. Clean, light cedar wood to calm the mind and ease tension.

Giguhl sat in a half-lotus position next to me, cradling

my cold hand in his claw. His eyes were closed while he waited for the rituals to be completed. Ever since I told him he'd be coming with me to the Liminal, he'd grown quiet, introspective. I guess I'd expected him to bitch and moan. But even the Mischief demon understood the gravity of our mission and felt the need to mentally prepare.

I was relieved that Rhea had insisted the Queen, Alexis, and the rest of the mages, faeries, and vampires stay outside the chapel during the ritual. It was hard enough to focus with the voices in my head reminding me that I had no idea how to win this battle. It would only have been worse with an audience. Even so, I felt their presence just beyond the walls. The tension, the speculations, the pressure.

Rhea's papery soft hands found mine. She looked into my eyes, her own dark with worry. "You need to call up your power. It will open a direct conduit to the Liminal."

A cramp pinched my clenched jaw. I licked my lips. Calling up my Chthonic energies was always unsettling. The blessing and the curse of my Chthonic abilities was that they were easier to access when I was under some sort of extreme emotional stress. Rhea had worked with me to be able to call them at will, but never were they as strong as when I was angry or scared. Which meant they should be a snap to command at that moment.

I took a deep cleansing breath and closed my eyes. In my mind, I played a montage of Maisie's greatest hits. The feral Maisie we'd liberated from that crypt. Remorseful Maisie, just after she realized she'd nearly killed Adam. Vengeful Maisie, Lavinia's executioner. Fugue-state Maisie, the murderer.

My chest swelled and my head swam as I reexperienced

those moments. I swam through the wave of emotions they brought up, diving down into black current.

Power rose up through the floor. Sizzled under my skin, rising up through my legs, my abdomen, my chest, my throat. My throat expanded and filled with the dark power.

As if from far away, I heard Rhea's voice. "Steady."

I opened my eyes. My vision was tinged red but super sharp. I noticed individual dust motes and the spider building a web in the rafters of the old chapel. I heard the heartbeat of a mouse hiding in the walls.

Hot wind rose, whipping my hair up around my face. Inside, I felt a door open in my solar plexus and the gentle tug of the in-between.

Maisie moaned in her sleep. Beneath her pale lids, her eyes jerked back and forth. Her breathing became more rapid.

"Don't leave her body." The voice that emerged from my lips was both mine and not mine. Deeper, darker, like a secret language.

Rhea put a hand over her heart. "I will watch over her corporeal form. You see to her spirit."

Confident everyone would be safe here in the mortal realm, I surrendered to the pull of the Liminal. "Giguhl, let's do this."

This time, the shock of arriving in the Liminal wasn't as sharp. I'd already seen the lunar landscape, the creepy crossroads with its ominous red flag, the horizons shimmering like a mirage. The light still hurt my eyes and the sharp air slashed my lungs. But something was different.

Me.

When I'd come before, I hadn't tapped into my Chthonic power. I was just me, Sabina, visiting a foreign place. But when I called up my power, I was more. The power of the Chthonic goddesses filled me: Melinoe and Persephone, Themis and Gaia, Hekate and Lilith. Their dark energies allowed me to see details I couldn't before.

A low-slung red moon loomed on the horizon. Black crows crouched in a skeletal tree. And long before the howl called to me, I felt the beast's presence. The beat of its heart called to me through the thin air. Its hatred burned my skin. Its green eyes flashed a warning. It paused, just beyond the horizon, knowing I was already tracking its progress. My awareness of it confused the beast. Frightened it.

Good.

I didn't have time to pursue shadow monsters. I had to find Maisie and free her from the prison of Cain's influence. I still wasn't sure how I was supposed to manage that trick. But first I had to find her.

And Giguhl.

"G?" I yelled. My voice echoed back at me like a taunt. Where the hell had that demon gone?

I turned slowly on the crossroads, looking for some sign of my wayward minion. But just then, a faraway shout reached my ears. Squinting in the odd light, I looked up. A gray speck rushed toward the ground from high above. The shouts grew louder the larger the speck grew.

I jumped out of the way at the last moment. Giguhl, in cat form, slammed to the earth like a tiny, hairless meteor. His body lay still in a deep crater in the center of the crossroads. Scrambling down the side of the hole, I rushed toward him.

"Giguhl!" I shouted, lifting his small, limp body.

The cat shook himself. "Thank the gods for nine lives," he groaned.

I frowned, checking him over for injuries. But other than his unfocused pupils, he seemed fine. "I'm glad you're all right, but I didn't tell you to change forms," I said. "Change back to the big-ass, scary demon, please." The last thing I needed was to face down Cain with a shivering feline.

"Red, this is the Liminal," the cat said, pulling himself out of my arms. He licked his paws and smoothed them over his head. "Normal rules don't apply."

Of course they didn't. Because that would make things easier. "Can you just decide to change into your demon form?"

"You don't get it." The cat shook his head. "I didn't choose this form. The Liminal chose it for me."

I sighed and shook my head. "Are you saying the Liminal has a consciousness and can impose its own will?"

"Trust me, Red. It's best not to question these things." He shrugged his naked shoulder. "Let's just go find Maisie, okay?"

I looked around the crossroads for some clue of where to begin our search for Cain and Maisie. But when a neon sign that said PSYCHOTIC MURDERER THIS WAY didn't appear, I knew it was time to try something else.

My next logical step would have been to call out for Maisie. But something, some instinct, told me to hold my tongue. A low-frequency pressure in my gut pulsed with the knowledge that monsters worse than the growling beast lurked in the shadows.

Two red dots appeared in the distance. Eyes. I braced myself, expecting Stryx. The vampiric owl had met an untimely end in New Orleans at the hands of a zombie I'd accidentally summoned, but that didn't mean he didn't make occasional appearances in my nightmares. Plus, the feathered demon had belonged to Cain, so it wasn't out of the realm of possibility he'd make an appearance.

Closer now. Low to the ground. I frowned. If the eyes belonged to an owl, they'd be higher to indicate flying. So if the eyes didn't belong to the owl, I reasoned, they must have belonged to one with four legs. "Look alive, G. We've got company."

I looked around for a place to set up a defensive position. But I had no weapons. Although judging from Giguhl's claim that normal rules didn't apply here, I wondered what good mundane weapons would do me anyway. And the desolate landscape offered little in the way of cover. So I stood in the center of the spokes with my fists clenched and my body braced for attack.

The creature reached us quickly. Faster than anything could have moved in the mortal realm. Jaw clenched, I waited.

Then, as if someone had pulled back a black curtain, the canine emerged into the light. Something about the dog seemed familiar. Like I'd met it before. Of course that was impossible, but still, the feeling the animal was an ally persisted.

"You now owe me two favors, Chosen." The dog's mouth didn't move, but I clearly heard the male voice in my head. At first, the words made no sense. I frowned down at the dog, wondering if this was some trick of my subconscious. "But I have to say, the sacrifice of such potent mixed blood almost makes it worth my trouble."

That's when I realized who the dog really was. "Asclepius?" I said aloud.

The big black head nodded. I should have felt reassured,

but my thoughts kept shifting like sand. Other voices whispered in my head. And every now and then, a flash of light or shadow would zoom by in my peripheral vision.

"Red?" Giguhl whispered. "What's going on?"

"Shh." I grabbed him off the ground and threw him on my shoulder. "Can you take me to her?" I asked the god.

Without another thought or action, the dog turned and trotted away. With Giguhl in my arms, I took off after him. "Red, seriously. It's probably not a good idea to follow strange animals around right now."

"Hush," I said. "I know what I'm doing." No, I didn't at all, but my instincts were guiding me now.

Soon the lunar landscape gave way to large gray boulders. Asclepius slipped between two building-sized rocks I hadn't seen before. He didn't glance back to be sure I was following. He knew I would.

The entrance to the cave gaped open like a mouth in silent scream. Asclepius's red eyes bathed the portal in blood light. "She's down there," the voice boomed in my head.

"Wait," I said. "Aren't you coming with me?"

"This is your battle," he thought at me. "Others will appear when you need them. Good luck, Sabina Kane. You'll be hearing from me soon. If you survive." With that optimistic farewell, the dog turned and ran off.

Just beyond the red haze, the darkness was absolute. Even my preternatural night vision couldn't penetrate the oppressive blackness. With a hand in front of me, I stepped forward. But when my foot lowered, it kept going.

A lifetime of throat-searing screams later, I landed on something hard and wet. I cradled Giguhl in my arms, protecting him from the drop. His little body shivered from something stronger than a chill. "Awesome call following the dog," he said in a voice as dry as the Sahara.

Ignoring him, I stood slowly and got my bearings. The top of the cavern rose high above like a cathedral ceiling covered in stalactites. I blinked against a pulsing blue light, whose source I couldn't locate. Shiny black crags made up the walls and stalagmites rose from the ground like onyx columns. Whispers echoed from farther in the cavern.

I hunched over and wove my way through the garden of rock formations. The air smelled like damp rock, wet metal, and fresh blood. The primordial scent was oddly pleasing. Comforting. Like coming home.

A black lake appeared ahead. Two onyx swans glided across the mirrored surface.

I blinked at the familiar image. I'd been here before. Back in October when I'd done my vision quest. Rhea had fed me a hallucinogenic tea to produce visions that eventually revealed me to be a Chthonic mage. Part of that trippy experience involved my entering a cavern that looked exactly like the one before me. I wasn't sure if I was seeing it again because the Liminal was reading my subconscious—or because the visions had actually been prophetic.

Either way, the similarities made clammy sweat crawl across my skin. Despite my fear, my feet moved toward the edge of the inky water. A white face with dead eyes appeared just under the glassy surface. The features and red hair were vaguely familiar. But as I tried to identify him from memory, another face appeared. And another. Soon, ghostly faces slammed up against the surface in groups of twos and threes, fives and tens. I recognized them now. Every one had died by my hand. These ghosts of sins past pounded on the barrier, their mouths open and screaming words I couldn't hear.

Through the jungle of limbs. Through the gaping, desperate mouths. Through the murky water, a light appeared. The tortured spirits ceased their frantic pleas. Surrendered to the inevitability of their watery tomb.

The pinpoint of light pulsed deep below the surface. With each passing second, the light grew in size and strength. The spirits beneath the water were drawn to the orb like swarming, ghostly moths.

The light rose and as it rose it grew larger, brighter. So blinding that I raised a hand to shield my eyes. Finally, it broke the surface in slow motion. The light morphed into a female figure in white. She rose from the water like a lotus from the swamp.

I fell to my knees.

All those months ago, when I'd first had this vision, I wasn't able to see the face of the female in white. Back then, all I knew was that she stirred up a deep well of regret. I knelt before her now and looked up.

She was so beautiful my eyes ached. Instead of the hollow husk of a woman I'd left behind in the mortal world, Maisie looked as healthy as she had the first time we met. Her cheeks glowed pink and her blue eyes sparkled. Her body had its natural curves under the white chiton. Her curly red hair shone like a shiny red apple.

Wait. That wasn't right. Maisie had straight hair that was streaked through with black, just like mine.

"Who are you?" I asked, suddenly unsure. She looked like Maisie but also like a stranger. One who was pure vampire.

"Shh." She placed a cool palm on my head. "There's no time. He's coming."

This goddess that looked like my sister, like me, made my memory of the real Maisie, the one lying back in the chapel, even more heartbreaking. Seeing what she might have been had I never entered her life. Never fucked with her path. Never exposed her to Lavinia Kane's wrath. Made my role in destroying her that much more stark and impossible to deny.

"Who are you?" I breathed again.

A voice spoke inside my head, as if the female shared a secret she didn't dare speak aloud. *Phoebe*.

My mother.

I'd never met her. I'd been born second that night fifty-four years ago. The night when the struggle to give me life ended in her death.

"I'm so sorry," I said, my voice cracking with emotion. "I'm so fucking sorry."

"Steel your spine, Sabina. Padlock your guilt. He'll feed off it and prevail." Her head jerked like a bird's. "He's almost here. Be strong, daughter mine. This is all a dream and dreams can be controlled." She touched the center of my forehead with her finger. "The Great Mother sends you her blessings and strength, but victory is not assured. You must survive to fulfill your destiny. No matter the cost. Do you understand?"

I nodded mutely. I had no idea what the hell was happening, but then maybe I wasn't supposed to. This realm was not the provenance of logic or reason. Emotion and instinct were the monarchs of this dark kingdom, this fortress of symbol. I closed my eyes, trying to herd my tangled thoughts.

A kiss as gentle as butterfly wings tickled my skin. When I opened my eyes, she was gone. My mother was gone.

"Sabina?" Giguhl whispered. "What the fuck is going on?"

A low growl echoed through the cavern. The hairs on

the back of my neck went stiff. I turned slowly to locate the source of the threat. Two glowing eyes peered at me from across the lake. Dropping Giguhl, I fell into my fighting stance.

Time slowed. Blood oozed. Pulse throbbed.

Thump...thump...thump.

The stag stepped out from the darkness, his red antlers and green eyes shockingly chromatic in the drab underworld. In the foreground, Maisie knelt on the shore. She wore a white chiton, the right strap drooping over one shoulder. She hummed to herself. Her melancholy tune drifted across the pool and reached my ears. The sound made static crawl under my skin.

"Maisie?" I called.

She didn't look up from the skull she cradled in her arms like a baby.

I started running before my thoughts registered the action. Instinct screamed for me to grab Maisie before the stag could reach her. I shot forward, directly across the water.

But with each step, the opposite shore grew farther away. My feet pedaled uselessly, like running on wet glass. The faces returned, taunting me from their wet grave.

My heart pounded and sweat beaded on my upper lip. The stag stood over Maisie now. She looked up and the beast stroked her face with its velvet muzzle. Her head shook from side to side, defiant despite her obvious fear.

"Maisie!" I screamed, but the sound shattered on the air. A movement along the shore caught my eyes, a flash of gray among the obsidian sand. Giguhl was making his way around the lake, unnoticed by the stag or Maisie. I snapped my mouth shut instead of calling to him.

Pull yourself together, Sabina. You control the dream, remember?

I stilled and gathered my powers in my solar plexus. Instead of fighting the parade of images, I lassoed my will and focused on my goal.

To the shore.

When I looked down, my feet were already on the black sands. The stag looked up, his green eyes widening. His head tilted. "I knew you'd come."

Ignoring the beast, I ran to Maisie. "We need to go." I pulled at her. I pleaded. I cajoled. And finally, I threatened. But she refused to budge.

As I struggled with my sister, the stag began to morph. Bones popped, skin stretched grotesquely.

Maisie fought me, scratching at my arms and face. Only instead of screaming or crying out, she laughed. Cackled even as she drew blood. "Not until it is done," she said in a singsong voice. I bent down to lift her and run like hell. The laughter cut off. "No! Not until it's done!" She kicked and rolled, falling back to the black sand.

"Sabina," a gentle male voice called. The sound of my name on his lips made my skin go icy hot. I looked up slowly to see not a beast before me but a man.

Cain.

His face, a study in masculine beauty, more perfect than Michelangelo's *David* or any of Hollywood's leading men. His olive skin emphasized his light green eyes, which glowed like poisonous neon. His long, red hair—the color of the shiny red apple that tempted Eve—fell across broad shoulders. The finely muscled chest formed a perfect V, tapering down to his sex, which stood proudly against his washboard abdominals. He had no shame over his nudity. Instead, he preened for me, like a peacock.

I stood slowly, my muscles taut in preparation for an attack. "Get away from her." My voice emerged surprisingly powerful despite the fear clawing at my throat.

"It's not her I want." He held out his hands. "It's you, Lamashtu. It's always been you."

"I am not fucking Lamashtu," I said, my volume rising. "I am Sabina Kane. And you can't have me."

His eyes darkened. "Oh, but you are her. Just as she is you. And you're both mine."

"Listen, asshole," I said, placing my hands on my hips. "It's time to move on already. Lilith chose Asmodeus. She doesn't want you either."

"*She is mine!*" His scream bounced off the cavern walls, making the stalactites tremble.

I flinched and moved to shield Maisie. "All right," I said, lowering my voice into what I hoped was a calming tone. I felt anything but calm, but I knew that angering him further would diminish our chances of surviving this confrontation. "Tell me what you want."

"You think you're so clever. I'll admit I worried when that mongrel god appeared two nights ago," he said, his mouth tightening in anger. Then as suddenly as the frown appeared, it dissolved into a grin. "Too bad you didn't protect her the next night."

My stomach cramped. He was talking about the incubation. The next night, I'd left without saying good-bye to Maisie, the night of Mac's mating. I'd promised my sister I'd come see her after that, but I had gotten so wrapped up in my own drama that she'd slipped my mind. But she obviously hadn't slipped Cain's.

"I didn't ask how," I said, raising my chin. "I want to know why. So I'll repeat: What do you want?"

He spread his arms and smiled a smile he probably

thought was charming. It turned my stomach. "You're going to free me from this infernal prison." He motioned to indicate the Liminal as a whole. "And then you're going to take me to Irkalla to claim what is mine."

My mouth fell open. "You can't be serious. Why would I release you?"

"Because if you don't," he said, his lip quirking, "I'll kill your sister."

"Not if I kill you first."

He tilted his head to the side. "I admire your bloodlust, my darling, but we both know if you kill me, your sister will die anyway. Along with the six other beings you love most in this world."

Images flashed through my head, the faces of those I loved. Who would the victims be? Adam, Giguhl, and Rhea, definitely. And the others? Pussy Willow, Georgia, Mac, Slade, Zenobia? Which of those would also suffer for my revenge? I couldn't stand the idea of any of them dying.

My fists clenched. Dammit! I wanted to raise my face and howl at the God of the mortals who promised vengeance sevenfold to anyone who killed Cain. How could a just God protect this beast? This murderer? "I won't break the spell!"

"You have no choice. Because after I kill your sister, I'll pay a visit to your mage's dreams and finish what your sister started on my behalf. I'll make him slit his own throat at your feet." He took a step toward me.

"Don't you fucking take another step!"

"Do you really want their blood on your hands?" Another step. "Again?"

I backed up, my legs bumping into Maisie's kneeling form. My heart felt like lead in my chest. "What makes you think I can access Irkalla?" I said, changing the subject to distract him from the idea of killing the people I loved most in the world. "Or that if I can get you there, that Lilith will go with you?"

"Because she has been waiting for centuries for me to free her from that bastard demon king."

"You're insane. She chose Asmodeus."

"She chose me!" His roar shook the stalactites. When the rumbling subsided, he smiled again. "Just as you must choose."

Panic rose in me like a flash flood. I had no idea how to talk him out of forcing me to make such an impossible choice. But just then, a flash of gray zoomed through my peripheral vision. Giguhl launched himself at Cain's face. The cat sunk his claws into his lips, his throat. With his teeth, he bit at the madman's eyes. Cain screamed like a little girl. He thrashed around wildly, trying to rip the cat off his head.

Magic rose in the cavern, making my ears pop. Cain morphed from his human form back into that of the stag. With a mighty whip of his head, the beast threw the demon from its muzzle. Giguhl slammed into a hard, rocky wall with a whimper. His little body slid limply down to the black sands, where it lay still. Too still.

"No!" I screamed. I launched myself at the beast. Willing a sword into my hand, I swung it at the stag's antlers. I couldn't kill Cain, but I sure as hell could make him bleed. The steel slashed just below the beast's right antler, lopping it clean off the scalp.

I spun, bringing the blade around for another punishing slice. This time the tip scored the beast's chest. Bright red blood stained the pristine white fur. I backed away, trying to make my way to Maisie. My only real choice now was escape. I needed to get Maisie and Giguhl the hell out of the Liminal before the beast could carry out his fucked-up plans.

Behind me, Cain howled. The same howl I'd heard during my first visit to the Liminal. The hairs on my arms rose. I heard him coming, his hoofs pounding the sand. I swung around, raising the sword. The steel reached its apex over my head at the same instant the stag slammed into me.

White lightning exploded in my chest. The air whooshed from my lungs. The left antler's three sharp points were impaled in the skin just over my left breast. Blood spray coated my torso and dripped from each of the wounds. But my broken ribs and torn muscles were nothing compared to the agony of knowing I'd just doomed us all.

Time slowed. The sword fell to the sand. My knees buckled. I clawed at the antler but I was too weak from pain and fear. Finally, the stag reversed direction, pulling the sharp points slowly from my flesh. I screamed. The pain was so intense my vision blackened. Gravity betrayed me and I fell face-first into the sands.

Magic snaked through the cavern once again as Cain changed forms. Bare male feet passed my face. As if from far away, I heard him talking to Maisie. I tried to yell, to warn her to run, but a violent cough racked my chest. I tasted blood on my tongue. My blood.

The male feet reappeared beside me. Two smaller feet beside it. I couldn't make out Cain's next words over the roaring in my ears. But in the next instant, Maisie knelt next to my face. She tilted her head to look me in the eyes. "Don't worry, sister," she whispered. A gentle hand wiped my brow. "It's almost over."

Then she lifted her wrist to her mouth and bit down hard

with her fangs. The world tilted and I was suddenly looking up at her. The haze of pain and confusion blurred my vision. A shadow leaned over me. My nose filled with my sister's familiar sandalwood and copper penny scent. I blinked to clear my eyes.

"Repeat after me, little one." Cain's voice came from far away, echoey and menacing. "*Ati me peta Babka.*"

I'd heard these words before. In the cemetery in New Orleans when the Caste members tried to summon Cain. It had to be the reversal spell to break Abel's magic and free the monster from his coma.

"No!" I yelled. "Maisie, don't!"

But my sister's eyes had glazed over. Cain controlled her now. And he was using her voice and our blood to free himself. She repeated the words in a mechanical voice.

"The blood," Cain commanded. "Now!"

Maisie raised her wrist over my chest. When the first drop of her blood landed in my wound, fire spread through my veins. My back arched up and a scream escaped my lungs.

Cain inhaled deeply, his chest expanding as if inhaling power deep into his center. "Good. Good!" He stepped closer to Maisie, urging her on. "*Wussuru Mahan ana harrani sa alaktasa la Tarat!*"

I strained to rise, to stop them. But I was too weak. My chest itched and throbbed hotly. "Maisie," I pleaded. "Honey, don't. Don't say it!"

Maisie paused, her mouth open to repeat the words that would free Cain. Her eyes flashed clear for an instant. "Sabina?" She sounded scared and confused. She began to pull her wrist away.

"Run, Maze!"

But Cain came up behind my sister. He placed one hand

on her shoulder. The other grabbed her bloody wrist and forced it over my chest.

Another searing infusion. I hissed against the pain as her blood mixed with mine. Cold sweat bloomed on my upper lip. My jaw cramped from lack of oxygen. I panted shallowly, struggling to fight off the panic attack.

Cain leaned over to whisper in her ear. "Almost done, my sweet. Focus."

Maisie struggled against him, her head shaking from side to side in frantic movements.

"*Wussuru Mahan ana harrani sa alaktasa la Tarat!*" A knife appeared in Cain's hand. The blade glinted evilly against the vulnerable skin at her throat. "Say it!"

She stiffened back into her robotic posture and her eyes glazed over again.

"No!" I cried. Hot tears burned my throat. Another drop of my sister's blood hit my wound like acid. Cain's form flickered and flashed. His full lips spread into a victorious smile.

"*Wussuru Mahan ana harrani sa alaktasa la Tarat.*"

It happened fast. The instant Maisie stopped speaking, Cain dragged the blade across Maisie's throat.

"No!" I screamed, my voice hoarse with fear and shock.

My sister's eyes widened and a gasp escaped her lips. Blood gushed from the angry wound. A gurgle escaped her mouth and more blood poured from her throat.

His form wavered again, going transparent. But Cain wasn't content to exit the scene without one final fuck-you.

"See you soon, Sabina Kane."

The air popped, signaling Cain's escape from the Liminal.

Fear shocked me into action despite the pain. Riding a surge of adrenaline, I lunged for my sister just as she started to slump over.

"Nonononono!" I ripped my shirt off my chest and pressed it against her throat. Wrapping my free arm around her, I forced my sister to look up at me. The whites of her eyes were impossibly large. Her lids flickered, like wings. "Honey, stay with me. Maisie?"

So much blood. Rivers of it. On some level, my mind demanded to know why her body wasn't healing the wound. I looked down at my own chest wound, which was already closing. Was it possible the spectral blood Maisie dripped into the wound was some kind of healing spell? And more important, could I do the same for her even though she was only in the Liminal in her spectral form?

I shook her roughly. "Maisie, you have to fight! It's just a dream!" I lifted my wrist to my mouth and slammed my fangs into the thin skin. Blood oozed thickly from the wound. Held it to Maisie's mouth. "Drink, Maisie."

Her mouth worked but no sound came out except a wet gurgle. She shook her head, turned her face away from the healing I offered. "Dammit, Maisie! You have to drink!"

I realized then that my blood and my magic couldn't save her. If she was going to survive, she had to consciously will herself to heal. She had to choose to live.

But her eyes told me the story. She'd already surrendered.

"No!" I screamed at her. I shook her harder, slapped her face. Forced her lips to part so my blood could find its way down her throat. But it oozed down her lips, her chin, her throat to mix uselessly with her own. "Don't you fucking give up!"

But her lips were already turning blue. Her muscles didn't strain. She blinked once, twice. I squeezed the material tighter around her neck, trying in vain to stanch the tidal wave of blood.

I looked around frantically, trying to find something, anything to help her. She shifted in my arms. I looked down to see her lids barely cracked. Her mouth moved. I bent over her to listen.

"No use," she breathed. "I died months ago."

My tears fell on her face like rain. "Maisie, please," I said through sobs. "Stay with me."

I rested my cheek on hers. But it was cold. So damned cold.

"Bina," she said, barely more than a breath. "Trust fate, sister." She coughed wetly, blood pouring from her lips. "Always with...you."

With one final breath, my sister's body sagged in my arms. "Godsdammit, Maisie! No!"

Her mouth fell open and a bright light escaped. The orb rose on the air and swirled around us once, twice, three times. As it spun, a deep blistering pain scored my left shoulder. I didn't flinch. Didn't shy from the pain. I was beyond feeling at that moment. Beyond self-preservation.

After the orb made its third lap, it rose high in the air before slamming down into the pool. The wake of its entry splashed a plume of black water high into the air. Then the light sank fast, until I couldn't see it anymore.

Maisie was gone.

My head fell back and I screamed my rage at the universe. Sobs doubled me over her body, already cold. I rocked back and forth, praying to every goddess I knew to bring Maisie back to me. I made outrageous promises and issued violent threats.

But she was gone.

I don't know how long I sat there, cradling her body and bawling. Time moved like oil in water. But eventually, I felt a warm touch on my back. It didn't scare me. I was beyond such weak emotions as fear. "Leave me, Giguhl."

The warmth didn't recede. "Sabina." The voice was feminine, rich, and dark. Definitely not Giguhl.

Blinking against the wetness clogging my eyes, I looked up.

"Daughter, it is time to leave this place." Phoebe glowed warmly, but her heat couldn't reach me.

I shook my head and squeezed my eyes shut. I resumed my rocking, faster now, more urgent. "I'm not leaving her."

"Sabina," my mother said. "She's already gone. Look."

I opened my eyes. My arms cradled nothing but air now. I stilled, but something deep inside me coiled to life. "Where is she?"

Phoebe smiled down at me. "At peace finally." My mother pointed to my chest, my heart. "But never doubt she is with you."

I licked my parched lips. "I don't understand." I choked on a gut-wrenching sob.

"The beast is free now. Until he is stopped, no one is safe. That is all you need to know."

"But I don't know how to stop him!" I cried. "I can't do this."

She lifted my chin with her fingers. "You can because you have to. He must pay for what he did to Maisie. He must pay for what he did to us."

Thunder rolled through the cavern. I cringed, wrapping my arms around my shivering body.

I swallowed my fear and frowned at her. "Us? Wha—"

Phoebe cowered and looked around, her eyes fearful. "There's not time. You must go." Her body went from solid to transparent. "Find the mage who calls himself Abel. He will help you." With that, my mother disappeared.

I sagged into the sand. My brain felt scrambled and my muscles useless.

Something rough, like sandpaper, scraped my cheek. With my eyes closed, I brushed at the annoyance. Another scrape, not painful exactly but annoying.

"Sabina," Giguhl whispered. "Wake up."

My eyes flicked open. "Giguhl?"

His little feline face was about an inch from my nose. "What the hell happened? Where are Cain and Maisie?"

The name made pain lance through my heart. I squeezed my eyes shut and clenched my jaw against the agony of the memories that rushed through my mind. I opened my lids and looked my minion in the eye. "Cain escaped."

"And Maisie?" But his eyes told me he knew. Instead of saying the words out loud, I shook my head. "Oh, gods!" He pushed his head against my chin and rubbed it there, both needing and offering comfort.

I pulled his little body to me, needing the warmth and the contact with something physical. Something real. Something I could trust.

He looked up, his eyes liquid with pain. "We need to get out of here. The others need to know."

I groaned and rose, carrying him like a football. But when I blinked and looked around the cavern, I realized the opening we'd entered through was gone. I spun around slowly. "Uh-oh," I said.

"What's wrong?"

"All the walls closed in."

The cat shrugged. "No problem."

"What do you mean, no problem?"

"Sabina," the cat said. "You don't need a door when

you've got a demon. Just say the words and I'll take us home."

I paused. With every ounce of my being I wanted to leave this place. This dank, black hole that became my sister's grave. But I suddenly didn't want to go back to New York. To face the disappointed and sad expressions on everyone's faces when I admitted I'd failed them. Here in this place, I felt broken and defeated. But once I returned to the mortal realm, this vulnerable, weak me would not be allowed to exist. Once I admitted my failures, there'd be no mercy. No comforting touches or words of encouragement. I'd released a psychopath on the world and doomed my own sister to death.

"Red?" Giguhl whispered.

I shook myself. "Yeah?"

"You're not alone. We'll handle this together, okay? No matter what waits for us back in the mortal realm."

"Can you flash us to New Orleans instead of the Crossroads?" If I worked quickly, maybe I could find Erron and he could get me to Abel in time to stop Cain. Then I could return to New York a hero instead of a failure.

The cat moved in my arms until his paws were on my shoulders and he looked into my eyes with his own. "I could, yes. But I think that's a mistake. I know it's going to hurt like hell, but you have to tell them what happened. They deserve to hear the truth. You can't just run away from it."

Why couldn't I have a demon who could lie to me every now and then? One who encouraged me to run from things I didn't want to face?

I looked down at the hairless cat demon who was my best friend in the world. The one who called me on my shit and always had my back. I didn't want any other demon by my side. "You're right."

His little eyes glowed with emotion. He cleared his throat and squirmed. "Now, say the words so we can get the fuck out of this hellhole."

I smiled. That was the demon I knew and loved. "Giguhl, let's go home."

The air popped and warped. In the next instant, we left the Liminal behind. Forever, I hoped.

36

The first thing I saw when Giguhl and I flashed back into the chapel was the empty floor where Maisie's body had lain before I left. For a split second, my traitorous mind dared to hope I'd been wrong. That maybe somehow my sister's death in the dream world hadn't also meant the death of her physical form. But before I could grab onto that wisp of hope, I was tackled.

The scent of sandalwood and the feel of Adam's fierce embrace demanded my full attention. I breathed in deep and willed my emotions to steady. I couldn't afford to break down now. I still had to get through my recount of the events in the Liminal. Still had to face all those trusting gazes and admit that I'd failed.

"Thank the gods," Adam said, his voice thick with emotion. "We thought you'd—" His voice cracked.

I pulled back to look in his eyes. In those depths, I saw the truth. Not only had Maisie actually died, but Adam and the others believed Cain had killed Giguhl and me, too. I opened my mouth to say . . . what? What could I possibly say?

"My turn." Rhea used her hip to push Adam out of the

way before he could tell me. She crushed me to her. "Don't you ever scare me like that again," she whispered fiercely.

I closed my eyes and surrendered to my need to be comforted. Rhea was as close to a real mother figure as I'd ever had. And right now, I needed every ounce of strength she offered. Especially since any minute now it would be withdrawn.

Over her shoulder, I saw Adam and Giguhl sharing a manly hug. When we'd reappeared, Giguhl manifested back in his demon form. He towered over the mancy, but looked as relieved as I felt for the support.

Beyond them, I noticed dozens of beings now filled the chapel. Everyone had frozen when we arrived and watched our tearful reunion. I knew it was only a matter of time before the questions started, but for the moment, I tried to block them out.

When I pulled away, my eyes throbbed with tears but I managed to hold them off. Unleashing the dam now wouldn't be helpful or pretty. I'd allow myself to fall apart later, but first I had to get through the next few minutes. "Where is she?" I whispered.

Rhea hesitated and pointed to a door off to the side of the altar.

Cold sweat bloomed from every pore. As if on autopilot, I turned and walked toward the wooden door separating me from my sister's body. From the corner of my eye, I saw the Queen move as if to speak me, but Rhea barked, "Give her a moment."

The door opened to reveal a smaller room with a single window. The stained glass formed a blue-and-red mosaic that cast my sister's shrouded body in a purple glow. The white gauze covering her was thin enough that I could make out her too-still features.

My knees trembled as I closed the door behind me, locking out the curious gazes of the audience in the chapel. The air here was heavy with cold and dust. I took a deep breath and turned toward the altar holding my sister. I kneeled on the low stone bench in front of the slab. Resting my forehead on the hard stone at her hip, I allowed the tears to finally fall.

They say that when you die, your life passes before your eyes. And as I knelt there, sobbing, it felt like a kind of death. Death of my illusions. Death of my hope. Death of my prayers for a happy ending.

Memories of Maisie, recollections of better times— short-lived though they were—flashed through my mind. The first time I saw my sister, singing that stupid Bob Marley song just before she ran at me with a huge smile and open arms. Her attempts to bond with me over girl talk and bags of blood. The way she'd tease Adam and she'd laugh indulgently at Giguhl's antics. The conviction in her blue eyes the night she told me she believed I was the Chosen. Standing back-to-back with her, fighting the vampires Lavinia sent to attack the mage compound. That night was the last time I'd seen my twin whole, just before our grandmother kidnapped Maisie and doomed her down the road that ended with her bleeding out in the Liminal.

Tears splashed my cheeks. Choking sobs clogged my throat. This was not the delicate cry of a civilized mourner. It was an angry outpouring of grief and rage.

Just before she'd died, Maisie had told me to trust fate. But how could I? In my experience, fate was a murderer. A ruiner of hope. A godsamned cosmic joke at my expense.

My left shoulder blade burned as if I'd been branded. "Always...with you," a voice whispered in my head. Maisie's voice. Her final words to me.

I might have been hallucinating. But it didn't really matter. Because the pain and that sweet voice filled me with a strength and calm I'd never known. I could sit there and beat myself with barbed, guilty thoughts or I could make things right.

"Maisie, I don't know why this happened. But I know you deserved better," I whispered. "I can't change the past, but I can affect the future. And I will not rest until you are avenged."

I placed a hand over my heart to sanctify the pledge I was about to offer. "Before the breath leaves my body and I join you in Irkalla, I vow on everything I hold sacred that Cain will pay for what he has done."

A warm breeze blew through the room, bringing with it the scent of sandalwood and lilies.

The door to the room opened suddenly. A shaft of light cut through the dark, bringing with it the sounds of voices from the main chapel. "Sabina?" Adam whispered.

I blinked against the intrusive light that stung my swollen eyes. Against the glow of the brighter room, Adam was little more than a shadow in the doorway.

"Red?" he whispered. "I'm sorry to interrupt but everyone's getting restless out here."

I nodded. As much as I wanted to put this off, part of me knew that if I stayed with my sister's body much longer, I'd lose my nerve to do what must be done. "I'm coming."

Adam hesitated before backing away to give me a chance to collect myself.

Placing a trembling hand over my sister's cold one, I swallowed. "Maisie," I whispered. "I know I wasn't the best sister. I know I failed you. If I could trade places with you, I would." I swallowed the new round of sobs that threatened. "And my biggest regret is that I never got to tell

you how much I admired you. How much you meant
to me."

I stood and lowered the shroud from my sister's face.
My lips felt hot against the icy skin of her forehead. "I love
you, sister. Rest in peace."

With that, I covered her back up and turned toward the
shaft of light in the doorway. Time to face the music.

"What happened?" Rhea asked, her voice kind but determined to hear the truth. "You were gone for hours."

I stood on the raised platform at the front of the chapel.
My tears were finally dry as I faced the dozens of beings
who filled the space—Rhea, Adam, Queen Maeve, Alexis,
and at least two dozen other mages, fae, and vampires. At
Rhea's question, my eyebrows rose. I knew Liminal time
was different than in the mortal realm but—I glanced at
the window. Holy shit, it was already afternoon.

I swallowed and looked around the room. At first, I'd
wanted to demand they leave. That the story I had to share
was too personal for an audience. But then I realized that
everyone in that room had a stake in the outcome of my trip
to the Liminal. So even though it was one of the hardest
things I'd ever done, I cleared my throat and shared the
story in a loud, clear voice.

I didn't stop until it was done. I told them about the
white stag and the pool. I told them about Maisie kneeling
on the shore. I told them about Cain's plans to enter the
Liminal and reclaim Lilith as his own. I told them about
the ritual Maisie performed that freed Cain. And then I
told them how my sister died in my arms.

The room fell silent. I backed away from the edge of the
altar and slumped against Giguhl. As the seconds ticked

by, pressure built in my gut. Any moment now, the accusations would begin.

Naturally, Queen Maeve—never my biggest fan—was the first to step forward. I gritted my teeth and braced myself. "Sabina," she said, her voice loud for all to hear. "I am the first to admit I had my doubts about your honor." I nodded and braced myself for the attack. "But I was wrong. Your sacrifices for the good of all the dark races will be the stuff of legend."

"B-but—" Shock made me stutter. "I failed. Cain got away and I couldn't save Maisie."

The Queen raised her chin and looked at me over her nose with an imperious stare. "Do not interrupt, young lady." I waited for her to continue. "We all mourn Maisie. Her loss will be felt keenly for decades. But you shouldn't blame yourself. Cain is a cunning foe, a manipulator of the first order. No one blames you for Maisie's death."

My mouth fell open. "Thanks."

She tilted her head. "Now, what resources will you need?"

"Wait," I said, having trouble keeping up. I didn't know if it was the exhaustion, the grief, or just the general fucked-up state of affairs, but I had no idea what she was talking about. "Resources for what?"

"For your mission," the Queen said. "Cain must be stopped."

Rhea stepped forward then. "Yes, get us a list and we'll make sure you have everything you need."

"Wait, you're serious?"

Rhea tilted her head and frowned at me like she was wondering if I had a fever. "Why wouldn't we be?"

Her eyebrows lowered. "My dear, I lived far too long and have seen far too many lives lost in this sad conflict between the dark races to joke. Cain is the biggest threat to our way of life that has ever existed. And if anyone can stop him, it's you."

I didn't know what to say. Sure, I'd already planned on going after him no matter what the Queen or anyone else thought. As far as I was concerned, the target on Cain's back had my name all over it. But I'd been prepared to have to fight for the right to be the one who went after Cain. I didn't expect to learn that everyone here believed in me and had my back. Their support went a long way toward easing my guilt and my fear. Now if someone could just do something about this black hole in my heart.

I pushed down my grief and focused on finding more answers. "What are you guys going to do about the treaty?" I asked.

The Queen and Rhea exchanged a look. "While you were gone, we had a chance to discuss that."

"We're declaring a state of emergency for the mage race," Adam said. "Aunt Rhea was elected as interim leader of the Council until Cain is out of the picture and a general election can be held."

My eyes widened as I looked at my mentor. She'd make an excellent leader for the race.

"Meanwhile," the Queen said, "Alexis and Slade Corbin will be searching for Persephone."

"What?" I said, my voice rising in shock. "Alexis and *Slade*?"

The vampiress came forward, her chin high. "When we realized Cain was behind all this, it was clear that Slade was never at fault. Besides," she said, her cheeks heating, "if Persephone is still in New York, I'll need his help tracking her down."

The corner of my mouth lifted. "I almost wish I could be there when you ask him for help."

"I just bet—" She paused, cutting off what was no doubt a brilliantly cutting retort. Taking a deep breath, she started over. "I'm sorry I, uh, accused you of murder and all."

I bit my lip. Her consternation was so un-vampire-like that I couldn't help but take pity on her. "Ditto, Vampira."

Our gazes locked for a few moments. All sorts of intangible things passed between us then. I still thought she was a hothead with questionable fashion taste. But I also knew she wouldn't be the worst ally to have on my side in a fight. If nothing else, she had a nasty right hook.

Rhea clapped her hands and turned toward me. "So, now that that's all settled, when are you heading out?"

I paused. "Tonight." My gaze shifted to Adam, who suddenly was very interested in his shoes. "I need to get to New Orleans to see Erron Zorn. He'll know how to get in touch with Abel."

Rhea nodded. "Sounds like the best place to start. You, Giguhl, and Adam can flash there tonight."

My head jerked up as her words sunk in. "Adam? You're coming?"

"Of course." He hesitated, as if something occurred to him. "Unless—do you not want me to come?"

Relief flooded me. I wanted him to come more than just about anything I'd wanted in my life. I'd just been worried that with everything that had happened between us he might prefer to stay and help Rhea run the race. "Of course I do."

Our eyes met and held. Words best left for a more private moment passed between us in that look. Words of forgiveness...and love. Maybe Giguhl was right before: Love alone isn't enough to fix a broken relationship. But without it, there was no hope. I knew I loved Adam, and judging from the look he was shooting me, he still loved me, too. I wasn't sure how we'd work through all our issues, but I knew I wanted to try.

I also knew that, other than Giguhl, there was no one I wanted by my side more for the biggest battle of my life.

Rhea cleared her throat. "Yes, well, now that that's settled, we'll expect daily reports on your progress."

I dragged my eyes from Adam and nodded. "Of course." I turned to grab my coat from where I'd left it on the altar.

Gasps echoed through the chapel. I paused and looked over my shoulder. Shocked stares greeted me. A cold chill passed over me. What the hell?

"Slap me on the ass and call me Dionysus!" Giguhl exclaimed. I looked up at Adam, whose mouth had fallen open. He approached me slowly, as if I might disappear. He and Giguhl reached me at the same time.

"What's going on?" I demanded. I craned my neck to look at the spot on my back where everyone was pointing, but Adam and Giguhl both yelled at me to stay still. Warm fingertips and a pointy claw prodded the skin of my left shoulder blade. "Guys?"

"Holy shit, Red," Adam said. "What the hell happened to you in the Liminal?"

I frowned. Hadn't we gone over this? "Wha—"

"You've got two birthmarks now!" Giguhl said, drowning out my question. I stilled, a chill spreading across my skin. A vague memory of the chaotic seconds surrounding Maisie's death flashed through my memory. The searing pain when the orb rotated around my body.

Rhea ran toward us then. "Oh, my gods," she breathed. "Sabina!"

I turned to her, accepting the embrace she offered. "This is a sign," she said.

"You and your signs," I said, trying to lighten the mood.

The air tingled with magic as Rhea summoned a mirror for me to use. I glanced back into the surface to see what they'd seen. My breath left me in a sudden rush.

Identical eight-point stars now scored both my shoulders. Is this what Phoebe had meant when she said that Maisie would always be with me? Had this birthmark been my sister's parting gift? Or was it just some other fucking arcane symbol I wasn't supposed to understand yet?

"What does it mean?" Giguhl asked.

I shook my head. My throat felt tight, but hope bloomed in my chest. The skin under the star felt hot, like a healing wound. I paused. It didn't really matter what it meant to anyone else, I guess. Because I chose to see it as a positive sign. A totem, a good luck charm. Proof that even though she couldn't be there in person, Maisie would always have my back.

"Whatever it means," Rhea said, her voice hoarse, "it's got to be a good omen."

I met her gaze and smiled. Finally, a reason to hope.

Adam cleared his throat and tried to covertly wipe the wetness from beneath his eyes. "The sun's going down so we probably need to motor," he said in a gruff tone. "Aunt Rhea, can you call ahead to Zenobia and let her know we're coming?"

"Absolutely," Rhea said. "I'm sure she'll be glad to see you all again."

Zenobia. Gods, I never thought I'd be seeing her again so soon. I definitely didn't think that when I did it would be under such dire circumstances. "I don't plan on being in New Orleans long," I said. "But we could probably use any supplies she can offer."

I saw Giguhl tense. Most likely at the prospect of seeing Pussy Willow again. But before we could deal with the ramifications of going to the Big Easy again, we had to begin the tough process of leaving New York.

"You guys ready?" Adam asked.

I grabbed Rhea in a tight, hard hug. "You be careful," she whispered. "Check in as often as you can."

I swallowed hard and nodded. "I promise."

"And, Sabina?" She pulled back with her hands on my shoulders. "Don't doubt yourself. You're ready for this."

"You don't know—"

"Hush now," she said gruffly. "Don't question your elders."

"Yes, ma'am."

With that, she released me and said her good-byes to her nephew. When she turned to Giguhl, she said, "You take care of them for me or I'll whip your scaly hide."

Giguhl chuckled and lifted the elder mage into an undignified hug. "You bet your sweet ass."

All around the room, awkward glances and sniffles punctuated the tension of the impending farewell.

Finally, Giguhl released Rhea. Turning toward Adam and me, the demon clapped his claws and rubbed them together. "All righty, let's get this quest under way already."

I smiled up at him. "Quest?"

He shrugged. "Sure, isn't that what you call it when someone rides off into the sunset to meet her destiny?"

I shook my head at the demon. "You've been watching too much TV again."

"All right, you two." Adam's upbeat tone was forced, and his red-rimmed eyes hinted at how much he was hiding. "Circle up and we'll be eating beignets in no time."

Rhea joined us in the circle, more out of solidarity than a magical need. Giguhl held my right hand. "On three," I said, forcing my tone to stay strong. Beside me, Giguhl and Adam nodded, giving me the all-clear.

"One..." Rhea's smile wavered.

The wind rose up, cold and harsh as a stranger.

"Two..." Adam squeezed my hand. Over his shoulder, I spied the tense, hopeful faces of the Queen of the fae, the vampire Enforcer, and the dozens of members of all the dark races who were putting their faith in us.

Through the haze of magic and the pull of time and space, I sent a little prayer to Lilith that this would not be the last time we were all together.

"Three."

Acknowledgments

*W*ith each book I write, the list of people I owe a thanks to grows, but then so does my gratitude. But instead of filling page after page with names, I'll just highlight a few special souls without whom this book wouldn't have been possible.

Devi Pillai: Thanks for everything you do to help me make this look easy.

Anna Gregson, Jennifer Flax, Lauren Panepinto, Alex Lencicki, Jack Womack, and the rest of Team Orbit and the awesome people at Hachette: Thank you for all your hard work behind the scenes to help me share my crazy stories.

Jonathan Lyons: Thanks for everything.

Rebecca Strauss: I'm looking forward to our adventures.

Maryam Houston: Amazing what a little wine can accomplish, huh? I can't believe all those crazy ideas we came up with actually worked! Be prepared, though, now you'll be required to help plot all my books.

Suzanne McLeod: You are a candidate for beta-reading sainthood for your quick turnaround and brilliant critique.

I feel lucky to work with you and smug that I get to read your amazing books before everyone else.

Margie Lawson, Susannah Curtis, Laurie Baltz, and Beverly Lindbo: You're an amazing group of women and writers whose passion and talent humbles me. Ladies, keep writing, the world needs to hear your voices.

Zivy and Emily: The older we get, the more I realize we're all three the pretty smart fools K.T. sang about. I love that about us.

Mr. Jaye: In addition to everything else you've given me, you've become a trusted advisor and bedrock of support for my writing. Thirteen years ago, even I couldn't have imagined how this would all unfold, but I wouldn't want anyone else by my side to face the adventure. ILYNTB

Spawn: You embody joy for me. Never stop being yourself. Always know you're loved.

Finally, thank you to all the readers and booksellers who champion these books. You all amaze and humble me.

extras

orbit

meet the author

Raised in Texas, JAYE WELLS grew up reading everything she could get her hands on. Her penchant for daydreaming was often noted by frustrated teachers. Later, she embarked on a series of random career paths before taking a job as a magazine editor. Jaye eventually realized that while she loved writing, she found reporting facts boring. So she left all that behind to indulge her overactive imagination and make stuff up for a living. Besides writing, she enjoys travel, art, history, and researching weird and arcane subjects. She lives in Texas with her saintly husband and devilish son. Find out more about the author at www.jayewells.com.

meet the author

introducing

If you enjoyed SILVER-TONGUED DEVIL,
look out for

BLUE-BLOODED VAMP

Book 5 of the Sabina Kane series

by Jaye Wells

Erron led us down narrow cobbled streets to a discreet wooden door set back into a stone building. A small, hand-painted sign advertised the name of the establishment: BAR SINISTER.

Erron opened the door. The scent of hops and barley mixed with the overpowering aroma of unfiltered cigarette smoke. Laughter and music fell out into the street like drunks on a bender. Erron entered without a word, leaving Adam and me to follow. Despite the bar being located in the center of Rome, the majority of voices I heard spoke with a British accent rather than Italy's mother tongue.

When I caught up with Erron, I yanked on his jacket. He stopped and looked at me with raised eyebrows. "What is this place, exactly?"

Erron frowned like I asked a stupid question. "A bar?"

"No," I said, huffing out an annoyed breath. "Why does everyone in here look like an extra from *Benny Hill*?"

"The owner's a Brit—from Liverpool, I believe. Lots of expat mages use the joint as a gathering place."

I exchanged a confused look with Adam.

"Well, that certainly relieves any worries about language barriers," Adam said with a shrug. Then he nudged me to follow the Recreant farther into the pub.

Erron sidled up to the bar and flagged down the barkeep. The guy had the physique of a potato. His ruddy cheeks and jovial expression made me like him immediately. "What'll it be, mate?"

"Three Guinesses," Erron said, as if we were in the British Isles instead of Italy.

The bartender toddled off to fill the order. Adam pulled up next to Erron. "I thought we were here to talk to someone."

"We are. But there's a way these things are done."

"Do you think it could be done a little quicker?" I said. "We're burning moonlight."

"Sabina, I know you're in a hurry, but this is Italy. Nothing happens quickly."

"I thought you said these guys are Brits," I grumbled.

"True, but *la dolce vita* tends to soften even the most type-A personality into complacence. You'll see."

I gritted my teeth and resisted the urge to remind Erron that we weren't in Italy on holiday. The mage might be a lot of things, but I'd spent enough time with him to understand that his laissez faire attitude was mostly an act. He understood the gravity of the situation more than most. After all, he'd suffered his share of losses at Cain's hands, too.

Three beers appeared on the bar in front of us. The bartender leaned against the wood with a smile on his face. He told us the total for the drinks. Erron handed him an unnecessarily large bill.

"I'll just be getting your change then," the bartender said, turning away.

"Keep it," Erron said, taking a casual sip from the pint.

"That's mighty kind of you," the bartender said. Instead of walking away, he leaned his elbows on the bar, ready to chat now. "You're Yanks, aren't ya?"

Erron smiled and nodded. "Visiting from New Orleans."

"Ah, well. Welcome to Roma! Is this your first time in Italy, then?"

I covered my sigh with a hefty swig of beer. Obviously, our British friend had seen the large tip as an invitation to pry.

"No," Erron said. "I've been here many times. However, my friends here are visiting for the first time."

The bartender's eyes, too shrewd for a man who looked like he bathed in whisky, gave Adam and me a once-over. "We don't get a lot of new visitors in Bar Sinister." Something about the way he said it made me think that "new visitors" was code for something else.

"We're actually here looking for an old friend," Erron continued. "Maybe you know him?"

Since the mage seemed intent on having a nice long chat, I decided to shuck off my jacket. The stuffy bar, combined with the hot air blowing between the males, made the bar feel stifling.

The bartender pursed his lips. "Maybe. What's this bloke's name?"

"Abel."

The instant the word fell from Erron's lips, the entire atmosphere in the bar changed. Nothing overt. No one rose to confront us or anything. More like a tightening of the air. A slight lowering of volume to the raucous conversation. Awareness. Yes, that's what it was. Everyone suddenly seemed very aware of us.

The bartender hunched down and leaned toward us. "Only Abel I ever heard of was that poor bastard got killed by his brother in the Bible story."

Erron's smile tightened. "Really?"

"In fact, I think maybe you're in the wrong place altogether."

"And what might be the right place?"

"I wouldn't be knowin' that." The bartender's lips tightened and his eyes were now as serious as life-or-death.

"This is a waste of time. This guy doesn't know anything." My aggressive tone earned me a sharp glance from the Recreant.

"If you'll be excusing me, I've got thirsty customers," the Brit said. "And I'll be asking you to leave once you finish your pints."

My mouth fell open at the dismissal. Erron kicked my ankle. I rounded on him but he shook his head with an expression that threatened pain if I caused a scene. "Let's go."

I slammed my pint on the bar and grabbed my jacket off the barstool. Erron had already turned to go, trusting I'd follow like a good girl. Adam stood nearby waiting to see my reaction. Part of me longed to stay and show these assholes who they were dealing with. But I could feel eyes on me. Could feel the magic hanging heavy in the air. Powers gathering, waiting for me to try something. These chaps might look like barflies but there was serious magic in that room. Erron, Adam, and I could have probably handled ourselves well enough to survive the brawl, but to what end? We'd still be leaving without the information we needed.

So with my pride dragging behind me like a piece of toilet paper stuck to my shoe, I stalked toward the door.

"Oy!"

I kept going, figuring that whoever had called out was trying to get someone else's attention.

"Oy! Mixed blood! Hold up!"

That stopped me. I turned slowly, my eyes narrow and my fists ready to defend. The bartender was rushing around the other end of the bar. He waddled toward me, his expression inscrutable but his movements anxious.

"What?" I snapped.

"What's this then?" he demanded when he reached me.

"What's what?" I'd run out of patience hours earlier. If he wanted to talk, he'd have to work for it. Behind me, I felt Adam's presence looming like a threat.

He lifted a hand. My hand shot out to stop what I thought was a strike. He paused and pulled back. "Relax, bird, I was just pointing to your back."

I frowned. "What about it?"

He frowned as if I was being purposefully obtuse. "What's your name?"

Jesus, this guy and his twenty questions. "I'm Sabina Kane. Who the fuck are you?"

The bartender smiled. A genuine one this time. "Well, well. This changes things then, doesn't it?"

"Listen, Mr. Belvedere, I'm tired and my patience ran out about a week ago. You got something to say to me, then say it."

"I think you and your friends need to come back to my office."

Adam stepped forward. "Two seconds ago you all but kicked us out of your bar. Why the change?"

"You know what? I don't give a shit," I said. "Let's go."

"Sabina—" Erron warned.

Belvedere ignored the Recreant and cocked an eyebrow at me. "You got a mouth, don't ya?"

"So I've been told," I retorted. "Come on, Adam."

"I got a message for you."

I plastered my poker face on. "Bullshit."

"Don't be like that. Can't blame a bloke for being careful. These are dangerous times we live in. Can't trust just anyone who walks in off the street."

I crossed my arms. "So why do you suddenly trust us now?"

The corner of the Brit's mouth lifted. "Because Abel told me a female bearing two eight-point stars on her back would be looking for him."

Cold sweat bloomed on my skin along with fear in the pit of my stomach. "How in the hell would he know that?" I'd received the second mark only a few days earlier and it was hardly common knowledge.

He shrugged. "I'm sure I don't know. Regardless, he said you'd go by one of two names."

I frowned. "What was the other name?"

"Maisie."

My skin crawled like someone had just played hopscotch across my grave. What. The. Fuck?

NIGHT SHIFT

The Jill Kismet Series Book 1

By Lilith Saintcrow

Jill Kismet. Dealer in Dark Things.
Spiritual Exterminator. Demon Slayer.
Not everyone can take on the nightside.
Not everyone tries. But Jill Kismet is not just anyone.
She's a hunter, trained by the best—and in
over her head.

Welcome to the night shift…

"Jill Kismet is, above all else, a survivor,
and it is her story that will haunt readers
long after the blood, gore and demons have faded
into memory."
—*Romantic Times*

The Jill Kismet Series

Night Shift

Hunter's Prayer

Redemption Alley

Flesh Circus

BLOOD RIGHTS

HOUSE OF COMARRÉ • BOOK 1

By Kristen Painter

Born into a life of secrets and service, Chrysabelle's body bears the telltale marks of a comarré—a special race of humans bred to feed vampire nobility. When her patron is murdered, she becomes the prime suspect, which sends her running into the mortal world…and into the arms of Malkolm, an outcast vampire cursed to kill every being from whom he drinks

Now, Chrysabelle and Malkolm must work together to stop a plot to merge the mortal and supernatural worlds. If they fail, a chaos unlike anything anyone has ever seen will threaten to reign.

◆

"Painter scores with this one. Passion and murder, vampires and courtesans— original and un-put-downable. Do yourself a favor and read this one."
—Patricia Briggs,
New York Times bestselling author

◆

HOUSE OF COMARRÉ

Blood Rights

Flesh and Blood

Bad Blood